Language of Thieves

Language of Thieves

Elizabeth Jackson

ROBERT HALE · LONDON

Typeset in 10/13pt Sabon
Printed in Great Britain by the MPG Books Group,
Bodmin and King's Lynn

This book is dedicated to the memory of Sally, my mother.
Her kindness and generosity knew no bounds.

'You are a child of the universe no less than the trees and
the stars: you have a right to be here.'

— Max Erhmann (Desiderata)

Acknowledgements

I would like to thank Jim Wight, Alice Galvin, Imogen Robertson and Alan Jones for their support and encouragement. Also, thank you to Robert Hale Ltd for taking a chance on me. And last, but not least, a big thank you to Edward, my husband. Without his endless support and gentle criticism, supplied with tea and biscuits, this book wouldn't exist.

Chapter One

Westmorland, June 1949

A dense carpet of white swirling mist muffled the sound of the horse's hoofs as the solitary rider steered his grey mare stealthily across the valley floor, then upwards toward the ridge that led to the valley beyond, through which the River Eden flowed.

Tobias Flint dismounted on reaching the sunlit brow. Stretching his tall lean body to its full height he scanned the mist-covered valley in the foothills rising towards the great folded bluffs of the Westmorland fells. The sun was streaming through Stainmore Gap into the great basin that drained into the River Eden which meandered north. He turned to look across to the far rim of the immense depression in the high land, an amphitheatre, where the slanting sun singled out Shap Fells and the Pikes guarding the eastern fringe of the Lake District. To his right he saw the clearing haze revealing levelling land of the Eden Valley. He savoured the moment, assimilating the wildness and wide horizons of this place he loved.

The sound of rippling laughter interrupted his reverie. He crouched down and crawled through the tall wet grass to a clearing where he looked into the valley below.

A girl of eighteen or twenty was mounted on a palomino horse. It had no saddle or bridle, just a makeshift halter. In the next instant the horse stepped tentatively into the shallow waters of the slow-moving river. Then, in one sweeping graceful motion, she lay back on the horse, and displaying absolute confidence in the animal, she raised her legs and rested her feet on its withers, her arms hung loosely by its sides.

Mesmerized, Tobias Flint gazed on in dreamlike wonder. The girl's face was framed in soft golden curls cascading down to the water. The plain fine white cotton shift she wore clung to her prostrate body exposing the outline of young generous breasts. Her eyes were closed and dark thick lashes contrasted sharply against her pale alabaster skin. And perfectly arched eyebrows suggested an element of surprise. The mouth that had been laughing was quite still now and her soft, velvety, plump lips twitched in a playful smile. He wanted to reach down and touch her, to kiss her.

He was so intent on a closer look he discovered he'd edged down the steep hillside further than intended and carefully began to ease his way back. The sudden call of a cuckoo split the air. Its song resounded throughout the valley causing his grey mare to whinny loudly. '*Blast!*' he cursed, losing his footing and slipped. He grasped at a tree root; it held him for a couple of seconds then snapped propelling him headlong down the grassy bank. Snatching at the undergrowth on his spectacular descent he arrived at the bottom clutching an assortment of weeds.

The girl sat astride her horse staring down at the unwelcome intruder with bright, clear green eyes full of surprise and alarm.

'Where the hell did you spring from!' she exclaimed. 'What d'you think you're doing here?'

'I might well ask you the same question, madam!' Tobias mumbled, scrambling to his feet brushing away mud and grass from his trousers.

He smiled, noticing a fine peppering of freckles across the bridge of her nose. She's got the greenest eyes I've ever seen, he thought, absorbing her every detail.

'This is private land. Have you permission?' she asked.

'So! What's the matter with you – can't you speak?' she snapped impatiently.

'What...? Er ... yes, I do have permission to ride on this land. And yourself, where are you from?'

'So you're not one of us, then?'

'Well, young lady, that all depends,' he grinned, 'on what *you* are one *of*.'

'Ah, yes, of course, I ... see now you ... er ... talk differently. For a moment, I thought you were from Appleby Fair, but I was wrong. I'll be on my way now.'

She turned her horse to leave but he grabbed the halter. She felt a tremor of excitement when he provided her with a lopsided smile, his soft grey eyes resting appreciatively on her.

'I answered your question,' he said, looking her steadily in the eye, 'now, how about you answering mine. Tell me, where do you come from?'

'I'm from Hampton, just outside Appleby,' she said politely, before adding crisply, '*Now*, if you'll excuse me....'

'Oh, yes, yes, I know Hampton.' He was fascinated by her and his mind sought desperately for something to say to detain her departure. 'And, tell me, did you honestly mistake me for one of those damned gypsies?' he asked, flipping his eyebrows.

Her face flushed crimson and her green eyes flashed rebelliously. She saw a gleam of mocking humour lurking in his gaze and a whirlpool of anger swirled within her.

'*Those damned gypsies*, as you call them happen to be my people!' she yelled fearlessly. 'Huh! Of course *you* couldn't possibly be one of *us*! I don't know how on earth I made such a mistake! I've never met a gypsy as ... as bedraggled as yourself at Appleby Fair, *ever*! And, another thing,' she added continuing her outburst, 'you'd better be off before you're caught riding on Mr Flint's land. He doesn't take kindly to trespassers. You'll be for it, mark my words!'

She tossed her head defiantly, her hair spilling over her shoulders. The cotton white shift rode up her thighs revealing slim, strong, honey-coloured legs that gripped the sides of her horse powerfully. She clicked her tongue and dug her heels in and the horse shifted restlessly. But Tobias tightened his hold on the halter and smiled at her with bland amusement.

'And what about you, young lady, *who*, may I ask, gave you permission?'

'Richard Flint himself, of course,' she replied haughtily, 'Many years ago. Not that it's any of *your* damn business!'

She yanked the horse's head freeing him from Tobias's hold and the animal backed away rearing slightly. She leaned forward and, whispering a command into the horse's ear, they galloped swiftly away.

Daisy Latimer returned from her ride breathless having galloped most of the way. She needed to put some distance between herself and that man. At first glance she'd thought him rather attractive until he'd opened his mouth, referring to those *damned gypsies*! What had they done to him? Nothing! He's no damn different from the rest of the gorgios, she concluded angrily. No wonder we're suspicious of everyone but our own!

She gathered up an armful of dry sticks from beneath the bow-top wagon and threw them on to the warm embers of last night's camp-fire. She raked it back into life and hung the heavy kettle on the prop positioned over the flickering flames.

Daisy looked at her surroundings and breathed in the cool morning air. Thoughts of the last hour diminished and her spirit soared with gratitude at being here among her people. She found the familiar buzz and excitement associated with Appleby Fair intoxicating and unparalleled. Her eyes scanned the field crammed with gypsy wagons. Bow-tops, open lots, flat carts and bender tents were dotted about the lush green countryside, adorning it with their bright alien colours. Flashes of reds, blues, yellows and greens lit up the field, a landscape daubed with all the brilliant colours from an artist's palette. The swifts had returned from their annual migration and wheeled recklessly in an enamel blue sky high above, their screeching song competing with that of the curlew.

The Romanies attending the fair had been on the road for countless days, some journeying hundreds of miles. Now, having arrived, family and friends were reunited; old acquaintances renewed, stories exchanged, and deals clinched.

Like a breath of romance the Romanies brought with them a taste of light relief to the simple workaday world in which the local people lived, social differences seemingly bridged – if only for a fleeting moment in time.

The low reverberating snorts and whinnies of horses tethered in clusters throughout the campsite conveyed their greetings to one another beckoning the day. Daisy's horse Chase whinnied softly in response. She walked over to where he was tethered and he muzzled his warm velvety nose in her open palms.

'Hello, my beauty. Are you hungry?' She fed him a titbit from her pocket and buried her head in his thick mane.

Chase had been her companion for eight years, but it seemed like only yesterday her father had brought him home. She was ten years old at the time. Her mother had died in childbirth a few months earlier along with the brother with whom she'd anticipated sharing her childhood.

'What do you make of him then, my sweet?' her father had asked her, laying the helpless foal beside her. 'Do you think you can look after the little fella? He's not very strong.' He'd shook his head despondently, 'His mother, poor old mare, she died of colic last night and this young 'un was sure to follow, so the farmer said I could tek 'im wi' me if I knew someone who'd care for 'im.'

'Oh, yes, Dad, I'll take care of him. I'll not let him die, I promise!' she vowed. Her eyes lit up with excitement for the first time since her mother's death. 'You'll be fine, little one,' she assured the foal stroking it gently.

'And what's his name to be?' Seeing his girl smile after all the recent grief moved him deeply.

Daisy thought for a long time before answering. She then pronounced with a valiant smile, 'Chase. I'll call him Chase, Dad, 'cos today, he's chased away some of the sadness inside of me.'

From that day forth Daisy devoted every waking moment to rearing the foal. And transforming her grief into love, they became inseparable over the years.

Samboy Latimer emerged from the wagon. His wild auburn hair streaked with grey tumbled about his suntanned face. He tied a spotted kerchief round his neck and walked to where Daisy sat by the fire. He dropped a kiss on her cheek then pulled up a wooden stool next to her. She handed him a cup of tea and a plate of bread and butter smothered in wild strawberry jam.

They sat in companionable silence where only birdsong, gentle snorts and whinnies, punctuated the stillness.

Samboy was a tall, well-built fellow with broad, straight shoulders. He had a kind, open face with dark intelligent eyes and deep laughter lines etched at his temples. His generous mouth gave the impression of a permanent smile, which could be disconcerting if he happened to be in a bad mood. His brown hands holding the Crown Derby porcelain cup and plate were rough and callused with years of labouring and the handling of horses. His rugged good looks turned the heads of many unattached traveller women attending Appleby Fair. Some hoped to pin him down for he was a fine catch with a good business. But he was content enough for the time being, raising his only child and having to be both father and mother to Daisy since the death of his wife, Mary.

Mary, who was not of Romany blood, married Samboy against her parents' wishes. They'd eloped to Gretna Green twenty years ago after falling in love one glorious summer at Appleby Fair. She was visiting the fair with friends and had just had her fortune told, when, stepping down from the fortune-teller's wagon, she had tripped on the bottom step. Samboy, who happened to be passing, saw her falling, rushed to her aid and caught her, holding her in his arms a while longer than was politely necessary.

After that moment they met secretly every day for the duration of the fair. He vowed to return the following year and marry her. He kept his promise, despite opposition from both sides. They married, presenting everyone with a fact they had to accept. Much to the surprise of their families, Mary and Samboy were happy regardless of their cultural differences.

Two years later they were blessed with the arrival of Daisy following an anxious pregnancy and difficult birth. Seven years later and against doctors' advice Mary fell pregnant again. After being in grave health for the nine months, she died in childbirth with their still-born son.

Samboy was proud of his daughter. When his late wife's parents had died, they had bequeathed them a cottage near the market town of Hampton, so she'd attended school from age five to fifteen and could read and write as well as any non-traveller. Daisy had attended school for most of the year, delighting her teachers with her keenness to learn. They didn't object when she arrived in school late in October when the gypsy fairs had finished, then abandoning lessons in May. For that was when the open road would call, summoning Samboy as it had his ancestors for hundreds of years.

'Big selling day tomorrow, Dad,' Daisy said, breaking the silence, 'Some grand horses to flash. I'll help you get them ready, eh?'

'Aye, Daisy, but first we'll go into town and stock up with a few provisions. And, if I'm not mistaken, it's somebody's birthday. We'll go an' 'ave a look in Danby's dress shop, eh?'

Daisy cringed. 'Oh, Dad, I'll be nineteen, not nine!' she remonstrated, 'Would you mind if I went on my own?'

She loved her father dearly, but the thought of him accompanying her to buy a new dress was too much. His excessive paternal protection was beginning to get on her nerves and resentment towards him was growing as he monitored her every move.

He'd also started encouraging his friends with unattached sons to visit in the hope she'd find one of them suitable for marriage. Most traveller girls were married by the time they reached the ripe old age of eighteen having already endured a lengthy engagement. But Daisy balked at the idea of being steered toward any man and would remain a spinster before marrying a man not of her own choosing.

'Of course I don't mind,' her father lied. ''Ere's some brass for yer, lass.'

'Thanks, Dad,' she said, stuffing the pound notes inside her pocket. She put her arms around his neck and kissed his cheek. 'I do love you, Dad,' she said guiltily.

'Aye, I know, lass,' he said, patting the soft white hand resting on his shoulder. 'Now, you watch out when you go into town by yerself!' The tone of his voice changed and rang with authority. 'There're some high-spirited young buggers flyin' about Appleby this time o' year! An' I'm not just talkin' about our own people, Daisy. So careful! D'yer 'ear me?'

'Yes, I hear you, Dad.'

Samboy couldn't believe the way the non-travelling lasses conducted themselves nowadays. Running wild, going out with lads, drinking in the pubs. Disgraceful behaviour! And he wasn't going to have his daughter influenced by such likes.

'Don't worry, Dad, I'll only be gone for an hour or so. I'll be back to get your dinner ready.'

Tobias Flint rode home at a leisurely pace. While meeting the girl had thrilled him it had also released long-forgotten memories from the past regarding the gypsy fair. He could recall how neither he nor his brother Hugh – or the staff for that matter – ever discussed the annual event. It was *taboo*! And, for some bizarre reason a wall of uneasy silence existed during fair time.

He had been away at school in Exeter from age six to seventeen. Then Sandhurst, followed by the God-awful war. No wonder I don't know anything about the fair, I've hardly been here. Damn and blast! I wish to hell I hadn't been so bloody rude to her. Well, if she's an example of the gypsy girls I won't mind going out of my way to see a few more of them, he concluded, smiling.

He was still smiling when he reined his horse to a halt in the stable yard.

'Morning, Dan,' he said chirpily to the stable boy who abandoned a barrowful of horse muck to attend his horse.

'Mornin', sir, grand 'n it is too.'

'Most certainly is. Tell me something, Dan, you've been around here all your life. Do you ever go to the gypsy fair?'

'Oh, yes. I always goes and watches t' 'orses, sir – when they're selling them, that is. I likes to watch 'em strike a deal. Yer never know 'ow much 'as been paid though.' His eyes were wide with excitement as he spoke, his fascination with the gypsies apparent.

'Really?' Tobias said intrigued.

'Oh aye, sir. Do yer know, they 'ave a strange language all of their own? And unless you 'appen to be one of 'em, they won't let you in – oh, no, it's like a secret society, that sort o' thing,' Dan imparted knowledgeably. 'They don't trust us gorgios though, yer know – oh no, they don't,' he said, shaking his head.

'Gorgios?' Tobias asked frowning, 'What the devil are gorgios?'

'Us! You an' me! We're the gorgios or flatties. That's what they call us non-traveller folk. Me now, ah likes the gypsies,' he disclosed sheepishly, 'Ah thinks they're a right decent lot, specially t'orse dealers.'

'Strange thing, Dan,' Tobias admitted soberly, 'I've lived here all my life ... and this fair has gone on for ... what? hundreds of years....' He sighed shrugging his shoulders. 'I know nothing, nothing at all about it, or its people.'

'No, sir, mebbe not; now yer father did, of course. Now 'e was very interested in the fair – and them travelling folk. I believe 'e got to know a few o' the families quite well. Sometimes 'e'd go down and 'ave a cup of tea with 'em on an evenin' – sit round t' camp-fires like, an' I've even 'eard tell that 'e joined in with their singsongs!'

Tobias raised his eyebrows his eyes as wide as Dan's, 'Really, Dan? Good Lord! I'd no idea, Mother's never mentioned it before,' he added.

'Oh, sorry sir, mebbe I shouldn't 'ave said owt like. I ... don't think yer mother was ower keen on yer father tekin' an interest in 'em like, I'm sorry, sir, don't be tellin' 'er I've gone and said anythin' p ... please, sir?' Dan stuttered, with a fearful look in his eyes.

'No, no, of course not, Dan, I wouldn't dream of it. Please, don't worry,' he added, hoping to mollify him.

Good grief, the lad's positively scared stiff! I wonder why? I think I'll take a look at this horse fair, see what it's all about. If Father enjoyed it, it must hold some interest. And what of the girl, I wonder? When did he meet her? And what decided him to give her permission to ride over our land? I'm sure she wasn't lying.

Tobias entered the house by the kitchen where Nellie, the housekeeper, was ushering a scullery maid to, 'get a move on'.

'Morning, Master Tobias,' she said, greeting him warmly.

'Morning, Nellie, hmm ... something smells good.' He lifted a lid from a pan bubbling on the stove and buried his nose in it.

'Come on now, out o' my way!' Nellie chided, shooing him with flapping arms. 'You know your mother doesn't like you coming in the back door – never mind hangin' around the kitchen. Now be off with you. I'll fetch your breakfast along soon enough.'

'Is Mother up?'

'Aye, she's in the mornin'-room, so get along.'

'Oh, you are a good 'n, Nellie, I don't know what this family would do without you,' he said, giving her a quick hug before disappearing to join his mother.

Nellie beamed with pleasure. She couldn't love Tobias any more had he been her own son. She had worked for and had lived with the Flint family for over forty-five years, witnessing many happy and some very sad events.

Eden Falls Manor had been in the family more than a hundred years with three generations being born there.

Richard Flint, Tobias's father, had died of a heart attack eighteen months ago. His eldest son Hugh had been killed in action at Tobruk. Tobias, by the grace of God, had managed to survive. When Tobias returned home from the war his father passed the entire responsibility of the estate to him before sliding into a deep depression, from which the poor man never recovered.

Nellie had no liking or regard for Richard Flint's widow, Lydia Flint. She'd been employed originally as personal maid to Richard's ailing mother. Destined for spinsterhood at twenty-eight, she was besotted with her employer. She was also an opportunist. Nellie had witnessed Lydia worm her way into the family. Watched her shameless flirtations, her throwing herself at Richard, and the eventual pregnancy. Oh yes, he'd married her, of course! What else could he do? It was his child and he wouldn't shirk his responsibilities. And Nellie didn't doubt that Lydia was fully aware Richard's ailing mother was too frail to withstand any family disgrace. Lydia would have held him to ransom had he refused to marry her.

Tobias made his way to the morning-room where his mother sat at a table in the large bay window overlooking the rose garden. She hadn't heard his approach and he paused in the doorway studying her intently. She was wearing a charcoal-grey skirt and a navy-blue blouse. The drab colours succeeded in accentuating her sallow complexion. Her greying brown hair was cut unfashionably short and brushed back severely from her face. It was a harsh face that must have smiled once upon a time to have attracted his father, he thought. But now it wore a permanent frown. Her mouth was encircled with deep vertical lines, formed from the years of bitterness they'd harnessed. Her cold, spiteful eyes now turned to look at him.

'Tobias! Have you been there long?' she queried sternly. 'God, you're enough to frighten anybody, sneaking up like that.'

'Sorry, Mother, I didn't mean to frighten you. And I wasn't *sneaking*.' He forced a smile and sat down opposite her. 'I've just come back from a long ride,' he said, changing the subject quickly. He didn't know why, but he had this tendency to irritate her, get under her skin, even when doing his utmost to please her. Not that he could recall her ever being pleased about anything.

During his childhood she hadn't exhibited an ounce of maternal love towards him in any shape or form. But it hadn't mattered, for what his mother lacked Nellie made up for a thousand fold. It was Nellie he ran to, Nellie who kissed him better, read him stories and tucked him up in bed at night; Nellie who kept him safe and made everything right. His childhood would have been an abysmal existence without her and he loved her dearly.

'I don't know why you have to go out riding so often. You're becoming more like your father every day,' she complained, 'Gallivanting all over the countryside mixing with locals, workers and … undesirables….'

'Is that such a bad thing, Mother?' Tobias interjected holding her gaze.

'What? You gallivanting all over the countryside, or mixing with riff-raff?'

'Neither. My becoming more like my father?' He hit a raw nerve and her eyes glinted bitterly for a brief moment.

'That's not what I meant, Tobias—'

'Well! What did you mean?'

'Don't you dare question me like that!' she shrieked. 'I'm your mother!'

He looked at her in disbelief. Yes, this was his mother! Her eyes flashed as white-hot anger took control. A vein pulsated rapidly in her neck and pockets of saliva gathered at the corners of her mouth.

'*And … you*! Don't you look at me like *that*!' she said, leaning towards him and screwing up her eyes, her face inches from his own. Her lips drew back to reveal clenched teeth. '*You … You and your precious bloody father! What you don't know about him doesn't bear thinking of*!' She spat out every word her voice a crescendo of bitterness.

'What … what do you mean? What don't I know about … about Father, *Mother*?'

Lydia leaped from her chair and stormed out of the room. She collided with Nellie in the doorway. The prepared breakfast tray she carried took flight, crashing to the floor with a resounding clang and food flew in every direction.

Tobias strode after her apologizing to a dumbfounded Nellie along the way. He raced up the polished staircase two steps at a time. On reaching his mother's door it slammed shut in his face. He turned the handle. It was locked.

'Open this door, Mother! I must talk to you.'

'Go away. I've nothing to say to you. *Please*, lower your voice!'

'Mother, you must tell me. What about my father? What is it you don't want me to know?'

'Tobias! Do you want the servants to hear you talking like this?' Her voice was a loud pleading whisper.

'*The servants*!' he now mocked, 'Huh! That's a laugh, coming from you. That's what *you* came here as, *remember*?'

'I won't talk to you while you're behaving like this. Go away, please!'

Tobias gave a frustrated thump on the door with a clenched fist and marched away.

He left the house by the front door cutting across the freshly mown lawns and past the paddocks toward the woodland that bordered the estate.

By the time he reached the wood and seated himself under a tree by the side of the stream his anger had abated. But his heart was heavy.

He glanced down into the stream where a large trout basked in a pool of sunlight. Its sleek body and slow, weaving motion for some reason reminded him of the girl he'd seen earlier that day. It brought a smile to his face. I wonder what she and my father spoke of, he mused. She's probably unaware of his death. I'd like to bet he was captivated by her. Maybe she was a regular visitor to the estate. Maybe they rode together. Ah, well, with any luck, one day I'll talk to her and get some answers.

He leaned forward snaking his body down the side of the bank.

'I'd wager she could tickle you out of this stream,' he said to the unsuspecting trout, and surreptitiously slid his hands into the warm, sun-drenched water. Placing his hands under the basking fish he tickled and stroked its underbelly. In the next instant with one sudden movement, he grabbed it with both hands and threw it on to the grassy bank. He picked it up and examined its fine markings. 'You'd make a first-rate meal for a family,' he said to the trout, 'but today is your lucky day. And, because of a certain young lady your freedom is secured.'

He leaned down and gently released the fish into the sunny shallows watching it dart away safely upstream. 'Goodbye and stay free, my friend.'

Tobias walked home by way of the fields where the hay turning was in progress. It was going to be a good year as the weather had been kind. The small tractor that had replaced some of the horses was making short work of the task.

His father had been a forward-thinking man with regard to modern agriculture. He was the first for miles around to have purchased a tractor, followed by a combine harvester. His workforce had dwindled but his profits had soared. Richard Flint had fast become one of the largest respected landowners in Westmorland.

He missed seeing the horses at work in the fields alongside the farm men and decided to keep two in reserve for emergencies. This proved to be a prudent decision in retrospect. When the weather was changeable during harvest time, or the tractor had broken down, a horse could quickly be harnessed and taken to the fields to do the job.

Occasionally a few gypsies would hang back after the fair looking for farm work thereabouts to earn extra cash. They were skilled horsemen and could be set on straightaway with a workhorse unsupervised.

Daisy sauntered down the main street of Appleby with the purchase of a new dress from Danby's tucked under her arm. She had settled on a cream cotton summer dress with a sweetheart neckline. It had patch pockets at either side and was exquisitely embroidered around the hemline in pretty red poppies. Mrs Danby said it suited her perfectly and suggested she also buy the cream shawl to match which she let her have at a reduced price.

She delighted in the warm sunny day that delivered swarms of visitors along with the travellers to the busy town that spilled out on both sides of the river. She wandered on to the twin-arched bridge spanning the River Eden to join the throngs of people who stood gazing idly over the parapet. The sparkling waters and the tranquil backdrop of old St Lawrence's Church added to the charm and intensity of a theatrical setting.

On reaching the bridge she looked over the parapet to the familiar sights below. A wave of fifty or sixty people swam and waded in the water alongside their horses. They washed them lovingly, thoroughly brushing their coats and manes. The horses delighted in scores of gentle hands. Daisy smiled to herself; she knew every person down there.

Her eyes moved along the river to rest on one person in particular. It was Roulson Adams. He was riding through deep waters further downstream astride a large Cleveland Bay. He turned his head sharply sensing he was being watched and appeared to look directly at her. He waved and she waved back.

'That yer boyfriend, luv?' a woman she didn't know enquired, nudging her with an elbow. 'My, but he's a bloomin' handsome brute, in't he?'

Daisy didn't reply although she agreed.

Yes, he is a handsome brute, she thought, studying him from her advantageous position. He was stripped to the waist. His deep-bronze, muscle-toned body glistened in the sunlight. She could imagine his jet-black eyes laughing and his wide mouth smiling back at her in the distance.

She watched him glide across the river and steer his horse up the river-bank before disappearing from view, merging with other numerous horses and riders.

She continued gazing in awe at those below. Young children swimming with their horses leaped from their backs racing one another to the water's edge then back again.

The spell was broken when an unexpected thunderous clattering of hoofs resounded on the bridge. Daisy whirled round to come face to face with Roulson Adam's horse. The animal was biting the bit and frothing at the mouth whilst prancing about wildly. Alarmed looks on the faces of those standing close prompted the rider to rein his horse back a few paces allowing people to retreat to a safer distance.

'Hello, Roulson,' Daisy said, taking hold of the horse's bridle. 'I thought it was you in the water below. Cushty gelding you've got; are you thinking of selling him on at the fair?'

He didn't reply but jumped down from his horse and stood very close to her. She could feel his warm sweet breath on her face, and the familiar aroma of horses mingled with his body sweat excited her. His shirt was slung carelessly round his neck exposing his broad chest where droplets of water trickled a pathway through the dark hairs; spellbound, she followed their descent to where the dark hair tapered below his belly-button.

'I knew it was you up on the bridge. I'd spot you a mile off, Daisy.' He spoke softly and reached out gently tucking a wisp of hair that had escaped back behind her ear. 'No mistaking that beautiful hair of yours,' he murmured, stroking it with the back of his hand.

She flushed hotly and bowed her head. Her heart quickened when he placed a finger beneath her chin raising her face to look at him. She stared into the darkest eyes she'd ever seen. He was the handsomest man around.

And Roulson Adams knew it.

'I'd better be going,' Daisy said, stepping back a couple of paces to disengage from his magnetic charm. 'Dad will be wondering where I've got to.'

'Are you walking back up the hill?'

'Er, yes, yes I am.'

'Well, come on then, I'll give you a ride.'

He took the parcel she clasped to her chest and climbed on to his horse. He held out his arm. 'Come on, grab a hold,' he said, winking at her mischievously. 'You'll be safe enough, I promise,' he added, laughing.

She looked about her where a crowd had gathered. Roulson, unable to resist an audience, burst into song.

'Daisy ... Daisy ... give me your answer do ...
I'm half crazy ... all for the love of you ... I can't afford ... a'

'Roulson! Stop it! Stop it *now*!' she pleaded.

'Well, come with me, or I promise you, it'll get worse,' he laughed, taunting her.

A moment later a figure stepped out from amongst the crowd and silence ensued.

'Is this man bothering you, madam?' a distinguished voice asked.

They both turned to see a smartly dressed man standing before them. It was the same man she'd met down by the river: Daisy recognized him immediately.

'And what the hell's it to do with you?' Roulson blared, jumping down from his horse. 'Bugger off and mind your own bloody business, if yer know what's good fer yer!'

Daisy stepped between them with her back to Roulson. She looked at Tobias, perceiving his every detail in an instant while wondering what he was doing here.

'No, this man isn't bothering me,' Daisy said coolly, dismissing him with a glance.

She turned to Roulson who was glaring challengingly at Tobias Flint. 'Come on, Roulson, let's go, can we, please?'

Roulson leapt on to his horse and held out a bronzed muscled arm for Daisy to grasp and climb up behind him. But first she turned to face the man who'd so readily insulted her people. 'I hardly recognized you cleaned up. You'd better watch you don't get yourself mistaken for one of us, especially dressed like that!' she added curtly.

Tobias grinned and looked on with envy as she grasped the strong arm that hoisted her up in one easy movement. They rode off but Daisy couldn't resist a furtive glance back over her shoulder. Tobias Flint stood in the centre of the bridge watching them. He smiled at her and waved before giving an elaborate, exaggerated bow.

She didn't smile back.

'You OK, Daisy?' Roulson asked. They had slowed to walking pace. 'Who's that gorgio making eyes at yer?'

'What? Don't talk daft, he didn't make eyes at me. He's someone who lost his horse down by the river when I was out riding the other day.' She didn't want to waste precious time talking about *him* when she was sitting this close to Roulson.

She relaxed her arms that gripped his waist. 'Hey, you shouldn't have done that!' she said crossly, prodding him in the back.

'Done what?'

'Embarrassed me out there on the bridge that's what! In front of all those people too. Can you imagine the talk going round the camp tonight? My life won't be worth living!'

Reports of the exhibition on the bridge would be common knowledge by the time she returned and her father wouldn't be pleased if he heard of it.

'Aw, c'mon, Daisy, I wouldn't hurt you – not for the world.'

He reined his horse to a halt on the grass verge and skilfully swivelled himself round to face her. 'I like you too much to do anything like that.' He looked into her eyes and held her hand. 'I was wondering Daisy … er … maybe …' he said, hesitantly, 'you'd maybe consider us … you and me like, that is, to be courting like?'

'Oh, Roulson, I'm flattered, but … I … don't think I'm ready for—'

'Hush, don't answer me yet,' he said, placing a finger on her wavering lips, 'Just think about it, OK?'

'OK, I'll think about it.'

He leaned forward and, taking her into his arms, tenderly kissed her trembling innocent lips. She closed her eyes to receive what was to be her very first kiss. She'd waited so long and she wanted it to be … perfect. It was. After what seemed like an eternity she opened her eyes to find Roulson gazing back into hers.

'That's yer first kiss, ain't it, Daisy?'

'Y … yes it is,' she admitted tentatively. Her heart thumped wildly and she prayed he wasn't too disappointed at her inexperience. After all, he was the most popular man around and all the lasses adored him, so wasn't she the lucky one?

'Well, don't look so worried, for God's sake! It was lovely, Daisy, just like you.'

'I'd better be getting back,' she said hurriedly, as the colour rushed to her face. 'Dad will be wondering where I've got to. I promised to help him with the horses today for the big sale tomorrow.'

Reluctantly he took her home.

Samboy was busy with the horses when they stopped near his wagon.

'Hello there, Roulson lad,' he said, smiling warmly at the young man he'd known all his life. He dropped the hoof he was cleaning and, taking a rag from his pocket, wiped the sweat from his brow. His smile evaporated when he saw Daisy climb down from behind him. He hurried towards her. 'Are yer all right? Has something happened?' he asked anxiously.

'No, no, I'm all right, really, Dad. Don't look so alarmed.' She retorted more sharply than intended wishing he'd not been waiting for her. 'Roulson gave me a ride back, that's all,' she added tersely, and, spinning round, spared her father the flirtatious smile she threw Roulson. 'Thanks for the ride home, Roulson – bye.'

'You're welcome, Daisy, ta-ra now.'

She saw the look of disapproval on her father's face and quickly disappeared into the wagon.

'Cushty stallion yer've got yerself there, Mr Latimer,' remarked Roulson. He climbed down from his horse and strolled over to where a black stallion was tethered. 'Best I've seen at Appleby in a year or two.'

'Aye, mebbe so,' muttered Samboy. He looked at the handsome good-for-nowt standing with his back to him admiring the stallion and was filled with an overwhelming desire to kick his arse! No! There was no way he was going to allow his daughter to get involved with such likes. Her mother would turn in her grave. 'Tell me, Roulson, what are you doing with yerself, nowadays?' he enquired.

'Oh, yer know how it goes,' Roulson replied, shrugging his shoulders, 'a bit o' this and a bit o' that.'

He's up to no bloody good, thought Samboy. Roulson's reputation for chasing women was no secret among the travellers. His good looks afforded him the pick of the bunch and there was no shortage of girls, married and single alike, queuing up for his attention.

'Well, I'll be seeing you, Mr Latimer, g'bye for now,' Roulson smiled and, leaping on to his horse, left.

'Aye, hopefully it'll be goodbye *for bloody good*!' Samboy cursed under his breath. He walked round to the back of his wagon and taking out his pipe lit it.

A gnawing feeling in his gut warned him *beware*. He'd seen the desire for his daughter in Roulson Adams's eyes. I'll protect her from that no good bastard at any cost, he vowed. She mebbe won't thank me now, but given time she will. Aye, given time....

Chapter Two

Daisy knelt at her father's feet. He held the bridle of a fine black stallion standing seventeen hands high. In her hand was balanced a pot of black dye and in the other a paintbrush. The right front fetlock was the only part of the horse that was white and Daisy carefully and meticulously painted out the white hairs taking great care not to spill any on the hoof.

'You've missed a bit, *there*!' her father snapped, pointing to where she'd missed some hairs. 'Now finish it off properly, they'll soon spot it.' He eyed her quizzically as she resumed the delicate operation. 'You don't seem to have yer mind on the job this mornin', lass. Remember, this is our big day an' we've seven 'orses to sell. Aye, 'e's too good for the shafts, this bugger. He'll make a cushty hunter if we can sell 'im to one of them gorgios. Yer never know, some posh nobs might be on the lookout for summat half decent.'

Daisy finished the final touching up to her father's satisfaction, then set about grooming the other horses for sale. Vigorously brushing them in turn her thoughts drifted to her encounter with Roulson. His kiss had thrilled her. If she closed her eyes she could still feel his breath on her face … his mouth searching hers…. She wanted more…. And he'd said he wanted to court her….

'Come on, lass, get a bloody move on and stop yer bloody daydreaming! We 'aven't got all bloody day, yer know!' Samboy barked impatiently.

'Sorry, Dad, I wasn't thinking.'

'That's the problem, Daisy, yer thinkin' too much! But not about the job you're supposed to be doin'. Now look sharp!'

Samboy was immediately annoyed with himself for snapping at her. Good Lord, man! What the hell do yer think yer doin'! She's done nowt wrong. All she's done is sit behind a bloke on a horse. Remember when you were young yerself kicking over the traces? By God, did you kick? Yer damn well stampeded! Now give her a bit of rein, man!

Daisy spotted a group of children playing in a distant corner of the field and decided to go and investigate their antics. 'Won't be long, Dad, I'm going to see what the bairns are up to over there and I'll fetch some water back.'

She tied the smartly groomed horse to the back of the wagon, picked up the empty water-jack and made her way across the field.

The party of children were crowded close to the hedge and she approached slowly.

Four young girls carried a wooden ammunition box left over by the Ministry of Defence which they must have pilfered from somewhere. The box was piled high with apple blossom and cowslips. A group of boys close by were standing guard over a freshly dug hole in the ground.

'What are you all up to?' she asked, taking them by surprise. Shocked, the girls spun round dropping the box in fright. Blossom and flowers flew like confetti across the field.

'Nuffin'!' the youngest girl protested angrily.

'Aw, now look what you've done!' exclaimed another. 'You've made us drop the bloomin' coffin! 'Ave you no respect, Daisy? We're 'avin' a funeral. We've got a dead rabbit 'ere an' it wants buryin'. We ain't doing nuffin' wrong, 'onest!'

'Aw, I'm so sorry,' Daisy apologized. She looked at the group of ragged children who belonged to the poorer gypsies. They lived in the crudely erected bender tents, scratching a living making pegs and paper flowers. Looking at them was a humbling reminder of how fortunate she was. Struggle for survival through a gentle winter in a gypsy wagon or bender tent was no mean feat and not for the faint-hearted. But there was nothing faint-hearted about this crew, she thought, looking at them. They'd poach: fish, rabbits, pheasants, and deer, given half the chance.

'Here, let me help you.' She knelt down and, gathering up the fallen petals and flowers, replaced them over the deceased rabbit that lay on a bed of hay in the box. She calculated it must have been dead a few days because it stank. She picked up the box and carried it to the shallow crater they'd carefully prepared.

'If you would like to put the earth back then we can say the Lord's Prayer. Would you like that?' she asked, smiling at their grubby familiar faces.

'Ooh yes, please, Daisy,' they chorused.

She knew most of them and their families; had even attempted to teach some to read and write. They would gather round the Latimers' camp-fire on summer evenings until dark. She'd supply pencils, paper, and simple reading material to feed their hungry minds ripe for learning. The gypsies didn't want their children mixing with gorgios therefore denying them access to local schools for the few weeks they camped in the area. But at the same time they were grateful for any tuition offered them by Daisy.

The hill was a swirling frenzy of horse flesh. Gypsy rivalry reached its zenith as the plucky bareback riders put their horses through their paces. The operation, known as *the flash*, consisted of riders trotting their horses down the hill and along the road at breakneck speed, displaying conformation and speed of their livestock.

Some riders were no more than ten years old yet were equipped with the equestrian skills of great horsemanship. The pride and joy combined with showmanship, shone from their faces as onlookers and potential buyers lined both sides of the road. Some stepped out for a closer look risking being kicked by flying hoofs.

'Hello, Daisy, yer dad's sent me to help you with the horses.'

'Oh, hello, Donny, thank you. Three are a bit of a handful, I must say.' She handed over two sets of reins and smiled warmly at the weird-looking man.

Donny Smith, known to everyone as Donny Cock-eye, had been part of her life for as long as she could remember, helping her father with the horses. He performed odd jobs in and around Appleby and anywhere he could find work; harvesting corn in summertime, potato picking in autumn, and a spot of road mending in winter. During the cold winter months when work was difficult to come by, Donny pulled his small bow-top wagon into Samboy Latimer's place and settled down in a secluded corner of the orchard, waiting for springtime and the warmer weather to arrive.

Donny led two horses for sale into the maelstrom of bidders. As he put them through their paces Samboy stood amid potential buyers waiting for offers. He didn't have to wait for long. With a few nods, hand slapping and gestures, horses were exchanged for cash and deals were clinched.

Next in line was Daisy. She stepped forward with confidence leading the black hunter stallion she and Samboy had doctored with black dye. The stallion was strong. He tossed his head high lifting her from the ground a few inches. Samboy handed her a riding crop and she flicked it lightly across the stallion's rump bringing him under control. She'd done this many times before and enjoyed the mood and excitement of the occasion.

Samboy didn't hurry anyone. He wanted people to take their time to scrutinize the fine animal on offer. The stallion had been the cause of many discussions around the campsite and the quantity of people encircling the horse demonstrated the animal's exclusivity and desirability.

'Hey! What yer doing, Samboy? Havin' a lass do a man's job!' one of the gypsies bellowed. Guffaws and sniggers from others ensued.

'And any girl could do your job, Diddy Dave. Doesn't take any brains to steal kindling from a wood!' Daisy retaliated. The crowd laughed louder than ever when Diddy Dave turned a bright shade of red and skulked off.

'Grand 'orse you've got there, Samboy, pity the pretty young filly that's leading 'im isn't for sale. I might be 'avin a punt meself!'

Laughter followed by a chorus of 'aye's'.

'No chance of that, Tommy,' Samboy retorted good-humouredly.

He knew from experience it didn't take much for fighting to break out amongst a gang of traveller men. And he'd no doubt a great many of these had visited the pub and downed a few pints prior to the sale.

'Now let's 'ave some serious offers. 'E's a fine stallion, and worthy of a good master,' Samboy said proudly.

Daisy continued putting the stallion through his paces. Holding on tightly she trotted him down the road before walking him back slowly, allowing potential punters time to cast a critical eye over him.

His black coat shone brilliantly as black coal. He held his head high with his ears pricked forward, a perfect example of his breed.

'Eighty guineas,' someone bid.

'One hundred guineas,' another called.

'Hundred and ten, that's me final offer to thee, Samboy.' Seth Connor stepped out from the crowd holding out his hand awaiting the proverbial slap to conclude the deal. 'And a better offer thee'll not get today.'

Samboy looked at the proffered hand and, smiling, shook his head. 'Not enough, Seth. Whitby Jet 'ere is the best hunter Appleby 'as seen in many a year. I'll keep 'im for myself before I let him go cheap.'

'Suit yerself, Samboy.' Seth gave Samboy a respectful pat on the back, 'If we can't strike a deal we'll not fall out over it, eh?'

'No, we'll not fall out, Seth, been friends all our life. Not that I wouldn't like yer to 'ave 'im like, 'cos a finer animal you'll never find. Now, if yer can manage to up yer offer a bit more ... mebbe....'

Samboy stopped talking. There was a sudden commotion followed by a hush.

'I'll willingly pay one hundred and twenty guineas for your horse, sir.'

Samboy was taken unawares by the well spoken voice and handsome offer of 120 guineas. He didn't have to search far to locate the man who owned the refined voice. He stood tall, at least six inches taller than the men surrounding him who'd made bids for Whitby Jet. He was dressed in riding breeches, a crisp white shirt with a silk cravat at his neck and a Harris Tweed jacket. His highly polished riding boots bore the muddy remnants of his walk up to the selling place.

'And who might you be, young man?' Samboy asked, eyeing up the stranger. He was just the sort of person he'd hoped would come along looking for the hunter. Here was a man who reeked of class; bore the stamp of someone born to privilege and wealth, from his well-groomed hair down to his highly polished boots. Aye, he won't be short of a bob or two.

'Mr Tobias Flint, sir. I am here by recommendation. I was told you had a fine hunter for sale,' he said, smiling appreciatively at the handsome stallion. 'And I can see I was not misled by that information. Would you maybe consider selling me the horse?'

All the while Tobias was mindful of Daisy standing beside her father. Her strong slim arms wrestled to hold the prancing stallion in check and he couldn't help but wonder why the hell nobody went to her assistance. He was about to do so himself when the vendor stepped towards him.

For a fleeting moment he could have sworn she'd smiled at him – or was he mistaken? Probably wishful thinking.

'Latimer. Samboy Latimer's me name.' He held out his hand and Tobias shook it.

'Do you think we can do a deal, Mr Latimer?'

'Aye, maybe we can,' he said, removing his cap and scratching his head, 'but, right now, I 'ave other deals to strike. Can yer come back in the morning?'

'Yes. I'll be here at ten o'clock if that suits you. I have business to attend to first.'

'Ten o'clock it is then, Mr Flint. Daisy!' He turned to where she stood, still wrestling with the horse. 'Let Mr Flint 'ere 'ave a look over the 'orse.'

Samboy walked over to where Donny Cock-eye stood holding the remaining horses for sale. 'Donny,' he said quietly, 'get yerself over there sharp an' keep an eye on our Daisy, will yer? He might talk like a gentleman, but I don't trust any of 'em – especially when they've got their eyes on my daughter!'

'Aye, I'll keep an eye on her, Samboy, all four of 'em!' he chuckled handing over the reins.

Samboy smiled after him. Donny's humble demeanour, ability to work hard, and friendly free helping hand to anybody who asked had earned him a great deal of respect among the travelling and Romany community.

'May I?' Tobias asked, relieving Daisy of the reins that held the tossing head of the powerful stallion. His hand brushed against hers causing her to bristle. 'He's a strong horse for a young lady to be handling ... but,' he added quickly, 'I must say, you do handle him exceedingly well ... having ... already witnessed your equestrian skills.'

'Do you want to take the horse for a trial ride?' she enquired, ignoring his compliment. Flattery was not going to erase his behaviour.

'Look,' Tobias said, 'I know, I was awfully rude down by the river the other morning and I am sorry, *truly* sorry. I honestly didn't mean to offend you ... or your people.' His voice was thick with emotion. 'Please,' he said, holding out his hand to her, 'can we start again? Friends, please?'

Daisy was struck silent for a moment by the magnitude of his question. How did a person shift from a position of blatant disrespect of an entire culture, to one of what ... acceptance? She knew for certain her father wouldn't consider selling him the horse if he knew. Not for a minute! She was about to decline and tell him to go to hell when, a look of sincere anxious solicitude on his face caused social distinctions to blur, creating an intimately connected moment. She couldn't explain what happened in that instant, not even to herself. Only in months and years to come would she recognize what had occurred. They were the seeds of love and trust being sown in her heart.

She looked down at the outstretched hand between them and, reaching out tentatively, she placed her hand in his. 'All right,' she said, aware of the physical contact when their hands touched and that he held on to hers longer than was necessary. 'Let's give it a try,' she said.

The black stallion snickered and a secret shared smile passed between them.

'He approves anyway. Thank you. Daisy, isn't it?'

'Yes.'

'And I'm Tobias. Now we've sorted that lot out,' he said, rubbing his hands excitedly, 'Let's take a look at this superb animal I've bought.'

The clatter of hobnail boots striking concrete indicated Donny's approach bringing their conversation to a close. Donny took the reins of Whitby Jet from Tobias and led him away from Daisy to some open grassland and gestured for Tobias to follow him.

A disgruntled Daisy stomped over to Donny. 'Haven't you the horses to flash for my father?' she snapped, 'I'm quite capable of seeing to Mr Flint here!'

'No. Yer father's seeing to them and 'e's asked *me* to help with Jet … and Mr Flint 'ere,' Donny said, ignoring her. She was livid. Here was the handsome squire paying her so much attention any young lass would feel the same, he thought sympathetically.

'Do you want to ride 'im, sir?' Donny asked Tobias, 'I can get a saddle for yer easy enough.'

'No, no, thank you, I'll try him out tomorrow morning when I collect him.'

Tobias turned to Daisy. 'Goodbye for now, I hope we will meet again, very soon.'

'Yes, I'm sure we shall. Appleby's a small place,' she added, smiling into generous grey eyes looking at her softly.

Someone was watching them from a short distance away. They were so wrapped up in one another that neither noticed Roulson Adams who quietly smouldered with envy of the squire with his bloody educated voice, fine bloody manners, and fancy bloody clothes!

Lydia Flint had spent most of the day in the rose garden. It was her favourite place on the entire estate, a show-piece, and every inch of it created by her: the planting, pruning, weeding and fertilizing. No one else was permitted to touch it. It was her stamp of identity at the manor.

She was well aware the staff didn't like her – or the locals for that matter – and she didn't mind in the least. The last thing she wanted to do was mix with riff-raff! She'd seen enough of them in her day having survived the workhouse, hunger and abuse. A string of horses couldn't drag her down those streets again.

Lydia had been born into abject poverty in the slums of London. She'd no recollection of her mother who dropped her off at the workhouse door when she was four years old or thereabouts. No birth certificate or documentation accompanied her that fateful day. She'd no knowledge of who her father was and the chances were, neither did her mother. Lydia endured ten years in that God forsaken hellhole working her fingers to the bone. In return she'd received a roof over her head, barely enough food to live, and unremitting sexual abuse from one of the overseers from age ten to fourteen.

Then she escaped.

She had planned her escape carefully for weeks and didn't leave empty-handed. The perpetrator who'd abused her for four years accidentally dropped his wallet in the store room one day. Lydia found it and kept it. The twenty-five pounds it contained assured her freedom from the workhouse and the opportunity of a new life. The new life it bought her was one of high-class prostitution. Ten years of depravity curtailed the flush of youth. She was known professionally to London society so would search for pastures new.

Then one day, quite by chance, she came across an advertisement in a newspaper for a position with a well-to-do titled family in Westmorland and Lydia applied for it. Having cultivated a refined accent and dressing smartly she managed to convince the Flint family of her capabilities without references and secured the position of personal maid and companion to the late Edwina Flint.

She snipped a rose and placed it among the rest she'd cut for the house. She had learned the art of flower arranging from Richard's mother. 'Now don't use red and white flowers on their own, Lydia, too much a reminder of blood and bandages from the war, dear,' she would chide, then instruct her to do what her own twisted arthritic hands could not.

Lydia had taken it upon herself to study Edwina Flint intently and, by doing so, inveigled her way into the upper echelons of society. She found the old girl an extremely demanding woman who had been spoilt rotten by her husband from the day they'd married.

After his father's demise, Richard had discovered that as well as the estate his mother was also part and parcel of his vast inheritance. He'd accepted his duty admirably, without rancour, but had no intention of being at his mother's beck and call so employed the services of a companion without delay.

Lydia attended to all her needs. She bathed her, dressed her, and humoured her. No, she held no fondness for Edwina Flint. The old girl was merely a means to an end, her meal ticket out of subservience. She found her way into Richard's bed occasionally; usually when he was too drunk to find it himself, or to decline her advances. She was delighted when discovering herself pregnant. Her ambitions at long last realized!

Not a soul knew the truth about her life before marrying into the Flint family. Richard went to his grave ignorant of her past. And although she'd borne him two sons it had never been enough to make him love her.

He had married her, hadn't he? Wasn't that enough! he'd yelled, when she accused him of having an affair.

With the passing of time Lydia couldn't help but overhear tittle-tattle among the servants. Her husband, they said, spent a great deal of time with the gypsy folk at Appleby Fair, and that he was fond of one family in particular, the Latimer family who had settled down not far from the town. Her suspicions were confirmed one summer's day when Richard arrived home with a pony for Tobias. The pony was being led by a gypsy. She had rushed out to confront him and screamed like a demented fish-wife at him in front of the staff.

'What is the meaning of this? Why do you have to humiliate me so? Flaunting your gypsy friends in my face!' she ranted.

Richard took hold of her arm firmly then led her back to the house not uttering a word. Lydia swore and struggled to free herself from his hold but he was too strong.

'Do you want a hand there, sir?' the gypsy asked, looking anxious for Richard.

'Don't you dare put your filthy, disgusting hands anywhere near me…you scum! Scum of the earth! I'll have you arrested if you come near me!' she yelled bitterly at the bewildered gypsy, then kicked out wildly at Richard catching him on the shins. He winced but held on to her tightly, hauling her indoors. He dragged her into the drawing-room still kicking and screaming and threw her roughly on to a chair. He poured a glass of sherry and shoved it into her hand.

'I'm going back outside now to finish my business with that gentleman, *yes*!' he stressed, '*gentleman*. And, I might add, more of a gentleman than a lady you could ever hope to be. And, from whom, I have just purchased a pony for our son.' He spoke with a steely calmness that unnerved her and she knew in that instant when she looked at him and saw the contempt for her in his eyes, that she would never be forgiven.

This was a side to the mild-mannered Richard she hadn't witnessed before. Something warned her to tread cautiously if she wished to remain at the manor.

'And, should you take it upon yourself to behave in such a way again – think carefully,' he assured her emphatically. 'Because, if you do, you will pack your bags and return to whichever gutter you crawled out from!'

When their eldest son Hugh was killed in the war, Richard's life also came to an end. He functioned to a degree, being a caring father to

Tobias and continuing to run the estate for his sake, his only surviving heir. But death became a welcome stranger, so deep was his grief. He no longer cared whether Lydia lived or died – nor she him.

Even in death he'd made no secret of his contempt for his wife, bequeathing her a small cottage on the estate for the remainder of her life plus a small income.

She resided at the manor only by grace and favour of her son.

Tobias guided his horse away from the main road and down the quiet lane which zigzagged towards the wood that led back to the manor. He reined his horse to a slow walk. There was a lot to think about. He couldn't remember when he last had such an exciting day. And what a day it had been. Seeing Daisy again and putting things right with her gave him hope. God is this what love does to a man? Could he bear it? he wondered, drowning in his senses.

Tobias arrived at the wood and, entering it, welcomed the cool, dappled shade.

Beneath the trees an ocean of bluebells and wild garlic carpeted the ground. He inhaled deeply filling his nostrils with their perfume.

A heron took flight a few yards in front of him flying directly over-head to where its nest perched precariously at the very top of an oak tree. Further on, something caught his eye and he climbed down from his horse for a further inspection. A crude snare had been placed across a rabbit run. 'Bloody poachers!' he said, cursing out loud. He removed it before remounting his horse and carrying on through the wood.

He was deep in the wood when his horse suddenly shied and swerved almost unseating him. A man appeared from nowhere stepping into the middle of the path blocking his way.

'What the devil do you think you're doing!?' Tobias shouted, jumping down from his horse. He looked at the man and a vague recognition registered.

'I'm giving you fair warnin': stay away from Daisy Latimer, she's spoken for,' the intruder said, glaring at him with jet black eyes.

'It's none of your damn business who I spend my time with! Get off this land right now!' Tobias ordered loudly, stepping forward. He pointed a finger directly in front of the man's face, 'You're trespassing!'

'Daisy is one of us,' the stranger continued, unfazed. 'The likes of you bring nothin' but bad luck and trouble to our people. You don't know our ways so don't meddle with our lasses – stick to your own kind.'

Outraged, Tobias pushed the man in the chest. '*Out of my way!*'

In the next instant Tobias was flat on his back taken by surprise by a mighty fist in his face. He sprang up on to his feet all set for the next swing from his assailant. He ducked and the man missed, then thrusting his leg between his rival's, he brought him to the ground. He leaped on top of him and the pair wrestled for a few minutes. Tobias had the upper hand.

'Had enough?' he asked the stranger struggling beneath him and gasping for breath.

The man nodded and Tobias stood up. He reached out his hand to help his opponent to his feet. The stranger grasped it, but once on his feet kicked Tobias full force in the groin. He fell to the earth rolling in agony.

The dark stranger walked over to where Tobias lay writhing and pressed his foot hard down on his chest. 'Got the message, 'ave you?' he asked and spat in his face. He then walked over to where Tobias's horse stood and clapped his hands loudly causing it to bolt. With one brief glance back at Tobias he strode away disappearing into the dense woodland.

Tobias lay for a long time before hobbling to the nearby stream where he washed the dirt and blood from his face before gingerly setting out for home.

Dan saw his boss limping into the stable yard hugging his stomach and ran to help him. 'Good God, sir! What's 'appened? I was just comin' to look fer yer. Yer 'orse came back ages ago! Here, let me take yer weight, sir.'

'Some bastard waylaid me in the wood coming back from the fair,' groaned Tobias.

'Who was it?'

'I'm not sure, I've seen him somewhere before but I couldn't quite place him. Someone to do with the fair I think. It'll come back to me, but one thing's for certain – he packs a bloody heavy punch.' Tobias laughed. 'Aagh! That hurts, now do me a favour, please, get me up to my room without anyone seeing me, will you, there's a good chap? I couldn't take Mother and the bloody awful fuss she'd make. Oh, and fetch some bandages from the first aid kit. I think I might have cracked a rib or two. The bastard got me in the ribs as well as the balls.'

Chapter Three

Nothing could dampen the warm glow Daisy felt the following morning. Not even the rain that threatened to transform the campsite into a quagmire. She couldn't get Tobias Flint out of her head. She'd lain awake for hours the previous night reasoning she owed nothing to Roulson. She was a free agent.

She'd risen early lighting the stove inside the wagon before preparing breakfast, climbing down from the wagon to get the eggs from a storage box alongside the kennel where Max, the faithful lurcher, resided.

All the eggs had vanished! And she was sure they had at least three dozen stored.

'Dad, have you seen the eggs?'

'Yes, under the wagon, lass,' he answered, 'Where they're always kept.'

'They're not there, Dad, an' I wanted to make a nice breakfast for you. The deals clinched yesterday are worth a celebration, eh?'

'Don't talk daft,' Samboy replied diffidently. 'Those eggs were there last night when I fed Max,' he insisted.

'Well, they're not there now so bacon and bread will have to do.'

'Bloody thieving gypsy bastards,' Samboy mumbled under his breath scratching his head. 'By the way I've got a job for yer to do, Daisy,' he said. 'We'll talk about it after breakfast, all right?'

'Yes, all right,' she replied, frowning, wondering what it was that required a full stomach.

She looked over to where Donny sat at the back of his caravan under a canvas canopy sheltering from the drizzle. 'Do you want a bit of breakfast if you haven't already eaten?' Daisy knew full well he wouldn't have had a decent meal since his last meal with them.

'That's real kind of yer, Daisy. Yes, thank you.'

'By the way, Donny, did you see anyone hanging round our wagon last night? All our eggs have gone.'

'No. I spotted one or two of Benny's kids but I didn't think they were up to any mischief; they were playing with Max.'

'Say no more, Donny. Benny's kids are always up to something at night when everyone else is asleep.' She couldn't help but smile. Benny's lot would have eaten half the eggs before extracting money from some gorgio for the remainder!

'Oh no, Dad, *please, please!*' Daisy cried. The tears streamed unheeded down her cheeks. 'Why now? There's another three days left of the fair. Don't make me go *now!*' she pleaded.

'Your Aunt Chrissie needs some 'elp. She's ill, Daisy. An' she's family, *remember!*' Samboy snapped. 'There's no one else to look after 'er, so pull yerself together and pack a few things. That's the end of the matter!' he added sternly.

His sister Chrissie had got word to him last night to say she was poorly and in need of help. He'd seen it as a God sent opportunity to get his daughter away from Roulson Adams an' that fancy bloke who'd got his lecherous eyes on her. He sensed trouble brewing and volunteered her services immediately.

'When ... when do I have to leave?' she asked, sniffing and wiping her eyes, already resigned to the fact he'd not be persuaded otherwise.

He looked at his watch. 'Two hours. Donny'll take yer to the station. You'll get into Thirsk and yer Aunt Chrissie'll send someone to meet yer to tek yer over to Hutton.'

Samboy put his arm around her shoulders but she shrugged it off. He was heartily sorry to be sending her away down to Yorkshire, especially before the fair was over. 'C'mon, love, you've always enjoyed stayin' with yer Aunt Chrissie,' he cajoled.

'How long am I expected to be there for?'

'That depends on 'ow fast yer aunt recovers. She's 'ad 'er appendix out an' she's weak. I would've thought it'll tek a week or two afore she's back on 'er feet.'

'Right,' Daisy retorted sharply, 'I'll pack, and ... and wait for Donny.' She turned away briskly and climbed into the wagon, her green eyes ablaze with tears of frustration. 'And don't bother to hang about waiting for me to go – I'd rather be here on my own till Donny comes.'

Samboy walked to where his horses were tethered. He didn't want her to see how sad he was at sending her away. He felt choked with emotion but resisted the tears and began methodically to groom one of the horses.

It's for your own sake, lass, he thought solemnly, plagued with internal conflict.

'Mr Latimer?'

Samboy turned to look at the stranger who'd imposed on his sadness. Daisy had left for Yorkshire with a stubborn refusal to heal the rift between them.

'And who might be asking?'

'My name's Dan, sir, I've come on behalf of Mr Flint from Eden Falls Manor who I works for. It's about t'stallion 'e bought yesterday from yer.'

'And where might 'e be? Said 'e'd be here at ten o'clock,' Samboy remonstrated, raising his eyebrows.

'Mr Flint sends 'is apologies but 'e met with an accident and couldn't come. I looks after the 'orses for 'im, so 'e sent me. I 'ave t'money on me, sir.' Dan reached inside his jacket pocket producing an envelope and handed it to Samboy. 'If you'd just check it's right, sir, I'll be on my way.'

Samboy tore it open, took out the notes and, licking his thumb, quickly counted them.

'That's all in order, thank you,' he said, stuffing the wad of notes into his trouser pocket. 'Here's fifty bob, give it back to yer boss, an' tell 'im it's a bit of luck money. It sounds to me like 'e's in need of a bit of luck. I'm sorry to 'ear about the accident. What 'appened? Nothin' too serious I 'ope?' he enquired politely. The squire seemed a decent enough bloke and he didn't wish him any harm – he just wanted him to stay away from his daughter!

'Well, er, yes, unfortunately 'e was set upon after 'e left 'ere ... beaten up 'e was,' Dan offered somewhat reluctantly. 'But, I reckon 'e gave as good as 'e got,' he added, thinking mebbe he should keep his mouth shut. 'I'm sure 'e'll be right enough in a few days. 'E'll be happier when 'e gets t'stallion. 'E's been raving about it back on the estate. Loves 'is 'orses does t' squire,' Dan announced proudly.

'Aye, well, come an' have a cup of tea with me an' we'll have you on your way back to your master with 'im. I think 'e'll not be disappointed. Give 'im my regards an' I hope he's feelin' better soon.'

'Also, Mr Latimer, I wondered if the young lady is 'ere. The lass who was 'elpin' you with the 'orse my boss bought?' Dan asked nervously.

'Now, why would yer wonder that?' His tone hostile, Samboy folded his arms across his broad chest.

There was a momentary silence. 'Er ... Mr Flint 'e ... er ... 'e ... asked me to give 'er this. It's p ... personal like,' Dan stammered.

'Well, she's gone away for a while!' snarled Samboy, 'an' I don't expect 'er to be back for a long time! *All right?*'

'Do you 'ave an address for 'er that I can give my boss?' Dan continued bravely.

'*No* I bloody well don't!' Samboy blared. 'Now, if you want me to send it on to 'er, I will, but I'm not 'andin' out any bloody addresses to anybody! She 'appens to be my *daughter!*'

'R ... Right, Mr Latimer, I'm sure that'll be fine.' Dan handed him the letter, doubtful it would reach the young lady in question. But he'd done his best.

'I won't stay for a cup o' tea if it's all the same to you, sir, I'd better be getting back. We're busy haymakin' an' a dry day is a precious one an' ... an' ... I'm sure you'll 'ave jobs to be gettin' on with yerself.'

'When can I see you again, Roulson?' the husky voice purred from the untidy bed.

'Soon, but mind you keep quiet about our romps. Don't want to give you a bad name now, do we?' Roulson chuckled playfully, slapping her bare backside.

'I'll come down and see you in Yarm in October when the fair's on, Roulson,' she said, slipping silently from the bed, wrapping her arms around his waist and preventing him pulling up his trousers. 'I miss you so much ... I can't wait all year, Roulson. I must, hmmm.... Please ... hmmm?' she pleaded stroking him.

Roulson glimpsed her reflection in the dressing-table mirror. What a bloody tart, he thought disparagingly, his sexual urge now satisfied. Her bleached blonde hair was stuck up all over the place, red lipstick smeared all over her mouth. Good God! He'd be ostracized from the travelling community if he turned up with Lill! She was a cosy handful admittedly, and the best jump a man could wish for, but that was as far as it went.

She'd taught him all he knew regarding the fairer sex. He'd been an enthusiastic and willing participant in her seduction of him as a mere lad of fifteen. She was twenty at the time, unattached, sexually ripe and available, welcoming him into her bed every year he visited Appleby Fair.

Gorgio women served a vital role for Romany bachelors like him.

He realized he'd made a big mistake coming back this year. But what the hell was a bloke supposed to do? There was no chance of sex with a gypsy girl before marriage. It was *forbidden! Taboo!* And should the male species manage to infiltrate any underwear he'd be married within a month! The girl's family would make certain of that, or he'd be beaten half to death by them.

Aw, Daisy, he thought, I wouldn't be here if I had you.

'I won't be going to Yarm this year, Lill. I might be going over to Ireland for the rest of the summer,' he lied. 'What you need, Lill, is a nice bloke from round here, one of your own kind.'

'Fat chance of that!' she sneered. 'All the fellas know you and me have been seeing each other these last few years. I'm soiled goods,' she added. 'And I don't want anyone but you,' she whispered, kissing his ear.

'Well, let's hope Daisy hasn't got wind of it!' he mumbled under his breath.

Two hours later Roulson crouched over his umpteenth pint at the bar of the seediest pub in town, a hangout frequented by the travellers during fair week.

The landlord had no complaints. Travellers and gypsies alike brought in good money for the short time they were here. Locals dwindled but his profits soared as the hard-drinking men downed pints faster than he could pull them. Some of them were trouble though like the one slumped over the bar now. But if he could get the rabble out on time, any disputes were settled outside the pub more often than not, or up on the hill, leaving the pub's fixtures and fittings intact.

One or two nodded their subdued hellos to Roulson, but in the main, they ordered their drinks then moved as far away as they could, or simply ignored him. They'd seen him like this before. Moody, drunk and objectionable, he was ready to fight anyone and everyone who got in his way – or who just happened to get on his nerves.

'What the 'ell's up wi' 'im?' whispered one of a group of men sitting by the window.

'God knows! He's had his oats today which is a damn sight more than any of us can say!' another guffawed.

'Aye, Lill must be fair knackered, he's been there all afternoon!'

'Well, 'e won't be much cop tomorrow afternoon by the looks of 'im now – I might drop in to see 'er meself!'

The bawdy laughter ceased momentarily when Samboy entered the low-ceilinged smoke-filled room. He went to the bar and ordered a half. He glanced across the room to where two inebriated gypsies stood propping one another up. They held on tightly to one another's lapels pledging incoherent allegiances, but too drunk to stand on legs threatening to buckle beneath them should either one let go. Samboy grinned and picked up his beer to retreat to a table. He looked at the man slouched across the bar next to him and saw it was Roulson Adams.

'You all right, lad?' he enquired.

Roulson raised his head slowly, his glazed eyes taking time to focus. He recognized Samboy and, attempting to stand, clumsily knocked over the stool he'd been perched on. Samboy grabbed him before swiftly repositioning the stool beneath him.

'Oh, Mishter Latimer, yesh, I'm fine,' he slurred, 'How's yershelf ... and – *hic* – my Daisy?'

'Daisy's well, thanks. She's gone to stay with 'er aunt in Yorkshire for a few months,' he lied. The last thing he wanted was him hanging around after the fair waiting for her return. There were many things about Roulson Adams he didn't like – and this was one of them. He drank too much than was good for him, unleashing an aggressive streak.

Aye, it's a good thing I've done sending Daisy to her aunt, he thought, congratulating himself on a prudent decision. Roulson Adams was nowt but trouble.

'Gone?' Roulson cried like an injured dog. 'Gone, without saying a word to me? I don't believe it!'

A silence fell across the room as his angry voice rose above the general conversation.

'Aw, she didn't 'ave time, lad,' Samboy said humouring him. ''Er aunt's ill an' has no other family. It was an emergency. I'm sure she thought you'd understand, Roulson, lad.'

'Yesh, of course I do – *hic* – Mishter Latimer, but she should've said,' he groaned, laying his head back down on the bar.

Samboy drained his glass. 'I'll be seeing you.' He patted Roulson on the back and left.

'Time, gentlemen, please,' the landlord called.

Roulson was the last straggler to stagger out of the pub. He urinated up against the pub wall before making his way unsteadily down to the river. Crouching, he glimpsed his reflection then ducked his head into the cool water diffusing the image. It was midsummer and still light, intensifying his vulnerability in his inebriated state.

'Walk it off, yer bloody idiot!' he said and headed for the quiet lane which skirted the town before leading back to the hill. It was a good two-mile walk and would help sober him up. He felt angry toward Daisy for leaving without a word. But most of all he was angry at himself and awash with shame. I should've kept away from Lill. Aw, an' caught drunk by Daisy's dad! What the hell was I thinking of! What will he think of me? God, I've made a right pig's ear of it this time!

In the fading light he could hear singing and laughter coming from the not too distant campsite. He stumbled upon a dry grassy mound beneath a heavily scented honeysuckle clinging to a hedgerow and sat down. He didn't want to see anybody in the state he was in and decided to wait until the singing ceased and people at the camp retired to their wagons. He closed his eyes and drifted off into a drunken dreamless sleep.

It was much later and Roulson woke with a start.

The sensation of a great weight pressed down heavily on his chest. 'Aw, God, what's happening!' he called out hoarsely, hardly able to breathe.

A giant dark shadow loomed over him. The crushing weight on his chest was that of a stranger's heavy boot.

'What the hell ... what do yer think yer doin'?' Roulson groaned in disbelief. He attempted to stand and push the weight from him, but the alcohol flooding his system prevented it.

'I'm warning you, that's what I'm doing!' The warning came with increased pressure on his chest. 'Keep away from Lill, or yer goin' to have me to answer to, *understand*?'

'Don't worry, you've no fear of that. I wish the hell I'd kept clear of her long ago ... arrrgh!'

The perpetrator dragged him roughly to a standing position and punched him full in the face before flinging him aside. Roulson managed to remain on his feet, as he staggered backwards to the wide trunk of a tree. The tree supported him, giving him a few vital seconds to focus. The man hurtled towards him. Roulson was ready this time. His knee came up to meet the charging head and, as the man's knees buckled under him, Roulson grabbed him. He rammed his head repeatedly into the trunk of the tree until blood ran through his fingers and the body became heavy and limp.

It was three hours later when screams and shouts alerted those asleep in their wagons and tents.

'*Fire! Fire! Help! Someone help!*'

People hurried from their beds to see a bow-top wagon engulfed in flames.

Mothers held their children close to them shielding their eyes from the blazing inferno. Men stood helpless after attempting to douse the leaping flames with limited supplies of water.

Roulson Adams's family stood with their arms around each other.

'It's our Roulson!' the mother cried. 'He was that depressed. He must've fallen asleep; drunk as a skunk he was. Gone ... gone ... forever! *Aaaargh* no! Roulson, me son!' she wailed.

Her husband and younger son flanking her, wrapped their arms about her and steered her into the caravan leaving the crowds to witness their tragic loss.

'Poor bloody buggers,' said one, shaking his head solemnly. 'What a bloody way to die. I saw him, the lad, earlier today – he was fair gone with the drink.'

'Aye, pissed as a fart he was when I saw him.'

'Well, he won't be depressed any longer,' remarked another. 'He'll be with his Maker, God love him and rest his soul.'

Samboy looked on quietly, saying nothing. He'd thought unkindly of Roulson, resenting his attentions to Daisy. But, he didn't wish the lad dead! God, Daisy, poor lass! I'll have to let her know somehow. But I'll wait a bit. No point in upsetting her and there's nothin' she can do anyway while she's at her aunt Chrissie's.

A posse of policeman arrived at the same time as the fire-engine, followed shortly by a black car driven by a detective. Samboy looked on as someone directed him to Roulson's family wagon where they explained what they believed to have happened. Old Ma Adams was too distressed to answer any questions and the detective gently touched her shoulder saying he was sorry and would call back later.

The police were not a welcome presence and, walking back to his car, the detective noticed all the travellers had returned to their caravans, that was apart from one man.

Samboy sat alone in the darkness outside his bow-top wagon cradling a cup of tea in his hands. The detective sauntered over to him. He looked familiar.

'Don't suppose you saw what happened?' the detective asked him.

'No, sir, sorry, I didn't. It's a rum do, this. The wagon was well ablaze by the time I saw it. But I did see young Roulson early evening ... be about seven o'clock. He was very drunk at the time. That's all I can tell you, sir.'

'Don't I know you from somewhere? I'm sure we've met before.'

'That you do, sir,' Samboy said, smiling at him. 'I broke a pony in for yer son ... be about a year or so ago.'

'Of course, Mr Latimer, isn't it?' The detective returned his smile. And what a fine job he'd done too of breaking the spirited Shetland pony. His young son was mad keen on riding and had ridden it every day since. From what he could remember, Samboy Latimer had a property not far from Appleby where he spent most of the year. And didn't he have a pretty daughter? He was highly respected hereabout, he recalled, and it was heartening to know he clung to his gypsy roots. They were a proud people the travellers; granted, there were undesirables among them but, didn't that go for the non-gypsies too?

'Well it's good to see you again, Mr Latimer. If you can think of anything that might help, I'd appreciate it if you'd let me know.'

'I'll do that. Goodnight to you.'

Samboy climbed back inside his wagon and into his still warm bed. He lit a candle knowing sleep wouldn't come for a long time. Something bothered him about tonight's events; all wasn't what it appeared to be. Aye, Roulson's mam and dad were upset … and yet … it all seemed a bit managed, all a bit of a show. Something just didn't fit, but he couldn't put his finger on it. And that detective knew something wasn't right. Best keep out of it, he told himself. We don't want involvement with any skul-duggery. After all, me and Daisy 'ave to live round 'ere after the rest of 'em 'ave buggered off back to wherever it is they bugger off to. Thank God Daisy isn't around.

No, I won't be sorry when Appleby Fair's behind us this year.

Chapter Four

The train pulled into the station where the platform was thronged with people waiting to return to outlying villages. It was market-day at Thirsk, a day country folk visited the town to do their weekly shopping, or to sell their goods.

Daisy stepped down from the carriage and made her way to the deserted waiting room where a fire burned brightly in the grate. Although it was June there was a chill in the air. She sat by the fire grateful for the warmth and silence.

Her eyes drifted to the enormous clock hanging above the fireplace. It struck five o'clock and her thoughts drifted to Appleby. They'd be building up their fires now getting ready to cook their evening meal. She closed her eyes. She could smell the rabbit stew ... taste the sweet baked potatoes, hmm ... dripping with fresh farm butter.

Her happy thoughts were interrupted by a rough shove on the shoulder.

'You Daisy Latimer?' a stranger asked gruffly.

'Yes, has my Aunt Chrissie sent you to collect me?'

'Aye, and thee'd better get a move on afore t'eavens open up, I've got t'orse an' cart waitin'.' He hurried from the waiting room leaving her to follow and carry her heavy cloth holdall to the awaiting transport.

The man's craggy face broke into a toothless grin when the sky black-ened and a loud rumble of thunder preceded torrential rain. 'Told you so,' he said, smugly.

The journey to her aunt's house was uncomfortable and miserable in the pouring rain and by the time they arrived Daisy was drenched to the skin.

'I'll be in fer me tea in an 'our or so,' the surly stranger announced, reining the cart to a halt outside the back door of the cottage. 'Yer aunt says yer gonna see to it, the cookin' like.'

Daisy glared at him dumbfounded. 'I beg your pardon? I don't know what on earth you're talking about! I'm not here to ... to look after strangers! I'm here to see to my aunt's needs!'

'Well, it just 'appens I'm no stranger to 'er,' he assured her. 'Been 'ere for nigh on two months now doing odd jobs, and she always meks sure there's plenty o' grub fer me – you just go and ask 'er,' he added, nodding toward the cottage.

'I'll do that!' she retorted, climbing down from the cart. She dashed through the teeming rain and into the house.

'Is that you, Daisy?' an anxious voice called. 'I'm in here.'

'Yes, it's me, Aunt Chrissie,' she answered brightly, passing through the scullery and kitchen to where the voice came from.

'I've got my bed down here in the front room, Daisy.' Thin arms emerged from under the patchwork quilt to embrace her niece. 'Thanks for coming, lass. I don't know what I would've done if you hadn't. Probably I'd have had to stay in hospital.'

Daisy saw she looked gaunt and frail. Being a diminutive woman, no more that five feet tall, she appeared even shorter in the big double bed. The dark-brown eyes smiled lovingly at Daisy, making her olive skin appear paler than it actually was. Chrissie's hair held only a trace of grey. The long, thick, black, glossy plaits were coiled round and round her head forming a coronet, giving her an imperial air.

Daisy had spied the large wooden water-butt positioned under a drainpipe near the back door to catch rainwater specifically for hair washing. Large jugs of water were carried in ceremoniously every two or three weeks before being heated on the old range in the kitchen. After the initial shampooing Chrissie then doused her hair in beer to produce a magnificent sheen.

Daisy smiled to herself. She loved the old traditional ways of her people and endeavoured to adhere to their customs. Many of the younger people hankered after effortless, more modern ways of living now, and who could blame them? It wasn't a comfortable existence. But being here right now with her dear aunt, she felt a deep sense of warmth and belonging. Change wasn't always a good thing, she decided.

'Oh, I don't mind coming to stay, Aunt Chrissie,' she said, returning her embrace and kissing the proffered cheek. 'That's what families are for.'

Chrissie felt the cold wetness of Daisy's clothes and shivered. 'Aw, you're sodden, lass! Get out of those clothes *now*, before you catch your death.'

*

Daisy woke early the next morning. Her eyes scanned the familiar little bedroom. Everything was exactly the same as when she had visited before. There was the small truckle-bed shrouded in a pretty rosebud counterpane with matching curtains and chair cushions. In one corner rested a marble-topped washstand and, next to it, stood a tall mahogany wardrobe. The fire she'd lit in the tiny cast-iron fireplace had produced enough heat to dry the clothes she'd hung on the rickety wooden clothes horse.

She walked over to the window and drew back the curtains. The sound of heavy rain lashing against the window-pane had woken her in the night, but now the sun shone brightly and raindrops glistened like jewels on the drenched landscape.

The cottage had been built about 200 years before on some elevated land on the outskirts of West Hutton. The slight elevation leant itself to wonderful views of the western hills. As she looked toward them she could see the early morning sun slanting on Penhill, and the clear wide entrance to Wensleydale and beyond.

'Is that you I hear moving about, Daisy?' Her aunt's voice prohibited her sliding into maudlin thoughts of home and what she imagined she might be missing.

'Yes, I'll be down in a minute, Aunt Chrissie.'

She threw on some slacks and a blouse then went downstairs to where Chrissie was sitting in a chair by her bed, a hairbrush resting on her knee. Her aunt's hair looked exactly the same as it had last night with not a hair out of place, signifying the arduous task of unplaiting, brushing and re-plaiting all that hair had already been done. What a mammoth under-taking! Daisy thought.

'I've made a pot of tea,' she said, indicating a tray on her bed. 'Now, Daisy, you remember the routine here without me havin' to tell you what needs doing. Lord knows, you've helped me here often enough. But there is one extra job I'd like for you to do for me, that's if you think you can manage it.'

'What's that, Aunt Chrissie?'

'Next Monday, I want you to take my cured rabbit skins to market, to sell.' She watched intently for her niece's reaction at being asked to assume such an important task. It was no mean feat to stand at a stall at Thirsk market for the day.

'They're all hanging up in the outhouse,' she continued, 'and there's just an odd skin left to finish scraping. Do you think you can do that?'

'Of course I can. I've been helping Dad sell the horses so I think I can manage to sell rabbit skins. And Dad's shown me how to mix saltpetre and alum to a paste. I cured a lot last winter … and I made a hat for myself,' she boasted. 'Maybe I can make one for you, Aunt Chrissie, before I go back home?'

'Aye, mebbe,' Chrissie said, pooh-poohing such notions. 'But let's get on with important stuff. Now, Caspar will be wanting a bit of breakfast about seven-thirty—'

'Who?'

'Caspar. The bloke who met you off the train? He's been helping me out a bit.'

'Caspar? What an odd name. Where's he from?'

'God only knows. Nowhere and everywhere if you get my meanin'. Gentleman of the road, that's what he is.'

Well, the sooner he's back on it the better, Daisy thought.

Caspar stood up and stretched his aching back. He was working in the vegetable patch when he heard her voice. He looked round to see it was the young 'madam'. She's nowt but a bloody pest. Better not spoil things for me. I can spend the summer 'ere if I play my cards right.

'I need some beans and a few potatoes for tonight's tea,' Daisy said, looking at the surly face that would curdle fresh milk. She couldn't understand why her aunt kept him on; she could easily do what he did – and in half the time!

He sneered and grunted. 'Well get the buggers picked! Yer've got a pair of hands, ain't yer?'

Daisy glowered at him and went to fetch a garden fork. She dug up the potatoes then quickly picked some green beans without another word before making a hasty departure.

'How long are you keeping Caspar on for, Aunt Chrissie? I could do his work now, and it would save you money.' Dangling the temptation of saving money was always the best ploy where her aunt was concerned.

'Yes, I know you could. I'll give him another week and by then I'm sure we'll manage between us.' There was a long pause. 'You don't care for him, do you, lass?'

'No, I don't. And I wouldn't trust him as far as I could throw him.'

A week later, Caspar was given his marching orders and left.

Daisy was loading up the cart for market while Chrissie stood by the horse going through a check-list.

'Now don't hang about, lass,' she said, wagging a warning finger at her. 'You set off back home at four o'clock whether you've sold up or not. You hear me now? I don't want to be fretting over you, I haven't the strength.'

'I hear you, Aunt Chrissie. Don't worry, nothing's going to happen to me. I'm looking forward to it. You've got some beautiful pelts and I'm sure they'll sell well.'

She climbed up on to the cart and, taking the reins into her hand, set off for market at a steady walk. As soon as she was out of view of the cottage where Chrissie stood watching them, she urged the horse into a fast trot.

The heat was oppressive and her hair felt wet and heavy with perspiration. She unloaded the pelts on to the stall then delivered the horse and cart to a stable behind the inn her aunt had used for years. Daisy poured water on to a handkerchief and dabbed her face and neck, wondering at the same time how on earth her aunt managed to do this at her age.

'Too 'ard work for thee, is it, lass?' said a gruff, familiar voice.

She spun round to see Caspar standing in front of her stall looking more unkempt than when she had last seen him.

'No, it's not! I thought you'd have been miles away by now,' she said frostily.

'You mebbe would've liked me to be miles away, but I like it round 'ere and it'll be Topliffe Fair soon. I might pick up a bit o' work there.'

He moved closer and the stench of stale beer filled her nostrils making her want to retch. She backed away slowly.

'I'll tell my aunt I've seen you,' she said, 'I'm sure she'll be pleased to know you are all right. Now I must get on.'

'Aye, you tell her that,' he said malevolently. Daisy shivered as she watched him disappear into the gathering crowd.

Creep! she thought.

It was nearly twelve o'clock before she stopped for a break after having sold a fair quantity of skins. Her aunt was obviously a popular lady at the market. A number of people had enquired after her health and wanted to know when she'd be back.

The stall next to her was laden with second-hand clothes. Her aunt had mentioned this stallholder was from traveller stock, and the local rag and bone man.

'If you need to go to the toilet he'll keep an eye on t'stall for you,' she'd said. And true to her word that's what happened.

'Off you go, lass, I can see to your stall an' me own for a while. Away you go and get summat to eat,' he suggested kindly.

Daisy thanked him and set out through the bustling market crammed with canvas-covered stalls listening to the call of market-traders.

The town boasted an ancient cobbled square encircled by a myriad of shops. It had two excellent hotels, ten pubs and a fine clock in the centre.

She treated herself to a new hair ribbon and some lace from a haberdashery stall before making her way towards Mill Gate to purchase a sack of flour her aunt requested.

She stopped outside the jeweller's shop and gazed in wonder at the array of silver, gold, and sparkling gems on display. Glancing through the window a young couple were scrutinizing a selection of engagement rings. The middle-aged man serving them said something causing the young man to laugh and the lady to blush. Daisy felt like an intruder on their special moment and quickly walked away. Instead of going directly to the mill she strolled along Bridge Street and on to the bridge spanning Cod Beck. She leaned over the parapet to glimpse shoals of minnows, tadpoles, and sticklebacks. Children were standing in the shallow margins of the river with fishing nets and jam jars secured on lengths of string, their eager faces set in concentration. Again Daisy was reminded of Appleby and the children laughing and playing in the River Eden.

Better get a move on, she told herself.

When she returned to her stall the man who'd been watching it for her said someone had come by asking for her.

'Did they say who they were, or what they wanted?' she asked curiously.

'No, some bloke who says he knows yer from Appleby.'

Daisy was puzzled. Must be that awful Caspar, she thought.

'Handsome bloke though. A right good-looking fella 'e was. One of us I'd say if I had to tek a guess.'

Daisy smiled to herself. One thing was for sure then, she thought confidently, it definitely wasn't Caspar.

'Well, he'll maybe call back. Thanks for looking after the stall. Looks like I've about sold out,' she said proudly, casting her eyes over the few pelts that were left. Aunt Chrissie would be pleased.

She folded and stacked the unsold pelts back on the cart and set out for home. It was just four o'clock, the time her aunt had said she must make her way back.

The horse whinnied in appreciation of the lighter load. Daisy clicked her tongue and flicked the reins, urging him into a fast trot.

It was two miles further when she turned right towards West Hutton that she felt sure she'd glimpsed a movement in the hedgerow.

'*Daisy*!' someone called out loudly, '*Daisy, stop*!'

Startled, she looked round frantically to see who was calling her name.

Within seconds a man leapt out from nowhere and darted in front of the horse. The horse shied and reared up, practically ejecting Daisy from the cart along with the rabbit pelts. The man grabbed the horse's reins and, using all his physical strength and expertise, brought the horse and cart to a juddering halt.

'Daisy, it's *me*!' the man yelled, raising his head which had been buried in the horse's mane. He tossed his wild dark hair back from his face. His eyes sought hers beseeching recognition. 'It's me, *Roulson*!'

'Roulson!' she screamed his name. 'What on earth are you doing here? I thought you were in Appleby. Has something happened? Is Dad all right? Tell me!'

'Your dad's fine, Daisy. Look we can't talk here, I must see you,' he said, glancing around to ensure no one else was about. 'I know where you're staying with your aunt. Can you meet me later? I'll see you about seven o'clock. Say you're going for a short walk before bed and I'll be waiting for you, OK?'

'Well, I'm not sure if … I….' Deceive her aunt? What a terrible thing to do! But there was an excitement and urgency about Roulson which was both dangerous and compelling.

'Please, Daisy, I can't explain anything now and … don't tell a soul you've seen me, promise?'

'All right, I promise I'll not tell a soul,' she whispered jokingly. 'I'll see you later. But you'd better let me get home now, or Aunt Chrissie will have the entire police force searching for me!' she added, laughing.

Roulson scurried away quickly at the mere mention of the police.

'You've done well, Daisy,' Chrissie said proudly. She'd just counted the takings. 'And I want you to have this,' she said, handing Daisy two pound notes.

'No, honestly, Aunt Chrissie, I don't want any money.'

'Well, if you don't take it, it'll be going into a post office savings account for you as soon as I can get myself to Thirsk.'

'All right, I'll take it, and thank you. I shan't waste it, I promise.' She kissed her aunt on her cheek and put the notes in her pocket.

'I know you won't waste it. I wouldn't be givin' you it if I thought you would.'

'I'll get on with tea, Aunt Chrissie. I bought a bit of fish in the market for us so you sit there and I'll soon have it ready.'

She hurried to finish her chores giving herself time to change before meeting Roulson. Her heart quickened at the thought of seeing him. I wonder if he'll kiss me. God! What on earth would Dad say if he knew?

'You all right, Daisy?' Chrissie called. 'I just asked you twice if you needed any help with tea.'

'Aw, sorry, I ... was just thinking about today and ... and ... what a good day it's been,' she fibbed, her face colouring with shame.

'Well, mebbe an early night will help. It's not easy standing a market. I should know, I've done it for many a year.'

'I'm not tired honest, Aunt Chrissie.'

Daisy promptly set the table, put the fish in the fireside oven then rushed out to the orchard to retrieve a line of washing she'd hung out before going to market.

With the chores completed and her meal finished, Daisy carried a jug of warm water up to her bedroom to wash before going out. She was accustomed to having strip washes when on the road travelling from fair to fair in summertime with her father. There was no bathroom here but the cottage proudly boasted an outside toilet. The toilet, or privy, as her aunt called it, was whitewashed twice a year. Daisy recalled with fondness it had been her job to cut up old newspapers into small squares before threading them on to a piece of string. The booklet of paper was then dutifully hung on a nail at the side of toilet and used as toilet paper. As a small child she could remember sitting for hours idly attempting to read bits of news from the small scraps of paper.

She opened the wardrobe and looked solemnly at the handful of clothes she'd brought with her, wishing she'd thought to pack the new dress she'd bought in Appleby. In the end she decided on the cotton slacks she'd worn for market and a clean, fresh-looking blouse of pale green silk. There was no point in arousing any suspicion in her aunt. Brushing her hair, she remembered the ribbon she'd bought that day and carefully tied it round her head. She was pleased with the result when she looked in the mirror. The pretty ribbon was a perfect match for the silk blouse.

She heard the clock in the sitting-room chime seven and quietly went downstairs.

Managing to avoid her aunt who had closed her eyes she crept past her. When she reached the back door she announced her departure. 'I'm just going for a walk before bed, Aunty, shan't be long,' Daisy called, crossing her fingers hoping she wouldn't detain her.

'All right, I'll wait up for you.'

She walked along the quiet road with the sound of a song thrush repeating its rich melodious tune. She looked up scanning the surrounding trees for its whereabouts. It was perched high in one of the trees lining the narrow road. As she lowered her eyes to the base of the tree Roulson stepped out from behind its broad girth.

Daisy smiled at the familiar figure waiting for her. Only Roulson could surprise a girl like that, she thought, appear like magic from behind a tree. She congratulated herself on being the one he chose to spend his time with, believing he could undoubtedly have any girl he wanted.

'C'mon,' he said, grabbing her hand and pulling her none too gently along the road.

'Hang on!' Daisy retorted, yanking her hand free from his. 'What's the hurry?'

'Look, I've got some transport,' he said impatiently, pointing to a small grey van parked along the road on the grass verge. 'Let's go for a drive and we can talk.'

She looked at her watch; it was a quarter-past seven. 'I can't, there isn't time. I have to be back before eight. Aunt Chrissie will worry as she'll be expecting me.'

For some reason this secret rendezvous with Roulson was not as she'd imagined.

His manner was brusque and any romantic notions she held were quickly dampened by his mood. Her thoughts in disarray, she wished she hadn't agreed to meet him and a sense of dread invaded her thoughts.

He saw the flicker of fear and uncertainty in her face. This is no time to make mistakes I've got to win her over! She's my chance to make a good clean break from Yorkshire. The coppers will soon be on my tail when they realize it isn't me who's been cremated in that bloody wagon! Roulson's family had purchased the van and registered it in his brother's name. The police were searching for a man using a horse and cart. But Roulson knew that even with his knowledge of secret places and hidden lanes familiar to wayfarers and gypsies, they'd find him eventually. He'd managed to keep a low profile so far with help from fellow-travellers, mainly cousins.

'Look, I promise yer I'll have you back in time, OK?' Roulson said. He gently took her hands in his, raising them to his lips and kissed them.

He provided her with an irresistible smile and little boy lost look. It had never failed him in the past and it didn't fail him now.

'All right,' conceded Daisy.

Roulson drove the van away from the village and prying eyes.

He drove to a quiet by-way commonly known as lover's lane, a place frequented by courting couples seeking privacy to indulge the art of kissing and sex.

When the sun went down and the moon came up couples were lucky to find a parking spot. Naked legs could be seen hanging over front seats and an occasional backside flashed in the moonlight; car windows steamed up rapidly with loving exertion.

Roulson switched off the engine and turned to face her. God, she's beautiful, he thought. She's no idea the effect she has on men – and I'm going to have her.

Daisy had been looking round the inside of the van while being driven along. The engine was loud causing everything to rattle and roll about making it impossible to be heard over the din. She saw that in the back were mattress, blankets, pots and pans. A tarpaulin was rolled up and tied to the roof. In the foot-well a bag containing clothes rested on top of a pair of boots. There was a sickly smell of sweaty feet and stale body odour. She wanted to open a window but wasn't sure how; she thought she might use the wrong handle by mistake and fall out so decided against it.

'There's something important I want to ask you, Daisy.'

'Well, before you ask me anything can you open a window please? It stinks in here! And then tell me first of all what you're doing here when Appleby Fair's on?'

He slipped his arm around her shoulders. 'I'm in trouble, Daisy. There was an accident at Appleby and ... and ... a bloke was killed. I had to get away.'

'Someone killed!' She shrank back in her seat. 'My God! Who? Who was killed?'

Shock waves shot through her body and her heart hammered loudly in her chest.

'I don't know who it was! *It was an accident*!   He was shouting now, his face black with anger. 'I didn't mean to kill him.... But, but ... he attacked me! And before I knew it we were fighting ... and ... and, he was dead. I can't go back there, not now ... not ever again. They'll put two and two together and ... aw, God, don't look at me like that, Daisy, *I'm not a monster*!'

'But if it was an accident they'll understand, surely! Once you've explained what happened!'

'Understand! Understand us gypsies!' he raged aggressively, his voice growing louder. 'Since when have we been understood by anyone, eh? Don't talk so bloody daft, Daisy! We don't count among the gorgios! *We're as welcome as … as … Jews in Germany*!' His rage unnerved her.

'Well, if you're not going back w … what are you going to do?' she asked. Her eyes were wide with terror. 'Y … you can't hide forever. They'll come looking for you and—'

'But that's it, Daisy, we can hide for ever … you and me. If you come with me we can leave, go away and get married and—'

'Come with you! Get married! What on earth are you talking about? I can't up sticks and come with you!'

'Yes, you can, Daisy. Marry me! Come with me to Southern Ireland. We can make a brand new life together.' His black eyes blazed fiercely.

'But I don't want a brand new life, Roulson,' Daisy interjected endeavouring to bring his insane suggestions to a close. 'I like the life I've got. Ireland? I don't want to go to Ireland – or anywhere else. Appleby's my home and always will be!'

Roulson couldn't have been more shocked if she'd hit him with a sledgehammer. He was floored without a punch. He removed his arm resting across her shoulders and slumped back into his seat. The ominous silence that ensued filled Daisy with horror.

'I'd better get you home, it's getting late.' His voice was calm, too calm, and his eyes looked at her without expression.

They drove back in silence to the cottage. He didn't look at her as she climbed from the van.

'Just one thing, Daisy,' he said, staring straight ahead, 'you haven't seen me, OK?'

'Yes, I promise. You know that goes without saying.' She hesitated, waiting for a response. None came. ''Bye then, Roulson. Maybe … maybe I'll see you at Topliffe Fair?' she asked nervously.

'Mebbe, mebbe yer will.'

Roulson watched her walk the short distance up the road to her aunt's cottage. Who the hell did she think she was? *Bitch*! That Caspar was right – she's nowt but a bloody stuck-up madam! And no one, no one crosses Roulson Adams and gets away with it. And *you* Daisy Latimer, are no exception! A plan began to form in his mind.

Chapter Five

Eden Falls commanded fine views across the sweeping countryside and the fells beyond. The large manor house built of sandstone stood four-square and was pleasing to the eye.

An old wisteria draped itself around the front of the house, wrapping itself casually about the stone mullioned windows with long, blue, pendulum-like flowers. At the rear of the house an archway led through to a courtyard and stables, two of which had been converted into garages for the automobiles now taking precedence over the horses. On the south side of the property, an elegant orangery had been erected about fifty years ago. It housed lemon, orange, peach trees and a grapevine. When in bloom the perfume from them permeated the house and gardens, triggering off blissful smiles among the staff inhaling the heady fragrance. Behind the orangery, a vast expanse of grass accommodated a tennis court and a croquet lawn where tennis parties were held regularly on the immaculate well-kept grass.

There was a time when the Flints were renowned for their hospitality, and neighbouring farmers and friends would visit. Some often stayed for the weekend having travelled a great distance. It was a time when the house and gardens burst with life and laughter, bringing sparkle and energy to the manor.

Yes, Richard Flint was sorely missed by all.

Lydia Flint looked out over the gardens from an upstairs window. Since quarrelling with her son a wall of tension had built up between them. It was he who should apologize for his disgraceful behaviour towards me *and* in front of the servants! But he hadn't, thus amplifying her bitterness and disparaging view on life and others.

She walked across the room and her stockinged feet sank into the deep silk pile of the Chinese rug which practically covered the whole of the floor. It was a beautiful room. She'd shared it with Richard for a few years until that fateful day ... the day she'd found him fraternizing with the gypsies. That evening he'd vacated the master bedroom and never returned.

The bedroom housed a four-poster bed that had come down through generations of the Flint family. There was a white marble fireplace with a pair of chintz-covered armchairs placed at either side. A fine walnut bureau stood in front of a window. An oak wardrobe ran the length of one wall in which her clothes hung on hangers next to those of the late Edwina Flint.

Lydia had kept her mother-in-law's clothes and on occasions wore them when alone in her room. She would squeeze herself into one of the many elegant evening gowns and dance wildly round the room imagining herself with Richard, and the envy of everyone. Such was her fragile state of mind at these times.

There was a scrunch of car tyres on the gravel and she went to the window. Tobias was heading down the drive and she wondered why he was out in the car again instead of riding that bloody horse he'd bought.

No one had told her of the attack her son had sustained and she was unaware of his injuries.

She looked at her watch. It was ten o'clock. Dan would be in the kitchen having his tea break with the kitchen staff. She pulled on a pair of outdoor boots and hurried down the stairs and out of the front door. Lydia trod slowly down the gravel path that ran by the side of the house before cutting through to the courtyard where the stables were.

She walked over to the stable that housed the newly acquired stallion which Tobias had purchased from some *damned gypsy*! Lydia felt her heart race and fill with hatred at the very thought of it! She put her head through the stable door. The horse turned to look at her before returning his attention to the hay rack.

'Here, boy,' she said, holding out her hand. Whitby Jet walked over to the strange woman and placed his nose in her hand accepting the small tit-bit. 'Don't get too comfortable,' she said, sneering cruelly at the horse. 'You're not going to be here for long, I'll make sure of that!'

The horse sensed something and stepped backwards. He pawed the stone floor and threw his head up, whinnying loudly, the whites of his eyes showing clearly.

'Steady. Steady, boy!' she said quietly to calm him. But Whitby Jet sensed the presence of evil and kicked the stable door causing Lydia to make a hasty retreat before Dan returned.

'What's up, lad?' Dan asked, puzzled at the sudden change in Jet. He saw the horse was distressed walking round in circles in the confines of the stable. He opened the door to enter but then decided against it when Jet reared up. He closed it quickly and looked enquiringly at the animal. 'Something's upset yer ... whoa there ... steady ... there's a good lad.'

In due course the horse settled down eventually allowing Dan to enter the stable and stroke him.

'There now ... what was it, old boy? Yer'll be fine. Let me tek a look at yer now.' He carefully examined each hoof before gently running his experienced hands over the legs and body. 'All seems OK with yer, lad, mebbe it's a bit more exercise yer needin'. We'll see about lunging' yer a bit. I'll be back later, boy.' Jet snorted as his fear abated.

Later that day, Lydia Flint walked to her car and passed Jet's stable. Dan was mucking out at the time when Jet suddenly fired up kicking over the wheelbarrow. He held on to his halter tightly and glanced over the stable door to see Lydia getting into her car; he realized then the cause of Jet's distress.

'Aye, Lydia Flint, eh? Ah should've guessed. I'll watch 'er, Jet; no wonder yer shit scared. Frighten any bugger that bloody cow would!'

Tobias parked his car in the town and made his way to where the horse sale was about to take place. He hoped to glean some news of Daisy while here, or, better still, learn of her whereabouts in Yorkshire.

Samboy had seen him arrive and monitored his movements from a distance while grooming the last of his horses to sell at the fair.

He seems a fine young fella, not unlike his father, Samboy thought. He'd been sorry to hear of Richard Flint's passing as had many of the travellers. The man had treated them respectfully and it had been reciprocated. The late squire had also shown great kindness to Daisy, giving her permission to ride on his land, aye, she'd be right sad to hear of him passing.

Samboy had decided against posting the letter to his daughter from young Flint, rationalizing it was for her own good.

Donny was making his way across the grass towards Samboy when Tobias Flint stopped to talk to him. He shook Donny's hand and Samboy saw the huge smile spread across his face which was animated throughout the remainder of the conversation.

Donny was pointing toward Samboy and Tobias turned and waved to him. Samboy raised his hand in acknowledgement and carried on grooming the horse. They walked over to him.

'Good day to you, Mr Latimer,' Tobias said amicably, smiling broadly.

'And to you,' replied Samboy. 'I'm glad to see that yer've recovered from any 'arm you encountered.'

'Yes, thank you. The weather's been most considerate to us this week, Mr Latimer. I expect business has been good for you.'

By, he's trying bloody hard, Samboy thought. 'Can't complain. What brings you back to the fair might I ask?'

'Oh, it's that time of year on the estate when haymaking is finished and the corn not quite ripe enough to harvest. Also ...' Tobias hesitated. 'I believe my father had many happy days here at the annual fair. And I can understand why, it's fascinating. He bought me my first pony from this fair, Mr Latimer. Pippin I called him. I had many happy years riding him about the estate.'

Samboy slipped into a more relaxed manner as the young man proved himself to be a genial fellow. 'Aye, I remember yer father well. I was right sorry to 'ear 'e'd departed. He was a grand man.' He saw the sadness in Tobias's eyes at the mention of his father and felt a genuine sympathy for him.

'Thank you, that's most kind of you,' Tobias replied softly. 'By the way, how is your daughter? Daisy, isn't it? I believe she was going to Yorkshire.'

'Ere we go, Samboy said to himself, I knew there'd be a bloody catch. 'That's right, she's gone to look after 'er aunt who's just come out of hospital, and, aye, before you ask,' he added sternly, 'I did forward yer letter to 'er. Now, if you'll let me get on I've got a 'orse to sell.'

Tobias didn't leave straight away. He decided to enjoy the pleasure of the warm sunshine and stimulation of the fair before returning home.

People had their wares for sale on show outside of their wagons and caravans. Baskets of pegs, lace, and arrays of artificial flowers made from bits of rags, paper and wire. On other stalls, Tobias recognized the brightly coloured Crown Derby and Royal Doulton china for sale. They had a number of rare pieces at the manor which had been in the family for many years and it was very expensive. His mother would die if she could see it for sale here.

He came upon a young, grubby-looking girl of about ten years old. She was sitting by a gypsy cart that, by the looks of it, had seen better days. She appeared to be in charge of half-a-dozen children younger than herself and just as bedraggled.

'Want to buy some lavender, mister?' she asked boldly, while wiping her runny nose on the sleeve of her dirty dress leaving a silver trail.

'I'd love to.' Tobias took some coins from his pocket and paid her for the sprigs of lavender. He gave her an extra sixpence, 'Here, buy some sweets for yourselves when you've finished selling, young lady,' he said, smiling at the family of children.

'Aw, ta very much, mister!' she exclaimed with delight. 'That's a right treat for us, ain't it? Now say ta,' she said, instructing the unkempt group.

'Ta,' chorused the youngsters, grinning madly.

He walked away carrying the neatly tied bunches of lavender.

Those kids maybe were dirty and bedraggled, he thought, but they have kinship and deep tribal roots which is a damn sight more than I have. I might own a manor house, land, and have servants to do my bidding, but when I go home from here it's to a humourless existence and a mother who grows more bitter and twisted with each passing day.

His despondency was interrupted. 'Tell you yer fortune, sir?'

He turned to where a dark-haired, olive-skinned elderly gypsy woman was sitting outside an immaculate, colourful, bow-top wagon. She smiled at him, a clay pipe filling the gap where once there had been teeth. Her dark hands rested upon her apron, the fingers heavily laden with sovereign rings. Enormous gold earrings the size of bracelets, dangled to her shoulders and around her neck hung strings of bright coral beads.

'I don't think so, but thank you,' he said, smiling at her.

'Yer've got a lucky face. Come on in, young sir, yer'll not regret it. Rose Marie is me name – I'm known all over the country for me gift of fortune-telling.'

Aw, why the hell not! He about turned and made his way toward the famous Rose Marie.

'And what will the pleasure cost me?' he asked, looking into the darkest eyes he'd ever seen. But they were kindly, knowing eyes that twinkled mischievously when she smiled back at him. He decided there and then he liked this woman. Whether or not she was a charlatan, he cared not. He wanted to spend some time in her company.

'Five shillings,' she said, her tone very businesslike.

'Five shillings, good Lord!' he exclaimed, 'That's a lot of money. You must be good.'

'I'm better than good,' she said confidently, 'I'm the best yer'll find.'

'Right. If that's the case, where do you want me?'

Rose Marie stood up from where she perched on a stool. She placed the clay pipe on a small ashtray then indicated the wooden steps leading to the inner sanctum of the bow-top wagon.

He had to duck his head and bend his knees to go through the door. On entering he gasped with delight at the beauty of it. It was crammed with the finest china and cut glass he'd ever seen; even his mother would be hard pushed not to be impressed, he mused.

The canvas roof of the wagon was lined in a quilted silk fabric, exquisitely embroidered in tiny flowers which must have taken months, or even years to do. Rich red velvet curtains hung at the tiny window. He was astounded at the delicate, intricate work visible in the construction and furnishing of the charming little house on wheels.

He sat down slowly, carefully avoiding knocking over any precious pieces of glass or china. Rose Marie read concern in his face and advised him not to worry but to relax.

She placed a flimsy bone china cup and saucer on the table between them. For the life of him he didn't know how she'd managed to produce a hot cup of tea within seconds.

'Go on, drink it. Don't look so scared, I'm not going to poison you 'cos you 'aven't paid me yet!' They both laughed and he relaxed a little. 'And I can't get to them tea leaves if yer don't get it down yer – and it's your lips that must drain the cup.'

'Right, right …' he said apprehensively, and quickly gulped the hot tea. He swallowed a few tea leaves causing a bout of coughing and choking. 'Sorry … sorry about that. I'm OK now.'

His index finger became stuck in the tiny handle. She leaned forward and gently released it.

'There now,' she whispered, and with a strange unnatural slow swirling motion of her hand – which appeared not to include any wrist action – she emptied the last drops of tea from the teacup into the saucer then held the cup in both hands as though ready for prayer.

She stared into the cup for what seemed an eternity. Her eyes assumed a faraway look. There was a hushed stillness within the wagon even though, outside, the place thronged with people.

A shiver ran down his spine when she placed the cup on the table and raised her head to look at him. The faraway look had vanished and was replaced with an intense gaze of concentration. This is serious stuff! he thought.

'*Change … there are going to be many changes in your life…. There is also deep sadness, but don't fear the change, it is good … good for all concerned.*' Her eyes held his gaze and she sensed a disturbance in his heart. '*Don't be afraid of the danger in your midst, but it is there … not for too long. You must ride the storms, storms in the near future. Your help will be much needed by someone....'* She took a deep intake of breath placing the cup back on the table.

Tobias could feel his heart racing. He was unable to move a muscle or to take his eyes from her. He made no resistance when she took his hand and turned it palm upwards in her own.

'Ah, a gentleman's hand,' she said, stroking her fingers over his soft palm.

Most of the hands she read were gnarled and callused from hard labour, the hands of men and women who were desperate for change in their lives. They wanted to hear about coming into lots of money, a way out of their poverty, hardship and misery that swallowed them up. Rose Marie could see that there was no way out for most of them.

She continued stroking the hand that lay in hers for a while before she spoke. *'You must guard against someone, someone close....'* She hesitated, unable to continue for a while and her lips moved as though in secret conversation with an unseen being. *'There is somebody who would harm you and there is also someone waiting for you to help them ... not a stranger. It's not too clear, but will be made so....'* She then looked up into his eyes and smiled. *'There is much love in your heart. I see you are waiting for the fortunate young lass to come and claim your love. She will, all in good time. There's nothing any good got in a hurry, young man, so be patient, and your patience will be rewarded.'*

The mystic spell dissipated as the Romany let go of his hand and stood up.

'Come and see me next year.' This was something she never asked any gorgio to do, probably because they always came back to her anyway for another reading. Yes, she had the gift of seeing into the future; sometimes it was a blessing, other times a curse, but for some reason she wanted to know how this man would fare through the difficult times ahead.

'I'll still be around then?' Tobias jested.

'You'll be around, young man, that's as sure as night follows day.'

Tobias was dazzled by the brilliant sunshine after the subdued light inside the gypsy caravan. He looked at his watch; plenty of time, no rush to get back, he said to himself ambling over to where the horses were being sold and stood behind a group of onlookers who were excitedly anticipating the horse sale.

Samboy was holding a fine skewbald gelding which would be useful in the shafts. Tobias smiled, watching the men endeavouring to negotiate a deal. One hand was held out, ignored by the other man – the hand was offered again along with a bid. Both men's hands went back and forth before eventually, after much talking, stamping, flamboyant arm and hand-waving gestures, Samboy's hand came down on the other with a sharp slap. A deal was struck followed by a great deal of handshaking and back-slapping.

Tobias was thinking of sauntering over to compliment Samboy on the fine skewbald he'd sold when he saw him take a wary look around then stride away briskly toward his bow-top caravan at the other side of the field.

He didn't know what possessed him, but he followed him discreetly, curious to know what he was up to. Tobias came to a sudden halt when he saw an attractive lady hurry toward Samboy. The couple laughed and hastened to his wagon, then disappeared into the back of it.

'Well, bugger me!' Tobias exclaimed, 'No wonder he wants Daisy out of the way – the bloody old rascal!' He couldn't help but smile and experienced a pang of envy, wishing it were he and Daisy clambering into the open-lot wagon.

'Oh, he's no rascal, believe me,' said a slow, measured voice. 'If anybody deserves a bit o' comfort, it's Samboy.'

Tobias spun round to see Donny Cock-eye standing behind him, eyeing him suspiciously.

'What? Oh, I do apologize. Please forgive me … I didn't mean to be rude.' Tobias stumbled over his words caught in the act of prying.

'I knows yer didn't. I shouldn't've crept up on yer like that, but I thought summat was wrong.'

'Well, you were right there. *I* was wrong for spying on the man and … and speaking out of turn, my only excuse being I … I … was thinking aloud.'

'Aye, well, yer'd better be off afore Samboy sees yer. He wouldn't tek kindly to bein' spied on.' He looked up and winked at the handsome young squire, adding, 'I'll say nowt.'

Samboy smiled down at the woman who lay sleeping in his arms after their pleasurable lovemaking.

Lavinia Cooper was a couple of years younger than himself and had been a widow for the last ten. Her late husband had been a close friend of Samboy's. They'd bought and sold horses from each other for many years. Then one day when John Cooper was breaking in a young colt he was kicked in the head and killed instantly.

It was about three years ago when his friendship with Lavinia deepened and, to avoid gossip, they decided to keep their courtship secret.

She stirred lazily and, opening her eyes, smiled tenderly at the handsome face looking down at her. He kissed her moist pink lips and held her close. Her body responded; her nipples hardening against his broad chest. He reached down caressing her full firm breasts and the need for her was ablaze in his loins once again. She broke free from him, throwing her head back, laughing.

'As much as I would love to, I can't lay here all day, Sam!' she said. Sam she called him when they were alone, or as they were now – making love. 'We'll be getting into bother one of these days found in bed together. All anybody has to do is come looking for one of us, lift up the canvas flap, and there we'll be – naked! Then what'd we do?' she exclaimed, feigning indignation.

He watched her as she climbed from the bed and began dressing. Her grey hair was tinged with a peppering of auburn. It was cropped short, unusual for a traveller woman, most favouring long plaits. Samboy liked it as it was. It suited her, making her appear quite boyish and cheeky even though in her early forties.

'I'll tell you what we'll do, sweetheart, we'll get married.'

'*Married*!' Lavinia exclaimed. 'Why? What's come over you, Sam?'

'You, Lavinia, you've come over me.' He reached to pull her back into the narrow bed. 'Come back to bed, Lavinia. Let's talk about the future, *our* future. We do have one, don't we?'

'Have you been drinking, Sam Latimer?' she asked, plonking down on the bed next to him.

'Aye, drinkin' in your beauty.' He held both her hands in his. 'I'm serious, Lavinia,' he said, gazing fixedly into her dark, intelligent eyes. 'Will you marry me?'

In answer, Lavinia leaned forward and kissed him gently on the lips. 'Yes, I'll marry you, Sam lad, an' make an honest man of yer.'

'Oh, you've made me a happy man, my love.... Now when?'

She placed her fingers on his lips, 'Now hush yerself and not another word about marriage till the end o' summer. We don't want to upset Daisy and ... and I want her to be happy for us. No, Sam,' she said, as he began to protest. 'Now promise me.'

'By, you drive an 'ard bargain, Lavinia, but I promise. I'll wait till September, but then we're to be married.' He grabbed her, pulling her down on top of him and they giggled like two naughty children. 'And then we'll belong to each other for the rest of our lives. I want you in my bed every single night God sends!'

Tobias drove steadily up the long winding drive. The acres of cropped grassland flanking each side of the road were quite spectacular this time of year. Copper beech, horse chestnut and cedar dotted about were grazed to the height of the cattle's reach giving the appearance of having been meticulously manicured.

The day was warm, the cattle lay in the shade of the trees lazily chewing the cud and flicking away the dratted flies with their tails. The ewes with their maturing lambs had recently been sheared and wallowed in the warm sunshine. The lambs' energy had not dispelled with the heat and they frolicked happily among themselves. A few small hillocks of grass-covered boulders enabled them to play king of the castle.

As he neared the house the gardener waved to him. Haven't seen old Matt for a week or two, he thought. I'd best check everything is all right. Feel a bit sorry for the poor old boy having Mother to answer to.

He parked the car and made his way to the gardens where he found Matt emptying a wheelbarrow at the compost heap.

'Everything looks perfect, Matt, you do an amazing job. I know Mother is pleased with the herbaceous borders,' he said, knowing it wasn't strictly true. She was constantly complaining about the management of the gardens, about Matt, and the rest of the staff.

'Mebbe she is, but she ain't too 'appy about *that*!' he said, pointing with a soil encrusted finger to a large bare patch in the centre of the border.

'Why's that then, Matt?' he asked in genuine ignorance, assuming some replanting was underway.

'Last night,' he said, still pointing to the bare soil, 'That there were stocked wi' the best lavender yer could get 'old of. An' I gets up this mornin' and the whole bloody lot's vanished! Gone! And God knows where, 'cos I don't! Unless them gypsies 'as teken it; nowt 'd surprise me.'

'I'll sort it out with Mother, Matt, please don't worry.' He patted the old man affectionately on the back and walked away quickly. He knew exactly where the lavender had gone. For hadn't he just bought some of it from the young lass at the fair? He laughed to himself. Mother will be hopping mad, he thought, but what the hell? It'll help her focus all that hatred that's eating her up.

*

A mist had crept up from the River Eden shrouding the old manor, creating an eerie, ghost-like appearance. It was 1.30 in the morning, the silence interrupted by the night sounds of an owl hooting and the trickling resonance of the waterfall running softly down the hillside behind the house. The dry weather had slowed the cascade of water considerably, but after heavy rains the transformation would be dramatic and the din of the waterfall would be deafening when it came crashing down through its rock-encrusted pathway.

The figure that crept stealthily under cover of darkness around the back of the house was cloaked in a dark raincoat and trilby hat, carrying a bucket.

The figure walked swiftly toward the stable block and, quietly entering, placed the bucket on the floor of one of them. The individual then backed away and waited.

Whitby Jet rose from the deep straw bed at the familiar sound of a rattling bucket being brought into the stable. The bran mash laced with molasses was a treat for any horse and Jet softly whinnied with delight before burying his head in the bucket devouring every morsel.

The figure crept back to the stable, reached in, retrieved the empty pail and quickly left.

Chapter Six

'Please, this way, madam.'

Detective Sergeant Keen steered the distressed woman into his office. He indicated a chair opposite him and asked a junior officer to bring her a cup of tea.

'Now tell me, Mrs Grant, you haven't seen your son for what? Three days you say? Is that right?'

'Yes, that's right. There's summat wrong, he'd never not come 'ome. It's them there gypsies!' she spouted venomously. 'He's never liked 'em an' one of 'em were seeing a lass 'e was sweet on and—'

'Now, let's take it slowly, Mrs Grant. You can't go round accusing people without proof. I know you're upset.'

He handed her his handkerchief and she wiped the tears from her eyes before blowing her nose loudly and passing it back to him. He shook his head. 'Keep it. Tell me now, was your son – Bob isn't it? – was he at the horse fair?'

'Well, no, but he was going to see Lill and she didn't turn up so he went for a pint. One of his mates said she'd been seeing one of them gypsy lads. Some real good-looking bloke that all the girls are talkin' about an' fancyin'. Then he'd got real mad and said 'e was goin' to sort 'im out and make sure this fella—' She knitted her brow trying to recollect the name she'd been told by one of Bob's mates. 'It were a queer name, Ronson, or summat like that. Any road, our Bob was gonna make sure 'e wouldn't show 'is face in these parts again.'

'Maybe he's taken himself off for a few days – decided to have a short break....'

'No! Never! Our Bob wouldn't do that – he's got a job of work to go to!' Mrs Grant insisted.

'Where does he work?'

'Local butcher's in town, bin there ever since 'e left school. A good job it is too. No, Bob would always turn up for work. There's summat not right, you mark my words, and it'll be summat to do with those no-good gypsies! They always brings trouble with 'em every year! Shouldn't allow 'em 'ere!'

She was relentless in her vitriolic tirade against the travellers. Poor buggers don't stand much of a chance when there are people like Mrs Grant in the world, he thought sadly. One would've thought with the appalling atrocities committed by the Nazis on the Jews and the gypsies people would have some compassion – but seemingly not. Racial hatred was still alive and kicking!

'I'll tell you what, Mrs Grant, I'll go back to the campsite myself today, ask a few questions, and then I'll call at your house, OK? Maybe by then your son will have returned.'

Three hours later Keen drove on to the campsite.

At a cursory glance it looked as though a lot of the wagons had already left.

He made his way to where Samboy's wagon was parked. Samboy stepped from behind the horse he was grooming at his approach.

'Good day to you, Mr Latimer.' Keen smiled and touched the front of his hat respectfully. 'I was hoping you might be able to help me.'

'I will if I can,' Samboy said, feeling none too happy about the detective seeking him out. The other travellers would be watching him closely from unseen locations about the place. Being courteous to the police was one thing, but being seen to be over-familiar with them, especially a detective sergeant, was asking for trouble from your own people.

'There's a man gone missing from the town; he works at the local butcher's.'

Samboy frowned and shrugged his shoulders. 'Sorry, I don't know who yer mean. I knows nobody from any butcher's. Sorry, but I can't help yer.'

Keen carried on talking, ignoring Samboy's dismissal of the matter. 'Well, his mother says she hasn't seen him for three days and that he had it in for someone. It sounded like it could've been that traveller lad, Roulson Adams, that he was after. But it appears his family have, er, left. Is that right?' He looked at the scorched earth and open spaces now devoid of any horses and wagons. 'Do you know where they've gone?'

'No. They could've gone anywhere. I don't think they wanted to be round 'ere after what 'appened, needed to go and grieve; get away from t' crowds, and pryin' eyes.'

'Ah, well, thank you Mr Latimer. I'll just have a walk round and see if anybody else knows anything.'

'Do that, but yer'll not get anything out of any of 'em. Waste o' time, tek it from me. The travellers stick together, Mr Keen. Even if they know summat they'll not tell. Sorry, but that's the way it is. I 'ope this missing bloke turns up – sad and sorry I am for 'is poor family.' Samboy shook his head sympathetically and walked away leaving Keen undecided whether to ask the other travellers for information. But, as he walked towards the caravans and wagons people turned their backs on him, directing their attention to daily tasks and melting away from view.

Keen climbed back into his car thinking Latimer was right. There was no way he was going to get anything out of them. God knows what he was supposed to tell Mrs Grant.

A police constable walked across to DS Keen when he'd parked his car back at the station.

'Hello, sir. I was hoping to catch you before I went off duty.'

The young constable was new to his post and eager to please.

'I picked this up the other day at the campsite,' he said, handing over a small, charred metal tin. 'It might help with your enquiries.'

Keen took the tin from the brown envelope then reached into his pocket for a penknife and prised it open. Inside was a selection of angler's flies which, by good fortune, were untouched by the fire and recognizable.

'Thank you, Constable. Tell me, where did you find it exactly?'

'In the middle of the scorched area under a pile of ashes I was raking.'

'Well done, Constable, thank you for waiting for me.'

Keen returned as promised and was in Mrs Grant's front room with a WPC.

Her son hadn't returned and she was growing more despondent by the hour.

'We'll put out an all alert in the area, Mrs Grant and maybe one of our officers will spot him.'

'Yes, thank you,' she said calmly. All the fight had gone out of her.

Poor old girl is worn out with worry and it looks as though there's no Mr Grant around, he thought. 'We'll be in touch tomorrow, Mrs Grant. Will you be all right on your own?' He touched her hand and the tears slid down her cheeks as she nodded.

He stood up to leave and, as he took his car keys from his pocket, the envelope carrying the tin of flies fell to the floor and sprang open. He bent down to retrieve it, but Mrs Grant reached it first and picked it up. Her eyes were transfixed on the object.

'What is it, Mrs Grant?'

'Where did you find this?' she asked, her voice a mere whisper. Her eyes held a faraway look.

'At the campsite. There'd been an accident and one of the traveller lads has been burned to death in his caravan. It was laid among the ashes. Why? Have you seen it before, Mrs Grant?'

'This belongs to our Bob! His dad and me – we gave it to 'im for 'is birthday. It was 'is twenty-first.' For a fleeting moment her eyes shone with happy memory of not so long ago.

'Look!' she said, excitedly now. 'There's the inscription. 'Is initials, we 'ad that done,' she added proudly. 'But what was it doing there … on the campsite? Burnt … among some … some ashes you say?'

She slumped back heavily in the armchair, her head, heavy with sorrow, moved from side to side refusing to believe what she had just heard.

'Have you anybody who can come and stay with you, Mrs Grant, family … a neighbour perhaps? Constable, you remain with Mrs Grant until something is sorted out. I'll go back to the station.'

'Yes, sir.'

He looked at the subdued, forlorn lady slumped in her chair and was filled with an overwhelming sadness. She knew her son was dead, and so did he. But how was it ever going to be proved?

A hundred unanswered questions raced through his mind: *where is Roulson Adams – the man supposed to have died in that wagon? Whose bones were taken for burial by Roulson's family, bones that will never be found again? And were his parents involved? What a bloody mess! I'll question every bloody one of them – even Samboy Latimer! Who do those bloody gypsies think they are? Closing ranks! They must think they're damned royalty!*

'Two days running! Becoming a regular haunt this place, eh?' Samboy said, grinning at the detective making his way toward him. 'I've already told yer I—'

'Never mind what you've already told me,' snapped Keen.

Samboy flinched at the sharpness of his voice.

'I'm here on serious business. Now, you can answer my questions here, or down at the police station. And quite honestly I don't mind which! That goes for everyone here on the campsite. Officers!' he barked, 'make sure no one leaves this site.'

Samboy removed his hat and ran his fingers through his hair. 'OK, let's 'ave yer questions then.'

'When did the Adamses leave?'

'The next night, I believe. I woke up the next morning and they'd up and scarpered.'

'Where did they go?'

'No idea, and that's God's 'onest truth. I only ever saw 'em at Appleby Fair. Probably gone down south, if I 'ad to tek a guess.'

'Did you see Roulson Adams that evening on the campsite?'

'No, I didn't. As I told yer before, I'd seen 'im earlier in the pub, fair drunk.'

'And you haven't seen him since?'

'Seen 'im since? Since he's died yer mean? What on earth d'yer mean? Are yer telling me 'e's not dead? Good God!'

'No, I'm not telling you anything, Mr Latimer. That will be all for now. Thank you for answering my questions.'

As he turned to leave, Samboy touched his arm. 'Look, if I can 'elp in any way I will, truly. I can imagine what's going through your 'ead with that other young fella missing. I take it 'e's not shown up yet?'

'That's right, Mr Latimer, he's not shown up.'

Samboy watched him walk over to another bow-top wagon to begin his questioning all over again. He hoped they'd hold nothing back, but he knew that hope was in vain.

Samboy rubbed the linseed oil into the leather harness which lay across his knees. His instinct had told him things were not as they seemed that night of the fire.

He had been into Appleby that morning and seen a picture of the missing man – and a sketch of Roulson Adams in the local paper. He was wanted for questioning.

A terrifying thought suddenly flashed through his mind – Daisy! Would he try and find her? God! He remembered telling him in the pub that night she'd gone to her aunt in Yorkshire. Hopefully he was too drunk to remember.

Samboy couldn't rest knowing Daisy wasn't under his protection. He arranged for himself and Donny to go down by train and bring her home. Donny said he'd willingly stay and help Chrissie for a while if she needed anyone and Samboy could pick him up at Topcliffe Fair which took place a few weeks from now. Yes, it would all fit in nicely, thought

Samboy. Lavinia was happy and willing to tend his horses and look after things here for a day or two.

They'd had a wonderful night of love-making last night knowing it would be a long while before they'd have any privacy. Samboy smiled, recalling the night of physical delights they'd shared and was sorry it wouldn't be repeated for a while.

Lydia was in the garden when she heard shouts coming from the stable block. She glanced up then carried on selecting and cutting flowers for the house, but the shouting continued.

'What a din!' she declared and walked to the stable block.

'Oh, it's you!' Dan said, when she put her head through the open stable door, 'Go and get Mr Flint as fast as you can!'

'Yes, *it is I!*' She enunciated each word and glowered angrily at the ignorant stable hand.' And you *will* address me correctly!'

'Aw, for God's sake go and get Mr Flint, will yer? Summat's 'appened to 'is 'orse!'

'*Good*! And you can go and fetch him yourself, *you ... you ... uncouth peasant!*' Lydia reproved striding away haughtily.

Dan rushed past her to the front of the house. He hammered on the door before thrusting it open and running into the hallway shouting for his boss.

'*Sir*, Mr Flint! Come quick!' he called, 'Are you there, sir?' He raced to where the study door flung open as he reached it.

'What is it, Dan?' Tobias asked, taking hold of his shoulders to steady the poor man bordering on hysteria.

'Quick! Come now! Jet's ill 'n I can't help him! 'E's real bad, sir.'

'Go back to the stable,' Tobias said in a calm voice. 'I'll be there in a minute or two, but first I must ring for the vet.'

Dan hurtled back down the hallway, the quickest route to the stable. As he opened the door Lydia was entering the house. Dan dashed past her accidentally catching the trug full of flowers she carried. It took flight, the flowers flew through the air and one landed unceremoniously on top of her head making her look quite comical. Dan would have laughed at the sight of her had he not been in such a sorry state.

'Sorry,' apologized Dan.

Lydia stood gaping with horror at the man she'd had just reproved. 'How dare you use the main door?' she screamed at the disappearing figure. By the time she'd recovered herself Tobias appeared striding down the hallway.

'Did you see what that ignorant lout did? He used the front door! You'll have to sack him, Tobias, he behaved in a most disrespectful manner toward me.'

Tobias sighed. 'There's an emergency, Mother! Can't you find something useful to do instead of finding fault with the staff at every bloody opportunity?'

'Tobias, there is no need to swear. Really!' she remonstrated.

'Oh, go to hell, Mother! I don't have time for your childish diatribes!'

Hurrying through the front door he sprinted all the way to the stable where he found Dan kneeling, cradling the head of the sick horse.

'How long has he been down?'

'He refused 'is food this morning but I didn't think it was serious like, 'e did seem a bit sluggish when I think about it. If only I'd—'

'Never mind, look, don't blame yourself you weren't to know. Tell me, then what?'

'I comes back and 'e's laid like this. Then I comes rushing for you.... Is 'e goin' to die, d'yer think?'

'I really don't know, Dan, but the vet will be here shortly. Let's hope he can do something, eh?'

'It's just a matter of time now, Mr Flint,' the vet said, shaking his head. 'I've done all I can for him. I'll call back tomorrow and – if he's still here – there's just a chance he'll make it.'

'Some sort of poisoning you say? Any idea what it was?' Tobias asked, as they walked to his car.

'No, sorry, I can't, not until we've run some tests. If he's been stabled since you bought him – it's rather puzzling; might be worth having a word with the previous owner.... Well, just a thought. I have to dash – got another visit to do, so good luck and I'll see you tomorrow.'

Tobias stood watching the car disappear down the drive pondering what could possibly have caused his horse to have been poisoned? He came to the same conclusion as the vet. He'd call on Mr Latimer. He won't like it, but I need to get to the bottom of this whether Jet survives or not. And maybe, just maybe, he might have some ideas on treating the animal.

Lavinia was busily grooming Samboy's horses. The sun was warm on her back and she welcomed the gentle breeze that had got up, cooling the perspiration on her forehead. Most of the travellers had left the field early, taking advantage of the good weather before it rained, rendering the field impossible for heavy, horse-drawn, narrow-wheeled wagons to move. When Samboy returned, Lavinia would pack up and travel down to the West Country for a few weeks. She'd meet up with family and friends before returning north when she and Samboy would make arrangements for their marriage and future together.

She smiled to herself thinking of Sam. A warm glow spread through her being making her want to shout and jump for joy. Never in a million years did she believe she'd find love again after John had been killed. Life had been difficult in those early months and family and friends had helped her enormously. She had had to learn quickly how to harness and drive the wagon – which had come as second nature to her. Sam had been the one who had advised her on the horses. He taught her all he knew, enabling her to carry on with the buying and selling of them.

The only cloud on the horizon she could foresee was possible opposition from Daisy.

She'd had her father to herself for many years and might resent another female appearing on the scene; but, Lavinia said to herself, Daisy was always pleasant and friendly toward her. So maybe, with patience and time, they'd become good friends and young girls needed a mother's guidance. Although Lavinia knew she could never take the place of her dear mother she could be a good second best.

She picked up the two water-jacks and made her way across the field to the standpipe where she filled them.

'May I help you?' The well-spoken voice belonged to a smartly attired young man.

'Thank you kindly, young man. It'll tek me all day to carry these back over there,' she said nodding to where the wagon was pitched. He insisted on carrying both lifting them as though they held nothing but fresh air. 'Aren't you the fella who bought the black stallion?'

'Yes, I am.' He smiled down at the lady flattered that she remembered him. 'Isn't this Mr Latimer's wagon?' he said, putting the water containers down.

'Yes it is, and that's mine.' She indicated a similar open-lot wagon pitched twenty yards away. 'Are you by chance looking for Sam?' she asked.

'Yes, it's quite urgent actually. Is he around?'

'No, 'fraid not.'

She filled a kettle and hung it over the fire. 'Now you'll stay and 'ave a cup o' tea with me Mister...?'

'Flint, Tobias Flint's the name.' He shook her hand and sat on the stool she'd pulled out from under the wagon.

'When will he be back?'

'Tomorrow sometime, 'e's 'ad to go to Yorkshire to fetch his daughter, Daisy.'

His eyes lit up and a smile played on his mouth when she mentioned her name. Ah, so that was it, eh? Lavinia thought, he's sweet on Sam's lass. Well I never!

'Anything I can help yer with? Did you want 'is advice on the stallion you bought? Mebbe I can help.' She saw concern on his face. 'If you need any advice on the horse, I knows me stuff, an' I should, aye, Sam taught me all I know. Now drink that,' she said, handing him the dainty cup and saucer, 'and tell me all about it.'

Tobias took a sip of the strong tea before relating what had happened to the horse. She didn't interrupt him and listened carefully to his every word making mental notes of all the details.

'And the vet thinks it's poison, eh? Not been out o' the stable, running in no field?'

Lavinia stood up and doused the fire. She took the half-finished cup from his hand leaving him somewhat perplexed.

'Right,' she said, 'I tek it that's your car?' She indicated to where he'd parked.

'Yes.'

'Give me two minutes and I'll come with yer. I think I know what Sam would do.' Without waiting for a response she disappeared inside the wagon. A moment later she emerged holding a large lemonade bottle full of sludgy green liquid.

'Come on then, we 'aven't got all day!' she chivvied. 'The sooner we get this down that 'orse's gullet the better!'

Tobias jumped to attention and they strode briskly toward the car.

'What's in the bottle?' he enquired, eyeing the unpleasant-looking contents.

'I'm not quite sure – it's a concoction that Sam uses to flush out any "impurities" 'e calls 'em. And if there's poison in that horse's system, this might just do the trick, and there again it might not, so don't be over hopeful Mr Flint.'

'Oh, please, call me Tobias. He wanted this woman's friendship. He liked her direct manner and no-nonsense approach. 'I am so grateful to you for coming with me.'

'Sam would do the same. We travellers wouldn't leave any horse to suffer if we thought we could do summat to ease its pain. It's in our blood, I suppose.'

*

Lavinia gasped in awe when the manor came into view. 'By, it's the grandest house I've ever seen. You must have a big family, Mr Flint?'

'No, sadly not, just myself and my mother, plus a few staff. And please, do call me Tobias,' he reminded her.

'And you can call me Lavinia.'

The car swept into the stable yard. They got out and walked across to the stable where Jet still lay with his head cradled in Dan's lap.

'Hello, Dan, any change in the old boy?' Tobias asked, kneeling down and stroking the stallion's head.

'No, no better. But no worse I think.'

'This is Dan, my stable man. Dan, this is Mrs Cooper, she is a good friend of Mr Latimer and has come to see if she can help. Now, Lavinia, what do you want us to do?'

She sat down on the straw beside the horse and lifted the closed eyelid before running her hands gently round the belly of the animal, stopping here and there adding a little pressure. Dan kept a close watch on her every movement, not sure what to think other than bewilderment at the squire bringing a gypsy to look at the horse. And a woman at that! Mebbe 'e's like 'is father! Eeh, an' if that cow of a mother of 'is finds out, there'll be all 'ell to pay!

'Right,' she said with authority, 'It'll tek the three of us to get this mixture into him.'

Dan seemed to know instinctively what was expected of him and held the horse's head back. Tobias forced open the horse's mouth while Lavinia poured the mixture deeply into its throat. Dan massaged Jet's throat until the horse gulped involuntarily and the mixture slid down his throat.

'What's the stuff?' Dan enquired, uncertain of this strange woman who appeared to be in charge of events.

'Not quite sure. But I do know a large part of it is young nettles that have been boiled. Sam doesn't disclose what's in some of his secret mixtures, otherwise 'e'd never sell any, would he?' Lavinia chuckled at her own joke. 'Well, that might do it. Stay with 'im one of you, will you?'

'Yes, I can sleep in t' stable, sir. I'll fetch a chair in. I wouldn't sleep if I left 'im so I might as well be 'ere.'

'Thanks, Dan.' Tobias stood up and brushed the straw from his breeches. 'Now would you care for a cup of tea, Lavinia, or a sherry?'

Tobias's invitation to the gypsy caused Dan to cough and splutter.

What the 'ell's 'e doin'? She'll go bloody barmy if 'e teks her into t' manor 'ouse! He held his breath, waiting for her reply and sighed with relief when she declined.

'That's very kind of you … Tobias.' His Christian name didn't sit comfortably on her lips, but she knew she'd be rebuked if she said Mr Flint. 'But I 'ave ter get back, there's no one to look after the 'orses and wagons with Sam and Donny both away.'

'Of course, I'll get you home straight away.'

'Thank you so much for all you've done for Whitby Jet, Lavinia,' Tobias said, as he drove into the field where suspicious eyes peered at them.

'Oh, you're welcome, lad. I hope he pulls through for yer, and for Sam,' she added. ''E'll be right upset about what's 'appened, but I'll 'ave to tell him.'

'Yes, do let him know.'

Lavinia ignored the peculiar looks from other travellers when she was delivered back to the campsite in Tobias's fine car. But their comments she couldn't ignore.

'Mixing with the gentry, are we now?' came a cutting remark, followed by, 'We'll soon not be good enough for the likes of you an' Samboy Latimer. Rather spend time with the gorgios than yer own kind!'

They'd watched the squire and seen he was smitten with Daisy, one of *theirs*, and they didn't approve.

'Don't talk stupid!' Lavinia countered defensively. 'That *flattie* 'as spent a lot o' money with Samboy. And he'll spend money again with him in the future! Who but an idiot would spurn business, eh?' She spat the words at them. 'The squire's money's as good as anybody else's! And, tell me, is there one of you here Samboy hasn't helped over the years in one way or another? No. So think on that afore yer start with yer nasty remarks!'

The talk stopped abruptly.

They knew what she said was right. And, if the truth be known, they were jealous of Samboy. He was a shrewd man, making more money than any of them in his horse dealings. He was also blessed with that rare quality of being able to talk to people from all walks of life in a free and easy manner, squires and peasants alike. Samboy was also renowned for his generosity of home-made herbal remedies and vast knowledge of horses. If one needed treating, or if someone required advice on breaking and breeding, he was there to help in whatever capacity he could.

In the not-too-distant future Sam would be her husband. She'd not allow anybody to blight the Latimer name which before long she would take as her own, and with great pride.

It was late evening when Samboy returned with Daisy. Lavinia didn't make a fuss when she greeted them although she longed to fling her arms around him and kiss him. The look of love which passed between them had to suffice. She'd prepared rabbit stew for them all and soon had it plated up in bowls. They sat on stools around her camp-fire and the conversation was convivial with Lavinia genuinely interested in Daisy's stay with her Aunt Chrissie.

'Now you get yourself to bed, Daisy. I'll help Lavinia clear away then I'll not be long before I turn in myself. We've had a busy day with you packing and sorting things out for our Chrissie.'

'All right, Dad. Oh, it's good to be home. I've missed you ... and everything,' she said, moving her arms in dramatic circular movements encompassing her surroundings. She hugged him and kissed his cheek. 'And thank you, Lavinia, for the lovely food and for taking care of Dad while I've been away. He's been telling me how kind you've been.'

Lavinia blushed. You bugger, Sam, she thought. Setting the scene for future events. 'Ah, think nothing of it, Daisy, your dad's always been helpful to me with the horses; least I could do. Good night, love.'

'Good night, Lavinia, good night, Dad.'

When they were alone, Lavinia related to Samboy what had happened regarding Whitby Jet and her visit to the manor with the squire.

He was shocked at what he heard, deciding he'd call there first thing in the morning. 'Will you come with me, love?'

'Yes, if you don't think Daisy will mind.'

'Why should she mind you comin' to 'ave a look at an 'orse with me? We've done that often enough in the past.'

'Surely you've noticed summat, Sam?'

'Noticed summat? What? What the 'ell are yer talkin' about?' he asked impatiently.

'The squire, Tobias Flint. 'E's fair smitten with 'er!'

'Smitten? With our Daisy, yer mean? Don't talk daft, woman!'

'I'm not talking daft Sam. And why shouldn't he be? She's the bonniest lass for miles around. And, I might add, he's not a bad-looking bloke himself.' Lavinia grinned at him. 'Quite enjoyed me jaunt in his car with him.'

'Just so long as yer didn't clamber in the back with 'im. I've heard tell these gorgios'll 'ave sex anywhere!'

They laughed and Samboy pulled her greedily inside her wagon and began kissing her deeply. He unbuttoned her blouse and cupped her breast, teasing her nipple until it hardened under his lips.

'Daisy will be fast asleep, Lavinia, please ... please ...' he begged unashamedly. 'I've got to have you.' Lavinia moaned with an equal longing and quickly hitched up her skirt. There was no time for preliminaries only an urgent desire to satisfy the sexual hunger in one another.

They parted with great reluctance that night, but both slept well.

Tobias woke early the next morning and straight away made his way down to the stables.

It wasn't only his concern for the horse that had kept him awake for most of the night, it was news of Daisy returning to Appleby. She would already be here, he thought, and wondered whether she would call with her father to see the horse. For Tobias was in no doubt Samboy Latimer would call today, anxious regarding the health of Whitby Jet. He would want to know whether the horse had survived or not.

All was quiet as he neared the stable and he feared the worst. Then came a gentle snort as he put his head through the door. It was a welcome scene before him. Jet stood munching his way through what looked like a bucket of bran mash with Dan fast asleep on a deck chair in a corner of the stable.

'Well done, boy!' Tobias quietly stroked his neck and Jet whinnied in response, waking Dan who fell off his chair.

'Morning, sir! 'E's made it, eh? I knew 'e would!' Dan said, smiling triumphantly. 'Them gypsies knows more than any vet, eh?' His face beamed with pride and appreciation of the traveller he now regarded as his new-found best friend.

'Well, they certainly know something about horses that's for sure. The vet will be dropping in sometime today, Dan. I'd rather you didn't mention anything about the ... er ... assistance we've had from the travellers, all right?'

'Aye, I understand, sir, I'll say nowt,' he assured him with a wink.

'Now, you get yourself to bed and grab a few hours' rest.'

'No! I'll not leave 'im today.' Dan said, flatly. 'I'll get to bed early tonight and that'll put me right. I'm that excited 'e's come through that I couldn't sleep.'

'OK, Dan, and thank you.' Tobias patted him on the shoulder, deeply moved by his employee's selflessness.

*

DS Keen left the station with a heavy heart. All his enquiries had drawn a blank. Two people missing and one of them presumed dead without any remains to examine.

Oh yes, they'd been clever, the Adams tribe with their charade of grief, the mother wailing and crying like a banshee, then the whole tribe of them disappearing with the burned remains. Surely they can't hide forever. Can they? The only witness, if any, would be one of their own. And there wasn't any likelihood of betrayal in the camp.

The DI from Carlisle had been on his back this morning yelling at him. 'Get some damned results! Those bloody gypsies get away without paying taxes, they're not going to get away with bloody murder as well! Are they?'

'I hope not,' Keen had said meekly, because he really didn't believe they'd catch the culprit without inside help from one of their own. Everything was conjecture and conjecture was not going to solve this crime.

'Never mind *you hope not!*' the DI snapped. 'Just make sure you catch this ... this ... bastard ... Roulson Adams, or whatever his bloody fancy name is! And question that trollop, Lilly ... whatever *her* bloody name is! Maybe she's hiding something. Damned woman probably sees him as some bloody hero for all we know!'

Keen made another visit to the campsite.

When he walked into the field there was an eerie emptiness. Apart from Samboy's wagon and one or two others, all had gone, as if spirited away. The only evidence remaining of the hundreds of gypsies and travellers who had gathered were patches of flattened grass where the wagons had pitched for a few days. And soon the grass would flourish to support grazing cattle and sheep again.

He wandered over to Samboy Latimer's wagon. Unable to knock on a door for attention he called out for him. 'Are you there, Mr Latimer? It's DS Keen. I'd like a word with you.' There was no reply. He was about to walk away when a young girl appeared and climbed down from the wagon.

'Hello, can I help you?' she asked.

Keen was taken aback by the softly spoken voice of the young lady. She had golden hair and the prettiest face he'd ever seen. He removed his trilby.

'Hello, I'm looking for Mr Latimer. His he about?'

'No, I'm sorry, my father's gone to see a horse up at the manor. Can I help you?'

'Oh, of course, I remember you now, but it must be a few years since I last saw you. Your father supplied us with a pony for our son....'

'I remember. Yes, it's been quite a while.'

'I understand you've been away for a few days, in Yorkshire?'

'Yes, I've been staying with my aunt.'

'Did you know that we're looking for two men, a local man and a Roulson Adams?' He saw her eyes avert from his, and her face paled. Her hand was gripping one of the shafts and he saw that her knuckles were white with pressure. Ah, yes, she definitely knows something, Keen thought. Maybe all is not lost after all. But, the chances are her father will be back soon and there's no way he'll permit his daughter to be questioned.

Time was of the essence.

'When did you last see Mr Adams, Miss Latimer?'

'I ... I really d ... don't know,' she stammered. 'Before I went down to Yorkshire, I suppose ... I saw him here at a sale. And I saw him riding in the river before that. Why ... why are you asking me?'

'And you haven't seen him since you returned, or when you were in Yorkshire?'

'*No! No*! I haven't! Now I'm busy, we're packing up today so I have to get on!' She turned and climbed back into the wagon.

Well, well, well, he thought. What have we here, eh? She's hiding something, that's for sure. Was Latimer aware his daughter was hiding something? Probably not, I'd say.

He returned to his car and set out for Eden Falls Manor to find Samboy Latimer.

As a matter of routine the vet had informed the police a horse had been poisoned at the manor and, as far as Keen was concerned, it was a good excuse to seek him out and question him further.

Lydia Flint heard the scrunch of tyres on gravel for the second time that morning. The vet had already been. She'd watched him drive away cursing the dratted man for saving the damned horse's life!

As she looked out from the upstairs window now she saw a smart black car pull up. An official-looking man stepped from it. Tobias walked over to him, smiled, then they disappeared into a stable.

She was attending to paperwork at her desk when, a few moments later, more noise interrupted her concentration and a distinct clattering of wheels and horses' hoofs sounded through the open window. It's like Piccadilly Circus, she said crossly, slamming her pen down on the desk.

She looked out of the window again. Aghast at what she saw, she leapt to her feet. Two damned gypsies. A man and a woman standing next to a horse and cart! She couldn't believe her eyes. Then, to cap it all, her son walked up and greeted them! He shook their filthy hands, bowing and scraping as if they were long lost friends!

The hazel eyes that glowered at the scene below held nothing but loathing, her mouth set in a thin grim line, her lips barely visible. *Oh no! He's not going to follow his father down that path! Mixing with scum! How dare he even think of it? Permitting them to drive up to the house! Let alone make them bloody welcome! How dare he?*

The rage building and exploding inside her couldn't be contained. Rage, like any energy, had to direct itself somewhere. She threw the papers she'd unconsciously screwed up into tight balls when looking out of the window on to the desk and stormed from the room.

Nellie was in the entrance hall polishing a table. She looked up to see her running down the stairs.

'Is everything all right, Mrs Flint?' she asked, seeing the wild look in her eyes which had become a cause for concern amongst the staff of late, especially Nellie. She'd meant to have a word with Tobias, but somehow it didn't seem proper. She thought he'd think she was sticking her nose where she shouldn't. But seeing the ferocious gleam in Lydia's eyes she wished she'd spoken out.

'No!' she yelled, '*Everything is all wrong! Have you seen those gypsies who have arrived by horse and cart? To the front of the house, Nellie! What is Tobias thinking of allowing such things?*'

'I wouldn't be overly worried, Mrs Flint. I believe they're just enquiring after the horse that was ill. He's a decent enough traveller that one. It's Samboy Latimer. He's a bit different to the others, so there's no need to fret yourself over—'

Nellie failed to placate her and, shrugging her shoulders, continued polishing. Nothing I can do, she sighed. Master will just have to deal with her as best he can. Maybe this'll make him realize there's summat not right with his mother.

Nellie had mentioned a name – a name that hurled Lydia's mind into a whirlpool of uncontrollable fury and jealousy. A name she'd *never* wanted to hear again as long as she lived! *Latimer!* How dare that woman come here! And with her husband! *It's too much ... too much! Richard, Richard, how could you?*

She marched out through the front door and into the bright sunshine.

The man and woman both stared at her as she walked toward them.

Lavinia stepped forward smiling and held out her hand to introduce herself to Lydia. Samboy also smiled, but it was fleeting. He saw a look of utter hatred on the woman's face. Within seconds, Lydia had closed the gap between them and struck Lavinia sharply across the face with a resounding slap!

'*How dare you come here after all this time, tempting my ... yes, that's right, tempting my Richard away from me! You ... you slut!*'

Everyone stood speechless unable to move for what seemed an eternity.

In the next instant, Tobias and Dan took hold of Lydia dragging her away screaming and shouting from a stunned Lavinia and Samboy. They hauled her back inside the house and Samboy put a protective arm around Lavinia.

DS Keen came out from the stable to see what all the screaming and shouting was about.

'Have I missed something?' he asked, looking about him blankly. He looked at the woman standing next to Samboy and wondered why she was holding the side of her face and her eyes were watering.

'Where's the squire? I haven't finished my business here yet,' he asked, flummoxed.

'Well, we've finished ours! Come on, love, we're off. The woman's bloody crackers!'

'Just hang on a minute!' Keen said, sternly. 'I want to have a few words with you about these two supposedly missing blokes. I think your daughter might know something we don't.'

'*My daughter!*' Samboy roared. 'What the 'ell's she got to do with anything? Come and see me later today if you must,' he conceded, 'but right now I need to get my friend 'ere back 'ome. We've had enough. I want to get away from this hell-hole!'

'Right, I'll be there about five o'clock.'

Keen stood watching the couple drive away on the horse and cart. It wasn't long before Dan appeared at his side.

'What on earth happened?' Keen asked him.

'Didn't yer see?'

'See what? I was in the stable.'

'Mrs Flint. She just walked out an' slapped that poor woman, she did –

smacked 'er 'ard right across 'er face! I didn't 'ear what was said, but it must o' been summat of a personal nature. Eeh, and that there traveller woman's just saved t' squire's 'orse!' He shook his head at the shame of it all.

Samboy guided the cart on to the grass verge at the side of the quiet road and reined it to a halt. He untied his neckerchief then doused it in water poured from a small bottle stored in the cart. Saying nothing, he gently dabbed the weal which glowed a vivid red on Lavinia's cheek. She winced at the touch.

'Sorry.' Samboy whispered softly, with eyes downcast.

Lavinia tenderly took his hand in hers and held it, putting her own pain aside. She looked at him. The shock of what he'd just heard from that vicious woman was alarmingly visible on his face.

'Sam, Sam love, that woman. She thought I was y-your Mary, didn't she? What is it, Sam? Do you know why she behaved like that? Did summat 'appen that you can't tell me?' she asked softly.

'I'm as flabbergasted as you are. Honest to God, Lavinia, I didn't know what she was talkin' about. But it appears my Mary wasn't as true to me as I thought she was.' He bowed his head and tears ran down his cheeks. 'She'd been 'avin' an affair with 'er 'usband. Richard Flint. Him who I liked and respected. I can't believe it!'

He raised his head and looked at her intently. 'Daisy must never know about what 'appened today. Promise me now Lavinia that you'll not say a word.'

'Of course, I won't, Sam. Don't you think I don't know it would break her heart?' She hesitated then continued, 'Sam, Mary did love you very much you know. I remember how she would talk about you ... with such pride.'

'That's enough now!' he interjected, silencing her with the sharp tone of his voice. 'I don't want to talk about 'er again. I don't want to 'ear her name mentioned! Now, let's get back. I've got that detective calling round later.'

He flicked the reins harshly and the horse threw his head up boldly, the whites of his eyes flashing, questioning his master's unusual cruel behaviour.

'Just don't harden yer heart, Sam.' The serious intonation in her voice made him turn to look at her. 'That is – not if you want us to have a future together,' she added.

*

The doctor was led into the study where he gladly accepted the whisky Tobias offered him.

He sat in an armchair and looked at the squire. One can't abandon the genes of a lifetime he thought, taking a large swig of whisky. He didn't envy the young man sitting opposite him. He had to shoulder not only the responsibility of the large estate but his mother's appalling mental illness too.

Frank Parks had been the Flints' family doctor for over thirty years and a close personal friend of Tobias's father.

Although Frank had never warmed to Lydia he nevertheless felt sorry for her. She and Richard had been incompatible from the outset. And when Richard eventually did fall in love, she, too, was unsuitable, a married gypsy woman at that! God, what a bloody mess! And now, here's Tobias getting himself involved just like his father, all over again! Was there any wonder Lydia had gone over the edge? How on earth do I tell him that his mother is stark staring mad?

It was at times like these he wished he'd chosen some other less taxing profession.

'Well, Frank, what can be done? My mother is obviously, er, not herself.'

Frank looked at Tobias sympathetically who appeared to have aged ten years in the last hour. 'I've got to be honest with you – how can I put it? – your mother is emotionally fragile.'

'You mean mentally unstable don't you? There's no point beating about the bloody bush, Frank; she's been behaving irrationally for years and now she's much worse. So, you're the doctor, tell me, what can be done?'

'All right, I'll give it to you straight. This is more serious than the usual nervous breakdown, if there is such a thing as a usual breakdown. I don't know how long she's been having these psychotic episodes. They are going to leave her feeling confused, distressed, and utterly exhausted. At these times, and I must stress this, so do try to understand, Tobias, she has no control over her thoughts. She will feel completely overwhelmed by the world around her. Also, I have to add, she could be a danger to herself and to others. Has she displayed any signs of violence?'

Tobias listened intently to everything Frank said. For a few moments he was unable to speak.

'Er ... yes, I mean, no! I don't know what you mean. Has she struck anybody? Is that what you're asking me?'

'Yes, or has she been more verbally abusive of late?' The look of horror on the squire's face was pitiful. But these things had to be said. 'There's no point pretending, Tobias.' Frank examined the empty glass he held, wishing it were full. He hated every moment of this but honesty was of the essence.

'It has been said to me on more than one occasion that your mother has … shall we say … verbally abused certain members of the staff.'

It hurt Frank deeply to reiterate unpleasant gossip and accusations, but what else could he do? He had to know the severity of Lydia's mental state.

Tobias rose from his chair and walked to the window. Long forgotten memories began to surface; her physical presence with an absent heart, sharp smacks on bare legs, angry shouts. And Father avoiding her as much as he could.

All these years he had taken her anger directed toward him as a personal affront, but now he could see there was a reason for her malevolence: his mother was extremely ill.

'I honestly didn't realize how ill she was. I truly didn't.' He walked back to his chair and sat down, fully prepared to take charge and face the problem head on.

'Can you medicate her, or what can you do to help her?'

'Not a lot I can do personally, but there are mental institutions with some excellent doctors who—'

'No! Definitely not! My mother is not going into a mental asylum. And no amount of coaxing or persuading will lessen my determination to keep her out of those places. That's *final*!' he said, his voice choked with emotion.

Chapter Seven

Roulson grinned at his reflection. The long black locks that had caused many a lady's heart to somersault were cropped short and dyed a dark-blonde making his skin appear pallid and unattractive. But he was delighted with his disguise; nobody would recognize him. Why, he hardly recognized himself!

From the moment he changed his appearance, he got two weeks' farm work close by, hoeing sugar beet. The farmer said he could stay in the barn and his wife would give him one good meal a day. So as far as he was concerned things were looking up. All he had to do now was bide his time until Topcliffe Fair. He'd no doubt Daisy and her father would turn up to sell the odd horse or two, as they did every year.

He would somehow get word to her to meet him. Surely she would have changed her mind by then and want to go away with him. The money he'd saved would get them away to Ireland where they could start a new life together. He'd thought of nothing else but her since the time they'd kissed that day he'd taken her home from Appleby – and no one else was going to have her! Yes, Topcliffe Fair could not come soon enough for Roulson.

It was one of those sparkling, dew-kissed mornings when you could taste the sweetness of the crisp clear air with every breath.

Daisy kicked Chase into a canter across the open field and the cool, early-morning air stung her tear-stained cheeks. She urged her horse yet again and he broke into a gallop – the hurt inside her took flight as she rode fast and free. It was balm for her soul. But right now all she wanted to do was put as much distance as possible between herself, her father, and that damned detective!

When she arrived at the river in the valley bottom she climbed down from her horse, kicked off her boots and rolled up her trousers. She waded into the water and, filling her cupped hands rinsed her face with the cool water. She paddled over to the large boulder in the middle of the river and sat down. The water was cold and she raised her legs, hugging her knees beneath her chin.

That detective had interrogated her as though she were a common *criminal*! But afterwards, when she thought about it, she supposed she was.

She hadn't let on to him or her father that she had seen Roulson during her stay in Yorkshire. Although she knew Roulson had killed the man presumed missing, she truly believed him when he'd said it was an accident and he'd not known his own strength.

Though any romantic notions she'd held for him had died, that didn't mean she'd give him away and tell the authorities where he was. She felt certain he'd be long gone from Yorkshire and disappeared south or to Ireland.

Then, her father had interrogated her after the detective had left.

'If you've seen that bloody scoundrel, you'd better tell me now, Daisy!' he'd yelled.

'I haven't! Anyway, you were the one who wanted me to go to Yorkshire. I can't do right for doing right.'

'You 'ave to know, Daisy, that Roulson Adams is no bloody good. 'E's a damned drunk and a thug,' Samboy had shouted at the top of his voice, wagging his finger in her face.

'Well, *I* haven't done anything wrong,' Daisy protested, in floods of tears, then running inside the wagon. She'd refused anything to eat and curled up in bed sobbing her eyes out for most of the night. Her father had sat in a chair by the camp-fire and drunk himself into a stupor before falling asleep under the wagon, bedding down with old Max, the dog.

She'd never known him drink too much before and it frightened her when she'd heard him ranting to himself. He was fast asleep this morning when she'd saddled Chase to come to this place, down by the quiet waters. A place she considered her oasis of peace.

She heard a noise. An elegant grey heron landed on the opposite side of the river. She remained still and quiet. The tall bird stood three feet high, adorned in grey and white plumage with yellowish legs and beak. It carefully and quietly scrutinized the water from the shallow margins for any movement, standing motionless on one leg, taking the occasional slow, steady step, so as not to disturb the water. Eventually a fish paid the price for its carelessness; the heron's kinked neck straightened with startling speed and the sharp bill speared its prey.

Her foot slipped clumsily from the boulder startling the bird which instantly took flight. It weaved its way gracefully through the upper swaying branches of the trees with its broad arched wings. She watched it until it flew out of sight. She hugged herself and closed her eyes, breathing in the pure pleasure of her surroundings. I love this place, she thought. It revives my spirit, helps me face whatever it is I have to face. I believe God created this little bit of heaven on earth especially for me.

She clambered up the side of the bank gathering dried twigs and branches on the way. No gypsy would walk past free kindling. It was free heat and cooking, while a hedgeful of brambles, or anything in Mother Nature's larder, was to the traveller and gypsy a stroll through a green-grocer's shop.

She bound the bundle of kindling together with thin, soft willow, crafting a makeshift handle and flung it over her shoulder, then mounted her horse and slowly headed for home.

He'd watched her thunder across the open meadow with terror in his heart.

She'd galloped her horse at breakneck speed and he worried for her safety, but neither she nor her horse faltered, not for a moment.

He considered riding after her to make sure she was all right and to tell her how sorry he was about what had occurred between his father and her mother all those years ago; tell her of the love he carried in his heart for her. But after yesterday, he just couldn't face her. The best he could hope for was, given time, she'd be able to look at him and not blame him for his father's dissolute behaviour.

He heard the distant whinny of a horse and guided his own back into the shelter of the small copse.

He smiled, observing horse and rider coming toward him. That was what he loved about her. The wildness tempered with gentleness. Where on this earth would he find a woman to equal her? I wonder, did my father feel the same for her mother?

And, if he did, who am I to cast aspersions on him?

As he watched her ride past, a pair of curlews took flight with warning cries driving the intruders away from their cleverly concealed, yet vulnerable nest on the ground.

He placed his hand over his horse's nose, muzzling his whinny. He needn't have bothered, Daisy's horse didn't shy at the disturbance and she gave her horse a congratulatory pat. He saw her face light up with a smile and he ached for her, wondering why love never followed a simple path.

When she'd faded into the distance Tobias ventured down to the river; unknowingly sitting on the same boulder, nursing not too dissimilar hurts.

DS Keen heard the clatter of hoofs and stepped out of his car. He'd been waiting for Tobias Flint to return from his ride.

'Thanks, Dan,' Tobias said, handing over the reins. He slipped the stirrups up the leathers and loosened the girth, wondering what the detective was doing back here again.

'I'm sorry I was unable to speak to you yesterday, Detective, we had a bit of an emergency. Now, what was it you came to see me about?'

'Yes, so I gather, I do hope your mother is feeling … er—'

'My mother is fine, thank you,' he said sharply, cutting him off mid-sentence. 'Now what exactly did you want?'

Well, that's you put in your place! thought Keen. 'Oh, it's about this poisoning of one of your horses. The vet reported it. Have there been any strangers about the place?'

'No.'

'No poisons left lying around … weed killer, anything that some unwelcome, er … trespasser might have picked up?'

'No, nothing,' Tobias stated emphatically. 'And if you're thinking for one minute it might be one of the travellers from Appleby Fair, think again. In fact, I don't believe anybody *deliberately intended* to poison my horse; it was probably some sort of accident.'

'That may be so, but I have to follow these things up, you understand.'

'Yes, I'm sure. Now, if you'll excuse me, I'm busy. Anything else you need to know, I'm sure Dan will oblige. Good day to you, Detective.'

Back in his study, Tobias poured himself a large whisky. He looked at his watch, eleven o'clock. A bit early, he thought, but I need it. He had two nurses to interview that afternoon. Both had been recommended by the doctor, saying they were highly trained psychiatric nurses with excellent references. Whoever acquired the position would be introduced as a companion for his mother, who had been quite heavily sedated for the last twenty-four hours.

A sudden knock on the door brought him back to the present. 'Come in.'

Nellie entered holding a tray. 'I know you've not eaten properly, so I've brought you a drop o' good broth. You've got to keep your strength up.'

She saw the dark shadows under his eyes and her heart went out to him. 'We're taking turns looking to your mother, so don't worry yourself there. And when you gets a nurse in for 'er, she'll be grand, so don't fret.'

'Ah, Nellie, you're the anchor as far as this household is concerned. I'm so grateful to you. All these years ... I don't know how you've put up with my mother's tantrums. The verbal abuse – you've never complained, not once. It leaves me speechless ... and ... and ... ashamed.'

Nellie walked round the desk to where he sat and hugged him, just as she always had. It was as natural to her as water to a garden. 'It'll be all right, lad, now come on, eat up afore these women come to be interviewed.'

'Nellie, will you do something for me?'

'Anything, all you have to do is ask.'

'I want you here this afternoon when I'm interviewing the two women, please. I know that your intuition and knowledge of others will be of great help.' Nellie began to protest. 'Don't worry, Nellie, you don't have to say anything but just sit there and listen, then afterwards, you can give me your opinion as to who you believe would be the more suitable. Would you do that for me, Nellie, please?'

'All right,' she agreed, 'on one condition.'

'What condition's that, Nellie?'

'So long as I don't have to open me gob,' she said, causing them both to laugh.

Tobias polished off another whisky before eating the lunch Nellie had brought him. He leaned back in his chair feeling the longed for effects of alcohol and closed his eyes.

He woke with a start when a loud knock sounded on the study door and looked at the clock. He'd slept for over an hour.

Blast! It must be those nurses. 'One moment please,' he called, quickly clearing away the whisky into a cupboard and popping a peppermint sweet into his mouth. 'Come in.'

Tobias was surprised to see Matt, the gardener, walk through the door. Normally the outside staff would use the farm office situated near the stable block if they had anything to discuss with him. This must be important, he thought.

'Sorry to bother yer, sir, but Nellie, she thought it best I sees yer in private, like.'

Matt looked uneasy, feeding his flat cap nervously through his fingers.

'That's all right, Matt, what can I help you with?'

'Well, it's this,' he said, producing a bottle of brown liquid from his inside pocket. 'It's weed killer, an' half of it's missin'. I ain't used it. I thought thee should know, what with yer 'orse being poisoned like. I didn't want yer to think it were owt to do wi' me.'

'Good Lord, Matt! You've been with us for years. Don't think for a minute I'd suspect *you* of ever doing anything untoward.'

Tobias regretted having drunk the second whisky and hoped to hell Matt couldn't smell his breath.

'That's right decent of you, sir, but like I says, I thought thee should know.'

'Thank you, Matt, now leave it to me. I'll make some enquiries. I'd rather you said nothing to anybody else if that's OK with you, especially that damned detective sticking his nose into everything. Appears to me there's enough going on around the place, without any added complications, eh?'

'I'll say no more. G'day, sir,' Matt replied, leaving more relaxed than when he'd arrived.

Tobias sighed and sank back into his chair. His fears were slowly but surely being realized. Was his mother so mentally sick that she would kill his horse he'd bought from the travellers? The answer was yes. She was capable of killing a horse – and in all probability, another human being, especially if Romany blood ran through their veins.

Opening the double doors he walked out on to the terrace and inhaled deeply. Must get my head cleared before the nurses arrive to be interviewed, he thought.

The study overlooked the rose garden his mother had created. Once again his heart sank – was there no escape from her madness? Maybe he was wrong. Maybe it would be better for her to spend the rest of her days in a mental institution. He bowed his head, admitting to himself there was no way he could ever allow that to happen, for there was no shortage of money. Apart from the farms making a handsome profit, there was the income from his grandmother. She'd come from a very wealthy family who had made a name and vast amounts of money in shipping. But, although money was not an issue, Tobias had been raised 'not to waste'.

His father had said, 'It would be unseemly to misuse wealth, especially when the world is struggling through war and famine.' Hence, there was money for evermore. It would take many generations to squander the Flints' vast amount of wealth, so if one nurse was not enough to constrain his mother, then two would have to be employed, or three, four, whatever it took.

*

That evening Tobias sat down with Nellie in the drawing-room, discussing the two candidates interviewed for the job and both were of the same mind in their decision.

A Miss Pettifer was their choice. She had first-class references from two former employers and was a bit younger than Lydia Flint. But, most apparent to Nellie and Tobias, was her non-professional appearance which was vital. She had to be seen as nothing more than a companion to Lydia.

Miss Pettifer would take her position at the manor in two days' time. She would live in and had been allocated a bedroom next to Lydia's. They would share the same upstairs sitting-room. A relief nurse would be employed once or twice a week, or when required, to allow Miss Pettifer time off, which, Tobias said, she would most definitely need.

Samboy had heard Daisy get up and ride away on Chase from where he lay under the wagon. After she left he crawled from his makeshift bed, groaning. His body was stiff and bruised from the uncomfortable night beneath the wagon; his head felt a thousand times worse. He couldn't hold his drink, never could, not even as a young man, maybe the occasional half-pint but that was it. But, alas, last night he'd drunk a lot of whisky and was now paying the price.

He squinted at the bright sun, shielding his eyes to look where Lavinia's wagon was parked. It appeared she was all packed up and would be leaving today. He hoped she'd forgive him for his stupidity in getting blind drunk last night. He couldn't bear the thought of losing her.

'Are you there, Lavinia love?' he asked, calling nervously. 'It's me, Sam.'

Lavinia was wide awake. 'I know it's you, you great lump, come on in. I'm just making a cup of tea.'

'Aw, I'm sorry; can you ever forgive me, Lavinia?'

She didn't reply for a few moments. She'd given what had happened a great deal of thought while Sam was unconscious beneath the wagon. 'I can, and I will, on one condition.'

'I'll do anything to put things right between you and me … and Daisy,' he added guiltily.

'Good. I'm glad to hear that. Now, when that daughter of yours comes back from her ride you tell her you're sorry, OK?'

'OK.'

She took his hand in hers. 'I know you've had an awful shock, Sam, finding out about Mary and that Flint bloke, but it's not the end of the world, is it?'

'No, it's not. But it would be the end of the world if you didn't want me any more.' He looked at her, his eyes shining with impending tears at the very thought of it.

'I'll always want you, Sam.' She leaned forward and kissed him tenderly and his heart overflowed with gratitude. 'Now, help me with my last bit of packing. I want to be away mid-morning.'

Daisy rode back into the field to see only a handful of gypsies ready to leave.

She and her father would also leave later today, returning to their cottage for a couple of weeks before making their journey south to Topcliffe Fair.

She could smell the bacon frying and realized she was starving. Her father had lit a fire and was cooking breakfast.

'Are you hungry, precious?' he asked, while she was removing Chase's saddle and bridle.

'Yes, Dad, I'm starving.'

He spoke as though nothing contentious had been said the previous evening and Daisy wasn't going to ask why. She hoped nothing more would be mentioned regarding Roulson. She hated lying to her father.

'Lavinia leaves today Daisy. I'm doing a bit of breakfast for her as well. Go and fetch her, will yer? It's about ready.'

Thank God for Lavinia, thought Daisy; she really was a good friend to them both. I'm surprised she hasn't remarried, but there again, Dad hasn't either. Now there're two people who could be happy together. They've so much in common. She smiled to herself wondering why she hadn't thought of it before. Come to think of it, they're always in and out of each other's wagons, discussing horses, drinking tea, I wonder....

'Hello, Daisy, are you all right, love?' Lavinia asked, interrupting her musings. 'Nothing like a long ride to sort out your thoughts and feelings, eh?'

'Yes, you're right there. Dad has breakfast ready for us. He says you're leaving today, I'll miss you. Do you think you'll manage to get to Topcliffe Fair?' she asked, as they strolled over to where Samboy was plating up bacon and eggs.

'No, not this year, love, but I'll visit you when you come back up home.'

'Good.' Daisy smiled at Lavinia hooking her arm through hers.

DS Keen parked his car then walked on to the campsite.

Everyone had left apart from Samboy and his daughter who were hitched up ready to go when Keen approached them.

'Leave all the talking to me, Daisy, right?' Samboy said, patting her hand.

'All right, Dad.' Relief washed over her. She'd got herself into a tight corner lying to her father about Roulson and would be glad not to have to say another word on the matter.

'Mr Latimer, I see you are on your way. Pastures new, eh?' Keen said.

Here was his only key witness: Miss Daisy Latimer shielded by her father.

'Look,' Samboy said, 'I'm not getting down from this wagon to talk to you, not because I'm rude, but because there's nothing to say. We've told you all we know. And personally, I 'ope you find the bugger 'cos if 'e's killed some poor innocent sod, 'e wants bloody locking up!'

'And what about you, miss, what do you say, eh?'

Daisy squirmed in her seat and moved closer to her father, sure the detective could read her mind.

'My daughter knows *nowt*! I asked 'er last night and if she knew anything she'd 'ave told me. Now, we 'ave to be off, that is, unless you intend arrestin' us?'

'No, I shan't be arresting either of you. But I must stress, if you do know of his whereabouts' – he looked directly at Daisy – 'and you don't tell me now, and at a future date I find you have lied, you will be charged with perverting the course of justice.'

He saw the look of fear in the girl's eyes.

'Thanks for the caution and good day to yer.' Samboy clicked his tongue and the wagon rolled away slowly. The sound of copper pans clinked tunefully as the wagon rocked and swayed when the wheels ran over deep, hard ruts in the grass.

Keen watched the wagon until it disappeared from view. He was at a complete loss.

This Roulson certainly had a hold over these women. Lill wouldn't have a word said against him when he'd questioned her, twice. And apparently the other bloke, Bob Grant, who'd gone missing, had had a soft spot for Lill for quite a long time. But she was that smitten with Roulson, believing one day he'd return and take her away with him.

As he looked around the empty field, it was as though the travellers had taken any meaningful knowledge of the disappearance of both men along with them. But, Keen mused, next year will arrive, Appleby Fair along with it, and who knows what will happen between now and then? He strolled back to his car with the inescapable realization that this case was on hold for the foreseeable future until somebody eventually made a slip-up, which they usually did, even the clever ones.

Daisy was happy to be home in Hampton for two weeks before leaving for Topcliffe Fair. There were numerous jobs to be done. The garden desperately needed weeding, and if she didn't keep on top of it, it would look like a jungle by the time they returned from Topcliffe.

Although it would have been more practical to have planted shrubs, Daisy loved growing flowers and herbs. She dried huge sprays of flowers in the late summer, displaying them about the window ledges, adding a splash of colour through the long, dark, winter months.

The lavender she would stuff generously into pretty, hand-made heart-shaped pouches edged with lace. The ladies would buy them from her to hang in their wardrobes or place in drawers for scenting their clothes. Often, she sold the lavender bags to local shops. Occasionally, people would drop by the cottage to buy her dried flowers.

But, more important to her than the flowers, was the precious herb garden she'd created a few years ago. These were grown for cooking and medicinal purposes. She harvested them in late summer, carefully drying and storing them in small, airtight, wide-necked jars and bottles. Each was labelled and kept in a dark cupboard in the cool pantry off the kitchen.

Countless people told her she had a natural aptitude when it came to herbs. She knew most of the names and their medicinal uses. Her father and Aunt Chrissie had handed down the age-old remedies to her that had been passed down to them through the generations.

The majority of travellers went along to doctors without a second thought now rather than relying on age-old cures that had stood the test of time. But individuals like Samboy, Daisy, and Chrissie, clung to the old ways, visiting the doctor's surgery as a last resort when the illness was beyond their knowledge.

She was hanging up bunches of parsley and mint to dry when her father came to say they would be setting out for Topcliffe the next day.

'But we can be there in a week, Dad,' Daisy grumbled. She'd hoped for more time to cut and hang the herbs which might go to seed if left. 'Twenty miles a day you said.'

'Well, we're goin' to take it a bit slower this time an' give the 'orses an easier ride. Anyway, it'll give you and me a bit o' time together an' we can have these 'orses in right grand fettle by the time we get there. We've the odd farm to call in at where I said I'd flash a spare 'orse or two at a couple of farmers on the way down. Yer never know, if I get offered a better price than we will at Topcliffe, I'll let one or two go. Make it a lot easier for us, Daisy, with only two to sell on at the fair, an' it'll mean we'll have a couple of days with yer Aunt Chrissie. I thought you might like that, I knows 'ow fond you are of 'er.' Samboy waited for her response.

'I'm sure you're right, Dad, it's just I was hoping to cut a few more herbs and do a bit more in the garden – but that'll all still be here when Topcliffe Fair's been and gone. And it'll be great to spend some more time with Aunt Chrissie.' She was pleased they were friends again and at ease with one another.

'Come on then,' she said giving him a friendly shove. 'Get a move on! Anyone would think you had time to waste.'

Samboy threw his head back and laughed. 'That's my girl. Let's get packed.'

The same evening, two men sat in a barn swigging bottles of beer together. Caspar had somehow managed to secure a job at the same farm as Roulson within Topcliffe parish about half a mile from the village itself. It was accessible by a long, private track used only by those living and working on the farm. It was the perfect place for Roulson. The two men worked, ate, and slept together in the same barn.

An unhealthy relationship had sprung up between them which was already proving injurious to Roulson's sanity. They were leading one another down a dark, dissolute path.

'Piss off for a couple of hours tonight, can yer, Caspar? The woman who fetches our grub is comin' round to have a beer with me about seven o'clock. She's needing a bit of company,' Roulson chuckled.

The woman he talked of had stayed on at the farm after the war, having come as a land army girl and grown fond of the area. The farmer and his wife thought the world of her. She eased the burden of house-work and helped out with all aspects of farm labour.

Roulson had no difficulty resurrecting his charm when required. After only a few visits to the barn with his meal, she was under his spell. A few years older than Roulson, she was destined for spinsterhood, leading a lonely life on the farm only meeting occasional itinerant workers like Caspar; it was highly unlikely she'd meet anybody suitable for marriage.

Roulson took full advantage of her lonely vulnerable position and wheedled his way into her affections. She brought him extra portions of his favourite food, double helpings of apple pie and custard, an extra Yorkshire pudding. Yes, he'd found a comfortable existence for now and it would suit him nicely until Topcliffe Fair.

'But she had a beer with you two nights ago,' Caspar complained. 'Do I have to leave?'

'Yes, yer bloody well do! She gets thirsty for my loving touch.' The beer was taking effect. Roulson laughed aloud, his night-black eyes shining with lust.

'Can't I watch?'

'No, you bloody can't! Just piss off! What are yer, a bloody pervert or summat?'

'I'll be quiet. I ain't 'ad any sex for a many a year – d'yer think she'd let me 'ave a go?'

'Aw, for God's sake, just do as I say; she'll be here soon and I don't want to see hide nor hair of you!'

Caspar stood up swaying unsteadily, cradling two bottles of beer in his arms. 'I'm warning yer, if it starts to rain I'm coming back inside, whether you're at it or not!' he said, staggering out of the barn and swearing under his breath.

He knew he'd better do as he was told because Roulson was the only friend he'd had for many, many years. In fact, the only friend he'd had since he was a young lad at school. He didn't want to upset him and lose his friendship.

Caspar sat at the back of the barn leaning against the brick wall warmed by the sun. He lost all track of time and, finishing his beers, stood up. He spat a gob of phlegm into a clump of vegetation and walked gingerly back into the barn.

To his great delight Minnie, the farm girl, hadn't left. She lay there completely naked next to Roulson. He quietly hid himself behind some sacks of meal, surveying her with drunken, lecherous eyes. They must've got it over with, he thought disappointedly. The bloody lucky sod! What I'd do to give her one, he said to himself excitedly. He unbuttoned his trousers and took his throbbing penis into his hand slowly relieving himself of the agonizing lust, while imagining himself buried deep inside her warm moist womanhood which was in his direct vision. He visualized penetrating her and the pleasure she received at having him inside her. His eyes focused on her large white breasts moving rhythmically with her heavy breathing. He wanted to hold them and kiss the huge dark nipples. As he watched, her legs parted and he saw their mingled love juices dripping from dark pubic hair and down her inner thigh. He ejaculated in a quiet explosion of utter pleasure.

Wiping himself he disappeared outside. Well, she can come visitin' whenever she wants, he said to himself.

Roulson's back was burning with the searing heat of the sun. He put his shirt on and continued hoeing the row of sugar beet. Caspar was twenty yards behind him working at a much slower pace on the next row. Roulson would be rid of him soon, but he would need him in a couple of weeks' time when Topcliffe Fair was underway. He would not be able to put in an appearance himself. He was well aware that the police would be looking for him now and keeping a low profile was a priority. He'd decided to go by the name of Bob Smith. Only Caspar knew his real name and would hold him back if he wasn't careful. The man had latched on to him for some reason, probably because nobody else bothered to give him the time of day – not that that surprised Roulson, for Caspar had a nasty streak, and he stank to high heaven. Yes, he'd soon be able to dispense with him.

Chapter Eight

Five days later Samboy and Daisy arrived at the village of Reeth which some considered to be the capital of Swaledale. It was a large village situated at the lower end of the dale. It boasted a couple of useful shops, a pub, and a generous village green in the centre, from where you could sit and watch Swaledale life pan out before your eyes. They tethered the horses to graze on the village green then stocked up with provisions before setting out to look for somewhere to camp.

It wasn't too long before they came upon an ideal stopping place about two miles the other side of the village by the River Swale and off the beaten track.

'This'll do nicely, Daisy,' Samboy said jumping down from the wagon. 'I'll see to the horses then take a walk along the river-bank. I might catch us a couple of nice trout for our supper, eh?'

'That would be nice, Dad. I'll get a fire going,' she said, confident he'd bring something back to eat.

After her father had left, Daisy paused in what she was doing. Looking westward, her eyes rested appreciatively on the magnificent view of the dale through which they had journeyed. The landscape was breathtaking. Bathed in luxuriant green dotted with trees, the fields were scarred with traces of the old man-made lines of neat stone walls which separated the crops from sheep and cattle. The sun was setting and the sky was ablaze with oceans of red and orange. They had travelled the same route every year and it would be a sin not to linger a while in this glorious dale. And every year she fell in love, all over again, with the indisputable beauty of Swaledale.

Father and daughter worked well together, both aware of jobs to be done without question: quietly seeing to the horses and storing the harness; finding water, and lighting a camp-fire. In all travelling families it was the same. No one sat about when there was work to do. Even the youngest children, from the age of three years old, would be given chores; whether it was cleaning harness, or gathering kindling for the camp-fire, there was always work to do. And that, in itself, created a huge cultural difference between the travellers and others. There was no doubt any child from a travelling family could fend for him or herself. By the age of five or six years old they were capable of hunting food and doing a day's work. That did not mean there was any lack of affection or care for the children, in fact it was quite the reverse. Children were an important consideration, perceived as sacred in the travelling community.

Samboy put his fishing reel inside the poacher's pocket of the jacket he wore. He had never actually fished using a rod with his reel. Poaching was a way of life, it was how they survived; they wouldn't recognize a fishing licence if they saw one.

He went down to the river with Max close at his heels. They'd had a couple of rabbits he'd managed to catch using ferrets on the way down from Appleby so a bit of fish would make a tasty change. He climbed down the river bank to where the clear water ran in dappled shade. Max sat obediently when told and Samboy took the fishing reel from his pocket. Taking the line he expertly threaded a ledger, then fastened a sinker on to the line, before tying on a hook from which three juicy worms dangled appetizingly. He lobbed the bait into a deep pool and waited. He basked in the silence and stillness of his surroundings and lit his pipe. He watched a dipper bobbing up and down on a cobble at the water's edge on the far side of the river; it flew away abruptly when a bright flash of blue marked the passing of a kingfisher. Within half an hour he felt the line tug and pulled the fish up to the bank where it surfaced and thrashed about. 'Go fetch, Max!' he commanded. Max leapt up immediately and, scrambling down the bank, brought the fish to him. He removed the hook before quickly killing the fish by bashing its head on a stone. Samboy then walked further upstream to another pool where he had a repeated success.

The sun was going down when he returned with the two large trout ready for the pot. He'd gutted and de-headed them at the river so as not to leave evidence of illegal fishing where they camped. Daisy had the camp-fire well underway with the potatoes already cooked ready and waiting to supplement whatever food her father poached. Her face lit up when she saw the fine trout her father had brought and soon she had them cooked and dished up.

They sat in harmonious silence listening to the sounds of the night. Samboy looked over at Daisy and was amazed at the difference in her since leaving Applepy. Her eyes sparkled and she'd sung with a light heart as they drove along the country lanes. It lifted his spirit to see her back to her old self. Thank God she's all right, he thought, hoping that Roulson had disappeared from her life. Wherever he is, it's likely he'll be hundreds of miles from Appleby or Topcliffe. By, that detective gave my Daisy a rough time ... I wonder, did he see summat I was blind to? Mebbe he did an' I'll never know, but one thing's for sure, this break will do her the world of good.

Max barked into the darkness and they both strained their eyes to see what had disturbed him. Samboy rose from his chair when a figure came into view in the firelight brandishing a large torch scanning the area like a searchlight inspecting everything in view.

'What yer after?' Samboy yelled, shielding his eyes from the glare of the flashlight. 'Turn that damn torch off, will yer, it's enough to blind a bloke!'

'Oh, I'm sorry,' the stranger apologized and turned off the torch. 'I didn't mean to startle you. I saw your fire when I was walking by the river and wondered what it was. I'm the river bailiff; I'm doing my rounds.'

Samboy blushed, grateful he and Daisy had finished eating their supper.

'We're just 'ere for the night,' he said. 'We're not causin' any bother to anyone. Mebbe you'd tek a cup o' tea with us, young man?' He smiled his most charming smile, disarming the bailiff immediately.

The man was taken aback by the offer and about to decline when he glimpsed Daisy rising from the stool she'd been occupying. The firelight illuminated her striking good looks. Her hair flashed with golden highlights and her slim body moved gracefully toward the wagon from where she fetched a cup and saucer as though already knowing his reply.

'Thank you I'd like that ... very much. Are you on your way back from Appleby Fair?'

Daisy hung the kettle on the iron prop and gathered up the plates by the fire. The bailiff glanced surreptitiously at the fish bones that lay on the plates as she leant to pick them up. Their eyes met momentarily and his look let her know he knew the fish had been poached. He smiled and she returned his smile ruefully, informing him, *we've eaten the evidence*!

'Yes, we are on our way from Appleby. Now, how could you tell that? It must be the bow-top wagon,' laughed Samboy. Daisy looked at the bailiff and they burst into laughter.

'We don't get many of those round here, I must confess. But it's a real beauty,' he added seriously. 'It must be wonderful living so close to nature.'

Daisy poured the tea and handed the bailiff a dainty cup and saucer. He thanked her and was moved at the ceremonial deference shown in the unexpected hospitality.

The bailiff stayed a while enjoying tales Samboy told. He was sorry when the time came to leave but went away with a renewed respect for the travellers, saying he'd look out for them on their way back from Topcliffe Fair.

'That would be very nice,' Samboy said. But I'll be fishing elsewhere, he thought.

It was Saturday afternoon four days later when Samboy pulled his wagon on to a grassy area on the west bank of the river opposite the Norman church in the village of Kirkby Wiske. They had stopped here many times over the years giving the horses respite before the last short leg to Topcliffe and arriving at Chrissie's refreshed from their long journey.

It held poignant memories for Samboy, memories he knew he had to revisit during his brief spell here. And if it's not this year it'll be next, he said to himself. And next year, I want to have Lavinia by my side when we make this journey down from Appleby.

'Shan't be long,' Samboy called to Daisy, two hours later when the work was sided.

'Do you want me to come with you, Dad?' she called out to the disappearing figure.

'No. I'll be back soon.' He didn't turn around, just waved and carried on walking.

The River Wiske was low and the flood-bank he walked along seemed out of proportion to the size of the river it had to contain. A pair of mute swans floated gracefully downstream on the slow current heading for a clump of reeds near the far bank where three cygnets wearing their dirty-grey down, swam about unaware of any danger.

'Don't fret,' Samboy said to the parents of the young swans as they gave him a warning hiss, 'I won't touch your babbies.'

He continued walking, soon reaching a fine old stone bridge.

It took him a while but eventually he found what he was looking for. There, etched deeply into the stone, covered in lichen, were a crudely carved heart and the initials *M* and *S* with the date, *1929*.

The years fell away. It seemed like only yesterday he and Mary had stood on the very same bridge declaring their eternal undying love for one another.

He leaned over the parapet and wept uncontrollably. His tears fell into the flowing waters of the River Wiske below giving vent to the hurt festering in his grieving, aching heart. The cries he wailed surrendered the agonizing pain carried inside of him since the terrible news dealt to him that fateful day. *'Mary, Mary ... why did you do it? Didn't you know how much I loved you? You were my life ... my ... my every breath. Oh, why?'* His questions drifted into the ether unanswered, but the need to cry them out was more central to his existence than any answer he could possibly receive. For he knew instinctively, it was not something lacking in him that had made Mary turn elsewhere for love, affection, excitement, or whatever it was she felt she needed and was denied, it was something unanswered inside herself that craved the need for an extra-marital affair.

He didn't know how long he stood there gazing over the bridge. All he knew was there were no more tears left to shed. He looked at his pocket watch and saw he'd been gone nearly three hours.

Strolling back, he felt cleansed, relieved. And one day in the not-too-distant future, he hoped he'd be able to find sincere forgiveness in his heart for Mary's betrayal. But, that time was not now.

The next morning after breakfast they set about cleaning the harness and grooming the two horses for sale and the two old faithful horses which pulled the wagon alternately before setting out for West Hutton to spend time with Chrissie. Farmers at both farms they'd called at on their way down snapped up the other horses, making travelling lighter and Samboy's pockets full of cash.

Their heads were bowed in concentration cleaning a rather grubby head collar so that they didn't see the woman approach.

'What on earth do you think you're doing here?'

The stentorian voice belonged to a woman who stood at a safe distance looking down her nose at them as if she'd stepped into a midden. She wore a smart navy-blue costume and a wide-brimmed hat with an imitation silk pink rose pinned to the side of it. About her neck hung a string of pearls. In her hand she clutched a matching handbag. The diamonds sparkling on her fingers caused Samboy to blink.

He looked into the cold grey eyes glaring back at him maliciously. 'I'm minding my own business, missus. What are you doin'?' he countered, continuing with the all important job of cleaning the leather.

'I, my man, have just come from that church,' she said pointing to it. 'And I couldn't help but notice you, and your – er – your trappings, for want of a better word!' she said, dismissively waving her hand at his wagon and horses. 'I do believe you are breaking the law, camping here. You should move on immediately.'

'Well, well,' Samboy said, rising to his feet slowly. 'That's really Christian of you – we'll move on when we are good and ready, and not afore! So tek that back into church with you and *pray on it!*'

'Well, I never!' exclaimed the woman, tossing her head and storming off.

'Bloody stuck up cow! Pity the poor bugger she's married to!' Samboy said to Daisy when she was out of earshot, and they both laughed.

Ten minutes later the vicar arrived in his flowing robes. Daisy and Samboy had watched her go straight back into the church. She must have taken it on herself to inform the vicar of the degenerates camping within striking distance of God's house.

'Good day to you, Reverend,' Samboy said, standing up respectfully and removing his cap.

'And a good day to you, sir,' replied the vicar, holding out his hand. His smile was warm and genuine. 'Please, I do apologize on behalf of the church for … for what can only be described as disgraceful behaviour from Miriam Drake. You are most welcome to stay here as far as I and the church are concerned. It's good to see this bit of ground put to some use.'

Samboy saw the poor man was sorry and embarrassed for what had taken place.

'That's kind of you, Reverend, but we'll be movin' on shortly anyway, regardless of Miriam Drake, or whatever 'er name is. We've travelled down from Appleby and we're on our way to stay with my sister, Chrissie Latimer; she lives in West Hutton.'

'Chrissie Latimer!' exclaimed the vicar.

'Yes, why, do you know 'er?'

'Know her? I most certainly do. Chrissie is one of the finest people I know. She doesn't come to our church, but she always has something to donate to our bazaar, or the harvest festival. Why, she even made a hat from some rabbit skins for my dear wife,' he declared. 'Please,' he beseeched, 'do come and have lunch with my wife and me at the vicarage today, will you? I know my wife would be delighted to meet you – she's so fond of Chrissie and drops in to see her occasionally.'

Samboy looked at his daughter who nodded, saying, 'I'd like to go, Dad.'

Samboy smiled at the vicar. 'That settles it then; thank you, Reverend. We accept your kind invitation.'

'That's wonderful! We'll see you in about an hour at the vicarage – will that suit you both?'

'That'll suit us grand, Vicar, we know where you live, thank you.'

An hour later Daisy and Samboy knocked on the front door of the vicarage. There was a warm welcome from the vicar's wife, who was obviously in awe of Chrissie.

'If our congregation was made up of people like dear Chrissie, none of Christ's children would be in want – she is a blessing in the world. Now tell me, Daisy....'

The vicar's wife didn't stop talking. She wanted to know everything about Daisy and Samboy. Where they lived? What did Daisy do each day? And was she happy? Was she looking for work elsewhere? Could they be of assistance?

As Samboy concluded later, 'She wants to know the far end of a fart and which way the wind blows! She means well, but people like 'er, well, they're better off helpin' folk that needs help and not the likes of us.'

'Thank you for your hospitality,' Samboy said, leaving their hosts watching them depart down the drive like long lost friends.

'Please, call in on your way back to Appleby if you have time ... oh, and do give our regards to Chrissie,' they chorused.

'Aye, we will do if we're comin' back this way. Thank you again.'

Samboy and Daisy looked at each other raising their eyebrows and sighing in unison when they walked out through the vicarage gate. 'Phew! That was hard work!' Samboy declared, wiping his brow in mock exasperation.

'Aw, they meant well, Dad. Nice to know Aunt Chrissie is well thought of, isn't it?'

'Aye, it is. Funny, ain't it? How someone like that stuck-up Miriam – or whatever 'er name is – doesn't 'ave that much clout where our dear Lord is concerned? Thank God.'

They set out for the last four miles to West Hutton with full stomachs and in high spirits even though stormclouds gathered in the western skies. A crack of thunder heralded a terrific downpour, the first in two weeks. The sky grew black turning day into night and Samboy slapped the reins spurring the horses on at faster trot. Fork lightning lit up the sky with its jagged patterns across the heavens.

'It won't be long now.' The comforting words from Samboy were to

himself as well as Daisy who was drenched to the skin. The horses struggled to hear his commands above the crash of thunder and driving rain.

'I'm sure Aunt Chrissie will have a good fire going, Dad, we'll soon
dry out,' she said, her voice barely audible above the squall.

'Aye, and thank the Lord we're not having to set up camp tonight.
Good timing, eh, Daisy?' Samboy grinned. Oh, it's good to be back on
the road away from all that's 'appened of late – even if the weather is
atrocious, he thought.

As quickly as the heavens had opened, dispensing volumes of water,
the clouds dispersed and the sun emerged, transforming the countryside
into a wet glittering terrain. By the time they arrived at Hutton they
resembled a pair of half-drowned rats.

'Good to see yer, Samboy,' Donny said, greeting him like a brother. It
was the longest he'd been away from his adopted family. That was what
Samboy and Daisy had become to him over the years, his family. 'Get
yerselves inside now and I'll see to the wagon and 'orses.' Donny fussed
about them like an old mother hen. 'Chrissie's got a right nice dinner
ready fer yer both.'

Samboy was about to protest and say they'd just eaten a huge dinner
at the vicarage.

'We'll look forward to that, Donny, won't we, Dad?' A mischievous
grin was in danger of breaking loose on Daisy's face.

''Ow's Donny done fer yer, our Chrissie?'

'Aw, he's been grand, Samboy. Best help I've ever had he is.'

'D' yer want him to stay back 'ere with you for a bit longer? I can
always come and get 'im when you're well enough to manage.'

'Yes, I'd like him to stay on a while, our Samboy. I don't feel quite up
to managing on my own just yet. He thought he'd give Topcliffe Fair a
miss this year, if it's all the same to you.'

'That's fine by me, our Chrissie.'

It was the next day at breakfast when Samboy noticed something
different about Chrissie. She appeared to have taken special care with the
way she dressed, wearing what could be described as her Sunday best –
a pretty summer frock without the protection of an apron. She flurried
around Donny needlessly. Had he got this? Did he want that? And is
everything to his liking? He, in turn, smiled his thanks, wearing a daft
lovesick grin on his face adopted by men in their youth. Donny helped
clear the table and with the washing-up which was unheard of back at
Appleby.

Daisy also noticed they got on like a house on fire. Chrissie was quite besotted with him. Her eyes followed him everywhere and she hung on to his every word. She couldn't recall either ever having been in a relationship before, never mind in love. Daisy was thrilled for them both. It might be a bit late in the day, but so what? If her Aunt Chrissie had found love, surely it was better late than never.

Donny had never looked so well and happy. He'd acquired a renewed energy and the years had fallen away, eradicating the deep lines from his face. His once cowed demeanour was something of the past. He now stood proud and erect.

Chrissie had let him have the spare bedroom, the first bedroom he'd ever slept in. In fact, it was the first house he'd ever slept in. His clothes were immaculately laundered and his hair professionally cut. Only his eyes betrayed what could be termed a handsome man. But even they didn't appear quite as crossed.

Samboy had pulled the wagon behind the cottage and tethered the horses on the grass verge by the quiet road. He and Daisy would normally sleep inside the cottage with Daisy in the spare bedroom, and Samboy on a makeshift bed in the sitting-room. But it was no hardship sleeping in the wagon this time of year, it was cosy and they preferred it.

At nightfall they opened up the canvas flap and they'd fall asleep gazing out at the moon and the night skies. Her father would point out the constellations of the stars and she would listen intently, dearly wishing to learn and remember. She would watch Venus rise and follow the moon, tracing her finger across the night sky locating the Great Bear, Orion, and the North Star. 'You'll never be lost if you know which is the North Star,' her father would say. This puzzled her; because if she looked up at the North Star she still wouldn't know how to find her way in the dark if she were lost. She'd never confessed this to her father, of course; it didn't matter to her, she just loved to listen to him teaching her the sky map.

Samboy was helping Chrissie dig up some early potatoes from the vegetable plot when curiosity got the better of him.

'You and Donny seem to 'ave come to be – er – very good pals.'

'We 'ave, yes,' Chrissie replied, blushing at her brother's inference. She hoped he hadn't noticed the closeness that had developed between her and Donny. To someone like Samboy, she supposed it all might appear reckless, and too sudden, especially for two middle-aged people, who, in the eyes of others, probably ought to exercise restraint and common sense.

When Donny had first come to the cottage, Chrissie had felt sorry for him. She'd met him many times before, often at Samboy's home, and at the Romany fairs she'd attended. But within a couple of days of him staying at the cottage, he'd surprised her. Donny had proved himself to be an intelligent conversationalist and a good companion. Chrissie realized she had grown lonely over the years and began eagerly to look forward to their mealtimes together, and to working side by side in the garden. Within a short time, both discovered a mutual affection for each other and their shyness had evaporated, replaced with a mature loving respect for one another. They considered themselves extremely fortunate to have discovered love at this belated hour in their lonely lives.

'Yer may as well be the first to know Samboy. Donny and me, we're a bit more than friends. We've found we like each other's company, and well, we might be together a bit more permanent like. *There*, so now you know!'

Chrissie's heart thumped wildly in her chest. He'd think she'd gone stark staring crackers! But, it was out and make of it what he will. She and Donny had become a couple.

'I'm right glad for yer, our Chrissie,' he said, surprising her and smiling warmly. He put his arms about his dear sister and hugged her close. 'You deserve to be happy, Sis, and there isn't a kinder, truer man than Donny. So if you're looking for my blessing, you 'ave it.'

'That means a right lot to me, Samboy, and I know it'll mean a lot to Donny. He's that fond of you an' Daisy; you've been his only family all these years, and now it's gonna be for proper. Let him know I've told yer, will yer, Samboy? And if yer can get a word with Daisy – mind you, nowt much passes that young lady, I'll bet yer she's figured us out already.'

Daisy was washing the dishes when her father gave her the happy news. She was overjoyed for them and went directly to her aunt and congratulated her. She asked when they were going to be married and Chrissie thought after the summer. Just a quiet register office ceremony; neither wanted any fuss, but they would ask the reverend from Kirkby Wiske to bless their marriage afterwards.

Daisy found it all very romantic. Imagine that! Her Aunt Chrissie falling in love, and at her age!

Lydia waited until Miss Pettifer left the room then spat the pill from her mouth, presumed swallowed as far as others were concerned. How she hated the prescribed medication from that doctor. It numbed her senses leaving her feeling extremely tired.

She didn't mind her companion too much. Miss Pettifer was a lively, intelligent woman, but for the life of her, she couldn't understand why Tobias had employed her.

It was necessary, Tobias had insisted.

As soon as I've got this awful medicine out of my system I'll feel much better, she told herself. They said I've had a nervous breakdown – what rubbish! Something's gone wrong. For some reason she felt angry that she'd lost something – or someone. If only she knew what or where she could find it! She wanted to strike out at those who tried to restrain her and stop her wandering about the house and gardens freely. And Tobias had asked her to keep away from the stables. This had caused her much concern. And when she did venture to the stables, that Dan – he'd looked at her in such a strange way. Yes, the doctors were not going to pump her full of sleeping draughts and pills. It wouldn't be too long and she'd be able to think straight again.

Her psychological decline was accelerating, any last hint of sanity, rapidly slipping away.

For a while Tobias thought his mother to be recovering quite well, but lately, there had been a marked difference. He'd seen a strange look in her eyes. She was watching people coming and going and listening to people's conversations but not partaking in them. Most odd, Tobias thought.

Eve Pettifer will keep a close eye on her, he reassured himself. She'll make certain she takes her pills. It's me; I'm worrying about nothing.

He considered taking himself down to the gypsy fair at Topcliffe, but realized it would be irresponsible of him the way things were at the moment with his mother. Anyway, Samboy Latimer wouldn't be pleased to see me, even if Daisy might.

Nellie was preparing dinner for guests, their neighbours Charles Shaw and his daughter Eleanor. They owned the nearby estate bordering Eden Falls, and an invitation for dinner was long overdue.

What I'd give to be having the Latimers over for dinner instead, Tobias thought, along with that delightful Lavinia. It would certainly be more interesting.

Charles Shaw and Lydia had high hopes of Tobias and Eleanor hitting it off and eventually marrying. Although he was fond of Eleanor and considered her a friend, there was no romantic inclination on his part toward her. On the other hand, Eleanor was besotted with him and he tried to discourage her by dating other girls in the area hoping to stamp out any romantic notions she might harbour.

He walked over to the back paddock where Dan was lunging Whitby Jet. He rested his arms on the top rail of the fence taking great pleasure observing the movement and beauty of his horse. The vet had been amazed at the horse's recovery, believing he had cured Jet. But Dan and Tobias knew differently. There was no doubt in their minds where Jet's healing had come from. As he looked on in wonder, his eyes roved over every facet of the cantering stallion. Suddenly he spotted something unusual and strolled over to where Dan stood.

'Just slow him down and walk him over there, please.'

Dan did as his master bade eyeing him curiously. He'd given Jet all the loving care and attention available, so what was the matter, Dan wondered, bring the stallion to a halt. Jet had broken into a sweat with the workout and looked extremely fit.

Tobias bent down and picked up a hoof. The hair on the fetlock had turned a dirty-grey colour.

'Well, bugger me!' exclaimed Dan, 'How the 'ell 'as that 'appened?'

'Yes, bugger me indeed! It appears all is not what it seems. They've dyed the hair on the fetlock, Dan, that's what.'

Tobias stood up and let the leg drop down. He turned to Dan who stood gaping, open-mouthed like an idiot. 'Close it, Dan, flies might be looking for a home.'

'Ah, I'm sorry, sir, I'm right surprised at that. I thought 'e were an 'onest bloke, didn't you?'

'Well, I did and I didn't believe him to be honest, if that makes sense. I would say they are honest people, who ... who make their living in a ... a not too dishonest way. Bending the rules is a way of life for them, and I for one, shan't hold it against them. Why? I would have still bought this magnificent animal from them whether it had one, two, or three white socks!'

Dan grinned, delighted his boss was not going to hit the roof, or, worse still, get rid of Whitby Jet.

'Mind you,' Tobias said, before walking away, 'I shall take it up with Mr Latimer on his return.' Just because, he thought, it will give me good reason to make contact again with the family and, with a bit of luck, Daisy will be around.

It was 7.30 that evening when the car containing Charles and Eleanor Shaw pulled up at the front of the manor.

Nellie opened the front door inviting them in. She ushered them into the drawing-room where a fire was lit against the chilly evening in Westmorland.

'I'll see to the drinks, thank you, Nellie. We'll dine at eight if that's all right with you, then you can get off to bed.' Tobias smiled his thanks to her as she left the room.

'She's getting old is Nellie,' he said, annoyed at himself for making excuses. 'I ... I, don't like to keep her up too late. Now, what will you have to drink?' he asked, clapping his hands.

'A dry sherry for me please, Tobias,' said Eleanor.

'And a whisky for me, old boy,' volunteered Charles.

'Yes,' said Charles, taking the whisky from Tobias and swallowing half of it in one gulp, 'you need someone young about the place to keep it in order.' He smiled, glancing over in the direction of his daughter, his intent blatant.

'Nellie has been with this family most of her life and will remain here for the rest of it if I have my way.'

'Quite, quite,' blustered Charles.

Bloody buffoon! Tobias thought, and looked to where Eleanor sat cradling her sherry wishing to hell she'd drink the lot and let herself go. I don't think I've ever heard her laugh, he recalled.

It was apparent she was heading for spinsterhood and she saw him as her last chance. And Charles was doing his damnedest to get them married. I'd be happier in a monastery! God, it was going to be a long evening, he thought, sighing deeply.

'How's your dear mother?' Eleanor asked politely. 'I did hear she hadn't been – er – very well.'

That's the understatement of the year, he thought. I'll bet they've heard she's gone bonkers. What an opportunity for Eleanor to inveigle herself into a position they consider needs filling, permitting the Flint family to appear normal.

'She's doing well, thank you. I believe the strain of the war and losing my brother had a more serious effect on her than any of us imagined. The war did that, Charles, didn't it? Destroyed so many lives, and not just the lives of those maimed or killed.' The buffoon didn't respond. 'But thank you for enquiring,' he added.

'Dinner's ready,' Nellie announced, poking her head around the door.

Thank goodness, Tobias thought, steering Eleanor from the drawing-room and into the spacious dining-room where a fire glimmered in the grate. The dining table was laid in all its finery. The polished silver glinted. Two candelabras, each holding five candles gave off a wonderful light.

'How superb,' remarked Eleanor, as she sat down. 'Your dining table must be the finest in Westmorland. And believe me, I've dined at many, but your family silver is by far the grandest I've ever laid eyes on.'

'Thank you, Eleanor, you say that every time.'

'Do I? Oh, how boring; do forgive me. Now, Tobias, tell us about this splendid horse you've bought from the gypsies. Everybody's talking about it and saying what a magnificent animal it is. Will you permit me to ride him sometime?'

Tobias was startled at the sudden interest in the acquisition of his horse. He'd bought horses before and she hadn't shown the slightest interest in them.

'Oh, I think Jet would be a bit too strong for you, Eleanor. He's a stallion and takes a lot of handling.' He noticed her blush at the mention of the word stallion. 'I may use him for breeding, but you're more than welcome to have a look at him though. We'll all stroll out to the stables after dinner, yes?'

'Thank you, I'd like that. But do tell me,' she continued, 'did you buy the horse from that frightful family who live in the village of Hampton not far from here?'

Something snapped in him. It was one of those mind-splitting moments in one's life when all you thought you believe in is washed away and your mind realizes a truth, not all truth, but truths that must be given space and acknowledgement.

Tobias looked at both his guests. He kept his voice calm. 'Actually, those frightful gypsies happen to be friends of mine.'

'Tobias! Honestly!' Eleanor threw her head back and laughed loudly.

So, you do laugh? Tobias thought, looking at her gaping mouth from which the sound of mocking high-pitched laughter exuded. What a pity it's at other people's expense.

Charles sat grinning having consumed far too much whisky and wine.

'Yes, honestly,' replied Tobias, unsmiling. 'The Latimers are good, decent people, and you do not only them but yourself, Eleanor, a great disservice mocking them.'

'You're serious, aren't you?' She stopped laughing and looked at him quizzically.

'Of course I am,' he said, smiling proudly. 'Now pass me your plates and I'll take them through for Nellie and I'll fetch in the cheese.'

They passed him their plates and he left for the kitchen.

'Really, Father,' whispered Eleanor, 'Tobias is behaving strangely, don't you think? How many in his position would actually run around after their servants to save them work? Do you think he's been contaminated with his mother's madness? God only knows if it would be wise even to consider him as a suitable father of any children he might sire.'

'Bit odd, I must admit, my dear, but, beggars can't be choosers. So better keep that in the forefront of your mind. We're struggling financially and the way things are going I might have to sack most of *our* servants, God forbid! And if you don't marry into money, *you*, young lady, or not so young now, are going to have to find yourself a position of companion or housekeeper somewhere! So, stop upsetting him!' he snapped.

'But, Father, I don't believe he is the least bit interested in me as a marriage prospect. And, to be honest, I don't think I could marry someone who held those thieving gypsies in such ... such high esteem!'

'Maybe you couldn't, Eleanor, but for God's sake stop being such a bloody snob. The chances are they'll have more money than you'll ever have.'

'Have you considered selling the estate, Father?' Eleanor asked.

'Considered it? I've damn well begged on bended knees! And your mother is not for moving. But, eventually, she'll have no choice. Not if she doesn't want to get up off her fat, lazy backside and work.'

'*Father*!' exclaimed Eleanor. 'How could you say such a terrible thing about Mother?'

'Quite easily,' Charles declared. 'I most certainly have no intention of finding work, not at my age. So it will be sell up or starve. The choice will be your mother's. Should common sense prevail and she decides to sell, then who do you think the obvious buyer would be? Tobias Flint, of course! Need I say more, Eleanor?'

'No, Father.'

Her heart sank as she imagined all the possibilities outlined by her father. She neither wanted to be Tobias's wife, nor did she relish the idea of finding work as a companion or housekeeper. All in all, life was not looking too rosy and her father was probably right, those damned gypsies would have more money than she. Her mother would just have to sell up. She would talk to her tomorrow and she hoped she would listen to the voice of reason.

Her thoughts came to an abrupt end as the man she knew not destined to be her husband, came back into the dining-room bearing cheese and biscuits decorated with bunches of grapes.

'Thank you, Tobias; you must be the kindest employer around.' She smiled a sickly smile at him as he placed the board in front of her. 'There are not many would consider the needs of their serfs.'

Tobias cringed at the expression which she deemed as kindly.

It was ten o'clock and the dinner party was coming to a close. It couldn't come soon enough for Tobias. He wanted rid of these terrible people, vowing it was the last time they'd be invited to dine at his table.

'Well, are you going to show me this superb animal of yours?' Eleanor asked.

'Yes, of course. Charles, are you coming?'

'No, no, if you don't mind I'll just rest here and finish my cognac. Excellent stuff, Tobias, I must get the name of your supplier.'

As soon as the pair had left the room Charles helped himself to another glass of cognac and a cigar from the box on the table. If Eleanor doesn't pull this off, he thought, this could be the last good cigar I'll ever smoke. I've no intention of rushing it.

It was dark outside when they crossed the courtyard to the stables.

Tobias opened the stable door and held up a lantern, throwing soft light into the dark stable. Jet snorted and, recognizing his master's voice, walked over to the door.

'Hello there, my beauty.' Tobias nestled his head in the horse's neck and stroked his mane.

Eleanor was quite envious of the horse, as she witnessed the affection Tobias showed him.

'I see what you mean, Tobias, he's a magnificent animal.' She was an accomplished horsewoman and knew he'd made a wise and excellent choice. 'I think you're right – he'd be far too strong for me, but maybe when he's a bit older you'll allow me the privilege of riding him?'

Her smile and appreciation was genuine and he recognized it. 'Of course, Eleanor. You will always be welcome here to ride any horse you wish.'

An unspoken understanding passed between them in that moment and Eleanor felt a sense of relief. She relaxed, allowing them to talk in a friendly easy manner without rancour.

It was as they were walking back to the house that Eleanor thought she heard something and turning saw a figure clad in a white robes run past and disappear round the back of the house. 'Tobias!' she exclaimed. 'Did you see that?'

'What?'

'There was someone in white, just now. They hurried across the court-yard and round the back of the house.'

'No, sorry, I didn't see a thing. Could be one of the servants going home.'

'No, this dress was white … chiffon … a ball gown or something like that.'

'I think the wine has gone to your head, Eleanor,' Tobias laughed. 'Come on, let's get inside, it's damned cold out here.'

Eleanor let it go. But she had seen something strange. It wasn't an apparition – it was more than that.

'I'm so sorry, Tobias,' Eleanor said, on reaching the front door.

'What on earth for?' he asked, knowing full well she'd been less than charitable.

'Sorry for making fun of your friends, the travellers. Sorry for being such a terrible snob. Forgive me?'

'I forgive you.' He put his arm about her shoulders and gave her a hug.

'Thanks, I needed that. You do know, don't you, that Father is hoping you'll ask me to marry you?'

Tobias was stunned at her directness and at a loss for words.

'Phew! Don't worry, Tobias. I don't want to marry you any more than you do me.' She laughed out loud and Tobias joined in. 'God only knows what Father will think! I believe I was supposed to seduce you out there in the stables!'

They both roared with laughter as they walked back into the house.

Hmm, that sounds promising! Charles said to himself, hearing them laughing as they came in. Something must have suited.

'Come on, Father, let's get you back home. I'll drive.'

'You will not! I'm quite capable of getting us home.' Charles struggled to his feet and weaved his way unsteadily to the front door. 'Lovely evening, Tobias, musht have a return match sshhoon, eh, old boy?' he slurred.

'Yes, that would be lovely,' Tobias said, humouring him and winked at Eleanor. She winked back and he smiled. If she'd been like this from the start I would probably have been quite keen on her.

Tobias walked outside with his guests and waved them off.

He felt relieved Eleanor had been open about her father's expectations. They might now be friends in their own right without anyone breathing down their necks, but, he had to confess, he had reservations and didn't really want to bother with the Shaw family again. The comments made about the gypsies had blotted their copy books and it would take a long time to expunge the damage.

*

Lydia had heard all that had been said in the dining room. And she'd seen them at the stables.

Once again she'd spat out the sedative given her and sneakily slipped it into the cup of cocoa Miss Pettifer was drinking. She had then gone to bed and lay quietly until Miss Pettifer had fallen asleep, thus giving her the opportunity to go about the house and grounds unsupervised. She had found it most humiliating having a jailer. Because that was what it was when not permitted to wander at will.

Lydia squeezed herself into her mother-in-law's wedding dress. It was too tight and the side seam ripped open. It didn't matter though, she still looked beautiful, she told herself, glancing in the mirror. Richard would fall in love with her all over again when he saw her – when he came back. He must be away on business, she supposed.

She walked through the rose garden and looked through the dining-room window and watched them. They couldn't see her in the dark, but she could see them. Why hadn't they invited her to dinner, she wondered? She could have danced with that silly little man – what's his name? She racked her brain, but couldn't recall it.

She had seen Tobias and Eleanor go to the stables and, after watching them for a while, she had became confused for some reason, and her head ached. She needed to go back to bed. That … that … Miss Pettifer is not doing her job – she should be looking after me properly and not letting me get cold. Going outside without a coat! Outside … on my own … like this.

She ran back to the house and upstairs where her companion was out cold. Lydia undressed for bed before glancing in the sitting-room where her companion was slumped back in an armchair snoring loudly. Lydia smiled to herself, going back to her bedroom for the night where sleep would not come – and her mind would not rest.

Chapter Nine

Daisy looked out of the back of the wagon to see that heavy rain had flattened the delicate flowers in the herbaceous border and Aunt Chrissie was struggling to rescue them. She dressed quickly and hurried out to assist her.

'You'll be away after breakfast then, eh?' Chrissie said. Their heads touched when leaning over, picking the flowers carefully so as not to damage them.

'We will, Aunt Chrissie, but I won't be feeling too sad to be going off without you this time. Not now you've got Donny here with you.'

Chrissie stood up straight, stretching her aching back, and looked down at her niece. Her glorious hair tumbled down, lost among the blooms. God keep her safe, she prayed silently. She's too beautiful for her own good and will cause many a heart to break.

Samboy had confided in her telling her about the trouble Roulson Adams had got himself into and that he'd been sweet on Daisy. He'd also told her about the squire who'd got his eyes on her. She'd envied her brother having such a lovely daughter, but now she wasn't so sure it was such an enviable position to be in. Daisy would take some watching where young men were concerned, she thought.

'Are you listening to me, Aunt Chrissie?' Daisy said. 'I've just asked if you'd like me to pick some vegetables for you that might have been damaged in the rainstorm.'

'Sorry, lass, my mind was elsewhere. Er ... yes, yes, let's go and see the damage.'

Daisy shook her head in mock rebuke. 'Is that what love does to you, Aunt, does it make you deaf?'

Chrissie laughed, placing her arm round her niece's shoulders and pulled her close. 'I don't know about deaf, Daisy, but it sure makes you daft!'

'I know you'll not need me to come and stay so much now you've got Donny, but—'

'What?' Chrissie exclaimed. 'Not be needing you? Why, Daisy? I'll always need you to come and stay, and don't you go thinkin' any different not for a minute! D'yer hear me? Good God, Daisy, the thought of seeing you less than I do already would fair break my heart. Now, give yer old aunt a cuddle,' she said, wiping her hands on her pinafore. 'And not another word about such rubbish, all right?'

'All right, Aunt Chrissie.' They embraced lovingly before making their way to the vegetable garden with arms linked in shared accord of their friendship.

Topcliffe was bustling with travellers when Samboy and Daisy drove up the main street.

Topcliffe Fair like other gypsy fairs was a meeting place where families and friends met each year, renewed old acquaintanceships and completed deals.

Farmers came to purchase new horses to pull their carts and carriages until quite recently. But, alas, the car and tractor had reduced the sale of horses dramatically, which were now often bought for pleasure rather than work.

The field by the River Swale was full, but Samboy managed to locate a site close to the entrance to unhitch his wagon, leaving ample room for people to come and go with their vehicles. It was a good spot. He was able to observe every person and horse that passed by, while in turn, they could admire the handsome pair of Cleveland Bays he'd tethered next to his wagon, which were sure to come under the covetous eyes of serious dealers. It was only a three-day sale and he'd no doubt he'd sell the bays at a good price.

His wistful eye spotted a cushty brood mare tethered further down the field and, if it was for sale at the right price, he'd have a bid. He hadn't bred for two or three years, but knowing Lavinia's magical way with mares and foals, it could be a sort of early wedding gift to her.

Daisy had seen the Maguire family down by the river. She hadn't seen them since last year and made her way over to see them. As a young girl she'd taken tea with the family often and had been friendly with their eldest daughter, Rebecca, who was the same age as herself.

Rebecca had married two years ago and now had two children. She and her Romany husband Nat travelled the roads in convoy with her parents and did the rounds of the gypsy fairs.

'Hello, Rebecca,' Daisy called, ambling down to the river.

Rebecca spun round holding both children, one in each arm. Daisy was shocked at the change in her. She appeared much older. Her hair hung in rats' tails and her clothes were stained with food and dirt. The children had dummies in their mouths caked in dried food. Daisy smiled at them and the little boy held out his arms to her.

''Ello, Daisy.' Rebecca smiled at her friend and handed over the squirming child to her. 'Ta, he's a bit heavy.'

'How are you, Rebecca? I see your family has increased.'

'Yes,' she sighed. 'Came as a bit of a shock so soon after 'im,' Rebecca replied, nodding to the baby she was holding, 'But I'm OK, ta. My, but you look grand, Daisy, dressed up all smart like. And yer hair's so pretty. It'll be you next!' she said, nudging Daisy with her elbow and she laughed. When she did so, Daisy saw that she had lost some teeth and she hoped Rebecca didn't hear her gasp or notice the momentary look of horror on her face.

'Er, maybe.'

'Aw, a lass as bonny as yerself won't be on 'er own for long. 'Ave yer got yerself a boyfriend yet?'

'No, not yet.' Daisy didn't want to get into talk about boyfriends or marriage. Seeing Rebecca like this was enough to put any girl off marriage for life.

'I 'eard tell that Roulson Adams was after yer, Daisy, is it true? And do yer know whether he killed that bloke up at Appleby? Yer wouldn't believe the stories that are flyin' round about him. He's supposed to 'ave been burnt to death, and now folks are sayin' that 'e's done a runner. Can you believe it, eh?'

Daisy wanted to do a runner. She wanted to run away from this woman she once considered to be a close friend. She'd come here to get away from all the questioning.

'I don't know anything, Rebecca. You probably know more than me. Look, I'm sorry to hand this young bairn back to you, but I promised Dad I'd help him with some jobs.' She handed the wriggling child back to Rebecca. 'I'll see you before we leave, eh? Give my best to the rest of your family.' She kissed her on the cheek and patted the head of the little boy.

'All right, tara then.' She watched her friend walk away and felt a stab of jealousy.

Daisy had everything, Rebecca thought, good looks and nice clothes. But most of all she's got her freedom, no kids or a sex-mad husband pawing and mauling your body every night. Wait till you're wed, she reflected resentfully, that'll put paid to yer clean clothes and pretty hair. The thought made her smile. She looked down at the two grubby infants in her arms. 'C'mon, bugger lugs, the pair of yers. Let's get you back and see what yer father's up to. Not a lot I should think.'

Daisy and Samboy sat over the camp-fire enjoying the company of some friends they hadn't seen for a long time.

'We're just goin' to 'ave a beer at the pub in a while, Daisy,' said Samboy. 'Will you tek the 'orses up Winn Lane and let them graze for an hour or so? Yer never know, there might be some local gorgios who'll tek a fancy to 'em.'

'Yes, I'd like to do that, Dad. Chase needs exercising and there're one or two friends I'd like to see.'

'Aye, good lass. I'll be looking out for yer coming back. I'll see yer when yer pass the pub, all right?'

'Aw, Dad, you don't have to look out for me coming back. I'll see to the horses and settle them down for the night. You have a nice time with your friends.'

She saddled her horse and led the two haltered Cleveland Bays from the field and along the road into the main street of the village. It was packed with people from the travelling community and neighbouring villages. The rhythmic clip-clop sounds of metal hoofs striking concrete invited appreciative looks from the many bystanders.

She was a striking picture. Her golden hair, ablaze in the evening sun, tumbled about her pretty face and shoulders. Her slim, lithe body didn't appear strong enough to handle three horses, but she had every confidence in Chase, steering him with the pressure of her knees, her hands free to maintain control over the two Cleveland Bays.

She slowed the horses to a walking pace as they made their way up the hill taking in the splendour of the village church rising boldly from the east bank of the River Swale. The large church was dedicated to St Columba, in its early Saxon time. The tall tower housed four bells, delighting her when they rang out for some special occasion that would coincide with the gypsy fair.

She continued past the church and, glancing down Back Lane, noticed a few horses being led to graze by traveller children. Daisy crossed the road and turned down Winn Lane.

It was quieter than she'd expected and she welcomed the silence. She dismounted and sat on a clump of dry grass. The warm setting sun blinded her and she lay back on the dry warm grass and closed her eyes.

The sound of the horses cropping placidly made a pleasant sound in her ears. She dozed for half an hour and woke with a start when one of the horses whinnied.

'What...? Who...?' She sat up quickly and, shielding her eyes from the low, blinding, setting sun tried to make out the person standing close by. He stepped in front of her blotting out the sunlight. She froze instantly.

'*Caspar!*'

'Glad to see you remember me.'

His ugly smile exposed a small amount of black teeth wobbling precariously in his gums. He licked his lips as his eyes devoured her body. He'd not forgotten how attractive she was and that she'd probably never had a man. If it wasn't for that Roulson, he thought, I'd take her right here and now; no bugger would 'ear 'er screams.

'I've got a message fer yer,' he said harshly, handing her a piece of paper. He grabbed her hand as she took the paper. 'Yer a nice-looking lass, Daisy, how about showin' a bit o' kindness to a lonely bloke, eh, for old-time's sake?'

Daisy cringed visibly and snatched her hand away from his.

'Don't you dare touch me you, you're ... you're ... *disgusting!* Whatever message you have you can keep it!'

She sprang to her feet and gathered Chase's reins pulling him close to her side for protection.

''Ere, tek it!' he said, shoving the piece of paper at her.

She took it and stuffed it into her trouser pocket before leaping into the saddle.

'Well, aren't yer goin' to read it?'

'Let me pass, or I'll run you down!' She felt braver now she was on the back of Chase with the two large bays flanking him.

Caspar stepped aside a few paces to let her pass. She dug in her heels and Chase took off at a canter with the bays following.

Well away from Caspar, she brought the horses to a halt. Her hands were shaking with fear and trepidation as she read the note he'd given her. It was from Roulson. The neat writing told her he'd found someone to write it for him. It read:

Dear Daisy

Please meet me tomorrow night, seven o'clock. I am leaving forever soon and I need to see you before I go, even if only to say goodbye. Sorry Caspar had to deliver this, but there was no other

way. Meet me at Maiden Bower tomorrow night at seven. I know
you won't let me down, Daisy,
Love Roulson

She folded the letter and put it back in her pocket. She looked back down Winn Lane, not sure she could, or even wanted to venture down there again. She would have to pass this way to reach Maiden Bower. All she wanted to do now was return to the safety of the camp-site and hope her father would be looking out for her riding past the pub.

Samboy was waiting at the side of the road.

'Where 'ave you been, Daisy? I was getting worried when everyone seemed to be back but you. Are you all right, love, you look a bit pale?' He took her hands in his. They were cold and shaking. 'What is it, Daisy?'

'Nothing, I'm all right, Dad,' she lied. 'One of the horses took a bit of handling; he didn't want to leave the good grazing. I'm tired, Dad, are you coming back with me?' she asked.

'Yes, I'll be along shortly, just got a bit of business to wind up with old Jake.'

Daisy went back to the field and tied up the horses. She filled the kettle and, hanging it over the embers to boil, set about preparing supper for her father. She wasn't hungry herself; any appetite she had dissolved along with her self-assurance at Caspar's sudden unwelcome appearance. She shuddered at the thought of him and never wanted to see him again. Should she decide to see Roulson, she would let him know how awful Caspar had behaved toward her, and Roulson would see to it that he never bothered her again. Her thoughts were in a whirl when her father returned and she didn't see him approach. She was anxiously wringing her hands and shaking her head.

'What's up, Daisy?' he asked, looking concerned.

'Oh! It's you, Dad!' Daisy jumped and crossed her hands over her chest to still her heart that raced rapidly.

'What's upset you, lass? Is someone botherin' yer?'

'No, honest, Dad, I'm just a bit tired, that's all. I suppose it's quite a journey from Appleby to Topcliffe.' She forced a smile and handed him a cup of tea. 'Some bread and jam there for you, Dad. Do you want anything else?'

'No, that'll do, ta. Now you're sure you're all right? We can get away early if you like.'

Her eyes lit up. 'Tomorrow, you mean?'

'Not tomorrow, no, but we can leave the day after. Tomorrow's an important sale day – the Cleveland Bays will make a cushty price for sure. I 'eard them bein' discussed tonight in the boozer.'

Samboy was sure there was something wrong. It's not like our Daisy, wantin' to be off afore a fair was over! I'll keep a close eye on 'er, he thought. She'd 'ad an upsetting time at Appleby, what with that bloody Roulson droolin' all over 'er and then disappearin' after a murder. And Squire Flint. Was Lavinia right, did 'e hanker after our Daisy? Why the 'ell didn't I 'ave a son? Would've been a lot less bother, I'd bet! Mind you, Roulson's parents wouldn't think that.'

He gazed across at her where she sat opposite. Unaware of him studying her, she stared blankly into the flames of the fire. She threw a few dry sticks on to it and they ignited instantly, throwing light and warmth about them. A fresh sadness had settled on her pretty face and she was preoccupied with something she didn't want to discuss with him. She needs a mother, Samboy thought sorrowfully. Maybe when Lavinia and me are married she'll feel she's got someone to talk things over with, things that a woman can't talk to a man about – especially yer dad!'

'So we'll leave the day after tomorrow, Dad, eh?'

'Aye, if that's what you want.'

'What?' Daisy looked up suddenly. 'Er ... oh, yes, I want to do that, Dad. It'll be nice to get back home and into a routine.'

'Does that mean yer'll not be wantin' to go to Yarm Fair later this year, Daisy?' He frowned in surprise looking at his daughter.

'Oh, I hadn't given it any thought, Dad, it seems such a long way off.'

'I suppose it is,' he agreed. 'Get yourself to bed, Daisy, I'll see to the horses and the fire.'

'Thanks, Dad.'

She went to bed leaving Samboy sitting by the fire. He lit his pipe and reflected on his daughter and the change in her today. She'd always loved the fairs they attended every year, and he couldn't imagine not going to Yarm in the autumn. He'd gone to Appleby, Yarm and Topcliffe Fairs since he was a babe in arms. Daisy too; she hadn't missed one since she was born. So what had happened to bring about this change in his lass? It wasn't Roulson, he'd be long gone and wouldn't dare show his face around here, or Appleby, come to that. Could it be the squire then? God forbid she'd ever get involved with suchlike. She's better off with one of her own. I'll be pleased to get home meself, and when Lavinia comes back from visiting her family down in the West Country, things will be different – I hope.

'*Move! Yer divvy gorgio! Get off the bloody road!*' the young man yelled at the woman who had wandered into the busy road.

The traveller lad was riding a piebald bare-back which was moving at a fast trot, lifting its front legs high, showing its ability for sulky racing. The young rider leaned back on the fine horse, his legs straight and thrust forward, taking on the typical style of riding when flashing a horse to sell.

'*Watch where you're bloody going!*' Someone else shouted.

All that concerned the young rider was putting his horse through its paces in the hope of an onlooker's interest in buying it – not injuring anybody during the process was somebody else's good fortune. Some stepped into the road as he rode past to admire the speed and conform-ation of the fine animal.

Samboy was next to follow the young man down the road. He struck an imposing figure riding a Cleveland Bay whilst leading the other. The crowd stirred, all eyes were on him and his quality horses. Every person there considering buying horseflesh knew him, traveller and gorgio alike. If you wanted to buy cheap – you didn't buy from Samboy, but took your chances with any other horse dealer there. But if you wanted guaranteed, quality horseflesh, from someone who looked you up the following year to see how the horse was faring, then you went to Samboy Latimer.

As he rode down the road he ascertained the potential buyers lining the way. He slowed to a walk enabling them to take a closer look at his horses.

A tall, elegant, gentleman farmer stepped out into the road and smiled at him. 'Good day to you, sir.'

'And to you,' replied Samboy. 'Are yer interested in one of my 'orses?'

'I'm interested in both of them. Now tell me, can we go somewhere and discuss a price?'

'Yes, we can, but allow me to finish showing them to the rest.' He smiled and winked at the middle-aged gentleman. 'You never know, you might not offer me a fair price then I'll be looking for another buyer.'

'Quite right, quite right. I'll wait by the bridge for you and see you in about half an hour. Dick Watts is the name, local farmer from Thorpe Farm, not far down the road.'

The young man flashing the piebald was on his return journey up the road and approaching fast.

'*Look out, Mr Watts*!' Samboy yelled. He leaned from his horse and, grabbing the farmer by his arm, pulled him brusquely to one side.

'Sorry if I were a bit rough,' he apologized, 'but he was goin' to wipe yer off the road.'

The farmer looked pale and shaken but managed to smile a thank you at Samboy before retreating to safer ground. The road had suddenly become a speedway for horses flying fast and furious as the fervour of the travellers reached fever pitch in flashing their prized horseflesh.

Daisy watched the proceedings in a desultory mood her thoughts elsewhere. She was undecided whether to meet Roulson later that day. It would be churlish of me not to go to say goodbye. I could ride down to Maiden Bower, see him and be back in an hour, she thought, burying her head into Chase's mane. 'What do you think Chase? Should I go and say goodbye to Roulson, eh?' The horse whinnied and she laughed. 'All right, we'll go together. I'll be all right if you're with me.'

Samboy was delighted with the price received from Dick Watts for both horses. The farmer was a fair man and was looking for a pair of hunters for himself and his wife. He would deliver them the next day on their return north.

Samboy gave his full stomach a satisfied pat. He'd enjoyed a supper of bacon bone broth fortified with lentils, pearl barley and potatoes.

'By, that was grand, Daisy,' he said. 'He'll be a lucky bloke who gets you for a wife.'

'Aw, Dad, you'll eat anything put on a plate in front of you and if you're not careful you'll get fat!' She laughed prodding his belly where his shirt strained at the buttons. 'So, will you wash the pots, Dad, while I take Chase up Winn Lane to graze for an hour or so?'

'Aye, you do that, lass. I'll see to everythin' 'ere. We'll get off in good time tomorrow and deliver them there 'orses to Mr Watts. Weather looks set fair for a few days,' he added, his eyes scouring the cloudless evening sky.

He'd be glad to get back home. There was plenty of work to do when he returned: four young geldings to break, liveried out to a neighbouring farmer while he and Daisy were down here, scrap metal to sort and take to the local scrapman, leather to mend and skins to cure: the list of jobs was endless.

Daisy felt apprehensive turning down Winn Lane. No one was around, but she kept glancing back over her shoulder expecting Caspar to step out from behind the hedge at any minute. Chase picked up on her nervousness and tossed his head to the side, straining to look at his mistress. The whites of his eyes flashed, displaying uncertainty as to where they were heading.

'Steady, boy, you're all right,' she said. Her calm words reassured the prancing horse and he continued at a steady pace.

At the bottom of Winn Lane they passed through a gate. Rising in the midst, Maiden Bower stood proud on an artificial moated mound, on which centuries ago stood a fortress, from where the Percy family reigned supreme.

Daisy steered Chase to the summit of the mound where she was able to view her surroundings from a vantage point. She shielded her eyes from the lowering sun and scanned the area. She spotted a grey van moving along the grassy meadow toward the river and recognized at once it was Roulson. It was the same van he'd had when she'd met him when staying with her aunt. She watched him drive down to the riverside where he stopped and tooted his horn.

She rode Chase across the narrow bridge spanning Cod Beck then dismounted, leading Chase toward the van. The van door opened as she neared and a man got out. Daisy stood stock still. She gasped, putting her hand to her mouth to stifle a scream. This wasn't Roulson, *this was a stranger*! The stranger smiled and a familiar voice spoke.

'Hello, Daisy, don't you recognize me?'

Roulson laughed at her reaction. Looking at her now it dawned on him it was her pretty face and virginal body that attracted him, and not the innocent, bashful attitude he'd found so appealing not so very long ago.

She stared at him in horror. The once handsome dark-haired gypsy was a blond-haired stranger. The warm, intoxicating good looks replaced with a face set in a stony hardness.

He walked towards her and she stepped back. Alarm bells sounded in her head. She knew in that instant she shouldn't have ventured here. Not without telling her father.

'Daisy, it's me! *Roulson*. Please, don't be frightened!' he pleaded.

'Hello. I'm sorry, it was such a shock to see you looking so ... so ... different.' She meant hideous, but guarded against voicing it.

'Well, I'm still me,' said Roulson. He shrugged his shoulders and put his hands in his pockets. 'Come down to the water's edge with me, Daisy. Nobody can see us talkin' there from the farm.' He nodded toward the farm from where he had just come. 'I'm working up there for the time being till I decide what I'm going to do. I'm sorry I 'ad to send Caspar with the message, but there was no one else I could trust.'

'Trust? You mean you trust that horrible man? He's despicable!' She shuddered, remembering Caspar's lecherous looks and the unhealthy advances he'd made towards her.

'He may be despicable to you, Daisy, but at the moment, as you can imagine, I'm a bit short of friends an' I can't be too choosy.' *You bitch!* he thought, looking at the spoiled brat he now believed her to be. *All you can think about is yerself.*

'What are you going to do, Roulson? Have you decided?'

'More or less, yes,' he answered, noticing the distaste for him in her eyes. 'I was hoping you'd changed your mind an' you'd want come away with me, Daisy. That's why I wanted to see you, but, by the look on yer face I'll take a wild guess that that isn't an option.'

A sardonic smile accompanied his words making her cringe and feel more uncomfortable than ever. His eyes looked peculiar and held a strange, glazed look. He sighed deeply and the fumes from his breath reached her nostrils; a strong smell of alcohol explained his glassy stare.

'I ... I ... can't stay,' she stammered nervously, 'Dad's expecting me back soon.'

'Not that soon, Daisy,' he corrected her, 'I suppose you told him you were goin' to graze your horse for a while? Don't forget, Daisy, I've been around these fairs for a lot longer than you have. So, come on, stay and talk a while. I'm leaving soon an' we won't be seeing each other again, I don't suppose.'

He held out his hand to lead her the few yards down the bank and she took it nervously knowing she couldn't outrun him. Chase was tied to a tree and she wouldn't leave without him.

It's probably best if I just sit down, let him talk a while, then he'll get fed up and be glad to be rid of me, she thought.

He sat down and, patting the grass with his hand, beckoned her to sit beside him. He laid back and closed his eyes. The cold silence was broken only by the sound of the river. Daisy's discomfort grew and her heart thumped loudly in her chest while her whole body trembled with fear.

'Nice and quiet down 'ere ain't it, Daisy?'

'Yes,' she answered timidly, 'but I really must be getting back.'

'*Aw, for Christ's sake! Stop yer bloody whining, will yer!*' Roulson barked, not opening his eyes, nor moving from where he lay.

Daisy slowly made to stand, but he sensed her movement. He spun round quickly and roughly pulled her back down. She fell back hard on the grass and was lying next to him. He laid an arm across her chest preventing her from moving. His eyes were still closed. Daisy felt the panic rising and wanted to be sick.

'Please ... please let me go home now, Roulson!' she whimpered.

'*Please, please let me go home now, Roulson,*' he mimicked. 'You're a pain in the bloody arse, Daisy. Do you know that? And a bloody cock teaser!'

'What ... what are you talking about? Let me go, please. What do you want with me when it's obvious ... you...you ... don't even like me? Let me go, Roulson, *please*! Dad will be looking for me soon!'

She made to move, but he was too strong for her. He rose up on his free arm and looked down at her. His eyes blazed with fury and she saw madness glaring back at her.

'There's only one thing I want from you, my girl, and quite 'onestly, I think I'll be doin' you a favour taking it.'

'What, Roulson? What do you want? Money?'

He threw his head back laughing insanely.

'*You stupid bitch!*' he snarled cruelly, then leapt on top of her.

As quick as a flash he produced a knife. He held it closely to her throat where the rapid beat of her pulse flirted with the sharp, pointed blade. 'One sound from you, girl, and you're a dead un!'

She couldn't move even if she'd wanted to. A silent scream echoed round and round inside her head so loudly she thought surely someone must hear! The awful terror that gripped her paralysed her body and mind. Roulson brutally ripped open her blouse and yanked off her bra. She felt his hands squeeze her breasts roughly and she winced at the pain.

'Like that do yer, Daisy?' he said, and tugged down her slacks. He tore the flimsy briefs she wore from her slim body and smiled lecherously, his eyes devouring her innocent body. He liked what he saw and licked his lips. Daisy almost blacked out with fear when he prised her legs apart and forced himself inside her. The agonizing pain was like a knife being plunged inside her again and again. Silent tears spilled down her cheeks as he pushed and grunted; she couldn't scream even though she was being torn apart – no sound came out; she wished he'd plunge the knife into her that he held at her throat. Death would surely be preferable to this! A final shudder from his spent body brought the violation to a sudden close.

He stood up and looked down at her. 'Sort yerself out and get home, Daisy. Oh, and a word of warnin' should you decide to blab.' He held the knife in front of her face turning it around, slowly and menacingly.

'I'll find yer, and I'll swing for you, and your father, so keep that in mind. I've got nothing to lose, they'd hang me anyway.'

Roulson stepped over her as if she were nothing more than a piece of litter lying on the grass and walked back to his van. He got in and drove off over the fields back to the farm where Caspar waited for him, eager to hear about his meeting.

Daisy opened her eyes when the sound of the engine finally faded away. She looked down at her violated body and sobbed. She limped down to the river with difficulty and rinsed away the blood and dirt from her inner thighs. How on earth was she going to get back to the wagon? She was sure she'd never be able to sit a horse again because of the bruising she'd sustained. She'd lost all track of time and when she looked at her watch saw it was ten o'clock! God! She couldn't tell her father; she couldn't tell anybody. Who would want her after she had been raped? No! No one will ever know about this, she decided, making her way back up the lane. The shame would be more than she could bear.

As she turned her horse into the main street of Topcliffe a police car whizzed past with its siren blaring. All she could think was thank God! They've found him and taken him away and locked him up for life. In those few moments her heart beat in normal rhythms.

The brawl had spilled out from the pub and into the evening sunshine when Samboy called at the pub for a beer while Daisy was grazing her horse.

The soldier and young traveller, grappled drunkenly.

Samboy recognized the lad. He was the one who'd almost mown down a woman in the main street that day with his horse.

A crowd had gathered, encircling the two men and exacerbating the unpleasant situation. It was difficult to tell which one was worse off in the scrap. The one in uniform was older and bigger, throwing heavier punches, but the younger man had left his mark on his opponent giving him a bloody nose. The soldier punched the lad on the side of his head and he fell to the ground with a resounding thud. Then he started to kick him. The crowd began to boo, and Samboy stepped in and pushed the soldier aside.

'Hey! You!' he bawled at the soldier, still kicking hell out of the young man on the ground. 'Hasn't there been enough killing for yer in the war without starting on one of yer own?'

'He's not one of mine! He's nowt but a bloody, loud-mouthed gypo! He shouldn't be allowed into public houses where decent people are trying to have a quiet pint!' The soldier wiped his nose on his sleeve, smearing blood across his cheek.

Samboy glared at the man and his blood boiled. Topcliffe Fair had always lacked the certain elegance that Appleby boasted and over the years more fights seemed to break out in Topcliffe. This was more often than not due to the soldiers stationed close by. They had plenty of money to spend on drink and the travelling lads visiting the fair drank heavily too during the few days they spent here. But it was the soldiers, not the travellers, causing trouble in the neighbouring towns of Ripon, Thirsk and Northallerton. So you couldn't blame them for that.

'Now listen 'ere, yer ignorant young bugger—!' Samboy stopped talking mid-sentence at the piercing sound of a woman's heart-rending scream.

'*Help! My babby's fallen in the river!*' came a cry from the bridge.

Samboy raced at high speed as fast as his legs would carry him down to the river's edge. He looked up at a woman standing on the bridge. She was waving her arms wildly and screaming.

'*My bairn! My bairn, quick! He's fallen in the river. Somebody save him please ... save him!*'

Samboy scanned the flowing waters. He spotted a bundle of clothing floating downstream. Without any hesitation he plunged in.

He didn't feel the coldness of the water. All he could see was a small bundle bobbing about on the river. He swam swiftly and, reaching the child, grabbed it firmly with both hands holding it high above him clear of the water. The water was deep coming up to his chest. Feeling his way carefully with his feet he waded back to the river-bank.

He held the child close and looked down into the pale, still face. *Please, God, let the poor babby live*, he prayed fervently. His prayer was answered when the child suddenly gasped and screamed. He looked up to see the mother of the child racing toward him, sobbing hysterically.

'Rebecca!' he exclaimed. 'The bairn's all right, hush ... hush ... he's going to be fine.'

She snatched the child from his arms and held him tightly to her.

'It was my fault, Mr Latimer,' she cried sorrowfully. 'I was looking over the bridge and the bairn started wriggling ... The next thing I knew' – she nodded to where she had just run from – 'I dropped him! I dropped my own child! I'll never be able to forgive myself.'

Samboy saw she was inconsolable and was pleased when her husband, though drunk, came and led her back home.

There were cheers, hand clapping and back-slapping as Samboy made his way back up the bank side.

'Well done, Samboy....'

'Let me buy you a pint....'

As he walked past the pub the soldier and traveller who had been fighting were stood side by side. They stepped forward to greet him. The soldier spoke first.

'Please, sir, accept my apologies, will you, for being so ... so ... disrespectful about ... your people? I've not seen such bravery in a long time, not since I was fighting in the war. And I feel quite ashamed of myself.' Samboy smiled and shook his hand.

'Thank you,' he said, moved at the soldier's modesty.

He then looked at the lad who'd taken what looked like a fair beating from the soldier.

'Well! Are yer gonna stand there gawping like a gormless gypo? Or take this man's hand in friendship and buy him a beer?'

The crowd erupted into laughter at Samboy's turn of phrase and the two rivals shook hands and walked back into the pub, their arms resting about each other's shoulders.

Samboy shivered. The water had been bitterly cold and he needed to get out of his wet clothes before he caught a chill. He looked at his watch and it was 10.30. Daisy will wonder where the hell I've got to, he thought and, making his way back to the field, he left the rest of the revellers to celebrate the rescue of Rebecca's child. Wait until I tell Daisy, he said to himself, by, she'll be that proud of her old dad!

Roulson collected his fishing rod and made his way back down to the river.

'Ain't it a bit late to be fishing? It's nigh on eleven o'clock,' Caspar said, picking up the beer bottles and following him.

'Nobody's askin' yer to come along – I like fishin' at night, anyway.'

Caspar stopped talking and followed Roulson. He was in a foul bloody mood, he thought. Mebbe if I get a few beers down him he'll cheer up a bit. 'E's not said a word about the young madam, mebbe she stood him up! By, that'll rile 'im.

They reached the river and Roulson sat down. He baited his line with worm and cast it into a deep pool. He smiled to himself glimpsing the flattened grass where he'd taken Daisy's virginity and felt no remorse. He was reliving the event when Caspar interrupted his thoughts.

'Did she turn up then?' he asked Roulson, licking his lips at the lustful imaginings crossing the threshold of his perverted mind. 'And was she a willing bit of stuff? I'd 'ave loved a go at 'er.'

'She said you were disgusting, Caspar. I think she's right about that, don't you?'

'I ain't disgusting. I just likes me oats, that's all – nowt wrong wi' that.'

'No, nowt wrong with that,' agreed Roulson. 'Only yer need to find someone yer own age.'

'Ain't nobody around my own age, not anybody wantin' sex any roads – they're all dead!'

Roulson threw his head back and laughed wildly. When he ceased laughing he sat up straight and looked at Caspar with a serious face and shook his head glumly. 'What will I do without you, Caspar?' he said.

'What do yer mean? What'll yer do without me? We're stickin' together, ain't we?'

'Aye, we'll stick together, Caspar. Look! Quick! I've got a bite!' They looked to where a large trout writhed to free itself from the taut line.

'Reach in and get it, Caspar, will yer? Quick, before it escapes. I've not brought my landing net and I don't think this line's strong enough to fetch this big bugger in.'

Caspar edged his way unsteadily into the shallow waters. The beer he'd drunk was taking effect and he swayed unsteadily to and fro with the force of the water.

'Don't think I can reach it from 'ere,' he said, holding on to a clump of grass with one hand while stretching to reach the fish with his other. 'Bring it in a bit closer, can yer?'

'You're all right, you've got your wellies on,' Roulson said, urging him on. 'Wade out a bit further. I'll get you if you're stuck!'

Caspar waded further out and the water rushed past his wellington boots. He turned to Roulson and asked him to reel the line in a few feet.

'Looks like that one's got away, Caspar,' Roulson laughed and, raising the fishing rod, dangled the naked hook in front of his face.

'Yer bastard!' yelled, Caspar.

He was about to make his way back to the bank when a sudden rush of water swept over the tops of his wellingtons. Roulson lifted his rod and, aiming it carefully, speared a startled Caspar in the side of his head, causing him to sway forwards and backwards, before losing his footing on the slippery stones on the river-bed. He fell backwards, the weight of his wellingtons filled with water and the heavy overcoat he wore both summer and winter alike, prevented him getting back on to his feet.

From the bank, Roulson sat watching him struggling to survive.

'*Help!*' he cried in desperation. '*Please ... please ... don't let me die!*'

Roulson slowly lit a cigarette and opened one of the beers Caspar had brought.

'Cheers, Caspar!' he called, laughing callously, watching him thrash about wildly. 'You won't be telling the coppers where I am now.'

Roulson appreciated he wouldn't be able to disappear safely without dealing with Caspar first. He couldn't trust him to keep his mouth shut especially when he'd had a few drinks.

He stood up and looked to where Caspar had given up the struggle. The current was rapidly carrying him downstream toward the confluence where the River Swale met the Cod Beck. This would carry him away from any prying eyes and he'd be long gone when the body eventually surfaced. He waited until the body had disappeared from view before gathering his things together, then headed back to the farm for one last night.

Roulson had crossed the line from which there was no return. Too much damage had been done. The moral list of do's and don'ts no longer existed for him. Acknowledging this in his innate self – it somehow released him from a bondage – a new freedom awaited him, albeit one of loneliness and mistrust of everyone, everywhere.

Chapter Ten

Tobias climbed out of bed and hurriedly slipped into his clothes. He glanced across at the woman who lay sleeping in his bed and wished to hell he hadn't invited her into it. They'd decided sex wouldn't spoil their friendship. He knew that was a myth but lust had got the better of him.

He gently touched her shoulder. 'Eleanor, Eleanor, wake up. It's time for you to go.'

She groaned and opened her eyes; her head hurt with every move she made. She looked about her and, realizing where she was, flung her head back on to the pillow, closed her eyes and sighed deeply.

'Oh, my God, Tobias! What have you done?' she asked, accusingly.

He stood up sharply. 'What have *I* done? I think this was your idea, Eleanor, not mine. If you recall,' he remonstrated, 'it was *you* who invited me to bed.'

'Thanks, you're a real gent.'

'Real gent or not, get your arse out of this bed before anybody sees you, OK?'

'OK. Can't have been that good, anyway, I don't remember a thing. Oh, God! Did anybody see me, do you think?'

'Firstly, the reason you don't remember anything is because you were too bloody drunk! And no, I don't think anybody saw us. Now, Eleanor, get a bloody move on.'

'Oh, Toby, does that mean you are not going to ask Daddy for my hand in marriage?' she teased him and, giggling, ducked her head under the blankets.

'And if I did, what, pray tell, would your answer be?'

'Why *no*, of course!' she said, laughing, and Tobias flopped down by her on the bed.

'Can we remain friends, do you think? I do hope so, Eleanor.'

'Yes, of course we can. What's a bit of sex between friends? At least we know we're not sexually compatible. Now, kiss me for the last time,' she said, dramatically pouting her lips, 'and I'll be on my way. Mind you,' she added, 'Father will be so disappointed, but I'm sure he'll get over it.'

'I'm sure he will,' he agreed, kissing her goodbye.

Lydia pretended to be asleep when her breakfast was brought in.

Late again, damn her! Must be my pills not suiting her, she thought. Well, now you know how I feel: they don't suit me, either!

She had managed to escape the watchful eye of her companion most nights, and last night had been a pleasant surprise for her. Tobias was seeing Eleanor Shaw. Thank goodness for that. It would stop his gallivanting and his infatuation with those gypsies. There was only that damned horse to get rid of once and for all, and then Tobias would be free from further influence. And maybe, just maybe, my Richard will realize his own stupidity and come home to me.

Somewhere in her confused, sick mind, Lydia was unable to accept Richard had died. She believed him to be taken up with some Romany woman called Mary, and his departure from the family home had to do with the gypsies. Tobias and members of the staff humoured her, allowing her to believe Richard would return home one day soon.

A knock on the bedroom door caused her to start. 'Enter.'

It was Tobias. 'Hello, Mother. Thought I'd see how you are and wondered if we might have dinner together tonight. What do you think? I could come up here, or maybe you would care to eat in the dining-room?'

She looked at him, mystified. 'Why would I not dine in my own dining-room? Isn't that where I always dine?' she asked.

Tobias saw the puzzled look in her eyes wishing he'd not bothered to come. He dropped a perfunctory kiss on her cheek. 'I'll have a word with Miss Pettifer, Mother, and see if she has anything planned,' he said, departing hastily.

Lydia nibbled at her toast thinking, what a strange manner Tobias has adopted – inviting me to dinner in my own home!

Tobias dropped in to see Eve Pettifer before leaving for his rounds on the estate. He knocked on the door of the upstairs sitting-room she shared with his mother.

'Come in.' Eve was finishing her breakfast. 'Hello, please, do come in and join me in a cup of tea.'

'Thank you. To be honest, I'm here because I'm somewhat concerned about Mother.' Tobias sat down, taking the armchair opposite her. He looked at her and couldn't help noticing dark circles around her eyes and that she looked extremely tired.

'Are you all right, Miss Pettifer? If you don't mind my saying so, you look awfully tired. Is my mother proving to be too much of a handful for you?'

She waved her hand dismissing the idea. 'No, nothing like that; your mother and I get on very well. But, of late, I do seem to have grown tired and for the life of me I don't know why. Probably some vitamin deficiency or something like that. Anyway, I'll have a word with Dr Parks about it, I'm sure he'll prescribe some pick-me-up. Now, tell me, what's this about your mother?'

'Well....' He hesitated, wondering whether should he go to Frank Parks instead and not bother her with his concerns. She raised her eyebrows impatiently, waiting for him to continue. 'Well, have you noticed she has been more confused of late? I thought she was behaving more normally – whatever normal is for someone like Mother – and ... and I wondered whether you had noticed anything different?'

'Not really. But maybe her medication needs reviewing. Shall I call Dr Parks and ask him to come and check her over? Maybe a blood test will help. Her lithium levels could have altered.'

'Yes, yes, if you'll do that, Miss Pettifer, I'd be grateful. What with the harvest upon us sooner than expected with all the hot weather we've been having, my time is spoken for, as you can well imagine.'

Yes, I can imagine, Eve thought enviously. I heard you and that Eleanor Shaw at it last night. And here I am, my sex life's over before it's even begun! I wish I was a bit younger – it wouldn't have been that Eleanor Shaw warming your bed!

'Must rush, Miss Pettifer, I'll say good day to you.'

'Er ... what? Oh...yes, and you too, Mr Flint.'

Tobias leaned against the door after closing it and breathed a deep sigh of relief, then asked himself was she really cut out for the job. God, she's almost as confused as mother.

Jet was saddled up ready and waiting when Tobias arrived at the stables.

He loved the horse. A strong attachment had developed between man and beast since the attempted poisoning. He rode Jet every day now that harvest was underway. The hot dry weather had ripened the barley early and all hands were busy, including a few of the traveller folk who had hung back after the fair, eager to earn some cash during harvest.

He called in at the estate office on his way out, collecting the half-dozen rabbits he'd shot the previous day. He'd left one with Nellie to prepare for themselves, and the remainder he decided to give to the workers in the harvest field.

The sun had disappeared behind a curtain of cloud when he rode into the field. The workers were taking a well-earned break and resting in the shade of a tree. He saw they had got on well with a great number of sheaves already arranged in stooks about the field.

He rode over to where the men gathered and climbed down from his horse. The men made to stand, but he gestured them to remain where they were. They'd obviously worked hard all morning and were in need of rest and refreshments. He knew, because as a young lad, his father insisted he work alongside the men in the field to experience first hand what was expected of one's workforce, and not to ask anybody to do anything you had not undertaken yourself.

'Good morning. Is all going well, Fred?' he asked his ganger in charge of the group.

'Aye, sir, grand weather for it. Never known us cut t' barley this early. We'll likely be finished in this field 'ere today and mek a start on ten acre tomorrow.'

Tobias reached for the sack hanging from his saddle and emptied the rabbits into a heap in front of the men. 'I wondered if any of you could make use of a rabbit or two.'

The dark, bright eyes of the gypsies eyed him suspiciously as they glanced covetously at the rabbits offered them, then, deciding it wasn't a trap, they smiled at him. He smiled back, pleased with his decision in fetching the rabbits. Save you having to poach! he thought.

'That's right kind of you, mister,' said one of the men taking it upon himself to be spokesperson.

'Aye,' chorused the others in agreement.

'And I see you're handling that cushty 'orse well. I was there when yer bought 'im from Samboy Latimer. 'E'll be right chuffed when I tells 'im I've seen yer out riding 'im.'

He found it refreshing. The gypsy spoke with a confidence lacking in most of his regular staff. He obviously considered himself of equal status and was not intimidated, clearly deeming him approachable. 'Well, you tell Mr Latimer I'm delighted with him.'

'Aye, I'll do that, and thanks again to yer, young man, fer fetching these 'ere rabbits.'

'You're welcome. Good day to you all,' Tobias said.

He didn't mount his horse but led him away across the field, stopping occasionally to inspect a stook of barley.

Frank Parks had been invited into the study to wait.

The housekeeper had said Mr Flint wouldn't be long. He looked at his watch. It was 5.30 and he was ready for a drink. The housekeeper had offered him tea but he'd declined hoping he'd be offered something stronger when Tobias arrived. As if his thoughts had been read, the door opened and Tobias entered the room carrying a full bottle of best Scotch in his hand. Frank stood up and they shook hands.

'Sit down, Frank, sorry to keep you waiting. I'll bet you can use one of these.' He poured two fingers of whisky into each glass and handed him one.

'Don't mind if I do, thank you, Tobias.'

They sat in silence for a few moments both savouring that first drink that eased away the day's tensions.

'Well, Frank, what do you make of her?'

'Who are you referring to, your mother, or Miss Pettifer?' Frank asked, with a note of sarcasm in his voice.

'That bad, eh?'

'All I can say is, until the results come back from the blood tests we've taken, that I do agree with you. There is a significant change in your mother. It's as though the medication has ceased working. And, dear Miss Pettifer, she appears exhausted. But, that could be iron deficiency as she indicated. As soon as the test results are in I'll be straight back and let you know. As for roping in more help' – he shrugged his shoulders – 'that's entirely up to you, but personally, I wouldn't bother for the moment.'

Frank was thinking selfishly. He'd taken quite a shine to Eve and he had a feeling it was reciprocated. He'd met one or two of these middle-aged, frustrated spinsters on his home visits. He could be just the cure they were looking for. He might be a good few years older than Eve – as she had invited him to call her – but so what? He still had lead in his pencil. And that cold fish he'd married had put a stop to any sex years ago. Yes, Eve might be grateful for some male company. He'd noticed she'd started taking extra care with her apparel and wearing a splash of make-up when she knew he was calling. She hadn't been at the front of the queue when looks were handed out, but she had magnificent breasts and good legs. Yes, I'm quiet, discreet – and bloody damned desperate!

'... thank you for coming at such short notice Frank,' Tobias was saying. 'Now, what about another drink before you go, old boy?'

'Hmm ... what? Oh....yes, why not indeed. Very hospitable of you, I must say.'

The weather broke on the second day on their return to Appleby, slowing down the horses considerably. A strong easterly gale had got up and the rain lashed cruelly at the horses.

No longer were Samboy and Daisy looking for grassy stopping places, but for more solid ground to camp on. They were only twenty miles from home and Daisy hoped they'd make it back that day.

The wind began to ease and the sun came out. Her eyes were oblivious to the rainbow Samboy pointed out, neither did her spirit lift to the dramatic scenery unfolding before her as they came over Bowes Moor.

This was usually a special time for her. A homecoming, when the Eden Valley stretched out before them, flanked by the Northern Pennines in the east, the Lake District to the west, and the southern hills of Scotland to the north.

'We'll keep goin', lass. I think we can make it afore nightfall, the 'orses 'ad a good rest yesterday. What do yer think?'

He was worried about her. He'd tried to get her to see a doctor before they'd set off for home but she'd flatly refused, saying she was going down with a cold and it was nothing to be concerned about; she wanted leaving alone.

'Yes, let's keep going, please,' Daisy replied, not raising her head to look at him.

When they got home she'd feel happier, he told himself. Lavina will be back soon; she might know what's bothering her. A warm, pleasant glow pervaded his body when he thought of Lavinia. He heartily wished she was there waiting for him on his return.

He handed Daisy the reins. The happy carefree girl he'd journeyed down with had vanished. She was pale and listless.

It was 9.30 in the evening when they eventually arrived home.

Daisy jumped down from the wagon leaving her father to see to everything, then hurried indoors to light a fire and prepare supper for them.

She was sitting over the fire nursing a cup of cocoa when Samboy came in. Daisy, handed him a plate of sandwiches. Standing up, she stated she was tired and needed to go to bed. He said that was a good idea and hoped she'd feel better tomorrow.

'But,' he said quite categorically, 'if you're not feeling any better in a day or two, Daisy, it's the doctor fer you, whether you like it or not.'

Daisy climbed into bed and wept her bitter tears silently into her pillow as she had done every night since the awful event.

If only I'd told that detective I'd seen him at West Hutton, they might've caught him before this … terrible … terrible … thing happened to me. And I can't tell anyone, he said he'll kill me if I did, and Dad.

She looked at the clock on the mantelpiece it was 2.30 in the morning.

She stayed in bed for the next two days. While her father was busy outside, she soaked her bruised and tender body in warm baths infused with lavender. The herbs she boiled and bottled for other people's ailments, she now sought for herself. Her emotional injuries were another matter altogether. No herbs could heal the mental suffering she was experiencing – only time would help heal this. But tomorrow was another day, and if there was no improvement in her, her father would take her along to the doctor and she didn't want to do that. The doctor might want to examine her, then he'd want to know how she'd sustained the terrible bruising on her inner thighs, back and buttocks. No, she'd get up tomorrow and carry on as best she could.

The next morning she rose early. She'd had little sleep but was determined to resume a daily routine and generate some normality back into her life, if not for her own sake than for her father's.

'You're up early, lass.' Samboy wasn't sure whether to be relieved or worried when he came downstairs to find Daisy up and about. The stove was lit and breakfast cooked. 'Are yer feeling better?' he enquired.

'Yes, thanks, Dad.' She turned to him and forced a smile. 'I need to get into the garden before stuff goes to waste.'

'Will yer be all right on yer own for the day? I've got some scrap to tek in afore I go and bring the 'orses back. Good thing you said to come back early, Daisy, there's that much work to be done.'

'I'll be fine, Dad. I'll pack you some food before you go.'

He smiled, thankful she was feeling better. She still looks a bit peeky though, but mebbe now she's up an' about an' eating she'll get some colour back into her cheeks. The thought comforted him.

Daisy worked solidly all morning in the garden, weeding, clipping, digging and cutting back the overgrown herbs which she would hang up to dry. It was only when she went into the house for lunch that she broke down and cried.

A knock at the door interrupted her weeping. She quickly rinsed her face in cold water at the sink before answering it.

'Hello, can I help you?' she asked the smart, middle-aged woman standing before her.

'I do hope you will forgive my just calling on the off chance of finding someone in.' Eve Pettifer was taken aback by the beautiful young girl. Surely this can't be the woman I've heard about, she's far too young. I expected a dark-haired, middle-aged, gypsy-looking woman. 'Someone in the town informed me that you are a very good herbalist ... or maybe it's your mother I need to be talking to?'

Eve couldn't help but notice the girl had been crying; her face was red and blotchy.

'No, it's me who's the herbalist, trained by my aunt. But if you're looking for someone ... er ... more professional?'

'No, no, I just thought you would be older, that's all.'

'Please, do come in.' Daisy said, stepping aside for her to enter the kitchen.

Eve was pleasantly overwhelmed by the heady perfumes that greeted her and inhaled deeply. The kitchen table was hidden beneath great mounds of colourful herbs all bundled together in preparation for boiling and drying.

'Would you like a cup of tea Mrs ... Miss...?'

'Pettifer, Eve Pettifer is the name. Yes, I'd love a cup of tea, thank you,' she said, smiling broadly at Daisy. 'Anything...anything, just to stay in this kitchen and wallow in the amazing fragrance of all your herbs.'

'It is a wonderful fragrance I must admit, but I suppose I'm so used to it, most of the time I'm oblivious to their perfume.'

Daisy cleared a space on the table and poured the tea. 'What is it you're looking for, Miss Pettifer? If it's anything serious I really do suggest you go and see your doctor.'

'No, nothing serious. It's just that I feel so exhausted most of the time. But I do sleep so well, too well, actually. I thought maybe a tonic or a pick-me-up. I'd prefer to take something herbal rather than a medically prescribed drug. You do understand, don't you? I've nothing against modern medical practices, but I prefer a more natural approach. That is, if you can think of something that might help me.'

'Please, have another cup of tea, Miss Pettifer, while I take a look through my notes and see what remedies I have already made up.'

Daisy disappeared into the large pantry off the kitchen where a long shelf stocked with bottles, wide-necked jars, and small paper packets were stored. Each one was carefully sealed, labelled, and dated. Ten minutes later she reappeared with a small bottle of mixture.

'I think this will do the trick, Miss Pettifer.' She sat down opposite her and placed the bottle on the table. 'It's a tonic I often recommend and I believe it will help you.'

The woman picked up the bottle and eyed the grey-looking liquid suspiciously.

'May I ask what it is, Miss Latimer?'

Hearing herself being referred to as Miss Latimer made her feel quite grand and professional.

'Yes; I don't normally discuss the ingredients, but I don't suppose you'll be setting up in opposition!'

They both laughed. 'I think not, Miss Latimer.'

'Please, do call me Daisy. Everyone else does.'

'All right, Daisy, now are you going to tell me what's in this?' she asked, shaking the bottle.

'It is a tincture of St John's wort.' Daisy grinned to herself. People's reaction to the concoctions she doled out often amused her and this woman's reaction was no different. 'And this,' she continued, 'is a list of things to avoid for the next two weeks while taking the tincture, nothing too serious.'

'Really, how extraordinary! And this will help me … you think? Well, I'm certainly willing to give anything a try.' Eve stood up to leave and walked towards the door. 'How much do I owe you, my dear?' she asked.

'Would half-a-crown be all right?' Daisy had a real problem knowing what to charge people. This lady was expensively dressed in a stylishly tailored costume with matching handbag and gloves. She came across as somebody able to afford to pay a reasonable rate. There were those who called for a remedy who had little money, she charged only pennies.

'That's fine.' Eve took her purse from her bag and dropped three shillings into her hand. 'Keep the change, my dear. I'm sure I'll come and see you again. It has been such a pleasure meeting you.'

'Thank you very much. It's been lovely to meet you too. Do you have far to go?'

'Not far, I borrowed my employer's car.' She nodded to where it was parked outside the gates. 'I'm companion to Mrs Flint, from Eden Falls Manor,' she added proudly.

Daisy gasped and felt her knees weaken. Miss Pettifer took her gasp as an indication of envy of her place of employment.

'Yes,' she boasted, 'aren't I the fortunate one to work in such a delightful place?'

'Yes ... yes, you are.' Her thoughts flew to the man she'd met on only two brief occasions. Tobias Flint. What would he make of her now? He wouldn't be so quick to flirt and be friends with her if he knew she'd been brutally raped.

Daisy sat at the kitchen table with her head buried in her hands. Her father would be back soon and she didn't want him to think she was still feeling under the weather, so she set about sorting the herbs and clearing the table ready for tea.

'Got a good price for that scrap I took into Fletcher's yard.' Samboy declared proudly.

He sat down and emptied his pockets on to the kitchen table. 'Count that when yer've got a minute, Daisy, and hide it somewhere safe, will yer?'

'I'll do it after tea, Dad. We're not expecting anybody, are we?'

'No. Tell me, what sort of day 'ave you 'ad, lass?' He saw her face was still downcast.

'Quite a busy day really and you'd have noticed if you'd looked at the garden, Dad, when you walked past it!' she rebuked. 'Apart from working in the garden I also had a visitor,' she added smugly.

His eyes lit up with interest, 'A visitor? Who?'

'A woman. She came to see me about a herbal remedy. Apparently somebody in Appleby had recommended me to her. So you're not the only one to have earned a bit of cash today.'

'Well. Come on then! Who was it, Dr Daisy?'

Daisy giggled. 'A Miss Pettifer. She works for the Flint family at Eden Falls Manor. She is a ... now ... what did she call herself? Oh, yes, that was it. Companion to Mrs Flint.... Dad! What is it? Are you all right?' All colour drained from his face turning it a deathly white.

'I'm OK. What ... what did the woman want?' he asked in a low voice.

'I've told you, Dad, a remedy! What is it? What's wrong? I only gave the poor woman a remedy because she was out of sorts and needed a pick-me-up.'

Who wouldn't be out of sorts being companion to that crazy woman, he thought. Just so long as nobody's said anythin' to my lass about the past – it can stay safely buried as far as she's concerned.

'Nowt's wrong, yer just took me by surprise, that's all. After that young squire bought that 'orse from us, I thought for a minute yer were going to tell me the dye had washed out from its fetlock we doctored! D'yer remember that, Daisy?'

'I remember Dad,' she said, but sensed that wasn't the real reason. He was holding something back from her and, if the truth be known, she really didn't want to know right now. Her damaged mind and body were incapable of withstanding any more problems.

A strong wind was blowing from the west.

Lydia looked out from her bedroom window watching the dark clouds scudding across a moonlit sky. The trees bowed in obedience to the strong breeze and the wisteria lashed noisily against the window-pane, stripping itself of what few flowers remained.

Her ghost-like reflection smiled back at her from the window and she nodded to it encouragingly – urging it on. *She'll be asleep now*, she whispered, *come, let's go out and play in the wind. Quick! Get dressed*! the babble of voices commanded.

She crept silently through the house and slipped out of the back door.

The wind snatched at the hem of the long dress she wore and snagged on a rose bush. She wrenched it free and examined the tear. This was her favourite dress, her wedding dress. It gaped open at the back where the zip would no longer fasten as it had done thirty years ago – exposing her skin to the cool night air.

'Oh! *I do hope Richard won't be too cross.*' Lydia clicked her tongue with irritation, fighting back the tears which threatened to fall. '*He loved me in my wedding dress.*'

The voices in her head called her. She hurried away from the house and gardens into the open fields beyond the drive. The wind blew and howled furiously across the unsheltered grassland. The sheep with their lambs watched the strange woman with curiosity from where they lay grouped together under the trees. Lydia ran to the top of a grassy mound where the lambs played I'm the king of the castle. She twirled around and around in a mad frenzy. The sound of her insane laughter was picked up on the wind and carried to where the sheep lay. They started bleating and ran to the other side of the field, seeking refuge from the unwelcome stranger.

The sound of a door banging in the wind woke Dan. He was unable to get back to sleep and decided he'd take a look around outside and check on the horses. He located the offending door that had come off its latch and was about to go back to bed when he heard the sheep bleating. Better make sure they're all right, he thought.

It was when he walked along to where the sheep were that he saw her in the moonlight. He could see her quite clearly. She stood on the mound spinning round unsteadily with her arms held high in the air; a forlorn imitation of a somewhat bedraggled ballerina. The sheep had dispersed, leaving Lydia spinning and laughing wildly. She hadn't seen Dan, who was undecided whether to wake his boss or go for Miss Pettifer.

In what seemed an eternity, but in fact was only seconds, he came to the conclusion that he'd keep an eye on her, hoping she would soon tire and go back to bed. He was aware, as were the rest of the staff, that the woman was quite barmy.

It was two hours later when Lydia returned to the house. Dan watched her unseen from a distance. He breathed a sigh of relief when she eventually went back in the house, allowing him some shut eye before the full day's work that lay ahead.

Eve Pettifer was feeling so much better. She woke up at six o'clock and made herself a cup of tea. She heard a shuffling noise coming from Lydia's bedroom when she came out of the bathroom and decided to take her a cup of tea.

'Morning!' she called, on entering her room.

'What are you doing coming at this time with my tea? You know seven o'clock is my time!'

Lydia was sitting naked in an armchair by the window in full view of anyone who cared to look up. Her face was smeared with make-up. The bright red lipstick she wore had been applied like that of a clown. At her feet lay a muddy mass of white silk and lace which Eve instantly recognized as the beautiful wedding dress Lydia had proudly shown her one day.

'Have you been out, Lydia?' she asked, quietly and kindly.

'No, I haven't!' Lydia snapped.

'Well, in that case, let me help you choose something pretty to wear and ... then I'll clean your lovely wedding dress for you, shall I?' All the time Eve kept her voice low while smiling at her.

'I don't know what happened to my dress – I think one of the gypsies must've stolen it and dirtied it. They do that sort of thing you know ... steal ... and lie ... an *unscrupulous lot*!'

'Yes, I'm sure you're right. Now, get dressed before you catch cold and we'll have breakfast together.'

My God! It's like talking to a child, Eve thought, guiding the wild-eyed woman back to her bed. She went into the dressing-room to find suitable clothes, and returning, discovered her in bed fast asleep.

There's no other way, I'll have to have a word with Mr Flint about extra staff, Eve decided, now that she requires twenty-four hour care. Goodness me! Disappearing in the middle of the night. God only knows where she goes or what she gets up to – she could harm herself, or, worse still, somebody else.

Chapter Eleven

Lavinia paused whilst dressing and looked at the clock on the dressing table. It was 6.30 in the morning and Sam had left ages ago to see to the horses.

She could hear what had become the familiar sound of Daisy retching and vomiting in the bathroom close by.

Ever since she and Samboy had returned from their brief honeymoon in Keswick, Daisy, had been suffering from morning sickness. Lavinia was concerned, yet at the same time unsure of approaching her. Although they enjoyed a good relationship, now she and Sam were man and wife it threw a different light on things, her loyalties lay with Sam, but on the other hand she knew instinctively Daisy needed an ally.

Lavinia and Samboy had married two months before. It had been a quiet affair with only Chrissie, Donny, and Daisy as witnesses. Samboy had informed Daisy of their plans to marry as soon as Lavinia had returned from the south. Daisy was fond of Lavinia and delighted in the prospect of her not only as a friend but also as a stepmother. She felt certain her father and Lavinia made a fine match and were right for each other.

Lavinia finished dressing and hurried into the kitchen to prepare breakfast before Daisy ventured downstairs. It wasn't long before she appeared, looking pale and glum.

'Good morning, Daisy. Now get that down yer and yer'll feel better.' She smiled sympathetically as she placed a bowl of porridge in front of her. Daisy said nothing and dutifully spooned it into her mouth. It was only a matter of seconds before she leapt from the chair and ran out of the back door to the outside privy.

She returned looking paler than ever. 'I'm sorry, Lavinia,' she said apologetically, 'but I don't know what's wrong with me, I can't stop being sick! It's happening every day now.'

She started to weep, Lavinia put her arms around her.

'Look, Daisy, I know it's none of my business, but I think yer ought to go and see a doctor. I know you've been sufferin' for a few weeks now. I've heard you being sick on a mornin' – thankfully, yer father's up and gone afore yer start. I'll come with you, my dear, there's nowt to fear. Let's go today, eh? Doctor Parks will be able to sort you out, he's a good bloke.'

Daisy looked solemnly at her and nodded. 'Yes, I'm sure you're right, I feel so tired and drained. We don't have to tell Dad I'm not well, do we, Lavinia? He worries so.'

'Not straight away, no.' Lavinia replied, uncomfortable with her decision of secrecy, but knew it was only temporary. The important thing now was to get her to a doctor as soon as possible. Please God, Lavinia prayed silently, don't let it be what I think it is.

'Well, Daisy, it seems you are going to have a baby.'

Frank saw the horrified look of disbelief on the pretty young girl's face as he delivered his diagnosis.

Daisy couldn't have looked more shocked if he'd told her she was going to die tomorrow.

'I ... I ... beg your p ... pardon. What did you say?' Her voice was a quiet whisper.

'I said you are going to have a baby, Daisy. You are at least three months pregnant. Surely you are aware that if you are having relations of a sexual nature it's inevitable that ... without precautions, you—'

'I'm not!' Daisy shrieked, finding her voice which was of complete denial. 'I'm not having *sexual* ... whatever it is you call it!' Her high-pitched shrieking turned into loud sobbing.

Frank Parks walked round from behind his desk and put his arm around her shoulders.

'Hush, hush, my dear, it's all right.' He opened the door and beckoned the receptionist. 'Go and fetch Mrs Latimer, please.'

Lavinia entered the doctor's surgery where Daisy was crying uncontrollably. She hurried over to her and hugged her closely.

'What on earth is the matter?' Lavinia looked from Daisy to the doctor and knew the answer. 'Are you pregnant, Daisy? Is that it?'

Daisy stopped crying for a moment and looked at her. 'How did you know, Lavinia?' she asked, a puzzled expression on her tear-stained face.

'Morning sickness, Daisy, it's a common symptom. Isn't that right, Dr Parks?'

'Yes, it is, Mrs Latimer. Now, Daisy, can you tell us who the father is?'

'*No!* There isn't one!'

'Don't be ridiculous, Daisy,' Frank Parks spluttered, 'Of course there's a father.'

'Can we go now? I don't want to be here any more.' Disregarding Frank Parks's questioning as to who the father was, she stood up and walked out of the door.

'We'll be in touch, Doctor, thank you,' Lavinia said, following Daisy out of the surgery and into the street.

Daisy walked fast, making it difficult for Lavinia to keep up with her. Her mind was in turmoil unable to take in the awful news and her head was spinning. They reached the bus station and waited in silence. It was only when they arrived home that Lavinia broached the matter.

'We have ter talk, Daisy. Yer father will be home soon and we have to tell him—'

'*No!* Please. Lavinia, don't tell him! *I beg you!* I don't want anybody to know.'

Daisy raced upstairs into her bedroom slamming the door behind her. She lay on the bed sobbing, her hands over her ears, endeavouring to block out what her distraught father would say.

Two hours later Lavinia climbed the stairs and knocked gently on the bedroom door.

'I've brought you a drop of nice broth, Daisy. Can I come in?'

'Yes.'

Lavinia entered and placed the soup on the side table then straightened up her pillows, before handing Daisy the bowl of broth which she ate in silence. When she'd finished eating, Lavinia settled her down comfortably, picked up the tray and made to leave.

'Lavinia?'

'Yes, love?'

'Thank you for everything. And I want you to know I'm so glad you're here. I don't know how I'd manage without you, especially now when....' Her eyes welled up again and Lavinia put the tray down and hurried to her side.

'It's all right, love. Come on now, we'll all pull through this somehow.' She sat on the side of the bed holding her close, allowing the poor girl's tears to spill forth. 'And as for yer father, don't worry about 'im – I'll tell 'im, and ... he'll ... he'll accept what's happened Daisy, I promise you.' Lavinia said crossing her fingers behind Daisy's back.

'Do you think so, truly? You don't think he'll throw me out?'

''Course he won't, lass, he'd have to throw me out with you!'

149

*

'What? *Pregnant*? Daisy? I don't believe you!'

'Well you'd better believe it, Sam, 'cos it's true.' Lavinia saw the disbelief in her husband's face. She'd rehearsed this moment many times over these last few days, but was still unprepared for Samboy's outrage.

'*Who*? Who's the bastard did this to my girl? Tell me, Lavinia!'

'I don't know, Sam, and that's the truth. She won't say.'

'Well, she's goin' ter tell me who the bastard is! Where is she?'

'She's busy in the stables. Sam, Sam, sit down a minute will you? I've got summat important to say.'

He was taken aback at his wife's composure. With a puzzled expression on his face, he did as she bade and sat at the kitchen table opposite her. She reached across the table taking both his clenched fists in her hands. They immediately opened and relaxed as she gently stroked them.

'I'm only going to say this once Sam, so listen to me carefully.'

She continued to hold his hands and looked sympathetically into the handsome, troubled face of the man she loved so deeply. 'Daisy needs you and me now, more than ever, Sam. Be kind to her. Love her, support her through this, and ... don't question her about who the father is, No ... no....' Lavinia raised her fingers to her lips pleading silence from Samboy who was becoming agitated at her request. 'Listen to me, Sam, please, hear me out.' She took a deep breath, knowing that what she was about to say jeopardized her own relationship with him. 'Should you decide to do otherwise, like hit the roof, chuck 'er out, or ... or ... anything other than help the lass – I will leave you Sam. And I'll take Daisy with me. I'll look after her, and the bairn she's goin' to have.' Her eyes never drifted from his as she spoke.

Dumbfounded, Samboy leaned back in his chair and removed his cap. He ran his hands restlessly through his hair before placing them palm down on the table. He stared at them for a long few minutes, his mind reeling. He looked up at Lavinia; the endless silence stretched between them and she felt her heart beating loudly and rapidly.

'I can't say owt,' he said, his throat constricting with tears. 'I'll see you later.' Samboy stood up sharply; his chair scraped noisily across the wooden floor. He picked up his hat and headed for the door.

'Where are you going, Sam?'

'*For a bloody drink*!' he blared, '*God*! I need to let off steam somehow!' He marched out of the front door and into the little Austin car he and Lavinia had proudly purchased. Daisy had watched her father leave from the barn. She'd seen the angry look on his face and covered her eyes in fear when he'd driven off at high speed, grit and dust flying from the screeching tyres. She walked back to the house where Lavinia sat at the table drinking a cup of tea. She was lost in thought and didn't hear her enter the house.

'You've told him, haven't you, Lavinia?'

'Hello. Come and sit down and I'll make us a fresh pot of tea. Yes, I've told 'im.'

'What did he say?' She held her breath waiting for the worst.

''E didn't say anythin'. 'E's gone to the pub.' Lavinia poured Daisy a cup of tea.

'Didn't he go crackers?' Daisy asked. 'I didn't hear him if he did.'

'No, he didn't go crackers, love'. I've told him unless he accepts what's happened – and supports yer through this – I'll leave him an' tek you with me.'

'You what? Aw, Lavinia, you can't do that! Or say that!'

'Yes, I can, Daisy, and I meant it – every word.'

Daisy looked across at this woman who was not only standing up for her, but also risking her marriage on her behalf. Her kindness was too much. Daisy felt a great lump catch in her throat and, unable to control it, burst into tears.

'There, there,' Lavinia said holding her in her arms. 'He'll be all right lass. If he was goin' ter blow his top, he would've blown it then. It might tek him a bit of time comin' to terms with what's happened, but he'll come round. I can feel it in my bones.' Lavinia smiled reassuringly at Daisy.

'Did you see him drive off? He was going hell for leather.'

'Aye, I did. Hope he can handle a car as well as he can handle a horse.'

Six pints later in the back bar of the Red Lion, Samboy lit his pipe. It was mid-week and the bar was quiet with only one or two drinkers with still a few bob left in their pockets before pay day.

He felt the anger and hurt slowly subside as the alcohol permeated his bloodstream. He had a lot of thinking to do before he went back home to face his wife and daughter. He drew deeply on his pipe and stared into the flames of the fire burning brightly in the grate. There was only one thing he knew for certain and that was he'd no intention of losing Lavinia. She was the best thing that had happened to him in a long time and he loved her passionately.

Who could the father be? There were only two men he could think of:

Roulson Adams, who was supposedly dead, or the young squire, Tobias Flint.

He was lost in his thoughts, unaware of someone sitting down next to him.

'Good evening, Mr Latimer, hope you'll join me in a pint.'

DS Keen put a glass down in front of Samboy.

'Ah, good evening to you too, Detective, and thank you, very kind of you.'

Samboy wasn't too sure whether he was disappointed or relieved to have had his thoughts interrupted.

'Cheers,' said Keen. 'How's the horse trade doing?'

'Not bad, not bad. Could always do with a bit more business.... Tell me somethin', did you ever find out any more about that missing bloke?' I may as well try and get some information out of the man seeing as I'm stuck with him for the time it takes to drink me beer, he thought.

'No, I'm afraid we didn't,' Keen said, shaking his head. 'Investigations are still going on though.' There was no doubt in his mind the body found inside the burned-out caravan was that of the missing man and not Roulson Adams. But he couldn't discuss any theories on the case with Samboy.

'I'm sure as time goes on all will be made clear. Funny how the truth has a way of establishing itself, wouldn't you agree with that, Mr Latimer?'

'Yes, yes, I would indeed, sir.'

The truth has a way of establishing itself, eh? Of course ... of course it has!

Samboy smiled at the detective and stood up. 'I have to go now,' he said, glancing at his pocket watch, 'but let me get yer a pint in afore I leave; it's been a real pleasure seein' yer again.'

Outside, Samboy breathed in the cool night air and walked unsteadily toward his car. Those few words from the detective had helped him make up his mind in what he was going to do. He'd go along with Lavinia's suggestion.

The truth will out. And when it does, God help him who's done this to my Daisy, 'cos I'll swing for bastard! he vowed and clambering clumsily into the car, fumbled drunkenly, inserting the key into the ignition.

'It's a damn sight easier travelling by horse!' he complained loudly when the car eventually burst into life.

The car weaved its way precariously under the inebriated guidance of Samboy along the dirt track road leading to the cottage. He heard a loud scraping noise behind him and, glancing through the rear-view mirror could see nothing untoward.

'*Bloody potholes*!' he cursed.

It was four o'clock in the morning when he woke with a start. He couldn't make out where he was. He looked about him and realized he was still in the car.

A warm sensation on his lap drew his eyes downward to where a hen lay sleeping.

'*God!*' he yelled. The alarmed hen shot into the air in fright, flapping its wings and clucking loudly. He quickly opened the car door and got out followed by the distraught hen.

'Bloody hell! How did that happen?' he said, scratching his head and looking at the car. He'd intended parking it in the barn not in the haystack. At the rear of the car dangled a tangled mess of yards of fencing with barbed wire still intact.

He had a splitting headache and for the life of him couldn't remember driving home. 'Better get meself to bed,' he said. 'God, I hope Lavinia isn't waiting up.'

He tiptoed upstairs and climbed into bed. Lavinia wasn't waiting up for him but she lay awake waiting for his return and felt his cold body snuggle up close to her. She turned and cradled him in her arms as a mother would a hurt child. He nestled his head in her warm breasts and slept peacefully.

Chapter Twelve

Frank Parks kept his head down and his jacket collar turned up as he crossed the busy road and entered the hotel.

She'd be waiting for him. Room sixteen. He checked his watch. He was fifteen minutes early so went into the cocktail bar where he ordered a double whisky. He picked up the courtesy newspaper and seated himself so he could see her walk past the reception desk and up the wide staircase.

He didn't have long to wait. Ten minutes and two double whiskies later he watched her from behind his newspaper; she passed the reception desk and walked sedately up the stairs. He drained the last drops of whisky from his glass before leaving the bar and headed after her.

'Excuse me, sir.'

Oh, God, I've been spotted! Frank didn't turn to see who had brought him to an abrupt halt and his heart raced violently. He was sure he was going to collapse with a heart attack there and then on the stairs. What would his wife and friends think? Here he was meeting a woman in a hotel in Penrith – he'd be struck off!

'I'm afraid I can't allow you to take the courtesy newspaper with you, but there is a newsagent just a few doors down. Now if you would like me to go and—'

'No, no, that's quite all right, I do apologize.' Frank turned round quickly shoving the newspaper into the bartender's hands and, sweating profusely, disappeared up the stairs two at a time.

'What time is your train?' Frank asked, looking at his watch.

'Four o'clock. Why? Are you in a hurry?'

Frank looked at his watch again. It was only two o'clock, they'd had wonderful sex, but he didn't fancy hanging about for two hours. 'No. But I do have to call in at the surgery to look at some notes of a patient I'm seeing tomorrow.'

'Well, you don't have to wait for me, Frank, I'm quite capable of catching a train on my own.'

'Yes, I know that, Eve, but I do feel somewhat responsible for you and I don't like leaving you here, on your own.'

'*Baloney Frank*! We both enjoy having sex, but, God, please don't talk to me like you would to your dependent little wife!'

'I'm sorry, I didn't—'

'Forget it, Frank. And stop bloody apologizing. I want to talk to you about Lydia.'

Frank raised his eyebrows, she had his interest now.

'You know I went to see that young gypsy girl to get a remedy for my tiredness?'

Frank nodded. He could hardly forget it, she'd chosen a quack before seeking his professional advice.

'Well,' she continued, 'I've discovered the reason for my fatigue.'

'Really? How intriguing,' Frank said sarcastically.

'Not that intriguing, Frank. The bloody vixen was spiking my cocoa.'

'Daisy? Spiking your cocoa? I don't believe it!'

'No not Daisy, Lydia. She's been slipping her pills into my cocoa at night, then when I've fallen asleep – or should I say, unconscious – she disappears into the night and comes back cold, bedraggled and dirty. God only knows what she'd been getting up to. Oh, do close your mouth, Frank.'

Frank was staring at Eve wide-eyed; his mouth gaped so much his chins fell into folds and rested on his chest.

'I didn't tell you at the time, because when I discovered what was happening, I confronted Lydia. She agreed to take her medication just as long as I didn't mention anything to her son. Well, I haven't mentioned anything to him, I've told you instead. But don't say anything to him, Frank, she appears to have calmed down a lot.'

'Well, well. I really don't know what to say Eve, I'm absolutely speechless.' Frank was shaking his head side to side in disbelief.

'That makes a change,' she snapped.

Frank walked over to where she stood looking out of the window into the bustling street below. She was tall, slim, elegant and proud, but Frank knew her vulnerability and drew her close to him. She responded, nuzzling her face into the side of his neck, inhaling the sweet fragrant aroma of tobacco mingled with his maleness and sexual contentment.

'I do care for you, deeply,' he whispered, gently rocking her to and fro in his arms.

'Yes, Frank, I know. It's just that ... that ... sometimes it's the only protection I have … from getting hurt … being sharp with you. I'm sorry, forgive me?'

Frank's forgiveness came with an affectionate kiss on her lips.

Eve gently pulled away from him aware he wanted to leave. She picked up her gloves pulling them over her ringless fingers. She glanced out of the window and gasped, placing her hand over her mouth. 'Frank, look, look, it's that gypsy girl!'

'Where?' asked Frank, craning his neck, his eyes scouring the street below.

'There. She's just going into the ironmonger's shop. Good grief! The girl's pregnant. You never told me, Frank.'

Frank managed a brief glimpse of Daisy before she disappeared. The poor girl was unable to hide her condition any longer and hadn't been back to see him since that fateful day he'd delivered her the news.

'How could I tell you, Eve? There is such a thing as doctor-patient confidentiality, as I'm sure *you* of all people are aware of. Anyway I haven't seen her for a few months, I believe she hides herself away at that cottage where she lives with her father and stepmother – poor girl, I do hope she is all right.'

'What about the father of the child? Won't he marry her?'

'I don't know who the father is – and she isn't saying.' Frank shrugged his shoulders. 'So, I suppose she'll have the child and put it up for adoption, or rear the poor little bastard herself.'

'Frank! Please don't talk like that about the girl. I thought when I met her she seemed to me to be the kind of girl who was quite … quite straightlaced, for want of a better word.'

'Yes, I know, Eve, but you can never tell with these gypsies – they're a different breed to the rest of us.'

'You damn snob.'

'Look, I have to go. I'll see you in a couple of weeks.' He peered out of the window looking up and down the street. 'Give me five minutes before you leave.' He kissed her on the cheek and left.

Eve watched Frank stride down the street and disappear from view. She kept her eyes focused on the ironmonger's hoping to catch another glimpse of the girl. When after ten minutes there was no sign of her, she left the hotel to do some shopping before going back to the manor. She walked into a nearby chemist and almost collided with Daisy in the doorway.

'Hello, Miss Latimer.'

Daisy looked at her, perplexed. 'I'm sorry, but do I know you?'

'Yes. I'm Eve Pettifer. If you recall I came to see you at your cottage in Hampton; you kindly supplied me with a herbal remedy for fatigue.'

'Yes, I'm sorry, of course, I remember you now.'

'Look, I'm just going to have tea in that café over there,' Eve said, pointing to a teashop over the road. 'Please, won't you join me? I'd be glad of your company.'

Daisy hesitated. She came to Penrith to avoid local people. She remembered this woman and had liked her when she'd called for a remedy. It would be refreshing to sit and talk to someone.

'Yes, thank you, I'd like that, Miss Pettifer.'

Eve smiled, taking the girl's hand and linking it through her arm. 'Come on then, Daisy, isn't it? And call me Eve, please.' She led Daisy to a table and ordered tea and toasted teacakes.

'Tuck in; it's so cold outside and I'm starving.' As usual after my sessions with Frank, she thought, smiling to herself.

'Yes, January is such a cold month. Tell me, Miss Pettifer ... I mean, Eve, did the remedy work for you?'

'Yes,' she lied, 'I believe it did – I'm certainly not as tired as I was.'

She studied Daisy intently. Pregnancy had certainly not dimmed the girl's beauty, quite the contrary, she was more beautiful than ever. Her skin glowed and her hair shone. But there was an irrefutable under-lying sadness in the girl's eyes, diffusing the brightness. Eve glanced down at Daisy's hands nimbly spreading the butter across the warm teacake and she quickly withdrew them placing them on her lap under the table.

'I'm sorry, did I embarrass you? I didn't mean to ... Daisy, look, I would like to be your friend.'

'Why? Why would you ... or ... or ... anyone for that matter, want to befriend me? I'm ... a ... a ... disgrace.'

'You're not a disgrace, these things happen. And why do I want you as a friend? That's easily answered: I like you. I have done ever since I came to your house that day last summer.' Eve reached for the girl's hand and held it. 'Look, Daisy, there are lots of unmarried mothers around – you're not on your own. People fall in love and—'

'I wasn't in love!' Daisy interrupted angrily, 'I ... I ... was attacked!' she added quietly.

There! She'd said it out loud for the first time.

'I haven't told anybody at all, please ... please don't say anything.'

Tears filled her eyes, so long had she waited to tell someone. She continued, 'Not even my father knows I was attacked ... and ... raped.

He would go crazy if he knew. He would hunt him down … and … and … probably kill him!'

'How dreadful, Daisy, you poor darling.' Of course this girl wouldn't be sleeping around – far too principled – gypsy or not, she thought, gently squeezing Daisy's hand. 'Well, your secret is safe with me, I promise. And should you ever want to talk about it, I'm here.'

'Thank you, Eve.' Daisy took a handkerchief from her coat pocket and blew her nose. 'I feel better already just being able to tell somebody.'

'Good, so eat up and we'll arrange to meet again. Here in Penrith if you like. I come once a fortnight, just for a change of scenery, of course,' she added quickly. God only knows what Daisy would think of me if she knew about my indiscretions with Frank Parks!

'I'd like that, thank you, Miss er … I mean, Eve.' They both laughed, and in that moment a bond was formed.

Daisy felt a sense of relief when she boarded the train back for Appleby. Although her father and Lavinia couldn't have been kinder or more considerate toward her, Eve Pettifer had done something special that day; she had made her feel acceptable in a world beyond the cottage where she'd hidden herself from prying, critical eyes these last six months, eyes that would look at her and label her a loose woman. But now she had a friend in Eve Pettifer, and what a difference that would make. She placed a gentle protective hand over the swell of her abdomen, smiling as the baby kicked impatiently for the long awaited acknowledgement if its existence. We're going to be all right, she said, silently, to the child she was now learning to love.

Tobias stepped out into the grim March morning and headed for the stables. It was 6.30. Dan would not be at work for at least another hour. He saddled Jet and rode out from the sheltered yard and into the open fields beyond where the cold north wind blew, cruelly stinging his face. He didn't bow his head against the strong wind, his jaw was set firm. His eyes glinted coldly as he surveyed the land ready for the plough. He urged Jet into a gallop across the valley floor and, before he knew it, had reached the brow of the hill and was looking down into the small valley where they'd first met. It drew him time and time again, like a magnet, clenching his mind in an imaginary psychological vice.

He hadn't seen her for months. Then one day, Frank had informed him casually that she was pregnant. Pregnant! He couldn't believe it! How could she? Frank also told him that she wasn't getting married and that there was no father. Was she crazy? Probably, he told himself. Just like my mother. But I was sure she was different, sure she felt the same way towards me as I did her; there was an unadulterated, beautiful innocence about her. For a moment his mind contemplated the sweetness of her and his heart faltered with an ache of intense yearning. He hung his head despondently and softly whispered her name. In the next instant he yanked the reins back in angry frustration and turned Jet for home, allowing the protection of indifference to replace the brief sensation of warmth and longing that had flooded his heart.

Back at the manor Lydia lay awake on her bed. She hadn't slept a wink all night.

Eve usually tried to engage her in conversation about her day off: what was new in the shops, where she'd been, who she'd seen. Lydia so seldom went anywhere, and never visited anyone, she believed it might help her feel less isolated. In passing Eve had told her of her chance meeting with Daisy in Penrith, and how much they'd enjoyed tea together.

Eve was completely oblivious to the loathing Lydia harboured for the Latimers. Her contact with the domestic staff was rare, other than with Nellie, so she was not privy to any below-stairs gossip.

During the next few days, undetected by Eve, Lydia managed to dispose of her pills, flushing them down the toilet.

Her inevitable descent into madness progressed, unabated.

How dare the woman associate with those damn tinkers. And then she has the audacity to ... to ... tell me! The woman talks as if she's quite proud of her acquaintance with this ... this Daisy! And did she say the girl was pregnant? I wonder ... is Tobias the father? God forbid!

Her tormented thoughts switched from one scenario to another before being suddenly interrupted by her companion.

'Good morning,' Eve said brightly, smiling at her. 'Need to wrap up warm today, Lydia, it's a biting north wind.

That's another thing, she thought bitterly, why does she have to pretend to be so damn chirpy all the time? And talk to me as if I'm a child!

'Why? Am I going somewhere? Or have we run out of coal?'

Eve laughed at what she thought was a joke. But when she turned to face Lydia, saw her face was quite serious. 'No, no, of course we haven't run out of coal. I ... I just thought we could go for a walk, the fresh air would be good for you.'

'Maybe it would but I'm feeling tired today. You go for a walk – I'll be fine on my own.' Lydia's mouth formed a sickly sweet smile. The last thing she wanted was for her to realize she wasn't taking her medication and report to Tobias. 'Maybe you'd read to me later this morning, Eve, my eyes are not good in this light. But first, let's have breakfast together, shall we?' she said, changing her voice to match Eve's cheery tone.

Chapter Thirteen

Two weeks had elapsed since Daisy's visit to Penrith and she hoped fervently Eve Pettifer hadn't felt rebuffed at her non-appearance at the café where they'd agreed to meet. Although so far her pregnancy hadn't been too much of an encumbrance, she felt unable to do more than what was basically necessary to get through the day. And a train journey to Penrith was out of the question.

Lavinia was cleaning the horse brasses at the kitchen table. Daisy sat across from her in the old, but comfortable wheel-back chair she'd requisitioned.

She looks tired, Lavinia thought, and still a month to go. I wish she'd see the doctor. 'I'll put the kettle on, love, you look done in. Why don't you go on upstairs and I'll bring you a cuppa up, eh?'

'I think I need some fresh air, Lavinia. I'll just go and have a stroll around the herb garden.'

'Well, don't be doing any weeding or anything, Daisy. I can do that for you, just say the word.'

She smiled at Lavinia. What a good friend she was, she blessed the day her father married her. 'I promise I shan't lift a finger.'

'Off yer go then and I'll make us a cuppa – so don't be too long, will you.'

Daisy threw on her old gardening coat and woolly hat. The wind snatched the door from her hand banging it shut.

Lavinia went to the window and watched her walk down the garden path toward the herb garden. She looked at the cuckoo clock on the kitchen wall, it was two o'clock. Sam would be back soon. She would tell him she was concerned for Daisy, and suggest the doctor be called in.

Lavinia hung the brasses which decorated the walls back on both sides of the fireplace. She threw another log on the fire and glanced at the clock. It was 2.30 and Daisy hadn't returned. She grabbed her coat and headed to the herb garden.

There was no sign of her.

'*Daisy, Daisy?* Where are you?' The howling gale smothered her shouts. She ran quickly toward the stables. '*Daisy*, are you there, love? *Can you hear me?*'

'*Here!*' came a weak pleading cry. 'I'm over here, oh, *help me!*'

Lavinia rushed to the stable from where the faint voice came.

'Oh! My goodness! Daisy! What happened?' The girl lay huddled on a bed of straw. Chase was standing close by, his head hanging down with the tip of his nose resting on her hair. Lavinia quickly led him to another stable before hurrying back to where Daisy lay hugging her stomach.

'I think … the … the baby's coming! … I'm so … scared. Help me … *please!*'

Lavinia gently assisted her to her feet. 'Come on, first of all let's get you back inside and into bed. Come on now, you're all right I've got you. That's it, lass, put yer weight on me, pet. Lavinia won't let any harm come to you.'

She slowly led a sobbing Daisy back to the cottage.

It was four o'clock when Samboy arrived home. He walked into the kitchen singing. His singing stopped when he looked to where Lavinia was tipping a large pan of boiling water over a blood-soaked towel.

His face drained of colour. 'What's happened? Is Daisy all right?'

'Yes … for now, but hurry, Sam, she needs a doctor. *Now, Sam!*'

Sam about turned and within seconds was driving as fast as he could back down the road.

Frank Parks followed a distraught Samboy back to the cottage in Hampton.

Samboy had managed to find his address, knocked on his door and begged him to come at once. The doctor's wife had been disgruntled. The mayor and his wife were coming round for drinks that evening and *what would they think?* Frank was grateful for the welcome disruption of what would have been a long-drawn-out, tedious evening.

'What else can I do?' Frank had said, feigning disappointment. 'I must adhere to the Hippocratic oath. Do give them my apologies, and you enjoy their company, my dear.' He'd pecked her on the cheek and left immediately.

*

Hmm, Frank said to himself on first inspection of Daisy, the gypsy woman is doing a good job here.

'It won't be long now, Daisy, before the baby arrives. I know you're in capable hands with – I'm sorry, I don't think we've been introduced, have we? Ah, yes, at the surgery, it's—'

'Lavinia, Lavinia Latimer, Samboy's wife.'

'Mrs Latimer, you are doing a fine job here. The baby isn't due for four more weeks, but Daisy is healthy, and the unborn baby has a strong heartbeat.

'I'll pop downstairs and put your father's mind at rest,' Frank said, taking hold of the young girl's hand and patting it reassuringly, 'Everything will be fine, my dear.'

Daisy nodded in response, too weak to speak.

Frank found Samboy in the kitchen looking pale and anxious. He stood up expectantly when he saw him appear and Frank placed a comforting hand on his shoulders.

'No, no, nothing yet. Stay where you are, Mr Latimer. I came downstairs to let you know she's going to be fine, but it might be a while yet.' He looked to where the kettle was hissing on the stove. 'Could I maybe trouble you for a cup of tea, do you think?'

'Certainly,' said Samboy and began brewing a fresh pot. 'Mebbe you'd care for a drop o' the strong stuff, Doctor?'

'When my work's finished that would be most welcome,' replied Frank, licking his lips.

They had been chatting amiably for half an hour when a piercing scream came from upstairs.

'Now, now, don't worry. I'll call you if you're needed,' Frank said.

He entered the bedroom and saw the baby's head was showing. Daisy was sweating profusely, gripping Lavinia's hand.

'Not long now, Daisy. *Push*, my dear – that's it, *push* as hard as you can.'

'I … can't! I … can't push … any … more. *Aaa. No! Help me, please. Aaa! Help me … Oh, Tobias!*' Daisy's face contorted with pain as she mustered up what strength she had left in her tired body for a final push which delivered her child into the world.

Frank and Lavinia looked at each other aghast when they'd heard Daisy's cry for Tobias. Lavinia glanced at the door and saw it wasn't closed properly. She hoped to hell Sam hadn't heard his daughter cry out Tobias's name, but that was unlikely; the cottage was small and the bedroom was directly above the kitchen.

'Congratulations, Mr Latimer! You have a fine, strong grandson,' Frank said, smiling, and shook Samboy's hand.

'Is she going to be all right, Doctor?' Samboy asked. He didn't want to get into any discussion about the child – not after what he'd heard through the kitchen ceiling a few minutes ago.

'She's fine. She'll need lots of rest and looking after for a week or two, naturally, but I'm sure your wife is quite capable. She's a fine woman, Mr Latimer – a natural born nurse, I'd say.'

'Aye, well, it comes from breeding 'orses. That's what she's done all 'er life – not a better 'orse breeder around,' Samboy boasted. 'Now do yer want that glass of whisky afore yer go, Doctor?'

'Yes, thank you, it's been a long night.' Frank looked at his pocket watch, it was just past midnight. Thank goodness I've missed the ghastly social evening at home; my time spent here has certainly been far from dull. Wait until I tell Eve what I've discovered – she'll be amazed. I'll have to swear her to secrecy, of course, because should Lydia Flint stumble across this news – all mighty hell will break loose!

'Are you going to go up and see your daughter and grandson, Sam?' Lavinia asked.

'No, not yet,' he replied. 'Let them both rest. I'll be seeing them tomorrow.'

Lavinia knew at that moment he'd heard Daisy call out for Tobias. Although she felt sorry for him, there wasn't a damn thing she could do.

'Well, I'll go up to bed, Sam, don't be long.' She rested her hands on his shoulders and dropped a kiss on his cheek.

'Aye, you must be worn out, love,' he said, smiling at her weakly. 'And … and … thank you for all your kindness, we'd have been lost without you. I'll be up soon.'

Samboy didn't go to bed, he spent the entire night in the kitchen, sitting over the fire and drinking tea. He had come to a decision.

'I'll be back in a bit, love,' he said to his wife when she came downstairs the following morning. 'There's a job I've got to go and see; some scrap that needs clearing from a local farm.'

Lavinia looked at him. 'You'll do what you have to do, Sam,' she said perceptively. 'Some things are none of my business.'

Samboy didn't look at her. 'Thanks,' he said and left.

*

Daisy looked down at her son laid in her arms. She climbed out of bed and took him to the window. 'Look, precious, this is your world.' She kissed his forehead and held him tight. 'And there goes your grand-father. I wonder where he's going?' She craned her neck and tapped on the window, but he didn't look up. 'He hasn't been to see you yet, but don't worry, my little one, he'll love you with all his heart when he does.'

She climbed back into bed just as Lavinia entered the room carrying a tray.

'Hello, you two,' she said, smiling. 'You eat some breakfast and I'll hold him for a while. Can I, Daisy?'

'Of course you can – you're his grandmother.'

'*His grandmother! Me?*'

Daisy passed the baby to her and tucked into the plate of food; she was starving.

'You'll be the best grandmother any child could have, Lavinia.' Daisy saw her eyes fill with tears. 'That is … unless … I'm sorry, maybe you don't want to be a grandmother – you're too young – I'm sorry.'

'What! Not want to be a grandmother? Ooh, Daisy I'd consider it an honour to be his grandmother. Thank you. Oh, I'm so touched I can't stop crying.' She took a handkerchief from her apron pocket and blew her nose loudly. The baby jumped with fright and began to cry. Daisy and Lavinia looked at each other and burst out laughing.

Samboy had no laughter in his heart when he turned the car into Eden Falls drive.

The bloody bastard's going to pay for what he's done to my daughter – I'll break his bloody aristocratic neck! No better than his bloody father. *Who the hell does he think he is*!

He arrived at the house and slammed on his brakes. The sound of flying gravel brought Dan rushing from the stables.

'Fetch yer bloody boss! *Now*!' Samboy yelled.

Dan quickly retreated to find his master, leaving Samboy by the side of his car pawing at the ground like an angry bull.

Within moments Tobias appeared, wiping his mouth with a napkin.

'Mr Latimer! Is everything all right? I mean Daisy. Is she all right? What is it?'

'What is it?' Samboy blared, 'You stand there and have the nerve to ask *what is it*!'

He couldn't contain his anger any longer and took a swing at Tobias who ducked and stepped back. Samboy lost his balance, falling to the ground with the force of his swing.

Tobias offered a helping hand, but he pushed him away.

'You bloody bastard!' Samboy growled, looking him directly in the eye. 'Yer think yer can get away with anything, don't yer? You bloody toffs!'

'Get away with what? Please, Mr Latimer, tell me what it is I'm supposed to have done, will you, and then maybe I can correct the situation?'

'Stop bloody pretending! As if you didn't know Daisy was pregnant with *your* child!'

'*My child*?' Tobias hung his head shaking it from side to side. 'Mr Latimer, if only it *were* my child, I'd do the right thing and—'

'Not yours?' he exclaimed. 'Not yours? If it's not yours then bloody hell, whose is it? Who … who could do such a thing to my daughter?'

Samboy brushed the dirt from his trousers. 'Looks like I've mebbe made a mistake,' was all he could say. An apology was out of the question; he just wanted to get away from the place.

Lydia woke up to the sound of gravel striking the bedroom window followed by loud voices. She climbed from her bed and went to see what had caused it. There was quite a commotion.

She could see them below, her son and a gypsy. They were arguing and the man struck out at Tobias. Lydia guessed immediately what it was about. He must be the father of the bastard the gypsy girl is carrying. I imagine he's come for money. She saw her son attempt to help the man to his feet and he shrugged him off. The gypsy then got into his car and drove away. *He has a car! A new car!* What is this world coming to when such people can afford a car?

'Well?' Lavinia said. 'What happened when you went to see him? I'm assumin' that's where you've been, Sam.'

'Says it's not his. 'E could be lying though.'

'I doubt it, Sam. You mebbe don't like the squire, but I think he's an honest man.'

Samboy bowed his head and sighed. 'I know, lass, I know. I'm just at a … a … loss as what to do for the best.'

'I know what you can do,' said Lavinia.

'Aye, and what might that be?'

'Get up them stairs and meet your grandson. They both need us now, more than ever. And, like Daisy says, I'm that bairn's grandmother,' she added, with an imperious toss of her head, 'and right proud I am of it, Sam!'

He rose from his chair and walked over to where she stood. He took her in his arms and whispered softly in her ear, 'Oh, my Lavinia, I love you so much.' He picked up the tray Lavinia had prepared and made his way up the narrow staircase, tapped gently on Daisy's door and waited.

'Come in,' Daisy called.

'Hello, love, it's me.' He walked over to the bed and, holding her face between his hands, kissed her on the forehead. 'I'm sorry I've not been up … but here I am. Are yer all right, my bonny lass? You can get well rested now, me and Lavinia are goin' to look after you and the bairn, I promise.'

Tears of relief sprang to her eyes. 'Thanks, Dad.'

She got up from her bed, walked over to the crib and picked up the baby. 'Come and meet your grandfather,' she said to him. 'I haven't decided on a name yet, Dad.'

Samboy sat himself down comfortably in the nursing chair waiting to receive his grandson. Daisy placed him in his arms. 'I'll have my soup while you nurse him, Dad.'

The baby was wrapped in a snow-white shawl pulled up around his tiny head to protect him from any draughts. He looked down at the baby and smiled. All thoughts of who the father might be melted in an instant. The infant was sleeping. He gently pushed the shawl away from the baby's head to take a closer look at him and he suddenly gasped.

Daisy flew across the room. 'What is it, Dad? Is something the matter?' she asked fearfully. He saw concern etched across her face and quickly composed himself. The last thing he wanted was for Daisy to be anxious. 'No, no, nowt's wrong, Daisy. My, what a fine boy he is. I'm sure you'll think of a name for him soon,' he said, handing the bundle of life back to his mother.

Samboy was in no doubt now as to who the father of the child was. The mass of black curls covering his tiny head confirmed it: the father was Roulson Adams.

When? When could this have happened? he asked himself countless times that day.

It was two weeks later when it dawned on him. He recalled the time they'd been to Topcliffe Fair. It was then there had been a significant change in Daisy; the change had occurred overnight.

He must've been there! That was why she'd wanted to come home early. She was upset about something. Did he take her against her will? *My God, I'll bet he did! The bastard!*

'Have you got a name for the young fella yet?' Lavinia was holding the baby while Daisy had her breakfast. He was five weeks old and she thought it time the little mite was registered and christened.

'Yes, I thought Ralph would suit him. What do you think?'

'Ooh, I like that. Ralph, Ralph,' Lavinia crooned to the baby. 'Yes, it suits him grand. He looks like a Ralph with his beautiful dark hair.'

'Good. Then Ralph it is,' Daisy said decisively. 'Ralph Samuel Latimer.'

'Aw, Daisy, yer dad will be fair chuffed.'

Samboy was exercising one of his yearlings, getting it used to the halter and the sound of traffic. He'd walked about three miles when a car passed him slowly then stopped further along the road. He thought the car looked familiar, and when the door opened and a man stepped out into the road he saw it was DS Keen.

'Good day to you, Mr Latimer,' Keen said, his greeting friendly. 'I saw it was you and couldn't pass without saying hello.'

'I'm just tryin' to get this young 'un used to these 'ere cars. Whoa! Steady boy!' The colt danced sideways and Samboy steadied him with his calming voice.

'Got your hands full there,' Keen said, stepping back a few paces.

'Aye, but 'e'll be worth the work I put in. He's for sulky racin' this one, already got a buyer for 'im.'

'I imagine you'll have a waiting list as long as your arm for any horses you break in, Mr Latimer.'

Samboy smiled at the compliment. 'I'm not so sure about that now. But I'm glad I've seen yer. Tell me, any fresh news o' that fella that went missin'?'

'No, I'm afraid not.' Keen said, shaking his head disappointedly. 'What about you, have you heard anything on … on … the grapevine?'

'I'll tell you something for nothing, sir, and that's this. Roulson Adams is alive.'

'Have you seen him?'

'No. And no one's told me either. But 'e's alive, believe me, and the sooner yer catch up wi' him and lock the bastard up, the better! Pardon me language, sir.'

'Why the change of heart?' Keen asked curiously.

'Can't say why, *but he's a bad 'n*!'

The colt flinched at the harsh tone of his angry voice.

Keen had heard Latimer's daughter had had a baby and wasn't divulging the name of the father. Gossip had it that it was Squire Flint. But maybe, just maybe, Roulson Adams was the villainous scoundrel. And Latimer wanted to avenge the disgrace brought upon his daughter. Can't say I blame him for a minute, if that's the case.

'How's your daughter doing, Mr Latimer? I heard you'd become a grandfather. Are they well?' Just a chance he'll let something drop, he thought.

'They're fine, thank you.' Samboy said flatly, bringing any questioning to an abrupt close.

'Two or three weeks ago, wasn't it? A boy I heard.'

'That's right, fifteenth of March,' was all he offered the detective. 'Now I must be off, this young 'un needs me time.' And touching the peak of his cap he strode briskly away with the young colt skipping playfully at his side.

Keen leaned on the side of his car watching him walk away into the distance. March the fifteenth, eh? Well I'll be damned, Beware the Ides of March.

A car pulled up outside the cottage and a well-dressed lady stepped out.

Eve Pettifer had heard from Frank that the baby had arrived. She had been concerned when Daisy hadn't shown up in Penrith at the café where they had planned to meet. She decided to buy a present for the newborn baby and deliver it personally, rather than send it by post.

An attractive-looking woman opened the door to her. She was possibly a little younger than herself, and had obviously been a real beauty in her youth.

'Good morning, I hope you don't mind my calling, but I've brought a present for the baby and was wondering how Daisy was.'

'Come in, come in!' Lavinia ordered. 'It's too cold to stand on ceremony, that north wind's perishing!'

'My name's Eve Pettifer—'

Lavinia didn't let her finish, she knew who she was. Daisy had told her all about her and how kind and friendly she'd been when they'd met in Penrith.

'Aye, I know who you are, Daisy's told me. Now tek yer coat off an' I'll put the kettle on and let her know you're here, she's just feeding the bairn. Oh, and I'm Lavinia by the way,' Lavinia said, wiping her hands on her pinafore. 'I'm married to Daisy's dad.'

'Pleasure to meet you, Mrs Latimer,' Eve said, shaking the extended hand.

'I'd say come into the front room, but it's too cold. The fire only gets lit on weekends in there, so I hope you don't mind us sittin' here in the kitchen.'

'Not at all,' Eve replied, smiling warmly. 'I remember when I came here once before how much I loved this kitchen. It was overflowing with huge bundles of herbs; the perfume was amazing! And now it smells of freshly baked bread. It's a superb kitchen, with a wonderful atmosphere.'

Daisy finished feeding the baby and went downstairs where Eve was having a cup of tea, and tucking into a huge chunk of cake. She and Lavinia were getting on like a house on fire, and Daisy was sorry to interrupt them.

'Oh, Daisy!' Eve exclaimed, enveloping mother and child in her arms. 'I'm so pleased to see you, and … and … oh, my, he's beautiful! May I hold him, please? I promise I won't drop him.'

'Of course. Sit down and I'll pass him to you.'

Eve sat down and Daisy placed the baby in her arms.

'He's so … so … tiny. Have you named him yet?'

'Yes, Ralph,' she said proudly.

'Ralph. Yes, it suits him – don't you think, Lavinia?'

'Aye, I do; it's a fine name for a fine boy.'

Eve tore her eyes away from the child, casting an envious glance at both women while feeling an absence deep within her. Looking down at the baby she knew this was the closest she would ever come to maternal fulfilment. She bowed her head and dropped a kiss, as soft as summer rain, on Ralph's forehead.

Lavinia gazed at Eve, and tears sprang to her eyes. She understood only too well what it was like to be middle-aged and childless. Her heart swelled with gratitude for Ralph, her step-grandson maybe, but a grandson nonetheless.

'Can I pour you another cup of tea?' Daisy asked, wanting to dispel the quiet sadness that had settled over them for some reason she was unable fathom.

'No, thank you.' Eve stood up to leave. Smiling, she handed the baby to Lavinia, then handed two neatly wrapped packages to Daisy. 'There's a gift for you too, my dear. I hope you like it. No … no … please, don't open them yet, wait until I've gone. And … maybe … I could call again sometime to see you both … and Ralph?' she asked, looking from one to the other.

'Oh, yes, please do,' Daisy said, with genuine delight.

'You're more than welcome,' Lavinia added. 'An' my husband will be right glad to make your acquaintance, I'm sure.'

They stood waving goodbye until the car disappeared from sight, then went back into the kitchen where Daisy opened the parcel for Ralph. It contained a white shawl of finest soft wool, a teddy bear, and three gold sovereigns.

'My! What generous gifts,' Lavinia exclaimed. 'She must be right fond of you, Daisy.'

'Oh, I do wish she'd waited so I could thank her.'

'Well, she did say she'd be back, so don't fret yerself.'

She carefully opened the gift Eve had left for her. Inside was a small black box. She opened it and gasped in astonishment.

'Oh!' Daisy exclaimed. Her hand shot up to her mouth. The small box held the most exquisite brooch. It was a diamond-encrusted horse, with green emeralds for the eyes and hoofs. 'Oh! Goodness gracious me! Lavinia! I can't accept this. It's … it's … too beautiful! Why? Why has she given me this?'

Daisy quickly put the brooch back in its box, pushed it aside and stood up. She began dashing about the kitchen clearing away the tea things. She didn't know the woman! What did she want of her? 'I'm going to give it back to her, Lavinia, that's what I'm going to do.'

'Sit down.' Lavinia guided Daisy to a nearby chair, sat down next to her and opened the box. She removed the brooch and examined it closely. 'I know why she's given it to you, lass.' She took Daisy's hands between hers and kissed them. 'She's no family as such, not to call her own anyway. No young bairns to spoil, or to comfort her in her old age. Can't you see, Daisy?' she pleaded in a sombre tone, 'It's giving *her* pleasure! She's not much different from me, really. 'Ere I am, well past child-bearing age, but I've been fortunate enough to have fallen in love, acquired you for my stepdaughter and … and … a precious grandson. So, no, Daisy, don't throw kindness back in her face, let her enjoy the pleasure of giving you a beautiful gift.'

Chapter Fourteen

'Are yer sure you'll be all right Daisy, yer haven't ridden for a long time. I can come with you if you like, Lavinia will manage the bairn, won't yer, love?'

Lavinia didn't reply and, glaring at Samboy, raised her eyebrows in exasperation. When was he going to get it into his thick skull Daisy was not a child anymore, but a mother herself.

'Be off with you, Daisy, Ralph will be fine with me and yer dad, *won't he?*' Lavinia cast her husband another warning glance. 'It'll do you good to get some fresh air, you've been tied to this house for over two months now; what with the bairn 'aving colic, yer've been fair worn out. I've packed some sandwiches – now off you go, lass.'

'Thanks, Lavinia, you too, Dad,' Daisy said, kissing the top of Ralph's head. 'Now, be a good boy for your grandma and grandpa, do you hear me?' Ralph wriggled and gurgled with delight at the sound of his mother's voice.

The man sat in the dappled shade of the trees by the river watching a lone white swan. With its angular beauty and ruffled lines it glided gracefully across the water. He'd seen swans here before, usually in pairs; he pondered idly whether this one had lost its mate. The swan turned its head sharply as though reading his thoughts and hissed noisily. Something had startled it. It ran swiftly on webbed feet across the water's surface like an aeroplane taking off on a runway. Its broad wings, spanning eight to ten feet, lifted the large white bird into the clear blue sky. His eyes traced it to a diminishing dot before lowering them back down to the river where he saw what had startled the bird.

She hadn't seen him camouflaged beneath the trees, and he watched her steady approach. She was seated sedately on the familiar palomino horse, treading cautiously through the shallow waters. He stood up and strode down to the river before she passed him by.

'Hello, Daisy.'

'*What!*' Her cry of alarm caused her horse to shy. Unprepared, she shot one way and the horse the other, depositing her unceremoniously into the shallow water! '*Oh! You bugger, Chase!*' she swore angrily.

Tobias hurried over to where she'd landed. 'Oh, Daisy, are you all right? I am sorry ... I didn't think ... I was so pleased to see you.'

'Nice way of showing it!' she retorted sarcastically. '*Ouch*! My ankle! I think I've sprained it!'

His mouth curved into a smile. 'It's all right, I've got you. Let's get you out of the river.' He swept her slender body effortlessly into his arms and carried her to dry ground.

'You'll have to get out of those wet clothes, you're drenched.'

'I will not!' she protested.

Ignoring her, he removed his shirt and tossed it to her along with the saddle rug he'd brought. 'Here, put these on, your things will dry in the sun. Don't worry, I shan't look. I promise,' he added, grinning.

Daisy, feeling uncomfortable, quickly removed her outer garments. She threaded her legs through the shirt sleeves, buttoned it up and tied a belt around her waist.

'OK, I'm decent,' she said, pulling the saddle rug around her shoulders.

'I know that,' he said, turning to smile at the sodden loveliness of her. She resembled a yogi master in his modified shirt, and a sexy one at that! He felt a stirring in his loins just looking her. He'd waited so long to see her again and there was no way he was going to destroy what friendship had been salvaged from what could only be described as a disastrous beginning.

'Now give me your things and I'll put them in the sun to dry. Are you hungry?' he asked. Not waiting for a reply he tended to her horse before walking over to where his own was tethered and returned with a hamper of food.

She watched him wander over to her horse. He was tall, lean and muscular in the white vest. His skin was fair. A down of light golden hairs covered his arms; she noticed the hard muscles of his biceps when he lifted the saddle from her horse. He was striding back towards her now with that lopsided grin. She let her eyes follow the strong, classic lines of his face; his nose was large but not too big, his square chin jutted out, but just far enough to display stubbornness. His unruly hair flopped down and he pushed it back with his hand revealing kind, laughing grey eyes. She was surprised at how at ease she felt with him. She didn't fear for her safety, not for a moment, which surprised her.

'Don't know about you, but I'm starving!'

Tobias sat quite close to her and handed her a sandwich and a cup of stewed tea from his flask.

'Thanks. I have brought food along with me, you know.'

'Good! We'll eat yours after we've polished mine off, eh?'

Daisy couldn't help but smile at this man, intent on being her friend.

'Thanks, for the shirt, you really didn't have to; are you warm enough?'

'No! I'm frozen, but it's worth it. You look much more attractive in it than I do. You could start a new fashion wearing it like that!' he joked.

'I doubt it,' she said, laughing. She was thoroughly enjoying herself.

'It's good to see you laugh,' he said, taking a cigarette and lighting it.

He leaned back against the trunk of the tree watching her closely as she sipped her tea. She's changed. Gone, is the spirited young girl who'd reprimanded him for riding on his own land that first day they met, a year ago. In her place, was a mature young woman, a mother, the promise of great beauty fulfilled.

'Please, Daisy, tell me to mind my own business if you want to' – he drew deeply on his cigarette, giving her a moment to shut him up, but she didn't – 'I heard you'd had a child a … a … boy, and I wondered, why … why … you didn't marry him?'

Both were silent, both deep in thought. He poured each of them another cup of tea, leaving her free to decide whether to tell him or not.

Daisy took the cup he'd handed her, nursing it in her hands. No more exhibitions of blushing or coyness now, she thought. Too much had happened over the last year. She wanted to surrender the cynicism that had soured her view of life these last few months.

'Do you really want to know?' she asked frankly.

'I do, that is, if it's not too painful for you.'

'No, not now. If you'd asked me six, *no, even four* months ago, it would have been impossible. But, I'm a different person now.'

'Yes, I know, I can see that. You are you're more … more—'

'Mature, is the word you're searching for I believe,' she said, grinning and raising her eyebrows, and they both laughed.

Tobias drew on his cigarette and waited.

'It happened when I went to look after my aunt, in Yorkshire,' Daisy began.

'I remember,' interrupted Tobias. 'Dan went to collect Whitby Jet, and you had already left. Did you get my letter? Dan said he'd given it to your father. He said he'd post it on to you.' He could tell by the puzzled expression on her face she hadn't received it. Bugger it, he thought angrily. 'Look, never mind about that, we're here now. I'm sorry, please, do go on.'

Daisy told him everything, holding nothing back. He was the first person to hear who the father of her child was and, God willing, the last. He was the second person she had entrusted with her heart-rending story. Somehow she knew, in him, she would find a loyal friend who sought no favour.

Tobias sat in silence, his eyes fixed unseeing in the distance. Every word she spoke pierced his heart, launching his thoughts and feelings into some unknown place and he was speechless for a few minutes. He was in awe of this strong, capable woman who had risen where others might fall. Like a phoenix rising from the ashes.

He looked into her green eyes which glistened with unshed tears. He lowered his head towards hers and her hand reached up and touched his face. His mouth tenderly covered her open lips and she responded hungrily, leaning into his passionate embrace, both mindful that there could never be a more beautiful moment in the whole of their lives.

Daisy reluctantly drew her body away from his.

'I ... have to go, Ralph will need feeding soon.'

'Ralph?'

'My son,' she said smiling. 'His name's Ralph. I'm still breast-feeding him, I must get back.'

Tobias had noticed her ample breasts and was aroused when he'd held her pressed close to his chest. He jumped to his feet as she made to move.

'I'll get your things for you. I'm sure they'll be dry.' He took her hands in his. 'And while I'm getting them, think of when I can see you again, please ... I won't take no for an answer. I must see you again soon. I won't allow you to escape from me, not ever again! OK?'

'All right,' Daisy answered with a smile spreading across her face like sunshine.

Lavinia was looking out of the window waiting for Daisy's return. If she didn't get herself back here soon, Sam would be out in the car looking for her.

'She's here! I can see her coming down the lane, I told you not to fret, Sam.'

'*And about bloody time!*' he yelled angrily.

'Now, Sam, behave yerself! Don't you go upsetting the lass. She's had enough grief to last her a lifetime, d'yer hear me?'

'Aye, I 'ears yer,' Sam replied, lowering his voice to appease her.

She always seems to know the right thing to say or do, he thought, so I'd better keep me mouth shut!

Lavinia walked over to the stable to greet Daisy where she was unsaddling the horse.

'Hello, love,' she said smiling warmly. 'Have you had a good ride? Get yerself into the house an' I'll see to Chase for you. Ralph's just now ready for a feed.'

'Thanks, Lavinia. I'm sorry … I … I … rode further than intended. I'll go and feed him.'

Lavinia's eyes followed Daisy back to the house. The girl looks flushed; mebbe she rode home a bit too fast, Lavinia thought, hanging up the reins next to the saddle. Then, she spotted the bag of sandwiches she'd packed for her that very morning which hadn't been touched. Well, well, Lavinia mused, there's summat afoot, or someone.

It was a bright, sunny October day with an autumn chill in the air. Daisy walked briskly from Penrith station to the cosy café.

He was there, waiting for her just as he had done every week since that glorious day in May down by the river, when they'd quite simply, fallen in love. She travelled to Penrith by train each week, and Tobias went by car. They met for lunch and afterwards took a long leisurely walk arm in arm. He would then drive her home, dropping her at a safe distance near the lane end, so her father wouldn't see them together.

But Tobias had had enough of all this secrecy. He loved her and she him. And today was the day, he'd decided, they were not going to meet in secret any more. His hand reached down and patted his pocket. No. If Samboy Latimer didn't like it, well, he could bloody well lump it!

He stood up as she walked over to the table for two tucked away in a corner of the room and pulled out a chair for her. They snatched a brief kiss before the waitress hurried over to take their order. Her face felt cold when he kissed her, so he took her hands, warming them in his own.

She's beautiful … and she's mine, he thought. There was a delicate pink glow on her face from the heat of the fire which burned brightly in the grate. Her brilliant green eyes brimmed with moisture from the cold air making them glisten and tremble.

As always, their time together passed all too quickly. Tobias ordered another pot of tea and Daisy looked anxiously at her watch.

'Do we have time for another cup?' she asked, with a frown.

'Yes. We have to make time today, Daisy. There's something important

I want to ask you.' He saw her chin rise challengingly and he smiled to himself. Why did she do that? Whenever he conducted himself seriously, she assumed a ... haughty attitude. Well, he told himself, life will certainly be far from boring with Daisy.

'I love you, Daisy. I have done from the moment I set eyes on you that first time by the river. Do you remember how cross you were with me?' he reminded her, grinning.

'Yes, I do.' Daisy laughed out loud and two elderly women sitting at a nearby table turned and tut-tutted disapproval of the young couple.

'Will you marry me?'

Daisy's laughter came to an abrupt end.

'Didn't think you'd be that upset,' he said. 'Isn't that what couples do if they love one another? Say something, Daisy, please. I've never known you at a loss for words.'

'I don't know what to say I ... I.... What about my father?'

'No, thank you, Daisy,' he said, shaking his head, 'I don't want to marry him.'

They looked at each other for a brief moment then burst into fits of laughter.

'Will that be all, sir? Here's your bill.' The waitress waited for payment then scurried off to fetch the gentleman's coat. She couldn't understand it. The couple had been coming in every week for months now, usually ever so quiet and refined, sitting in the corner, holding hands. Just goes to show how people can change.

Tobias and Daisy left the café still in fits of laughter.

'Come on, Daisy, We'll go and have a coffee in that hotel over the road.' He grabbed her hand and, weaving through the throngs of people busy doing their shopping, went into the hotel lounge bar.

'Well? What's it to be, Daisy? Is it a no and coffee ... or yes and champagne?'

'Aye, I'll marry you Tobias Flint, on one condition.'

'Conditions now, eh? And what might that be?' There was no one about, the lounge bar was empty. He pulled her close, their faces almost touching. He inhaled her sweet breath when she gasped with delight at his touch.

'Don't expect me to change – that's all, Tobias Flint.'

'I wouldn't want you to change, Daisy Latimer.'

'Ah–hem, excuse me, er ... can I get you anything, sir, madam?' the young barman asked.

'Yes, thank you, champagne, and the best you have.'

Tobias surreptitiously reached inside his pocket and produced a box. He opened it and removing the diamond cluster ring, slipped it on to her finger.

'Oh,' she gasped, 'it's beautiful, Tobias, and it fits perfectly. How did you know what size?'

'I didn't. It was my grandmother's. I hope that's all right, Daisy. If you want me to buy—'

'No,' she said kissing him, 'I'll be proud to wear your grandmother's ring.' A lump came to her throat and she swallowed it. Today was not for tears.

'I suppose I'll have to get used to your extravagant ways,' she teased.

The champagne arrived. Tobias was thanking the waiter when he spotted Frank Parks hovering about the bar.

'Frank! Frank!' he called, beckoning him. 'Please, please, come and join us in our celebration.'

'Ssh,' said Daisy, blushing.

'No, no more secrecy remember? We're engaged now, Daisy.'

'What!' Frank spun round on hearing his name. His florid complexion and shocked expression made his eyes bulge and appear enormous.

'Come on, Frank, have a glass of champagne.'

Daisy looked beyond the doctor to the open door. Walking gracefully through it into the bar smiling broadly at the doctor, was Eve Pettifer. She hadn't seen Daisy and Tobias sitting there. She only had eyes for Frank Parks and, sidling up to him, placed her arm affectionately on his, the nature of their relationship patently obvious. Daisy had no idea!

Eve had become quite a regular visitor to the cottage. Her father had grown fond of the seemingly starchy spinster as well. She brought presents for baby Ralph, spoiling him at every possible opportunity. Now, here she was, meeting the doctor on the sly. What would Lavinia make of that? And her father! He wouldn't have her over the threshold if he knew.

Tobias's jaw dropped. They stared at each other in disbelief, and for a long while both were unable to speak. He wished to hell he'd not called Frank over to join them and that he and Daisy could just sneak off. But it was too late. Frank and Eve had been caught, red-handed. Poor buggers, Tobias thought.

Eve Pettifer turned to see what was causing Frank such consternation. Her hands shot up to her mouth in horror. Frank looked at her and whispered something before walking over to where the couple sat, speechless.

'Ah, Tobias, Daisy, lovely to … er … see you both,' he said, looking over the rim of his glasses. He was equally shocked. What on earth was the man doing? Being seen in public with a *gypsy girl*! What on earth was he thinking of? He'd heard a bit of gossip, but didn't expect it to amount to anything, not like this. No, by God! Drinking champagne too.

'Miss Pettifer and I, er, we just happened to bump into each other in town, didn't we, Miss Pettifer?' he said looking across to where she stood dumbfounded, for confirmation of his lie.

'What? Er ... oh! Yes, yes ... and I needed to discuss something, er, about the, er, medication I'm on.'

Eve took a deep breath and walked nervously over to where the young couple sat with open mouths. 'Daisy, how lovely to see you,' she said, and shaking her boss's hand looked beseechingly into his eyes, before placing an affectionate kiss on Daisy's cheek.

'Did I hear a celebration was in order?' Frank asked, looking from one to the other.

'You most certainly did, Frank. Waiter! Two more glasses, please,' called Tobias. 'Daisy and I,' he said proudly, taking her hand in his, 'have just got engaged.'

The waiter brought two more glasses which Tobias filled to the brim. He saw Frank was desperately in need of sustenance, his eyes were about to pop out of their sockets. Tobias smiled to himself. He was aware Frank Parks was a pompous ass and he'd be disappointed in his choice of fiancée, as would his mother. Oh, his damned mother! He'd forgotten about her.

'Well, congratulations, and good luck to you both,' Frank said half-heartedly, thinking they'd need all the luck they could get when his mother got wind of this!

'Thank you, Frank. I'll tell Mother tonight, Eve.' Tobias said, as though reading Frank's thoughts. He'd rather Eve was about when he gave her, what in his mother's mind, would be tragic news.

'Congratulations!' Eve said, raising her glass. 'You couldn't have chosen a lovelier girl, or marry into a finer family. I can vouch for them all; they're good friends of mine.'

'Thank you, Eve.'

Frank cringed, and tipping the glass of champagne to his lips, drained it dry. He was relieved when it was instantly replenished.

A full, watery moon drifted in a dark-blue sky.

The poacher sat quietly under a canopy of branches, patiently waiting for the pheasants to go up to roost. He could hear the scraping and rustling sound of them approaching through the undergrowth. He had no gun or dog, just a catapult, ready loaded with a ball bearing, and his expertise to use it.

The flapping of wings and loud calling of korr-kuk korr-kuk preceded the vertical flight of the roosting pheasants. Unmoving, in his advantageous position, he raised his catapult, slowly taking aim. There, perched high up in the branches, silhouetted in the face of a poacher's moon, sat the unsuspecting pheasant.

Thwack! Then, *thud*! The cock bird landed heavily to the ground.

'Got ya!' Roulson Adams moved swiftly and, plucking the bird from the ground, deftly crushed its skull between his forefinger and thumb assuring its demise.

He ran quickly, weaving his way between the trees of dense woodland. The gamekeeper was renowned for being keen this time of year. Moneyed men from the cities and surrounding areas paid vast amounts to gather for a day's shooting; killing hundreds of birds for killing's sake, often leaving many to rot where they fell. The gypsy, on the other hand, killed for the pot, to feed himself and his family, never killing anything harmless in life or useless in death.

The band of gypsies Roulson had tagged on to were regular visitors to the wood. He couldn't afford to be picked up by the police for poaching – or anything else. Not when the hangman's noose awaited him!

Dark, inquisitive eyes turned to watch him when he returned to the campsite down a secluded byway, in the foothills of the Wicklow Mountains, south of Dublin City. He hid the pheasant under his jacket. He'd no intention of sharing his kill with any of them.

He held no fondness for them. He thought them a dirty bunch of idle buggers, yet to witness one of them taking a wash or do a day's graft. They were entirely different from his own people, back home in England.

God, how he missed them! Occasionally, a cousin would find him, tracking him down by bush telegraph, bringing him welcome funds from his mam and dad, and news from back home. He'd bought a horse and a small cart with some of the money, thus enabling him to move about the county, and conveniently attach himself to bands of gypsies to hide behind.

He threw the dressed bird, along with potatoes and turnip he'd managed to steal from a nearby farm, into a pot suspended over the fire. He tossed the raw guts to a dog that had crept close to where he'd been dressing the bird. 'Get on, yer bugger! Tek it away!' he snapped. The mongrel bravely gathered the guts into its mouth and scampered off.

Roulson swigged from a beer bottle. Besides him, there were four families in the group consisting of sixteen people, eight adults and eight children. The authorities didn't appear to bother them, he'd noticed. They didn't shunt them around like herds of diseased cattle, which had become a common occurrence back in England.

Roulson's cart was positioned in such a way as to screen him from view of others. He needed their cover for anonymity, but not their friendship. Besides, he couldn't understand a bloody word they said. The mix of Romany cant and Irish became an unintelligible babble.

The pheasant and vegetables were cooked and he transferred them to a tin plate. He pulled the black woolly hat from his head and tucked it into his pocket. His thick black hair had grown back more lustrous than before he'd cut and bleached it. His thoughts revisited the day down by the river with Daisy and his black eyes glinted bitterly. She was to blame for all that had befallen him. If only she'd come away with him, he wouldn't have to be biding his time here, like this. He'd heard she'd had a bairn, a boy, last March, and according to his sums, he was in no doubt the bairn was his. He'd thought about it a lot. He'd like to have some kin alongside of him, and a son would be grand company. Why, he'd be able to teach him to ride, poach, fish. They'd be the best of friends.

'Muskras ha' bin lookin' for ye.'

'*What?*' Roulson exclaimed, looking to where the sudden interruption had come from.

A scruffy young boy belonging to the family directly opposite stood staring at the plate of food he was enjoying.

'*Muskras!*' repeated Roulson. 'The coppers, yer mean? What did they want?'

The boy shrugged his shoulders and continued to stare at the plate of food.

'Here,' Roulson said, shoving the plate and remainder of his meal into his hands. 'Now, speak very slowly, and tell me what you 'eard. Slow now,' he reminded him.

The boy was ravenous and stuffed his mouth full of food rendering him speechless for a moment.

After swallowing the mouthful he took a deep breath in preparation.

'Oi-heard-dem-ask, ooh-wos-it-dat-wos-stoppin'-'ere,' he said enunciating each word.

'And who did *they* say was stoppin' here?' Roulson asked the boy.

'Dey-said-dey-did-nat-know,' he concluded, giving himself a swift nod of approval for delivering what he believed to be perfect English.

'Are they comin' back, d'yer know?'

He shook his head. 'Oi-don't-tink-so.'

'Well, if they do come askin' about me, remember to mang nix. Now yer know what mang nix means, eh?'

'Yis-oi-do. Dat-means-ti-say-nottin',' the lad answered proudly, grinning from ear to ear.

'That's right. Now, this is for you.' Roulson took a generous half-crown from his pocket and dropped it into the boy's grimy open palm.

The following morning the young lad peered out from the back of his wagon. The mist was clearing and he saw that the man had absconded. Only the ashes of a camp-fire and patch of compressed grass suggested the tell-tale signs of someone having camped there.

Chapter Fifteen

May, 1951

'**N**o! *You can't do this to me, Tobias*!' Lydia grasped her throat in disbelief. '*Please, I beg of you*!' she pleaded, falling to her knees.

Tobias looked down at the pitiful sight of his mother. 'Oh, get up Mother, please. I'm not doing anything to *you*. I'm sorry if I've disappointed you, but I love Daisy, and we intend to marry next month whether you approve or not.'

Lydia stood up. Her steely, pinprick eyes glared at him angrily now. Tobias's heart hammered in his chest. Her eyes didn't waver and when she spoke, there was a tremble in her voice but she didn't look away.

'Daisy! What kind of name is that?' she yelled, spraying his face with spittle. 'A weed – that's what it is – nothing but a damned weed!' She smiled cruelly at the look of horror on his face. 'Well, boy, what have you to say to that? Cat got your tongue, has it?'

Tobias spoke softly. 'No, Mother. Why don't you rest awhile, and we'll talk tomorrow.'

He left her room quietly. As he walked down the stairs, a loud, insane cackle echoed ominously from her room along the galleried landing. A maid waiting at the bottom of the stairs for him to pass looked at him alarmed, with eyes like a frightened fawn.

'It's all right, Meg,' he said, recognizing the young girl. 'Mother's having a difficult time. Please go to Miss Pettifer's room, will you, and tell her to come to the study – that is, after she's attended Mrs Flint? Thank you, Meg.'

Tobias poured a sherry for Eve and a large whisky for himself.

'Thank you for coming, Eve. How is she now?'

'I've given her a sleeping pill and she's taking a rest. I really can't understand it. She's not been too difficult of late but, I suppose....' She shrugged, lost for words and her voice tapered to a silence.

Tobias looked across at her and smiled warmly. 'I know I don't owe you an explanation, Eve, but I want you to know. I truly love Daisy, and nothing, or anyone, including Mother, will dissuade me from marrying her.'

'Oh, yes, yes, I quite understand.' And she did. Because of the absence of love in her life, she was only too quick to recognize its existence in that of others. 'Maybe ... maybe, she'll come round to accept in time—'

'No, no, never in a month of Sundays, that's for sure,' Tobias interrupted shaking his head.

'You're probably right. If you, or Daisy for that matter, need my help in any way, please, just say.'

'Well, there is something I need to discuss. Are you happy here, Eve?'

'Oh yes, of course. I love being here,' she answered, reassuring him. She had no intention of leaving the position she held.

'The thing is, after the wedding, Mother will be moving into the dower house on the estate. I haven't informed her as yet, but will do so as soon as she's feeling better. And, of course,' he added, reaching his main concern for this talk with her, 'I hope you will stay on. More staff would be employed, of your choosing, and you would have overall responsibility of hiring and firing. I know it's a lot to ask of you, and I shan't hold it against you if you no longer wish to stay here.'

He waited nervously for her response and took a large drink from his glass.

'That sounds most satisfactory, Mr Flint,' she said, smiling at him with genuine pleasure. 'And when will the move take place?'

'As soon as possible; next week if that suits you?'

'Wonderful!' Eve said standing up. 'It may be the best thing for your mother. A whole new environment with nothing to remind her of— Oh, I do apologize, how thoughtless of me.'

'No, not at all. I quite agree with you. The further she is away from here, the better for her – and Daisy and me,' he added ruefully.

'I'm sure you are wise to make these changes. Daisy will certainly appreciate your decision, I mean, consideration.'

'Please, have another sherry,' he said, refilling her glass. 'And if you'd start interviewing people for relevant positions immediately, I'd be grateful. Here's to the future, Eve.' He leaned over and touched her glass with his own.

'To the future,' she smiled.

Appleby Fair, June.

Tobias woke up to the dawn chorus of birds nesting in the trees about the house.

He dressed and went downstairs before the staff had risen, helping himself to tea and toast. He quickly scribbled a note for Nellie saying he'd breakfasted and would be back for luncheon about one o'clock.

The clip-clop of Jet's hoofs in the courtyard alerted Dan who appeared wiping the remains of breakfast from his mouth on his sleeve.

'Mornin', Sir.'

'Morning Dan, don't worry, you're not late, it's me. I was up early and thought I'd take Jet for a gallop. While I'm away he'll have to be lunged regularly, he's not used to being cooped up. Oh, and get the farrier out, he needs shoeing again.'

'Yer won't 'ave to give 'im a second thought. I'll mek sure he's well looked after. A big day for yer tomorro', sir, what wi t' weddin' like.'

'Yes, a big day, Dan. Hope you and your girlfriend – it is Meg you're seeing, isn't it?'

'Aye, yes, sir,' Dan replied blushing bright crimson.

'Well, you are both invited to the small reception we're having.'

'That's kind of yer, sir, me and Meg'll look forward to it.'

The unwelcome clouds rolled away to the east and the morning mist evaporated in the warm June sunshine. Tobias gave Jet his head, and he raced across the open fields. On reaching the boundary of the estate he brought him to a halt and dismounted. He picked up a clump of mown hay and smelled it. Hmm, perfect for gathering in, he thought, inhaling deeply.

The sound of thundering hoofs invaded his peace. He turned to see his neighbour galloping towards him. He grabbed Jet's reins who whinnied excitedly at the approaching horse.

'Hello, Toby. I thought it was you in the distance.'

'Hello, Eleanor. Not like you to be out and about this early,' he said sarcastically, pretending to look at his watch.

'Oh, I do get out of bed early sometimes. I'm pleased to see you. I understand congratulations are in order, that you're getting married.'

He could hear the displeasure in her voice.

'Yes, tomorrow, actually.'

'*Tomorrow*! Oh, I'd no idea it was so soon. Well, congratulations, Toby, and … is it the young gyp— I mean traveller girl?' Her expression was one of anger, but her voice was remarkably cool.

She knows very well who I'm marrying, he thought, looking into the spiteful face for a long, still moment. He'd heard she'd met some wealthy landowner from Yorkshire. Well, he was welcome to her – and her bloody family, who would in time, bleed the poor unsuspecting sod dry.

'It is the traveller girl, yes, and her name is Daisy. Actually we're having a bit of a do at the manor afterwards, Eleanor. Nothing too grand you understand. We'd be delighted if you'd come; most of the staff will be there,' he added, grinning mischievously, and watched her flinch with horror at the thought of it.

'I … I … couldn't possibly.… But thank you all the same. Sorry I can't stay and chat, but I'm expecting Bernard; he's coming up from Yorkshire this afternoon.'

'Bernard?' he enquired teasingly.

'Yes. Bernard Fotheringham, Sir Percy's son. We've been seeing quite a lot of each other of late.'

'You must fetch him over sometime, Eleanor. Daisy has family in Yorkshire; I'm sure they'd have lots to talk about.'

She squirmed awkwardly in her saddle. 'Quite, quite, I'm sure. Well, must dash, Toby, 'bye.'

You stuck-up bitch, Eleanor! Daisy's worth a hundred of you – no, a thousand, Tobias thought, watching her disappear over the rise. And I once thought we'd be friends; *once*! What a mistake that was.

He walked over to where Jet stood flicking his tail, sweeping away flies settling on his rump, and cropping at the short sweet grass he'd found. He patted the black sleek neck and Jet raised his head, whinnying softly. A lump came to his throat and with it, an overwhelming desire to see Daisy. Mounting his horse, he turned him for home.

It was two o'clock in the afternoon. Tobias made his way to where he would find Daisy and her father. Hostilities had finally ceased and he was an acceptable visitor at the family home. At first, Samboy had been mortified at the prospect of Daisy marrying him, but, with Lavinia's patience, and guiding wisdom, her husband eventually acknowledged that his daughter's happiness was more important than his own imagined honour. Tobias realized Samboy would never fully trust him – how could he? He was a gorgio, and not one of *them*. But, Samboy had reasoned in his own mind, Daisy had her mother's gorgio blood running through her veins, so it was only natural she'd be attracted to *them*.

The warm June sunshine had delivered hundreds of people on to the hill which was a riot of colour where the gypsies gathered.

Tobias's eyes moved with exactitude over the sea of heads. A mane of golden hair caught his eye, and he strode towards it, his heart quickening as he neared.

Observing her in her natural environment where she belonged, and at ease, he felt fearful and questioned whether she would be happy in his world. Then he recalled the condition she'd stipulated the day he'd asked her to marry him, 'Don't expect me to change', she'd said. He'd no doubt, watching her now, she'd meant every word.

She wore riding breeches with a neat white shirt, and strong riding boots. He gazed at her with pride as she leant down, picked up the heavy piebald horse's hoof and proceeded to clean it with a hoof pick. He saw the diamond ring she wore flashing brilliantly as her hands moved deftly about the horse.

He strolled over to where she was and casting a shadow across her, caused her to look up crossly, ready to protest. Her face lit up and coloured with excitement when she saw it was him.

'Oh, Tobias, how wonderful to see you. I didn't expect to see you until tomorrow What is it? Have you changed your mind?'

'Of course not, silly. I just had to see you, hold you. I couldn't wait another day. I hope you don't mind. I love you so very, very much.'

His eyes brimmed with tears of joy and when he blinked, they didn't fall, but settled like dew drops on his lashes. The joy in her own heart equalled his and, reaching up, she cupped his face in her hands, kissing him softly on the mouth. His arms encircled her slim body, drawing her closer to him and inhaling her familiar smell, his manhood stirred with pleasure.

'This won't sell any horses, lass. Come on, get a move on! Yer'll 'ave more than enough time for gawpin' into each other's *yoks* – er, sorry, I mean eyes,' Samboy added, correcting himself. He had to think before using gypsy lingo in the squire's presence, and he found it wearisome, like talking to a foreigner. But, he had to admit, he'd turned out to be a decent bloke – and not once did he doubt the man's genuine love for his daughter.

'I'm sorry, sir, just thought I'd call in to and see if … if … Daisy or you, required anything before the big day tomorrow.'

'No, thank you. But please, do you have to go? Why not stay and watch the sale?' Daisy grasped his hand tightly not wanting him to leave. Tomorrow seemed an eternity away.

'There is something I have to do now. So, I'll see you in church tomorrow morning, darling,' he said, dropping a light kiss on her lips. ''Bye, Sam, see you in the morning.'

'Aye, ta-ra, lad.'

*

Tobias walked through the throngs of people to where jumbles of gaily coloured gypsy wagons were parked. His eyes searched doggedly, as he weaved in and out between the wagons. A middle-aged gypsy riding bareback on a skittish skewbald, and leading another six horses, three on either side, trotted past, nearly swiping him off his feet.

'Watch it, mister!' He'd pulled the herd to a chaotic stop and eyed Tobias suspiciously.

'I don't think I was doing anything wrong,' Tobias said, defensively.

'Yer might tink dat, but dese 'orses are big brutes, and der loikes of you should stay out o' der way, if yer value yer life,' he said, in a thick Irish accent. 'Wot is it yer be lookin' fer about der place?'

Tobias wanted to laugh but refrained. 'I'm looking for a fortune-teller who goes by the name of Rose Marie – do you know where I might find her?'

'Dat oi do, she be over dere,' he said, pointing to a wagon tucked between two larger ones.

'You be der toff from der big 'ouse who be marryin' Latimer's girl?'

'Yes, I am,' he answered, with a puzzled expression. 'Why, do you know them?'

'Oi do, yis – an' oi have a word of advice fer yer, young fella.'

Whether or not Tobias wanted this advice, something told him he was going to get it.

'Don't be weddin' beneat' yer station dat's moi advice. C'mon my beauties.' The gypsy clicked his tongue and urged his horses into a trot leaving a stunned Tobias gaping open-mouthed at the retreating ensemble.

He strolled across the field to the fortune-teller's bow-top wagon. She was sitting on the bottom step smoking a clay pipe. She'd seen him long before he'd located her and had mused over what the Irish tinker might have said to him.

'Good day, madam.'

'Rose is me name. Save the madam stuff for those as needs it,' she said, the pipe still in her mouth.

'Rose it is then,' Tobias said, responding politely, duly chastised.

She rested her eyes on the handsome gorgio standing before her who had every tongue wagging at the fair. But my, he looks so much happier than the last time I saw him. Must be two years now, she calculated.

His eyes sought hers and she saw a sudden flicker of anxiety.

She got to her feet. 'Let's get on with the job in hand, young man. I'm aware yer in a hurry, what with getting married tomorrow.'

'How on earth do you know that?' he asked.

'You're the talk of the fair, young man, everybody knows!' she said, smiling.

He followed her into the hallowed sanctuary of the wagon. The china teacup appeared within seconds which he drained before handing back to her.

A silence settled upon them when she looked into the cup. The tea leaves gave rise to her psychic interpretation and Tobias watched intrigued as her dark expressive eyes looked up to meet his own warm gaze.

'You've chosen well. Others might think differently, but she's the one and you'll be happy together, but remember, love doesn't always follow a sensible path.'

She cast her eyes downward looking into the leaves again. After a long, silent pause, she smiled to herself, the deep lines etched in her face spread even deeper.

'*Three babbies I see, three fine bairns. Aye! And they're yours!*'

His heart pounded. It's as though I'm not here, he thought. Her preoccupation with what she saw transported her to another place, somewhere in the future. Without looking at him she put the cup aside and, reaching across, took his left hand in hers. She stroked her fingers across the palm of his hand. The peaceful silence suddenly crashed. An ill-omened, ghost-like presence filled the air between them. Rose Marie bristled and held on to his hand tightly as he tried to pull it away.

'Judging by the look on your face, it must be serious,' he said, with nervous laughter, but she didn't hear him.

'I see a stranger among us. Beware, he's up to no good. He's looking to harm you and those you love!'

Tobias tried to free his hand from hers, but the grip held fast.

'Shhh ... hush. A softer path is coming. Be patient. Yer can't go walking on green, peaceful plateaux forever, not without the pain in your heart. No one can.'

The gypsy's brow knotted worriedly and she continued, her eyes drawn upward by some invisible force. '*I see a fire blazing and rough seas, an' ... someone's coming. They bode evil. You will be tested – the both of you. Hold firm now....*'

Her voice tailed off and the words died on her lips. She'd seen two dead bodies, one in the remains of a fire, the other in a river-bed.

The fortune-teller chose not to tell him of the impending deaths, and releasing his hand, the spell was broken.

Tobias fished in his pocket unable to find the correct change. He dropped eight shillings on to the table in front of him and, apologizing, left hastily. The feelings present in the air were claustrophobic, threatening to overwhelm him.

The woman got up and followed him outside, but when she looked for him he'd disappeared.

If Tobias had thought gypsy Rose Marie was going to weave some special kind of magic for *him*, he'd led himself down an illusory path of make-believe.

Daisy saw him from a distance. She slapped the reins, spurring the glossy thoroughbred on at a faster trot.

'Tobias!' she called loudly, but he hadn't heard her. He was walking at high speed, his hands buried deep inside his trouser pockets. She was on top of him before he saw her.

'Didn't you hear me calling?' she asked.

'Sorry I—'

'What is it? Something's happened to you. Where have you been?'

'Nowhere, honestly, Daisy. I ... I just wanted to take in the fair, that's all.' He couldn't tell her where he'd been and certainly not what he'd been told by the fortune-teller. 'Please,' he said grabbing her hand, 'let's walk a while and sit somewhere quiet for a few minutes, can we? Look, over there,' he said, pointing to a patch of grass away from the wagons and people milling around.

'OK, just a few minutes though. Dad gave me explicit orders, Amber here,' she said, looking at the horse, 'is next on the list for sale.'

'A beautiful animal,' Tobias said, immediately attracted to the horse. He circled the chestnut mare, appreciating its perfect conformation. He tied it to a branch and lifting its leg, began inspecting its fetlock.

'Oi! What do you think you're doing?' she asked.

'Just checking that's all, making sure she hasn't been doctored,' he added, grinning, and let the inspected hoof fall to the ground.

Daisy pushed him playfully. He dropped to the ground laughing and, joining in his hilarity, she sat down beside him. They lay back on the grass shielding their eyes from the sun with one hand and holding hands with the other. Large puffs of white clouds scudded across the sky giving welcome respite from the blinding sun.

I hope the weather stays fine for tomorrow, Daisy thought, and, turning her head, looked at her future husband.

His eyes were closed but he felt hers upon him, a smile played about his mouth. 'Having second thoughts, Daisy?'

''Course not, silly, you?'

''Course not, silly you, too.'

They laughed, rolling over to face one another. He raised himself up on to one elbow, his face only inches from hers. A memory came flooding back when he'd first seen her two years ago – when he'd wanted to reach down and kiss her ... and now, here she was lying next to him, soon to be his wife. His blood stirred and, closing his eyes, he kissed her, feeling the beat of her heart in his own lips. When her arms encircled him drawing his body closer to her, he wondered if she was aware of the power she held over him, and he drew back from her. He opened his eyes and saw that her own were filled with bright tears.

'I love you so very much,' she whispered softly.

'I know, and I love you. We are going to be so happy, my darling, it's a new beginning for the three of us.'

Chapter Sixteen

Lydia looked at the clock on the mantelpiece, it was 5.00 a.m.
She viewed her surroundings. She'd been relegated to the dower house with a retinue of staff, hired by Eve Pettifer, no less! When did her son decide she was incapable of hiring and firing? When he'd decided to marry *that gypsy scum*! That's when! Her face became distorted with contempt.

She walked over to the mirror on the dressing-table, 'How nice for you both,' she said demurely to the reflection. Then her voice suddenly changed, to one of derision. 'Out of sight out of mind, eh?' she said, throwing her head back, laughing hysterically. 'Well, my little newly-weds, you may think you have me locked away here at the dower house, but I'll find a way.'

There was a knock on the door. 'Is everything all right, Mrs Flint? Do you need anything?' asked an unfamiliar voice.

'Yes, er, I mean no, no I don't ... thank you,' she added sweetly. So many bloody people about the place, it's no wonder I don't know any of their damned names! She glanced at the clock again, 5.30. They'll be married in five hours, 'Too late then, Tobias,' she said bitterly. 'You'll tie a knot with your tongue you won't undo with your teeth.'

A knock on the door, a short wait, then another knock. Eve entered.

'Hello, Lydia, I thought you might be awake so I've brought you a cup of tea,' she said, sitting down uninvited in the armchair next to her bed. 'It's chilly, Lydia, do you want a robe?'

'No, thank you,' she said, climbing back into bed.

'Beautiful morning,' Eve commented, looking out of the window. The sun was climbing into a clear blue sky throwing beams of sunlight through the trees surrounding the lovely dower house.

Eve loved the house. At first she'd been dubious about moving from the manor, but from the day she'd moved in, she'd felt at home here. And Mr Flint hadn't exaggerated the amount of staff she could employ either.

Lydia now had round-the-clock supervision, albeit from a distance for most of the time, so as not to cause distress, allowing her the illusion of independence.

The extra staff made Eve's life a piece of cake really, affording her freedom to come and go at will, as she would today. It was the wedding and she'd been invited. She was excited and had splashed out on a new outfit, and new hat and shoes. Frank would be attending, of course, and, much to her relief, without his wife. His wife had stated she'd rather die than be seen socializing with such riff-raff! Frank had confided to Eve. He was delighted – it meant he could have a good time.

She couldn't claim to have fallen in love with Frank with the passage of time, but they'd discovered a sexual satisfaction which had intensified after she had left the manor. He dropped in most days after his rounds, sometimes managing to stay over, under the pretext of a patient's impending death. It was at these times she recognized she could never live with him, or any other man for that matter. Men were far too invasive!

Lydia was watching Eve intently. She'd heard them, she and that bloody doctor, going at it like dogs on heat, night after night. Did they think everyone was deaf? And, she'll be going to the wedding today, I've no doubt.

She'd slipped into Eve's room one day unseen and inspected the new outfit she'd bought specially for the occasion. While there, she'd discovered her pills tucked away inside a drawer and returned surreptitiously one evening, swapping the tablets with similar sized pain-killers.

'No good can come from it,' she said waspishly, shaking her head.

'What?' Eve exclaimed. She looked at Lydia, the expression of disdain on her face made her cringe. 'No good can come of … what?'

'The marriage. That's what!' she said, looking grave and staring ahead blankly. 'You can't make a silk purse out of a pig's ear.'

Eve shuddered. Well, *you* should know, you wicked old cow, she thought. Thank goodness you won't be there to spoil it for the young couple.

Daisy stood at the bedroom window looking toward the paddock where the horses grazed. I'm going to miss this, she thought. She looked about the bedroom she'd known for most of her life and had shared with Ralph for the last two years since his birth.

He was sleeping peacefully and she tiptoed over to the cot. Her face softened with a smile looking at her son. His raven black curls were a startling contrast against the snow-white pillow. His complexion was creamy as buttermilk kissed with a blush of peach, and dark thick lashes rested above chubby healthy cheeks. She leaned over and dropped a gentle kiss on his forehead; his perfect cupid-bow mouth twitched into a smile.

It was six o'clock when she went downstairs where Lavinia had laid the table for breakfast. She was in her rightful place, Daisy thought. She was standing with the sunlight bursting through the kitchen window lighting her up, like some heroine from the last century. Lavinia wore a white, high-necked blouse with flounced sleeves, and a cameo brooch pinned to the front of the high ruff collar. Her outfit was swathed in a large apron, protecting her clothes for the wedding.

'Lavinia, you look beautiful!' exclaimed Daisy, 'but isn't it a bit early to get ready?'

'I want you to have time for yerself to get ready, so I thought if I got meself decked out first, I'd see to Ralph. Yer dad needs to get a move on,' she added, anxiously looking at the clock on the mantelpiece, 'He's not over keen on preening himself. Oh, Daisy, thank you for tellin' me I look nice,' she said, giving a twirl.

'I'm going to miss you so much, Lavinia.'

'Rubbish! We're five minutes drive from you, or a fifteen-minute ride – depending' how yer like to travel. Come here, lass.' Lavinia opened her arms and Daisy walked into them; enveloping her she hugged her tight. 'There now, lass, come on, no tears … please, not today.'

'I'm sorry, Lavinia,' she sniffed, 'I am happy … it's just that the manor is so big and' – Lavinia reached into her pocket and handed her a hand-kerchief – 'and … what if they don't like me?'

'C'mon, sit down, I'll mek us a cup o' tea and you can talk it through, eh?'

They hadn't heard Samboy come in. He stood in the doorway looking at the pair of them crying.

'Cryin'? It's yer wedding, lass, not a bloody funeral yer goin' to!'

'Aw, shut up, Sam!' Lavinia said casting him a warning glance. 'Let the bairn cry. You cried when we got married,' she reminded him sternly.

'Ooh, Lavinia, love, you do look lovely,' he said, noticing where her blouse was exposed. 'Don't she look grand, Daisy?'

'Yes, Dad, she looks lovely.'

Lavinia blushed as both pairs of eyes rested on her.

'Never mind me, get a move on, the pair of yers! Sam, mash that tea – Daisy, stay where you are.'

'Ganda, Ganma!' Ralph appeared in the doorway terminating Daisy's tears, all attention on him.

Samboy lifted him into the chair next to himself at the table. I'm gonna miss me grandson sorely, he thought. He'd never considered Roulson, the boy's real father; he himself had been father to the boy. Ralph accompanied him about the holding, watching him feed and groom the horses, mending fences. Ralph had been his constant companion since he could walk. There was a strong bond between them. He felt tears prick his eyes and quickly blinked them away.

'I'll still fetch Ralph to stay for one or two days a week, if that's OK with you both?' Daisy said noting the silence that had fallen across the table when her father looked at Ralph.

'That'll be champion,' Lavinia said and, walking behind her husband's chair, rested a hand on his shoulder. 'Won't it, Sam?'

'Aye, champion, lass. I'll save some of me jobs he likes helpin' with for when he comes. We'll 'ave a cushty time together, eh, son?'

Ralph giggled when his grandfather rubbed his head. Wriggling, he snuggled up closer to him.

I've been so fortunate, Daisy thought. Dad and Lavinia have been wonderful to me as well as devoting themselves to Ralph. When she left this happy home today, her way of life would change considerably, but, she told herself resolutely, I'll remain the same. Not harbouring any misconceptions of who she was or where she'd come from, she hoped, would pave the way for a peaceful existence at the manor. She hadn't met his mother. Tobias had tried to explain her mental state to her quite a while ago, and said she was to live in the dower house, along with Eve, and other staff, and that she need never worry about her. She was unsure as to what he meant by that. But, nevertheless, Daisy felt sorry for the poor woman, even though somewhat relieved that their paths wouldn't cross.

She had been introduced to Nellie a couple of weeks ago and had taken to her at once. Her no-nonsense attitude had been a comfort, reminding her of Lavinia.

The grandfather clock struck 7.30 a.m. Nellie was already up and in the kitchen busy preparing breakfast for Tobias. They'd arranged catering staff to come in to prepare the small reception as it was important to Tobias that Nellie attend the wedding.

'Morning, Nellie.'

'Mornin'. Won't be long and I'll fetch it through for you.'

'Not today, Nellie, thanks all the same, it'll be fine here. I hoped you'd join me – there's something I need to discuss with you.'

'Aye, well, pull up a chair.' She knew what he was doing. He didn't want her trailing after him. Her legs were giving her fair gip these days, particularly her knees.

He'd brought his young bride-to-be to meet her last week, giving her a tour of the manor. Nellie had to admit she didn't approve of him marrying beneath himself, especially into a gypsy family, but, on the other hand, the girl appeared quite ... genteel, Nellie supposed. A damn sight more genteel than that woman his father had wed! Nellie thought the lass seemed nice enough, and it was obvious to anyone they loved each other – so, God willing it'll work. Ah, well, here it comes, he wants shot of you. I'll make it easy for him.

'Too much of a liability, am I now? I know I can't move about as fast as I used to an' the stairs play havoc with me legs, but it's all right, I'm ready for off an' to make way for someone younger....'

Tobias was staggered. His mouth fell open and he was speechless for a few seconds.

'What? Leave here? Good grief, no! Nellie, nothing was further from my mind. Please,' he assured her, leaning over and taking hold of her gentle, worn hands.

'Well, I'd understand if you need someone younger—'

'Most certainly not!' he said sharply. 'What I had in mind was employing extra help for you, here in the kitchen,' he said, looking around at the huge domestic domain she'd run superbly for years. 'And, I'd hoped you wouldn't mind helping Daisy. Show her the ropes, and such like. This place is so much more than she's used to, as you can well imagine, quite daunting after living in a tiny cottage, or the ... gypsy wagon.'

'If that's what you want, I'll do it with pleasure.'

'And should the time arise, and you feel it's too much, Nellie, this will always be your home. You won't ever leave us, Nellie, will you? You've been like a mother to me.'

A lump caught in his throat and he was unable to utter another word.

Nellie's eye too filled with tears. 'I know,' came her choked reply.

Samboy held the car door open for Daisy. He'd never felt as proud as he did at that moment. A great many horse dealers and their families had come from the fair and stood outside the church to watch. After all, they'd said, it wasn't every day one of our own marries into gentry.

Daisy was striking. She wore the palest green satin dress with a sweetheart neckline and a full skirt which fell just below the knee. The bodice of the dress was embroidered with appliqué velvet flowers in the same shade of green, with a matching lace, short-sleeved bolero jacket. She carried a bunch of sweet peas and lilies of the valley tied up with a ribbon, freshly picked from her own garden an hour ago.

A group of scruffy-looking children stood by the lych-gate. Daisy recognized them immediately. They were the ones she'd caught burying the dead rabbit a couple of years ago.

'Hello,' she said to them smiling. 'How nice of you all to come. Did you walk?'

'No, we came on our 'orses – they're over there,' one said, pointing to where a pair of untidy skewbalds were fastened to a tree near the church wall.

'We made this fer yer this mornin', Daisy, an' wanted you to 'ave it.'

From behind their backs, the two older ones produced two daisy chains.

'Oh, thank you, you're so kind. They are just what I need, because I didn't have anything for my hair.'

Daisy carefully placed one chain around her neck, and the shorter one on top of her head. The children smiled with delight. She bent down and kissed each one on their grubby cheeks.

'C'mon, lass, you can't be too late, the lad will be waitin' fer yer,' Samboy said impatiently.

'All right, Dad. Now listen, my dad will bring some treats along for you tomorrow to the fair, won't you, Dad?'

'Aye, if you say so.'

''Bye,' she said to them and, hooking her arm through her father's, walked towards the church.

Tobias cringed as the tone-deaf organist blasted out her painful rendition of 'Ave Maria'. He turned and grinned at Frank, his best man, sitting beside him on the front pew. The organist continued to offend people's ears for the next ten minutes, then paused when someone whispered in her ear, 'The bride's here.'

Frank stood up and steered Tobias to the designated spot before the altar. The organist began belting out a tortured version of Mendelssohn's *Wedding March*, announcing the bride's arrival.

His mouth dried and his heart beat frantically in his chest.

She was down the aisle and by his side in seconds. The moment he laid eyes on her he feared he'd wake up and his perfect dream would end. He saw the daisy chain positioned on top of her golden hair, carried regally as a queen would a crown, another, strung around her neck rested on the gentle swell of her breasts peeping above her neckline. He smiled; only she could get away with daisy chains and still manage to look beautiful, he thought, smiling.

'I now pronounce you man and wife. You may now kiss the bride,' couldn't come quick enough for Tobias. The pompous vicar had displayed dreadful snobbery when he'd visited him about the marriage, and all he wanted to do now was vacate his church as soon as possible, before the dreadful organist struck up again.

But instead, somewhere from the back of the church, soothing music resonated, penetrating the entire building. Its haunting quality stilled the tongues and minds of everyone. Tobias saw surprise on the faces of the vicar and the organist, who pursed her lips petulantly. He smiled in gratitude for whoever it was had the good sense to arrange such a pleasant interlude.

By the font at the back of the church stood Donny Cockeye, playing the fiddle as confidently and expertly as any trained musician. The strains of 'Danny Boy' were accompanied by the travellers who had gathered outside, their fine voices reaching the ears of those inside who vacated their pews and inched closer, to hear him play.

'Isn't he amazing?' Daisy murmured.

'Nearly as amazing as you,' Tobias whispered, slipping his hand around her waist.

When Donny's playing reached a gentle trembling crescendo, applause of appreciation echoed round the church. Additional hand-clapping greeted the bride and groom when they walked out from the church into the bright June sunshine.

A sudden gust of cold wind whipped the posy of flowers from Daisy's hand transporting it unceremoniously on to a nearby grave. Laughing, she hurried over to retrieve it. Bending down, her face drained of colour when she saw the lichen-encrusted writing etched on the leaning gravestone, 'Here lies Adam's son'. Daisy gasped in disbelief. What can it mean? she thought fretfully. God, what have I done?

'Are you all right, my love?' Tobias had walked over to where she was crouched, 'You've turned quite pale. What is it, my darling?' He eased her to her feet and drew her close.

'Oh, it's nothing, honestly, I'm fine … Just got a bit cold inside the church, that's all. Come on, Husband, let's go and enjoy our wedding party,' she joked, attempting to shrug off the sense of foreboding taking root.

*

Meanwhile, across the Irish Sea stood a tall, dark man looking back over the water toward Westmorland and his beloved Appleby, with an aching heart. His black eyes glinted menacingly against the bright sunshine. He smiled to himself.

'I'm comin' for yer one day soon, Daisy,' Roulson vowed. His ominous words are conveyed over the ocean on a westerly wind.

Chapter Seventeen

Black clouds rolled in from the east throwing a blanket of darkness over the whole place. A strong wind got up and whistled through the trees surrounding the garden.

Large blobs of rain began to fall. The woman did not move, but turned her face skyward to stare at the gathering blackness of the approaching storm.

At the sound of her name being called in a shrill voice, she turned violently, her face black with anger. A woman walked towards her at an urgent pace.

'Mrs Flint, Mrs Flint, quick! A storm's coming. We must get you indoors.'

'Who the devil are you?' Lydia asked bitingly. She didn't recognize the stranger. So many new people about the place. Where's that Eve? Ah, yes, I remember now – at *my* son's wedding, that's where, she thought bitterly. Can't keep track of the flighty spinster nowadays.

'I'm Janet. You remember me. I'm on duty to look aft— to be with you,' she added, hastily correcting herself, 'And I'm under strict orders not to leave you alone. We could play dominoes, if you like.'

Huh! Who the devil does this patronizing cow think I am? Some bloody idiot to be told what they can and can't do? Well they can *all* go to hell, she thought, because that's where *that trollop* who's married my son will end up by the time I've finished!

'You've no idea what I like or don't like, neither do you bloody care!' Lydia spat, smiling spuriously.

The machinations for revenge having already taken root in her mind, the doors of madness flung wide open. Lydia stepped through them with glee.

Janet shuddered and averted her eyes, grateful to be here only for twenty-four hours' emergency cover, whilst the staff enjoyed the wedding party.

Miss Pettifer had said the staff would return shortly after the reception and she wouldn't be alone with Mrs Flint for long. Thank God! Janet thought, as they made their way across the lawn towards the house.

She glanced obliquely at the woman in her charge. The rain had flattened her wet hair to her head and the sinister expression on her face was enough to frighten anyone. As soon as she's changed into dry clothes I'll give her a sedative, Janet decided.

But Lydia knew the game well having played it many times, and it would be easier with this new nurse. She popped the sedative into her open mouth, duly lodged it under her tongue, then spat it out at the first convenience.

It was 11.00 p.m. before the house eventually fell silent.

She'd overheard them all downstairs, laughing in the kitchen, drinking the left-over champagne. And the more they laughed the angrier she grew.

'Not in my worst nightmare did I ever imagine such a thing would happen!' she said to the reflection in the dressing-table mirror, 'Turned out of the manor house to make way for ... for a bloody gypsy! It's unheard of!'

She went to the cabinet where Eve kept a supply of sherry and poured herself a large glass. That lot downstairs will never smell it on me, not after what they've consumed. Told to abstain whilst on medication. 'Not had a tablet for weeks,' she said out loud. 'And I feel better than I have done in months.'

Janet put her head round the door and peeked at her sleeping patient before retiring to her bed.

Lydia lay for a long while before slipping from her bed fully dressed. She looked in the mirror and daubing on some lipstick, smiled at herself in approval.

The clock in the hallway struck two.

She left through the back door. The rain lashed against her face. The wind had spiralled to gale force, making it difficult to walk, but less likely to be heard. She threaded her way through the trees before striking out into open grassland. From here she could see the manor rising above the trees. It was a slow arduous trek in the howling gale.

Lydia reached the shelter of the stable yard.

Before retiring, Dan had double checked the stables, securing doors, and anything that might take flight in the storm. He'd had a grand day, he thought, climbing into bed at midnight, and drifted into a deep, champagne-induced sleep.

The feed store was fastened tight. Lydia hurried to the workshop, returning with a crowbar. She smiled, grateful for the storm masking the din she created. She forced the door open, oblivious to her bloodstained hands cut to ribbons in the process.

Once inside, she secured the door and lit the candle she'd brought with her. Finding the bag of oats she emptied some into a bucket before smothering them in molasses.

Outside, the wind had changed direction and whistled loudly through the yard. There was a loud bang and she quickly retreated into the feed store and waited.

It wasn't long before Dan appeared wearing pyjamas. She hid behind the sacks of oats. The blood pounded through her body with excitement. Not now, she prayed, listening for him, not now!

Dan located the noise, a stray metal bucket crashing against the cobbled ground. He picked it up and set out to take it back to the feed store. On the way he shuddered against the cool wind, and, changing his mind, turned and went back home.

Lydia, agitated, waited another fifteen minutes before deciding the coast was clear.

She went to the stable and slowly and carefully opened the top half of the stable door. Jet heard someone approach and stood up at the sound of the door opening. He tossed his head nervously when Lydia's face lit up in a violent flash of lightning, turning night into day.

'Come on, boy,' she said softly, a patina of evil masking her smile. 'I've got something tasty for you.' Jet snorted pawing at the stone floor. He turned his head sideways, his eyes observing her with suspicion. She lifted the bucket over the door so he could smell the oats and molasses. He walked forward and, sniffing the contents, he whinnied appreciatively.

Her movements were slow and measured when entering the stable. She was under no illusion and realized this intelligent horse was regarding her warily. She walked over to a corner of the stable, placing the pail on the floor instead of the metal ring provided.

After a few moments and complete stillness, Jet turned his attention to the oats. Lydia quickly gathered up some straw in the opposite corner and waited. Jet paused to watch her for a moment then returned his attention to the contents of the bucket.

Lydia saw her chance. She reached into her pocket and, taking out a match, struck it and lit the straw.

Jet spun round immediately it ignited. Lydia made a dash for the open door but Jet lashed out with his hind feet before she reached it, kicking her to the ground.

Within seconds the stable was ablaze, the flames leapt up the wooden manger and into the hayrack.

Lydia lay helpless, unable to move. Her back was broken. She glimpsed the open door through which Whitby Jet escaped. Her insane laughter spewed forth – then the fire engulfed her.

Dan stirred and opened his eyes. He sat up in bed sniffing the air. Am I dreaming, he asked, or do I smell smoke? He jumped out of bed, put on his dressing-gown and went outside. His jaw dropped on seeing the leaping flames and he ran swiftly to the stables.

Jet's stable door was wide open. He hurried to the house and hammered on the door.

'Fire! Fire!' he yelled. Within seconds lights went on and people scurried from their beds and out of the front door.

The first person to appear was Frank Parks. Eve had stayed the night at the manor at Tobias's suggestion, and Frank, deciding to take advantage of the situation, spent the night there too.

'What the devil's happened? I'll phone the fire brigade immediately,' Frank spluttered, taking charge of the situation.

'Quick! An' I'll get the other 'orses safe an' put 'em in't field.' Dan said, wondering at the same time, what the 'ell's the doctor doin' 'ere?

'Anyone missing?' Frank asked Eve. She'd appeared at his side looking aghast. He'd made the emergency call ten minutes ago and could hear the fire-engine sounding in the distance.

'No, I ... I don't think so. Why would there be?'

'Well, you'd better check. And get over to the dower house fast! Make sure everyone is all right there.'

Eve agreed and taking a car from the garage arrived at the dower house in minutes. Everyone was fast asleep when she let herself in through the front door. A door slammed shut somewhere downstairs as she entered. She walked through to the kitchen to see the back door was unlocked and the floor wet with rain and leaves, blown in from the storm.

She raced upstairs and, knocking gently before opening the door, she walked into Lydia's bedroom. 'Oh no! Please! Lydia!' she exclaimed, finding it empty. 'You haven't!'

She sped from Lydia's room and woke both the nurses meant to be on round-the-clock duty. She demanded Mrs Flint's whereabouts. Both were embarrassed at having misplaced their patient whom they were highly paid to look after.

'Well, which of you saw her last?' Eve demanded, looking from one to the other.

'Me, I did,' Janet admitted meekly. 'She seemed all right, to me. I gave her a sleeping pill and then when I went back in to check on her, she was fast asleep, and I assumed she was fine.'

'Fine? Fine, you say? She most certainly was not fine! That's why you are both employed to help look after her! Bah! Anyway, pack your cases, the pair of you, and leave at first light. Your wages will be forwarded in due course.'

'She's not there! Lydia's gone! Oh, Frank, what do we do now?' The fire-engine had arrived and the fire was under control. He put his arm about her shoulders and steered her indoors.

'The police will be here shortly. I'm sure they'll find her. You know what she's like, Eve, taking off in the middle of the night roaming the grounds.'

'I've got a really bad feeling this time though, Frank.'

Frank looked at Eve, anxiety etched across her face. He'd got a bad feeling for himself as well this time. The staff had seen them emerge half-dressed from the same bedroom. If my wife hears of this I'll have hell to pay, he thought. She won't leave me. Oh no, that would be too easy; she'll have me pay through the bloody nose with my cheque book instead – demand a new three-piece suite, or some fancy, expensive gadget for the kitchen which is all the rage and all the best people have. Still, it was worth it, he supposed. Eve was damn good company in bed, never tiring of the adventurous sex games he liked to play.

'Shall I contact the hotel where Tobias and Daisy are staying?' she asked Frank.

'Good grief, no! There's nothing he can do from up there in Edinburgh – the man's on his honeymoon. All we need to do is find his bloody mother.'

'Frank! Please, don't swear about it.'

'You're beginning to sound like my wife,' Frank snapped, regretting it the moment he'd said it. 'Oh, Eve, I'm sorry, I—'

'Well, don't be sorry, Frank! You can bet your life it won't happen again!' she exploded, and stormed off leaving the bewildered doctor scratching his head.

The next morning the search for Lydia Flint was called off when charred remains of a body were discovered in the burned-out stable. Jet was found unharmed two miles away in a neighbouring field, settled happily alongside a mare in season, that he'd no intention of leaving, the farmer informed Dan.

DS Keen couldn't help a feeling of *déjà vu* when looking at the charred remains of the body on the stable floor. He'd spoken to the doctor, nurses, and the woman supposed to be in charge, a Miss Pettifer. The doctor had insisted on contacting Mr Flint himself, didn't want some stranger informing him of his mother's possible demise, he'd said.

Keen still entertained doubts as to the identity of the woman until forensic came back with evidence. He recalled the last time he was here, must be two years ago now. The stable lad related that Mrs Flint had come rushing from the house and, for no apparent reason, had slapped Latimer's lady friend across the face. Yes, the woman wasn't right in the head then. He'd heard gossip that the squire wouldn't have his mother put away so he'd hired a team of helpers to care for her – not that it'd done a fat lot of good. Ah well, the young couple will have a better chance making their marriage work if it is you lying there, he thought furtively, eyeing the burnt corpse.

Tobias sat on the side of the bed looking down at his wife sleeping peacefully. I'm the happiest man on earth this morning, he thought, smiling at her. Their night of love-making had been wonderful. She'd responded with innocent enthusiasm, delighting in the union of their bodies which carried them to sexual heights and beyond. She stirred, pushing the silk sheet from her. She wore a fine white cotton nightdress with skimpy straps. The front was cut low, exposing the tops of her milky white breasts. She opened her eyes and smiled, and he slipped back between the sheets drawing her close. He felt her long silky hair against his bare chest and ran his hands along her supple body. She writhed with pleasure at his touch; their bodies were on fire with desire for one another.

'Make love to me again, please,' she murmured softly in his ear.

'The pleasure's all mine, darling.'

'I don't ... think ... so.... Ah ... wonderful....'

It was an hour later when the hotel manager asked Tobias, would he mind coming to his office? There was an urgent phone call from a Dr Parks.

'I'm sorry, sir, is it bad news?' the hotel manager asked Tobias whose face had drained of all colour when he came out of the office.

'Er, yes. I'm sorry, do you know when the next train to Appleby is, please?'

'I'll find out for you, sir.' The manager went into his office and returned in seconds brandishing a timetable. 'Tomorrow morning, ten o'clock.'

'Thank you, I'm sorry to say we will have to leave, emergency at home.'

'I will have your tickets here at reception waiting for you in the morning.'

'Thank you, that's most kind.'

He could hear Daisy singing in the bathroom when he went back to the room. He loosened his tie and the top button of his shirt. He couldn't quite make out what she was singing, something of Mario Lanza's. he tried to concentrate on the words but his mind was in turmoil and all he could think was, *it's my fault*.

The singing stopped abruptly. Daisy stood in the bathroom doorway looking at him for a few seconds, shocked at the transformation that had taken place in a matter of minutes.

She rushed over and knelt beside him. 'What is it? Tobias, what's happened? Please, say something, darling!'

He shook his head numbly. She took both his hands in hers and held them to her breast.

'What did Dr Parks want to talk to you about, Tobias ... Tobias?'

He felt a prickling of unshed tears gather behind his lids. 'The ... they believe my mother might have died ... in a fire. They're n ... not sure ... yet if it's her body ... It doesn't sound like me saying this, Daisy. It can't be true, surely! We have to return, there's a train back in the morning. I'm so sorry.'

'Oh, my darling, how dreadful for you. Yes, we must go home immediately.' She cradled him in her arms, rocking him back and forth, his silent tears wetting her breasts. She experienced pangs of guilt at her surprise at his distress, knowing he held no fondness for his mother. But she was his mother, Daisy told herself, he's bound to have some sort of love for her. It may be different, but, nevertheless, he loved her – and she him, in her own crazy way.

Tobias hardly said a word on the journey home but they both managed to laugh when he told her about Whitby Jet busily servicing the farmer's mare, free of charge.

*

Tobias looked down at the coffin that held his mother's remains. He dropped a handful of soil on to it before stepping back to allow others to follow suit.

The small group of mourners, mostly staff, stood a respectful distance away from the family. Eve stood alongside them, looking quite out of place. She was elegantly attired in a black calf-length coat and a chic box hat with a short veil concealing her eyes.

Not a tear in sight, Tobias thought sadly, glancing at the apathetic expressions on their faces. She'd exercised her position of power over them callously, spiteful to every one of them to the bitter end; yet, they'd remained loyal – not to Mother, but to my father and me.

Daisy had been talking to Eve, but now she walked over to where her husband stood and hooked her arm through his. Tobias thought she looked magnificent dressed in black. It enhanced everything about her; her skin appeared paler, her hair more golden, and her eyes greener. He patted her hand and smiled at her. Everything's going to be fine – just fine.

Chapter Eighteen

Two years later.

The storm had abated when the fishing boat dropped anchor in
Port Logan Bay.

Both men were relieved to see the Mull of Galloway come into view.
A force five gale had accompanied them for most of the journey across
the Irish Sea. The small vessel was tossed about relentlessly in the roaring
waters, causing the skipper to consider turning back. But when he'd
suggested this to the stranger aboard, he was furious and demanded they
continue. He'd been paid handsomely for bringing the man over the
rough sea to Scotland. But all the same there was something suspicious
about him and he wouldn't be sorry to see the back of him.

The fisherman lowered the painter into the water and rowed his
passenger ashore.

The attractive port was deserted. A flat-bed lorry was parked close to
the jetty. A man climbed out and waved to them.

Roulson Adams walked up to where his brother waited and jumped
into the lorry. His dark eyes scanned the immediate area, 'Anybody seen
you hangin' about?' he asked.

'No, yer'll be safe enough round 'ere, our lad. Come on, let's get yer
back to see Mam and Dad. It's been a bloody long time.'

'Aye, and don't I know it.'

'We've found a cushty stoppin' place, our lad. It's only five miles from
Appleby, so's our dad can sell his 'orses. It's as quiet as a graveyard,
Roulson. Some deserted farm buildings, an' there's water laid on!'

Roulson nodded and grinned, wishing he'd put a sock in it. He'd
hardly spoken to anyone since he'd left and listening to his brother prat-
tling on made his blood boil. But, oh, it was good to be back on home
ground, he thought, detaching his mind from the inane chatter.

'Are yer tired?' his brother asked looking at him.

Roulson closed his eyes and rested his head against the window not bothering to reply. A welcome silence ensued, allowing his resentful thoughts to surface. Resentment toward *her, Daisy Latimer*! It had eaten away at him for four long years. And now, his mother was ill, insisting on his return. His dad had got a message to him saying she'd get better if only he'd come home. He didn't mention he was coming back anyway.

He had got unfinished business – and a son.

'Mummy, Mummy!' Ralph called excitedly, racing across the lawn in bare feet as fast as his legs would carry him. His shiny black curls bobbed about his head in an unruly fashion. In one hand dangled a worm, in the other, a handful of pansy heads.

'Oh, thank you.' Daisy smiled at her son as he pushed the flower heads into her hand. 'And what a large worm you've got there. Give it to Mummy.'

'No!' Ralph said, snatching his hand away and holding it behind his back. 'That's for Daddy to fish with,' he said proudly.

'All right, sweetheart, let's go and find him.'

'Carry Ralph!' the boy whined, suddenly tired.

Daisy bent down awkwardly and put on his shoes. She stood up placing her hand into the small of her back, massaging the ache. The baby wasn't due until September, and at six months, she was already as big as she was full term with Ralph.

Tobias, her father, Lavinia, and the staff were delighted at the prospect of another child running about the place. They adored Ralph, especially Eve, who had stayed on to help with the running of the house. But Ralph's favourite person on the entire estate was Dan. Dan led him out on the small Shetland pony Samboy had bought him for his second birthday.

They found Tobias in his study going over some papers.

'Daddy, look!' Ralph proudly offered the dead worm to his father.

'Thank you, Ralph.' Tobias ruffled the boy's hair and placed the worm on top of the mantelshelf. He dropped a kiss on Daisy's cheek, 'Are you all right, you look tired?'

'I am tired. Would you mind finding Eve and ask her to see to Ralph, please? I'll go and have a lie down.'

'Good idea. Come on, young man, let's go find Eve. I'm going over to the fair, darling – thought I'd take a look at the horses, see what's on offer. Maybe have a word with your father and Lavinia.'

'Good idea. Tell them I'll drive over to see them next week when the fair's over and they're back at the cottage, will you?'

She had learned to drive last year and also taught Lavinia. The cars afforded them greater freedom, the distance between their homes covered in minutes.

Daisy sat watching the two most important people in the world to her, walk through the open French windows into the rose garden. Never in her wildest dreams did she believe she'd know such happiness. He'd astounded the town in marrying the golden-haired gypsy girl two summers ago, and she the travelling community by marrying gentry. She continued to watch them walk away, Ralph's short legs running to keep up with his father's slow walk. The boy was looking up at Tobias. He laughed out loud at something Ralph said and a lump caught in her throat. He was a wonderful husband and father, accepting Ralph as his own.

She settled back into the large comfortable leather chair and sighed contentedly. A soft breeze drifted in through the open windows, I'll just rest here for a while then go to bed she said to herself and, closing her eyes, drifted into a deep sleep.

She woke fretfully and looked at her wristwatch – she had slept for over an hour.

'How are yer, Daisy?'

She froze at the sound of his voice. Fear ran through her veins. She spun round. Sitting in her husband's high-backed leather chair at the other side of the desk, glaring at her with black eyes under a cloud of black hair, was Roulson Adams. Her heart faltered and her hands shot up to her mouth to stop herself screaming.

'Well? Aren't yer goin' to say hello to an old friend?' His voice was low and full of venom. 'Or is it, out of sight out of mind. Eh?'

'How ... how d ... did you get in?' she stammered, finding her voice. She couldn't move or think – only stare.

'Easy,' Roulson answered sarcastically, nodding to the open windows. 'Daisy ... you should be more careful – yer never know who's hangin' around nowadays.'

'Well you can get out or I'll scream!' she blared, overcome with a moment of bravery, 'There are ... are people ... staff about the place, and....and my husband will be back any minute.' In her mind's eye she tried to calculate who would be around, but, more to the point, who would hear her should she scream?

'Oh no he won't. Now don't lie, Daisy, it doesn't suit you. He's at the 'orse fair. I've seen 'im – right 'appy 'e looks too. *So shut yer gob if yer know what's good fer yer!*' He smiled to himself, taking pleasure in the power he held over this woman who'd turned his head then ditched him. Now, here she was trembling with fear in his presence.

'Doin' all right fer yerself, eh?' he said, taking in the expensive furniture and ornaments that adorned the room. He looked out over the grassy lawns and to the ancient trees that surrounded the beautiful house. 'I noticed yer'd gone all la-di-dah like.'

'Don't talk nonsense!'

'Ah, that's what I mean. Yer wouldn't 'ave talked like that afore. *Don't talk nonsense*,' he mimicked.

'Well, what is it you want, money?'

'I've seen 'im, Daisy.'

'Seen who?'

'Our son. That's who, *my* son!'

'What on earth are you talking about?'

''E's mine, Daisy. 'E mebbe sounds like you, but 'e's my bairn, my son. I'll never be dead as long as 'e lives. But that's not mine,' he said, looking down at her swollen abdomen.

'*You … you miserable creature!*' she hissed, '*Your son? You'd sire nothing but pigs!*' Daisy placed her hands protectively over her stomach.

'*Shut your mouth!*' he snarled. Hatred twisted in his gut and he moved to where she sat, waving a clenched fist in her face.

'Don't you threaten me!' she countered, rising to her feet. 'I'll go to the police and have you arrested – just like that!' She snapped her fingers loudly in front of his fist.

He lowered his fist his face mere inches from hers. 'Yer sounds just like a friggin' gorgio now, Daisy. My, my how you've changed.'

'It's a pity you haven't changed! 'Cos you're still the ignorant pig you were all those years ago! Now get out!'

There was a rapid knocking at the door before the handle was tried – It was locked. He'd turned the key in the door when he'd sneaked in.

'Mrs Flint? Are you in there? Are you all right? I thought I heard shouting.' The handle rattled as Nellie tried again to open the door.

Roulson clamped his hand over Daisy's mouth, 'One word from you and the kid in yer belly will be out afore its time!' he whispered, cruelly.

'I'm all right Nellie. Just had a sleep. I'll be out soon … I'd love a cup of tea, please.'

Nellie frowned, that's not like her she thought, wanting a cup o' tea in the study. Still, there's no accounting for pregnancy, hormones all to bloomin' pot! Raising her eyebrows she made her way back to the kitchen.

'She'll be back in a few minutes. You'd better go, and quick. If it's money you want, you can have it, but don't ever come back here, or I promise, I'll 'ave the muskras on to you!' She said, lapsing into her native tongue, reminding him she was no weak gorgio to be threatened by the likes of him.

'Some'ow, I don't think yer'll do that, Daisy. After all, you didn't tell them where I was before, did yer? And there's that son o' mine. Yer wouldn't want owt awful to 'appen to 'im now, would yer?'

He'd found her Achilles heel.

'Please, please don't hurt … my … son, Roulson, I beg of you … please,' she pleaded.

'Ah, yes, that's right, beg. I'm not sure what I want from you yet, but when I decide, I'll let yer know.' He was playing with her fear. 'In the meantime,' he said, placing the flat of his hand across her mouth, 'keep that shut.'

He slipped out through the open doors and sloped away across the lawn.

Daisy sat stock still listening to her own heavy breathing. Thoughts raced round in her head producing a tangled web of fear and disbelief. Should I tell Tobias, Father, or the police, she wondered? She stood up to unlock the door for Nellie and the room began to spin. She sat back down again quickly. I must relax for my baby's sake. Tears sprang to her eyes at the thought of her unborn child, and Ralph. Well, if it's money he wants, he can have it. With the money left me by my mother and grand-parents, and Tobias's generous allowance, I've at least £2,000 in my account. Yes, that should do it. I'll get the money out of the bank tomorrow, keep it safely hidden until I see him again, then he'll be on his way. So I shan't tell anyone about him coming here. Why worry Tobias or my father? He'll be gone with the rest of the travellers by the end of the week. Now, I must pull myself together before Tobias comes home.

In the back of Daisy's mind, lurked the ever-present fear of his return.

Chapter Nineteen

Daisy looked at the calendar on the bureau, it read 1 July, exactly twenty-one days since Roulson's unwelcome intrusion into her peaceful life.

All the gypsies had left Appleby more than a week ago, her father had informed her. Roulson hadn't returned. She reasoned that fear of recognition and capture prevented him doing so.

Tobias eyed his wife standing next to the bureau. He felt something was troubling her, unless it was, as Nellie said, the heat and pregnancy taking their toll. But it was more than that, she looked solemn and preoccupied. God, she's lovely, he thought, staring at her. Head held high, straight back, regal and beautiful. Pregnancy enhanced her loveliness.

'You OK, Daisy?' he asked, getting up from behind his desk. He walked over to where she stood and wrapped his arms around her.

'What? Yes, just thinking, that's all. It's nothing.' She lifted her face and Tobias kissed her lips. The unshed tears sitting in her eyes hadn't escaped him and he promised himself a quiet word with Frank tomorrow when he called.

A car pulled up on the gravel and Tobias released her from his embrace.

'That'll be Lavinia.' Daisy's face lit up and, hurrying from the room, she paused in the doorway, 'Will you join us?' she asked, glancing back at him already knowing his answer.

'No, I'll leave you ladies to it. Give her my love.'

The two women embraced then Daisy led Lavinia along the hallway and into the drawing-room. It was an elegant room with floor-to-ceiling windows draped in heavy chintz curtains piped in gold. A grand piano sat at one end of the large room. At the other, several easy chairs in the same chintz and two comfortable sofas were situated before an enormous white marble fireplace where the grate was already laid ready to put a match to.

'Eeh it's a grand room this, Daisy,' Lavinia said, her eyes darting from one end of the room to the other.

Lavinia said the same thing every time she visited, which was at least once a week, sometimes twice now that Daisy found it impossible to fit behind the steering wheel of a car.

'That's why we come in here,' Daisy said, guiding her to a chair, 'because it's your favourite room. Now, sit down and tell me all your news before Ralph knows you're here and devours you.'

Lavinia eyed Daisy thoughtfully. The lass looked tired and there was something else about her, her thoughts were elsewhere.

Lavinia spoke calmly, conveying her thoughts. 'What's botherin' yer, lass? Summat's wrong; d'yer want to tell me about it?'

'Wrong? I don't know what you mean?' Daisy replied shakily with a hollow laugh.

'Yer worried about summat. It's not just me, love, yer dad's noticed too, and he's fretting.'

'Well, you can tell him to stop it. There's nothing the matter with me. It … it's the pregnancy, and…and the heat gets me down. Honestly, I'm fine, please, let Dad know I'm OK, will you? I don't want him worrying about me. Oh, look,' she said, pointing excitedly to the window. 'Here's Ralph and Eve.'

Daisy's welfare was instantly shelved when Ralph spotted his grand-mother through the drawing-room window.

The summer heatwave broke violently with the onslaught of a heavy storm.

Roulson secured the framework of the bender tent he'd erected with hazel branches from a nearby tree before jacketing it with a tarpaulin.

His family had departed south immediately after the fair, leaving behind a horse and cart for his use. They'd begged him to go south with them, pleading he'd be conspicuous travelling alone, they'd warned. But he was adamant in seeing to some, *unfinished business*, he'd called it. He was beyond warning.

The horse whinnied fretfully when the thunder crashed loudly directly overhead followed by forks of lightning. Roulson crawled reluctantly from the tent into the raging storm and walked over to where the piebald was tethered. He spoke softly to the terrified animal and led him into a derelict building, 'Come on now … steady my old boy, there … there….'

Back under cover he divested himself of his wet clothes and wrapped a horse rug around his damp body. God, I'm fed up with hangin' around 'ere'. I've waited long enough! There was a cattle market tomorrow at Penrith, an' *Mister fancy pants* will be there as usual, according to that farm worker I was talkin' with. Aye, I was lucky there, 'e was a bit loose with 'is tongue.

He stared into the darkness rolling a cigarette, his eyes narrowing vindictively. She offered me money, so I'll 'ave that too. A plan began to form, and a sardonic smile spread across his face as the scene played itself out in his warped mind.

The storm abated in the early hours, but the adrenalin continued coursing through Roulson's veins, robbing him of sleep.

He reached the manor at four o'clock in the morning, walking the last half-mile on foot. He left his horse covertly tethered in a small copse and made his way to a shed in the orchard where he'd hidden before, and settled down on a dilapidated armchair to eat the bread and cheese he'd brought. The front of the manor house was visible from where he sat, watching and waiting. It was 7.30 when the curtains were drawn back in two first-floor windows. He paused in his eating. The food stuck in his craw, causing acid to rise when the morning sun caught the reflection of her golden hair. He could see her outline but not the expression on her face. But he could guess. She'd feel safe now, believing him to have left, smiling at *him* in adoration with those green laughing eyes, and her son, *my son*, would be calling *him, father*.

He'd watched his son playing in the garden. Ralph was his name. He knew because he'd heard her call him. Well, at least she got the R right, he thought. But when 'e's with 'is proper family an' away from these gorgios, he'll be known as young Roulson. Aye, we'll be a proper family, my mam an' dad will be right glad to 'ave their grandson with 'em on the road. Roulson's daydreaming was interrupted by the sound of tyres on gravel. Tobias was pulling away down the drive; Daisy and Ralph stood in the doorway waving until he'd disappeared from view.

Roulson kept low behind the beech hedge running alongside the house. He could see into the study window where he'd found her asleep the last time, but she wasn't there. He edged his way unseen to the front of the house and, looking through the window, saw her resting in an armchair. Her eyes were closed and her hands rested on her protruding abdomen.

He rapped on the window with a pebble.

Daisy sat up quickly. The blood drained from her face when she looked to the window and saw Roulson standing there. He put a warning finger to his lips.

She walked across to the window.

'What do you want of me?'

'I want money. You asked if I wanted money, well I do. I want to get away – now open this bloody window an' give me the money an' I'll scarper.'

Daisy opened it reluctantly. He stepped through, pushing past her and into the drawing-room.

'Wait here,' she said, drawing back from him. 'I'll go and get the money, but I have to lock the door in case someone comes in.'

He reached the door before her. 'No funny business, Daisy. Don't forget, I can do a lot of harm to you and yer family before the muskras catch me.'

'No, there won't be any funny business. Just don't come back here ever again. And if you do, I shan't hesitate in telling the muskras, regardless of the consequences.'

'I won't be back. That's somethin' yer can bet yer life on, or yer son's,' he added smirking.

She left the room and turned the key in the lock before going to her bedroom where the money was safely hidden in a suitcase.

'Are you all right, Daisy?'

Eve Pettifer was in the hallway. Daisy had walked straight past her without seeing her.

She stopped and spun round, her face pale and anxious. 'What? Sorry, Eve, I didn't see you there.'

'Sure you're OK? You look concerned about something; can I help?'

'No! I'm all right, honestly. Where's Ralph?'

'He's in the kitchen with Nellie, making fairy cakes,' Eve said, smiling. 'I'm going to take him out for some fresh air soon.'

'Where will you take him?'

'To the dower house, where I always take him. We'll feed the birds and the cat … Daisy, are you sure you're all right, my dear? You seem, upset.'

'I'm fine, thank you. I'll see you with Ralph at lunchtime.'

Daisy swept down the hallway. Eve watched her hover outside the drawing-room door until she'd passed from view. She heard the key turn in the lock and wondered what on earth could be wrong. It can't be too serious, she speculated, or Mr Flint wouldn't have gone away for the day.

Eve entered the kitchen where Ralph, covered in flour, was licking a wooden spoon smeared with butter icing. Nellie smiled guiltily and, grabbing a damp cloth, wiped his face.

'Petty!' Ralph yelled with delight.

'Sorry he's a mess, Miss Pettifer, I couldn't keep 'im out of it.'

'Don't worry, Nellie, he'll be dirtier still by the time we've fed the birds and cats. Come on, young man.'

Ralph clambered down from the chair and, taking hold of Eve's hand, they made their way to the dower house. She loved this walk with Ralph, which they did most days. It took about fifteen minutes. Ralph was an inquisitive child. He chattered about anything and everything, asking questions ranging from why are there clouds in the sky, to, can I have a deer to ride like Santa Claus?

As Ralph toddled across the lawn, Roulson watched him. Daisy had her back to the window, unaware of him watching her son and, when his eyes lit up, she assumed it was at the £2,000 she'd just handed him.

'They're all used notes and can't be traced.'

'Very generous of yer, I'm sure.' He stuffed the money inside his shirt and buttoned it up.

'No, it's not generous of me. I want rid of you. *I despise you*!' she said vehemently.

'Everybody despises me, Daisy, that's why being me is exciting! Ah, but there was a time, Daisy, when—'

'Leave! Now!' she yelled, not wanting to hear anything from the past. That's what he was, the past and that's where he was going to stay!

'I'm going. Tara, Daisy.'

She watched him slope across the lawn through tears of rage burning her eyes. She had no fear of him now. Oh no, she felt nothing but pure hatred for him.

The sun was at its zenith. Eve secured Ralph's sunhat.

'We'll take the short cut by the wood, Ralph? Are you hungry?'

Ralph nodded and his sunhat fell forward covering his eyes. Eve laughed, and he kept on repeating the action until she stopped.

'Come on, young man, Mummy will be waiting for us,' she said seriously and, taking his hand in hers, they set off.

Roulson heard their laughter and chattering from where he'd hidden behind the wide trunk of a tree as they approached.

He waited until they passed by, then like a cheetah stalking its prey, he crept up behind them.

Eve heard something and turned round quickly. The thick wooden club came down heavily on the side of her head, felling her instantly.

Ralph stood very still, staring with disbelief at his beloved Petty lying on the ground. His bottom lip trembled and his eyes filled with tears. 'Petty! Petty! Get up ... please....'

'Hello, son. I've come to tek yer with me. I'm yer dad.'

'Noo! Mummy! Noo! Arrgh!'

Roulson grabbed the screaming child and tucked him under his arm and ran. The boy continued to scream.

'Shurrup! You'll get a bloody good hiding if you don't be quiet!'

He was instantly silenced by the stranger's cruel words, and through tear-drenched eyes, looked on as the safe, familiar surroundings gave way to unknown terrain.

Daisy looked at the clock and frowned, it was one o'clock. It's not like Eve to be late, she thought, and went out to the stables to find Dan.

'Dan, would you please go and find Miss Pettifer, I think she must have lost track of time; lunch is ready.'

Dan set off for the dower house taking the route favoured by Eve and her young charge. He was walking alongside the wood when he came across her. She staggered towards him with blood pouring from her face.

'Dan! Quick! Someone's taken Ralph. He hit me with something, and I ... I don't know what happened ... Help me, Ralph....' Her voice trailed off as she collapsed in his arms. He was a strong man and gathering her up in his arms, headed back to the manor.

Daisy saw them approach and ran outside.

'Where's—? Oh, no, where's Ralph?' Her eyes searched Dan's then she looked at Eve. Her eyes opened slightly.

'Daisy, Daisy, quick get some help. Now. Help. Some man, a gypsy, he's ... he's taken Ralph. Hurry. So ... so ... sorry....' she murmured, before passing out.

'Quick! Take her inside and get the doctor. What time is it?'

'One forty-five.'

'Right. Call the police after you've rung the doctor, Dan, tell them Roulson Adams is in the area and he's taken my son. I'm driving to Penrith to fetch Tobias.'

The discomfort of being wedged behind the steering wheel became apparent when she pulled into the auction mart and couldn't get out of the car.

She wound the window down and shouted for help from a passing farmer on his way to the sale. 'Excuse me, but can you go and find my husband, please? It's urgent,' she said holding her stomach. 'His name's Tobias Flint, he's selling cattle.'

The farmer took one look at her swollen abdomen. 'Right away; madam. I know the squire, I've bought gimmers from 'im afore.'

'Good. Now hurry please … please, now!' she pleaded.

Tobias appeared in a matter of minutes. He opened the car door and eased her out. 'What's the matter?' he asked anxiously, 'is the baby on the way?'

The words tumbled from her mouth as she related what had happened.

When she paused to take a breath, he demanded, 'Why didn't you tell me he came to our house? A bloody murderer! And you said nothing!' His jaw tightened. 'Let's get going – we must find Ralph.'

He helped Daisy into the passenger side of the car and a cold chill gripped him when he saw the dark shadows beneath her eyes, and a new gauntness in her tired face. Oh my God, thought Tobias, she could lose the baby.

'Everything will be all right, Daisy, we'll find him, I promise you,' he said, patting her hand.

But it was too late, his words had cut through her like a knife. The guilt she felt was beyond comprehension.

'Just drive,' was all she could manage to say. Her pulse was beating rapidly and, resting her hands on her abdomen, she prayed a silent prayer for both her children's safety.

She hadn't slept all night. The police had questioned everyone, including herself and Eve, who, thankfully, had recovered and was able to answer questions, giving a description of the man. She was in no doubt the abductor was Roulson. She reported all the information she had on him to DS Keen, no longer fearing the consequences of aiding and abetting. If she had to go to prison to save her son, it was a small price to pay.

The police search party scoured the estate and surrounding area to no avail, apart from finding Ralph's sunhat. Daisy held on to it willing any minute trace of her son left on it, be it a bead of sweat or a microscopic hair, to be brave. Mummy was coming to rescue him.

She sat in an armchair in the drawing-room. A cloak of silence wrapped around her as she stared through the window into the distance. The voices of others in the room muted, allowing her thoughts to break through. Please, don't hurt him, Roulson. I love him so much. Please, if you have a shred of decency left in you, give me our son back.

*

Ralph stopped crying and Roulson handed him a slice of dry bread with a lump of cheese and a cup of water. The boy refused it, shaking his head. He hadn't spoken a word since they'd arrived back at the camp.

'Eat,' Roulson yelled, 'and do as yer father tells yer!'

Ralph jumped at the harshness, picked up the bread and nibbled it before drinking the water. He looked at his dirty hands and rubbed them on his grubby shorts trying to clean them.

Queer bloody kid, Roulson thought. She'd 'ave 'im a right nancy boy. I reckon I got here just in time by the looks of it. 'A bit o' muck won't 'arm yer. Get that scran down, then we're gonna go south so's yer can meet yer proper granny and granddad.'

The boy's head bowed low and huge teardrops plopped from his eyes on to his dirty knees.

'Stop yer gennin' and pack some stuff up! 'Ow old are yer? Three years if my reckoning's right! You're old enough to do a bit o' graft, so get a bloody move on. I won't stand for idle buggers!'

The cart was packed with enough provisions for a few days and yoked up to the piebald ready for departure. Roulson scooped Ralph up and plonked him on the front of the cart, his short legs dangling freely. He'd cut the boy's hair short and dressed him in some ragged clothes he'd managed to retrieve from a dustbin. Roulson climbed up next to him. Yes, he thought, pleased with the transformation. Nobody would guess for a minute he didn't belong to the gypsies.

''Ere, wear this, and keep yer 'ead down!' He yanked a woolly hat down over Ralph's short black curls.

He'd planned a route that would take them all the way, avoiding busy roads and towns, with the exception of Appleby. He decided to wait until dusk when people had finished work and had gone home. There would still be enough light to guide them away from the main road once through the town.

Samboy and Lavinia spent the night and the next day at the manor.

On hearing of Ralph's abduction they were distraught, searching for him all day. Now they had to return to the cottage to bed down the horses before coming back to the manor, where they'd stay for as long as needed to support Daisy and Tobias.

Samboy pulled the car to a halt in Appleby by the river. The sun had set on what should have been a perfect day. He placed an arm round Lavinia's shoulders and she hugged his waist. Holding hands they strolled down to the water's edge and sat on the cool grass, neither caring it was damp. Tears flooded their eyes blurring their vision and Lavinia leaned her aching body against Samboy, taking comfort from his closeness.

Both were reluctant to move. They sat until a mist descended over the river as the evening cooled, penetrating their stiff aching joints.

'Come on, love, we'd better make a move.'

'Do you hear that?'

'What?'

'Shh, listen,' Lavinia said, craning her neck. 'There it is again.'

'Yes, I do hear summat,' Samboy said, standing up.

The clattering of cartwheels sounded. It grew louder, accompanied by the familiar clip-clopping of iron hoofs and the crack of a whip striking the air. Lavinia shuddered.

'Someone's just walked over me grave, Sam,' she said, but he wasn't listening.

'Come on!' He grabbed her hand. 'Let's get up on the bridge, lass, and see who it is. They're comin' at an 'ell of a speed! A bit late in the day I'd say to be out wi' a horse and cart, it's gettin' dark now.'

They hurried along the road and on to the bridge.

'Sam! Look!' Lavinia cried, pointing to an obstacle in the centre of the bridge.

A block of masonry had fallen out of the wall and rolled into the centre of the bridge. Samboy rushed over and tried to heave it out of the way, but it was too heavy.

The crack of a whip sounded again – echoing through the evening mist. It was followed by the distressed whinny of a horse gathering speed. Samboy and Lavinia looked at one another, alarm written on their faces.

'Get out the way!' he called to his wife. 'There's a bloody idiot on the loose. I'll try an' warn 'em!'

He rushed to the other side of the bridge. A horse and cart loomed into view advancing through the mist at full gallop silhouetted against a darkening sky.

Samboy flapped his arms wildly shouting, 'Stop! Stop! The bridge is—'

But the horse kept coming. He saw a man driving the cart and alongside him, a child, perched and clinging on for dear life.

They were only yards away when Samboy recognized him. Roulson!

'*You bastard*!' he roared, looking into coal black eyes of the devil himself. He glanced at the young passenger sitting beside him. His heart stopped when he caught sight of the terror-stricken face of his grandson. Ralph's eyes lit up for a brief moment when he saw his grandfather.

'*Granddad*!'

'No … *no*—' came Samboy's agonizing cry as the cart flew past him and on to the bridge.

He spun round just in time to see the cartwheel hit the boulder. What happened next appeared in slow motion. He froze in terror as the horse leapt over the parapet, followed by Roulson holding the reins. The cart was left, wedged between boulder and bridge. Samboy, struck with horror, ran over to the cart and searched for his grandson. He wasn't there. He looked over the bridge and scanned the water below.

'Sam!' Lavinia cried. 'Sam! I've got him!'

Samboy looked up to where Lavinia stood on the other side of the bridge, holding the limp body of Ralph in her arms. He walked towards her slowly, afraid of what he'd discover. He saw she was sobbing loudly and his grandson lay unmoving in her arms. Please, he prayed, not my Ralph….

'Sam,' Lavinia said, placing the child in his arms, 'he's goin' to be all right. Aren't yer, little fella?' She looked down at the boy. 'Open yer eyes, Ralph, it's me and yer granddad. You're safe.'

Ralph slowly opened his eyes, 'Granddad!' he sobbed, wrapping his small arms around his grandfather's neck and burying his face into him.

People had come from their houses to see what all the commotion was and were gathered on the bridge.

'What about the horse?' someone shouted.

'Tek Ralph to the car, love. I'll see what's to do.'

The crowd parted and made way for Samboy. He leaned over the parapet looking to where the piebald horse dangled from its tangled leather traces. A guttural sound escaped its mouth where froth was forming rapidly. Directly below the horse, Roulson lay floating in the river, face up. Samboy reached into his pocket and retrieved his penknife. He leaned over the bridge as far as he could and cut the leather traces. No one saw the satisfaction on his face as his knife passed through the leather.

The horse plunged solidly on to Roulson, who opened his eyes fleetingly to witness his own end.

Samboy walked to where his car was parked. Lavinia was holding the piebald horse that had swum to safety. He took a halter from his car and put it on the horse before securing it to a nearby tree.

'Come on, Ralph, let's get yer back home, yer mother's waiting.'

He took a last look at the crowded bridge, then his eyes glanced across the river to where a familiar figure stood looking back at him. He raised his hand and waved before getting into the car.

DS Keen waved back, conscious it was a thankful Samboy Latimer who drove away.